DEADBALL

DEADBALL

A Metaphysical Baseball Novel

DAVID B. STINSON

Library of Congress Control Number 2011940478

ISBN 978-0-98-366890-9
ISBN 0-983-66890-6

Published in 2011 by:
Huntington Park Publications, Inc.
103 N Adams Street
Rockville, MD 20850-2256
www.huntingtonparkpublications.com

PRINTED IN THE UNITED STATES

First Edition
10 9 8 7 6 5 4 3 2 1

Cover Photograph, front and back (*black and white image*):
Image Id # Z24.80, Courtesy of the Maryland Historical Society

Cover Photograph (*color image*): *David B. Stinson*

Cover Design and Imaging: *Jim Morris*

HUNTINGTON PARK PUBLICATIONS, INC. · MARYLAND

ACKNOWLEDGMENTS

The author would like to thank the following family members, friends, and colleagues who generously gave of their time and talent to critique my many drafts and rewrites of *Deadball*:

Steve Quinn, Paul Wellons, Jan Stewart,
Patty Bartlett, John Kelly, Ruth Kelly,
Bob Reutershan, Peter Brown, Sameer Yerawadekar,
Jim Colbert, James W. Stinson, Jimmy Stinson,
Dick O'Connor, Andrei Kushnir, Ray Perez,
Matt Hurwitz, Alan Lo Re, Bob Kirschman,
Michael O'Connell, Kevin Johnson,
Greg Allen, Eric Platt, and David Rogers.

Thanks also to Jim Morris for his assistance
in designing the cover and book layout.

"To Understand, First You have to Believe."

Matty O'Boyle

PROLOGUE

⚾ ⚾ ⚾

A Moment in Time
August 1989

The wooden planks of Silver Stadium's dugout bench were smooth as polished brass, buffed to an imperfect shine from years of minor-league ballplayers riding the bench waiting for their turn at bat.

"In the hole," said Byron Bennett, one of the many players who had ridden that bench. It was a phrase he had been uttering to himself since before he could even remember, four or five times a day, every day. It was just one of the many rhythms of the game he would miss.

Only a few hundred fans were on hand that night, the last day of August 1989, the last game of Byron's professional baseball career. The teams were scheduled to play one final game the following day, but a warm front approaching from the west had forecasters calling for rain. With both teams out of the hunt for the playoffs, the likely rainout would not be made up.

Byron knew he would not be invited back for another season. He had seen it coming for the better part of the summer. The team's owners had said nothing to him directly, but their silence spoke volumes. And so, on that warm, late summer's evening in Rochester, New York, the time had come for Byron to let go of the game, or, more to the point, the time had come for the game to let go of him.

Waiting in the bottom of the eighth inning for what would be his last at bat, Byron rubbed his hands along the front of the wooden bench beneath him, his momentary solitude interrupted when the batter at the plate took a called third strike and the umpire punched him out. Approaching the bench, the failed batter tossed his helmet out of frustration, almost hitting Byron in the legs. Nothing personal.

Byron nodded as the batter walked past, but they exchanged no words. "Gotta protect the plate," called out the bench coach in an authoritative, gravelly voice from the far end of the dugout. Byron paid no attention to his teammate's annoyed response.

The next batter, standing by the dugout, pounded his bat handle against the ground, dislodging the donut weight from the barrel of the bat. He strutted like a rooster to home plate and took a couple of practice swings before stepping into the batter's box.

Byron pulled his bat out of the rack and walked up the dugout stairs, each step more purposeful than the last. "On deck," he said to himself, as he took his place inside the faded lime of the batter's circle. He picked up a rag coated with pine tar and worked the sticky, carbonized concoction over the handle of his bat. Tossing the rag to the ground like a smoker discarding a cigarette, he gripped the handle and swung the bat several times. After completing this timeless ritual, Byron rested the bat on his shoulder and took a long look around the old ballpark.

The Rochester Red Wings had played their home games in Silver Stadium since 1929 – 60 years of baseball history hidden in every corner of the ballpark. For the past two seasons, Byron had made the place his home. Most ballplayers loathed the old stadium, with its cramped dugout and minor-league accommodations. Not Byron. He considered it an honor to play in such a historic ballpark, with the ghosts of players long departed hovering over the rafters and clinging to the light stanchions.

Byron felt no nervousness waiting for his turn at bat,

butterflies having left him some indeterminable time long ago. The pitcher for the Scranton Red Barons threw only fastballs, apparently lacking confidence in his late season ability to get any other pitch over the plate for a strike. Byron had watched the opposing hurler's offerings for most of the seventh inning and agreed with the pitcher's assessment.

After working the count full, the batter fouled off three straight pitches and then drew a walk on the ninth pitch of the at bat. With two outs and the Red Wings down 2-1, Byron represented the go-ahead run.

"Now batting, the third baseman, number 17, Byron Bennett," rang the public address system. The words bounced around the stadium, tailing off somewhere in the darkness above the lights. A smattering of applause greeted Byron as he stepped to the plate.

On most days, Byron tuned out the din of the crowd. On that particular night, however, he let it all in. It wasn't much of a din.

"Come on, Bitty, just a hit," yelled a fan in the stands behind him.

"Just a hit" was all Byron was looking for and, in actuality, all he was capable of. Perhaps the fan knew this. Scant few home runs had flown off Byron's bat during his years in the minors. As a corner infielder, his lack of power was the excuse most thrown about by management for why he had never received a call up to the majors. Blasting a home run off the stadium lights looming above right field, à la Hollywood's version of Roy Hobbs, wasn't going to happen.

Come on, now, Byron thought. *Get your head in the game. Focus.* After watching the pitcher's first offering sail low and away, a ball, Byron stepped out of the batter's box and swung his bat twice before stepping back in, crowding the plate. *Okay pitch*, he thought. *Waste one, brush me back*. The pitcher obliged, throwing Byron a fastball up and in, backing him off the plate and making the count 2 and "O" – a hitter's count. *Gotcha now*, Byron thought.

The pitcher's third offering, a belt high fastball, was just off the plate. Byron swung late, fouling the pitch off. "Dammit," he said, as the ball sailed high into the stands along the first-base side and careened around the empty seats like a pinball sprung into play. A spectator jumped two rows of metal benches and, after grabbing the ball, thrust it aloft as if he were a conquering hero returning from battle with the severed head of a vanquished foe. Those around him acknowledged his achievement with enthusiastic applause.

The next pitch, again low and away, Byron took for a ball, making the count 3 and 1. He watched the pitcher's fifth offering catch the outside corner of the plate, bringing the count full. *Damn*, he thought. *Nice pitch*.

Asking for time, Byron stepped out of the box and rested his bat against his knees as he adjusted his batting gloves. The gloves felt fine; Byron just wanted to buy some time, slow down the pitcher, and take it all in one last time. It was, for Byron, a moment to remember – a moment he could return to in later years, when he no longer stood in the batter's box, when he found himself missing the game.

The stadium lights cast shadows in the stands, hiding the few spectators sitting on the metal benches underneath the large over-hang running along the first and third base lines. Byron looked out past the red oval Genesee Beer sign above the scoreboard in left field. The night sky seemed exceptionally dark.

Out beyond the stadium lights a new moon - invisible to Byron and everyone else in Silver Stadium - rose over the western horizon. *The last at bat of my meaningless minor-league career*,

Byron thought. He felt like the moon.

The umpire brought Byron back to earth. "Come on, batter, let's go." A handful of fans applauded as Byron stepped back into the box. "Hit it up the middle, Bitty," yelled a fan behind him.

"Alright," Byron said to himself. *This is it. Make it count.*

The pitcher nodded his head at the catcher's sign, although Byron didn't know why the two bothered to communicate at all; everyone in the ballpark knew the pitcher was looking to throw yet another fastball somewhere around the edge of the plate.

Everyone was right. As Byron swung at the pitch, his torso drew perpendicular to the plate just as it had countless times before. With full extension of his arms, he drove the ball out over the shortstop. His signature hit – a single in the gap between the left and center fielders that Byron could stretch into a double.

With two outs and the count full, the runner at first was off with the pitch, dashing around second base and sprinting toward third. The centerfielder was quick to the ball and rifled a shot to the cut-off man. Ignoring the third base coach's signal to hold up, the runner hustled around third and barreled toward home. Byron rounded second base, hoping to divert the cut-off man and draw a throw. The shortstop would not be fooled and, instead, sent a sharp strike home to the catcher. The runner was out at the plate and the inning over.

"Damn," said Byron, clapping his hands in disappointment as his body came to a halt.

Walking toward first base, Byron yanked off his batting gloves and shoved them inside his helmet.

"Tough break, Bitty," said the first base coach as Byron handed him his gear. "You'll get 'em next time."

Byron nodded his head, not bothering to let on that he knew there would be no next time.

In the ninth inning both teams went quietly, three up, three down. Watching the final at-bats unfold, Byron sensed his teammates had little interest in extending the season, even if for only one more inning.

After the last out, Byron remained on the bench, staring at the field before him as fans trickled out of the stadium. He watched a father wait patiently as his kids hunted for souvenirs in the seats behind the visitors' dugout. The stadium lights continued their slow burn as the grounds crew unrolled an expansive white vinyl tarp to protect the field from the approaching front that threatened to arrive any minute. The enormous plastic sheathing floated over the playing surface like waves of billowy clouds, before resting upon the worn, late- August infield.

Byron rose from the bench and picked up his bat and glove.

"Hey, can I have a ball?" yelled one of the souvenir hunters who had made his way over to the home dugout.

Byron poked his head out over the top of the dugout and gave the kid a long look. He glanced around the dugout, but there were no balls to be found.

"Here," he said, handing the kid his professional model Louisville Slugger. "I won't be needing this anymore."

The kid, speechless at first, blurted out a "Thanks!" as he turned away, sprinting back through the maze of empty, red plastic box seats toward where his father stood.

Byron knew the significance of his gift, for he too was a collector. Although such largesse was not out of character for him, in giving away the primary souvenir of his last professional at bat, Byron had surprised even himself.

Heading back toward the stairway to the clubhouse at the end of the dugout, Byron heard the boy's excited yells. "Look what I got! Look what I got!"

As he sauntered down the clubhouse steps, Byron heard the first heavy drops of rain pelting the infield tarp like marbles falling from the sky. The outfield lights cut out in rapid sequence, covering the field in a sheet of darkness.

Then the rain began in earnest.

Chapter 1

🟤 🟤 🟤

A Grand Baseball Palace
May 1999

Byron had heard no voices telling him to take a Sunday drive to the Harwood section of Baltimore, nor could he articulate why he found himself obsessing about Union Park, wanting to know its exact location. As a diehard Charm City baseball fan, Byron knew the history of the game and Union Park's importance to the deadball era, but never before had he thought it necessary to stand where the ballpark once stood. Indeed, he figured it a fair guess that few fans - no matter how much they loved the game - would be interested in taking a day trip to the former site of a ballpark erased so long ago by the passage of time.

Maybe it was the impending demise of Memorial Stadium - the Orioles' more recently abandoned ballpark - that had him thinking about such things. It bothered him that the city, either through design or indifference, would let slip through her fingers such an important historical and cultural artifact. One of Byron's most treasured childhood memories was standing in a crush of fans outside Memorial Stadium after a game as Paul Blair, the Orioles' fleet-footed centerfielder, towered above him, signing his program. Excited and not wanting the moment to end, Byron handed the program back to Blair, which the centerfielder dutifully commenced signing again, until he realized he already had autographed the item, thus leaving half a signature - a second "Paul" - just below his fully signed name. Although the memories of that day remained with Byron regardless of Memorial Stadium's ultimate fate, the idea of the Grand Old Lady of 33rd Street becoming another lost ballpark saddened him nonetheless.

Whatever the cause of his latest obsession, for Byron, Union Park no longer was some obscure sports reference layered within the pages of long-forgotten baseball texts, and his drive to Baltimore that Sunday afternoon was more pilgrimage than day trip. Driving north from downtown Baltimore, Byron imagined a similar spring day 100 years earlier - throngs of people making their way to Union Park, up Greenmount Avenue to Huntingdon Avenue, now 25th Street, coming by bicycle or on foot, by street car or horse and buggy, the sights and sounds of the ballpark rising in the distance.

Union Park was located at the intersection of East 25th and Guilford Streets, some 20 blocks north of Baltimore's Inner Harbor. The cluster of row houses built in the ballpark's place provided no hint of that corner's once glorious past. No historical marker noted the corner's significance to the people of Baltimore only 100 years earlier. Yet on that spot once stood the home of the National League Baltimore Orioles. It was there that future Hall of Famers John McGraw, Hughie Jennings, Willie Keeler, Wilbert Robinson, Joe Kelley, and manager Ned Hanlon brought the world championship of baseball to Baltimore three years in a row, from 1894 to 1896.

Baseball remained in Byron's blood some ten years after the end of his minor-league playing career. Now a salesman for the Baysox, an Orioles' minor-league affiliate in Bowie, Maryland, Byron spent much of his free time reading anything he could find on the history of baseball in Baltimore. With no wife or kids, and his dance card typically unencumbered, he had little trouble finding the time.

After exhausting the local libraries and area used-book stores in search of anything mentioning the old Orioles, Byron had turned his attention to the collections of the Babe Ruth Museum and the Maryland Historical Society, scrolling through old microfilm of the Baltimore Sun and the Baltimore News-American, researching and piecing together a timeline for the Orioles at Union Park.

Constructed in 1891 by Orioles' owner Harry Von Der Horst, Union Park fell out of use when the National League dropped its Baltimore franchise after the 1899 season. Although the city fielded a professional team in 1901 as part of the newly-organized American League, the reconstituted Orioles, with only McGraw and Robinson back in the fold, played their home games at a different park several blocks away. Union Park, still under control of the National League, went unused, abandoned, a victim of league animosity between the long-established National and the upstart American. Byron could find no newspaper account of the ballpark's demolition, but he had determined from area land records that Union Park met its demise about 1910, lasting less than ten years as a major-league venue.

The neighborhood surrounding the ballpark offered Byron several clues as to the ballfield's former location. Comparing photographs of Union Park to buildings surviving from that era, he was certain he had found the spot. The infield, once located near the southeast corner of East 25th and Guilford Streets, faced out toward East 24th and Barclay Streets. The architecture of the timeworn, brick, row houses - built where the wooden grandstand once embraced the infield - suggested they were constructed sometime during the second decade of the 20th century.

Falls Alley, situated mid-block between Guilford and Barclay and running north to south, allowed Byron an unobstructed entrance into what was once Union Park's playing field. Row houses on either side of the alley's entrance dated to the time of Union Park, as did the row houses on the southwest corner of East 25th Street and Barclay. Byron recognized those houses from old photographs of Union Park. They provided him a historical reference point for his research.

Behind the houses immediately to the west of Falls Alley, in what was once the infield, was a parking lot. Immediately to the east, in what was once left field, were rows of brick garages. It all seemed to Byron a rather inglorious use of such historic land. He took a picture of the parking lot and the garages, for posterity.

Standing in the area that was once third base, Byron thought about John McGraw, who long ago roamed the hot corner for the Orioles. Having played third base himself, Byron felt a particular kinship with the 5'6" McGraw, whose physical size and make up was similar to Byron's not quite 5'9" frame. "If only I'd been born one hundred years earlier," Byron used to tell his teammates, "I would have made it to the majors." Byron knew all about McGraw and his fiery, aggressive style of play. One of the greatest players of that era, McGraw's lifetime on-base percentage was third all time. As player and manager, he helped develop baseball strategies designed to win at any cost. "Inside baseball" it was called. Tellingly, he set the mark for being tossed out of the most games, having been ejected 131 times.

Byron lingered for a moment in the alley, kicking at an imaginary dirt infield and pounding an imaginary glove with his right hand. Sensing that he was being watched, he scanned the backyards and the windows of the surrounding buildings. Seeing no one, he turned in the direction of home plate and crouched into a defensive position, as if awaiting the next pitch to an imaginary batter.

I know I'm being watched, he thought. He straightened his body and looked around a second time. *I should get out of here.* As he turned to leave, he realized he could not move his feet. *What the hell's going on?*

A deathly silence enveloped him. He sensed the presence of a thousand ancient faces watching him, their voices yelling, cheering, but he heard nothing. It was as if the past and the present had converged and the memories of all that had once transpired there 100 years earlier somehow remained, frozen in time, and he was part of it.

Byron's heart pounded and his muscles tensed. He closed his eyes to try to calm himself. But in his mind, he saw the transparent image of a distant baseball player moving in rapid succession, like something out of a black-and-white kinetoscope movie reel - first tagging a base runner, then arguing a call with an umpire, then grabbing a base runner's pants belt as he rounded third, slowing the runner's approach toward home plate.

As the image faded, Byron opened his eyes. The alley's pavers and asphalt were gone, replaced with dirt and grass. Disoriented and breathing heavily, his heart still racing, he looked down at a worn base path, following it with his eyes toward home plate. The ghostly outline of a ballfield flickered briefly like the image on a television screen losing reception. "It's happening again," he said to himself, his voice raised and tense. "This can't be." As the words were leaving his lips, the base path, the grass, and the intermittent ballfield all vanished, as if Byron's expressed disbelief had convinced the ancient images to depart. The alley's pavers and asphalt reappeared beneath his feet. "I've got to get a grip. This is a parking lot in Baltimore. Nothing more."

Byron took a deep breath. Able again to move his feet, he

sat down on a discarded plastic milk crate. As his heart rate and breathing returned to normal, he thought about what had happened, hoping to make sense of what he had seen. But it made no sense, and he knew it.

He stood up and walked slowly toward the area that was once home plate, anxious and uncertain whether the ballfield's apparition might reappear. According to his calculations, home plate was located in the alley behind the row house at 313 East 25th Street. The three-story brick structure sat within the footprint of the grandstand. Its postage-stamp backyard was once foul territory behind home plate. Byron took several pictures of the rear of the house, including the basement door and stairwell, the chainlink fence surrounding the backyard, and the alley where home plate once sat.

Heading east on 25th Street, away from the row house, Byron wondered whether anyone else had drawn similar conclusions about the historical significance of the unmarked alley. He wondered whether the owner of the row house knew his home was built on hallowed ground.

With a mixture of trepidation and excitement, Byron walked the perimeter of the old ballpark, scanning the row houses and front yards for anything out of the ordinary. As he approached Barclay along East 25th Street, he passed the area that was once the left-field corner. The row houses on the west side of Barclay sat in place of Union Park's massive wooden bleachers. The houses on the east dated to the time of Union Park.

Byron pulled out of his pocket a copy of a photograph taken in 1897 during a championship game between the Orioles and the Boston Beaneaters. In that famous photo, the row houses on the east side of Barclay loomed like ghosts over left-center field. On that late September afternoon, more than 30,000 spectators had jammed Union Park – the greatest number ever to attend a baseball game up to that point in time. Seeing those row houses, relics of a bygone era, Byron imagined their rooftops packed with fans, or cranks, as they were called back then, hoping to catch a glimpse of the action on that late summer's day.

He continued his walk, stopping at the corner of East 24th Street and Guilford to take a picture of row houses sitting in what was once Union Park's right field. Long ago, the Orioles' wood-slatted clubhouse sat in that corner, perched atop Brady's Run, a creek that ran along the back of right field.

Byron wondered whether people sitting in the kitchens and living rooms of the houses built in place of right field ever saw images of ballplayers like Willie Keeler, the Orioles' diminutive right fielder, chasing down a fly ball and hurling it toward home plate. Known for hitting the ball "where they ain't," Keeler set the National League consecutive-game hit streak record of 44 at Union Park in June 1897. Legend has it that Keeler, when playing right field, kept an extra ball or two hidden in the high grass, just in case he needed a quicker retrieve to catch a runner trying to score. Because right field sloped away from home plate toward Brady's Run, the umpire standing behind home plate could not see the illicit cache of baseballs hidden in the grass.

After completing his circuit around the old ballpark, Byron stopped in front of the house he believed marked the location of home plate. To all outward appearances, the dwelling was the quintessential Baltimore row house – a three-story brick facade with a wood-framed front porch connected to the neighboring structures on either side. On the first floor, underneath the front porch roof, were two picture windows to the left of a plain, wooden front door unceremoniously enclosed by a 1970's-style metal screen door. On the second floor, a three-frame bay window sat perched above the front porch. Ornate brownstones above the three windows on the third floor suggested an owner of some affluence when the dwelling was built. The current state of the house suggested something less.

Wooden steps leading from the sidewalk to the front porch were painted red, although Byron would have chosen orange and black, the colors of both the original and modern-day Orioles. He took a picture of the front of the house, making sure to capture the ornate, gold-painted house number - 313 - adorning the glass transom above the front door.

As he was putting his camera back in its case, Byron heard someone call from the direction of Falls Alley: "Hey, you with the camera!"

Byron looked to his left and saw an old man emerge from behind the alley.

"What were you doing in my backyard?" yelled the old man.

"Me? Nothing," said Byron.

"Well, then why were you taking pictures of my house?"

"Because your house is, well, actually, I was taking pictures of the whole area." A bit shaken from the inquisition, Byron added, "There used to be a ballpark here . . . ."

A puzzled expression came across the old man's face. "Oh. Are you a player? You look so young. I didn't recognize you."

"A player?" asked Byron.

"Yeah. A baseball player."

"I used to play, but not anymore."

"Well, go around back. But, give me the camera. You know the rules."

"My camera? What rules? I'm not giving you my camera."

"Listen, I don't have time for this. If you don't give me the camera, you're going to have to leave."

"Well, I'm not giving you my camera."

"Then you better leave." The man turned back toward Falls Alley. "I'm getting too old for this," he said, shaking his head.

"Excuse me, sir," Byron called out, following behind the man. "What's your name?"

The man did not answer.

Byron caught up and walked alongside him. "My name's Byron Bennett." Byron held out his hand.

The man stopped and looked at Byron, ignoring his outstretched hand.

"From what I can tell," said Byron, "your house is located about where home plate used to be."

"You think I don't know that? It's the bane of my existence."

The old man resumed his walk and soon disappeared around the corner.

"That guy's crazier than me," said Byron to no one. "And I thought I had issues."

Wait a second, he thought. *I said that out loud. Man, I hope nobody heard me.* It was one of the downsides of Byron's living alone for so many years - his proclivity to verbalize his thoughts.

Heading back toward his car, Byron thought about the old man's question. *Am I a player? I wish.* He stopped on the sidewalk in front of the man's house and kicked at some loose dirt near a tree beside the road, dislodging a piece of metal sticking out of the ground. Never being one to pass up the opportunity to examine a crusty, metal object, Byron picked up what turned out to be a crushed, steel beer can. *I doubt this is left over from Union Park*, he thought, tossing the can back on the ground.

In the dirt underneath where the can lay Byron noticed a smaller piece of metal, about the size of a bottlecap. He picked it up, too, peeling away several layers of hardened clay covering its surface. "It's a coin!" he said, again verbalizing his thoughts. On the front of the coin Byron recognized Miss Liberty, surrounded by 13 stars, visible above a date. On the reverse was the Roman numeral "V" surrounded by ears of corn and the words "United States of America." *A vee nickel,* he thought. *How cool.*

He moistened the coin with spit and wiped it on his T-shirt. "No way," he said, reading the coin's date: 1899 - "the Orioles' last season here." He finished cleaning the coin, amazed by its near mint condition.

Again sensing he was being watched, Byron looked back toward the old man's house and saw the front window sheers sway to a close. *I wonder what else is buried here? If only I had a shovel.* Byron wrapped the nickel in his picture of Union Park and stashed it in his front pants' pocket for safe keeping.

CHAPTER 2

Table for Two

Two blocks east of Union Park's former site was the Stone Tavern, another of the many time pieces dotting Harwood, whose past, like the buildings surrounding the vanished ballpark, lay buried beneath its current facade. The building's distinctive Little Tavern shape suggested its former incarnation as a "Buy 'em by the bag" hamburger shop. Now encapsulated in Formstone, that plaster-based, counterfeit rock unique to East Coast cities like Baltimore and Philadelphia, the former "dine-in or carryout" shop no longer specialized in greasy sliders, featuring instead modestly-priced selections of chicken and fish.

Hoping for a cup of coffee, Byron pushed open the arched, wood front door and stepped inside the restaurant's tiny interior. The place was empty that Sunday afternoon with the exception of a man behind the front counter and a patron sitting in a back booth reading a newspaper. A murky sheen covered the wood-paneled walls, compliments of years of grease percolating out of the kitchen grill and fryers. Byron placed his hands on the counter and cleared his throat, hoping to gain the attention of the man standing with his back to the counter. "Excuse me," said Byron.

The man's lack of response, and his Miles Davis-like determination not to face his audience, suggested he had little interest in any additional sales that afternoon.

"Excuse me," said Byron, trying again to gain the man's attention.

"Sorry, we're about to close," said the man, still with his back toward Byron.

"I was just hoping for a cup of coffee to go. You got any left?"

"I'd have to make a pot. You gonna buy a large?" asked the man, turning to face Byron.

With his beak-like nose, wide, toothy grin, and comically bad brown toupee, the man bore no physical resemblance to Miles Davis. The man did look, however, as if he kept himself in good shape.

"If you make it, I'll buy it," said Byron.

"Alright then," said the man.

Byron watched him shuffle off, half expecting him to commence a full-tilt sprint toward the end of the counter and slide, feet first, into the kitchen, as if he were stealing second base. After the man disappeared into the back - walking, not sliding - Byron leaned against the counter and took a quick look around the small confines of the restaurant. His eyes fixed on an area above the window in front of him. *You've got to be kidding*, he thought, his mouth agape. A large wooden sign proclaiming "UNION PARK" in faded Edwardian script hung serendipitously on the wall. With part of the "r" and most of the "k" missing, the sign's jagged, uneven border suggested the relic had been ripped from a larger structure.

"Would you look at that, it must be a sign," he said, proud of his lame pun.

"Hey," Byron called out to the man in the kitchen, "where'd you get the Union Park sign?"

Before the man could answer, the patron sitting in the back booth said, "It's mine. It ain't for sale, so don't bother asking."

Byron looked over at the man, an older gentleman wearing a wind breaker and a Giants cap. A shock of white hair, lightly yellowed by the sun, protruded from underneath the man's hat and over the top of his large, ancient ears.

"Is that sign original?" asked Byron. "You know, is it from *the* Union Park?"

"That would be my guess," answered the man.

"Where'd you find it?"

"I picked it up in my travels."

"I'm surprised it survived all these years," said Byron.

"It was luck, really. Someone found it in the subflooring of a house they were gutting down the street. They had to piece it back together. I figure when they tore down Union Park, they must have salvaged wood from the grandstand and the fences to build houses in the area."

"Which house did they find it in?" Byron asked.

"I don't remember which one. It was near the corner of 25th Street and Guilford."

"We're out of coffee," interrupted the man behind the counter. "Sorry."

"No coffee? Horrors! Nothing for me then." The man shrugged his shoulders and disappeared back inside the kitchen.

"So why's the sign hanging in a dive like this?" asked Byron.

"I've got no place else to put it. I knew the owner, so we hung it here."

"Who, that guy over there?" asked Byron, pointing to the man in the kitchen.

"Nah, different owner."

"Aren't you afraid it will disappear?"

"Son, at my age, I don't worry about things like that."

"You know, it belongs in a museum."

"Oh, believe me, them folks at the Babe Ruth Museum would love to have it, but I ain't selling."

"Have they tried to buy it?"

"No. They don't even know it exists."

"Mind if I sit down?" Byron asked, pointing to the empty booth across the table from the old man.

"Be my guest."

"My name's Byron Bennett." Byron held out his hand as he sat down.

"I'm Mac." Mac raised his hand and gave Byron a short wave, avoiding his outstretched hand.

"Nice to meet you, Mac."

"You're not 'Bitty Byron Bennett' are you?"

"I, I am," said Byron, shocked that the man knew who he was.

"You used to play third base for the Rochester Red Wings."

"I did. I'm surprised you'd know that."

"Oh, I follow all the Orioles, major league and minor, past and present. So what brings you to Harwood, Bitty? Is it okay if I call you Bitty?"

"You know, I never liked that name."

"Why? It's a great nickname."

"I'm just thin-skinned, I guess. My first year in pro ball, a teammate who was like a foot taller than me started calling me 'Itty Bitty.' The name stuck and after a while, it got shortened to 'Bitty.' No pun intended."

"Kind of like 'Wee Willie Keeler.'"

"Yeah, I guess," said Byron. "So if you don't mind, call me Byron."

"Byron it is. So what brings you to Harwood, Byron?"

"Union Park." Byron pointed to the sign.

Mac smiled. "Now, why would a kid your age care anything about a place like Union Park?"

"Because I love baseball - the history of the game - and I have way too much free time on my hands."

"Well, there's worse things you could be doing with your time, I guess."

"I'm not sure my ex-wife would agree with you."

"She's not a fan, eh?"

"Not like she used to be."

"So what have you heard about Union Park?" asked Mac.

"What I've read about it, and the pictures I've seen."

"It's a shame more people don't make an effort to learn about the past. There's a lot to learn, if you know where to look."

"My ex used to say I was living in the past."

"Well, if you like the past, you've come to the right place. It's everywhere around here - you just have to know where to look, how to train your eyes."

"What do you mean?"

"Well, this restaurant, for example. Before it was built, there was a house here. I can still remember how the house looked before they tore it down. The house may be gone, but I can still see it 'cause I remember how it used to be. Of course, most people don't see things that way anymore."

"People tear down history all the time," said Byron. "Look at Memorial Stadium. It will be gone before you know it."

"Same thing happened in Harwood. This place used to be the center of baseball in Baltimore."

"Because of Union Park?" asked Byron.

"Yes, but there were others, too. Harwood is littered with old ballparks. Huntington Park was across the street at Greenmount and 25th Street." Mac shook his finger in the direction of Greenmount, which ran north and south outside the window where they were sitting. "The 'beer and whiskey league' Orioles played there," he said.

"'Beer and whiskey?'" Byron asked, "I think I remember reading something about that.

"They were with the old American Association - the teams were allowed to sell booze at the games," said Mac.

"The start of a great friendship - baseball and beer," said Byron.

"Three blocks up Greenmount was American League Park – the AL Orioles played there two seasons before they left for New York."

"Oriole Park," said Byron, trying to impress Mac with his baseball knowledge.

"Yup, it was called that, too."

"Do you have any idea how long Union Park lasted after the Orioles left?" asked Byron.

Mac paused a moment, folding his hands in front of him. Leaning forward, he said, "It depends what you mean by 'lasted.' You want to know a secret?"

"Sure."

"It's still there," said Mac.

"What is?"

"Union Park."

"What do you mean Union Park is still there?"

"I can still see it, on game days, that is."

Oh Lord, thought Byron. *Another crazy old man. This day's getting weirder and weirder.*

"I can see everything," Mac continued, "people in the stands, ballplayers playing a game. Everything."

"You mean like how you can still see the house that used to be here, where this restaurant is now," said Byron, trying to make sense of Mac's outrageous claim.

"No. It's more than that," said Mac.

A chill came over Byron, much like what he had felt when he saw the ballpark's images earlier that afternoon. "How's that possible?" he asked.

"It just is."

"Can you see it now?"

"No, not this minute. I'm sitting here in this restaurant. I can't see through walls."

"How often do you see it?"

Mac started drumming the table with the fingers of his right hand. "Look, it comes and it goes, okay? You don't understand. I shouldn't have said anything."

"Wait - Mac - don't get me wrong. It's just that, Union Park's been gone a long time."

"I guess I misjudged you."

"Misjudged me?"

"The park may be gone, but its memory lives on," said Mac in a defiant tone. "At least for me it does."

"Well, you're lucky then."

Mac picked up his copy of the Baltimore Sun and pushed himself out of the booth. Disappointment filled his face.

"Mac," said Byron. "Wait a second." Mac adjusted the collar of his jacket and headed for the door, ignoring Byron's plea. Byron raised his voice: "Mac, don't leave."

Mac stopped and turned toward Byron. "What?" asked Mac.

"I think I know what you're talking about." Byron paused for a moment to gather the courage he needed to tell Mac what he had seen that afternoon. "When I was in the alley behind 25th Street, I had this feeling I wasn't alone, although I know I was. It kinda freaked me out, so I closed my eyes. When I opened them I could have sworn the alley I was in had turned from pavers to dirt and then back to pavers. Man, this sounds crazy even as I'm saying it."

"Perhaps I didn't misjudge you," said Mac, sitting back down in the booth.

"Then, when I was walking around the neighborhood, I met this guy who told me he'd seen ballplayers in his yard."

"Stocky guy with white hair and mustache?"

"Yeah. About your age."

Mac smiled. "He's actually younger than me. His name's Murph. We worked the grounds at Memorial Stadium together for just about six seasons."

"Really?" asked Byron. "When?"

"I started right after the Orioles arrived in '54 - long before you were born."

"He wanted to know why I was taking pictures of his house."

"And why were you?"

"I told you, I was looking for Union Park – you know, where it used to be. From what I can figure, home plate would have been behind his house."

"Sounds about right. Murph's house is on the third-base side of the grandstand. It wasn't much of a grandstand, though, compared to places like Memorial Stadium and Camden Yards. It looked more like a minor-league ballpark, at least by today's standards. Even after it burned down in '94 and they rebuilt it with a second tier, it still seated only a few thousand people."

"It was the first ballpark with assigned seats," said Byron, again trying to impress Mac with his baseball knowledge.

"Yup. Mr. Von Der Horst bought some old theater seats and stuck 'em behind home plate. It was great until it rained - then the upholstery would get soaked and smell something awful."

"I read that he put in a beer garden where he sold his own beer," said Byron.

"Yeah, I never much cared for it."

"Von Der Horst beer? I didn't know they still made it."

"They don't anymore. It's been a while."

"Murph wanted to know if I was a ballplayer," said Byron. "Why do you think he'd ask me that?"

"You'd have to ask him. You used to be a ballplayer. Maybe he recognized you."

"No, he didn't recognize me. He even said as much."

"Well, I recognized you, if it's any consolation."

"That's true, you did."

"Guess I better be on my way," said Mac. "The Orioles are playing Boston, you know."

"They are? Boston?" asked Byron, surprised. Byron suspected Mac was confused about the game. But not wanting to further alienate him, he decided not to say anything more about it. "By the way, what's with the Giants cap?" Byron pointed to Mac's hat. "Harwood being the 'center of baseball' and all."

"Oh, this?" Mac pulled on the bill of his hat. "I lived in New York for a while. I guess you could say I'm a fan of both teams, the Giants and the Orioles – before the Giants moved to San Francisco, that is." Mac stood up from the booth and headed toward the door.

"Hey, Mac. If you don't mind, let me have your telephone number – maybe we could go to a game sometime."

"I don't have a telephone, sorry."

"Where do you live?"

"Around," said Mac as he walked out the front door. Byron stood up and nodded to the man behind the counter, who had been listening to their conversation.

"Do you remember Union Park?" Byron asked.

"Not like Mac does. Of course, if you ask him, he'll probably tell you he remembers Abraham Lincoln's stop at Camden Station on the way to Gettysburg," said the man, chuckling to himself.

"So you're saying he's crazy?"

"No. Mac's an old man who remembers what he wants to remember."

The man followed Byron to the door and locked it once Byron left the restaurant.

Driving south on Greenmount, Byron kept replaying in his mind Mac's claim he had seen the old-time Orioles play at Union Park. For Mac even to remember a game from the Orioles' last year there would have made him at least 110 years old. While Byron thought Mac looked generically old, he didn't think Mac was 110. Still, Mac's description of Union Park sounded authentic, at least when considered in conjunction with the few pictures of the ballpark he had seen. Perhaps Mac had seen those pictures, too.

Heading west out of Baltimore on Route 40, Byron turned on WBAL to catch the end of the Orioles game. Baltimore was playing Minnesota, not Boston, just as Byron had suspected, and the game was already in the seventh inning. *By the time Mac gets to Camden Yards,* Byron thought, *the game will be just about over. I hope he's not too disappointed.*

Byron arrived home and collapsed into his favorite chair – a gold-plush La-Z-Boy recliner bequeathed to him by his late grandfather. More brown than gold, and with much of the plush worn away, the chair had taken on a shape all its own. Emptying his pockets onto the side table, Byron rummaged through the contents looking for the nickel he had found in front of Murph's house. He unfolded his picture of Union Park and found inside a corroded piece of metal.

Wait a second, he thought, examining the object. *It was*

a nickel. What is this?

Byron tossed the piece of metal back onto the side table. He picked up his copy of Lawrence Ritter's *Lost Ballparks* and started flipping through the pages. The book made no mention of Union Park, but did include a chapter on Memorial Stadium.

Later, he switched on the television to the *ESPN Sunday Night Game of the Week* – the Chicago White Sox were playing the Anaheim Angels. John Miller's lyrical voice floated out of the television and across the room, lending excitement to an otherwise mundane, one-run ball game. *That guy could make watching mildew grow sound exciting.* Turning off the table lamp, Byron pushed back the La-Z-Boy as far as it would recline. The glow of the television filled the room. Byron fell asleep as the Angels scored two more runs in the bottom of the seventh.

CHAPTER 3

Bitty and the Babe

There were times in Byron's life when he felt as if he were meant for a different era. As a child, he listened to the stories of his parents and grandparents and tried to imagine what it would have been like to live during the first half of the 20th century. He read history books, watched old movies on television, and collected antique toys and vintage baseball cards. His youthful fascination with the past developed into a passion for history and an appreciation for everything old.

Baseball became his main obsession, which is why he knew about places like Union Park. Why, when he met people like Mac, he gathered as much from them as he could, as they reminisced about days gone by. Mac, however, offered something more than mere reminiscence, for he claimed he could see the past, that he could still see games being played on a ballfield erased from the landscape a century earlier. For Mac, the past was still present - a proposition Byron found fascinating.

It also was a proposition with which Byron was not unfamiliar, for he, too, had experienced similar, fleeting "moments," as he called them, when it seemed the past became present. Two such moments during his formative years stood out. Both involved Babe Ruth, who, like Byron, was born and raised in Baltimore.

The first occurred in Ellicott City, Maryland, when Byron was ten years old. Although the town was by then a tourist and shopping destination, a century earlier it had been a prosperous mill town, one of the largest in the state. Andrew and John Ellicott founded Ellicott Mills along the banks of the Patapsco River in the 1770's and many of the buildings there dated to the early 1800's, lending the town an authentic, rustic feel.

Byron always looked forward to his family's trips to Ellicott City, where they visited his parent's friends, the Reutershans. Their house was built in the late 1800's and, over the years, had served as both a residence and an antique shop.

Across the street from the Reutershans' house was St. Paul's Catholic Church, perched on a hill overlooking Main Street. A tall, grey, granite steeple at the front of the building offered entry to the church on three sides. Ornamental rose windows adorned the steeple above the three separate entrances, each with a set of green-painted doors. One mid-October day, when his family was visiting the Reutershans, Byron took his dog, "Miss Tree," for a walk around the church. The dog's name was a tribute to the day Miss Tree, a stray, first showed up at his house. Byron's parents tried without success to locate the dog's owner and, unable to solve the mystery, named her as such and let Byron keep her. Byron, then a small boy, pronounced her name with two, not three, syllables.

Byron and Miss Tree climbed up the 20 worn, granite steps - Byron counted each one - which led from the sidewalk to the church's east entrance, and took seats on the top step. While Byron was watching a train approach the B&O Railroad station that bordered the city's east side, the church doors burst open behind him and a young couple appeared, arm in arm, smiling and laughing. The sound of a pipe organ playing Mendelssohn's "Wedding March" emanated from inside the church. The commotion startled Miss Tree and she began barking. Byron scooted to the side, pulling Miss Tree along with him, and put his hands around her mouth in a failed attempt to silence her.

Byron looked up at the couple as they passed. The groom towered over him, dwarfing his small frame. With his thick lips, wide nose, and olive complexion, the man looked like a young Babe Ruth. In the fall of 1914, some 60 years earlier, Ruth and his first wife were married at that church. Ruth had just completed his first year of professional ball, beginning the season with the International League Baltimore Orioles and closing with the American League Boston Red Sox, a rapid rise through the baseball ranks.

Byron waved to the couple as they descended the steps. The groom turned around and gave him a wink. Miss Tree continued barking. In the small parking lot at the base of the church steps there appeared a Packard S-38 touring car with thick whitewall tires and an open roof. Byron watched as the happy couple slid into the back seat and the car roared out of the parking lot, disappearing as if evaporating into the air before it reached Main Street.

After staring for a moment in disbelief, he stood up, still confused as to what he had seen, and looked down at Miss Tree, who appeared equally confused. "Did you see that?" Byron asked his attentive companion.

Byron walked over to the church entrance, pulling several times on its worn, cylinder-shaped, brass door handles, but they were locked. He knocked, but no one answered. Abandoning the doors facing east, Byron ran down the 20 granite steps, past the entrance to the church basement, around to the other side of the steeple, and up another 21 granite steps - he counted each one - to the doors facing west. Miss Tree followed suit, barking all the way. Byron pulled on the handles, but those doors were locked as well.

Unable to gain entrance to the church, Byron ran back to the Reutershans' house with his dog in tow and told his parents he had seen Babe Ruth and his bride coming out of St. Paul's. His parents didn't believe him. He told them Miss Tree had seen them, too, but his dog could not corroborate the story. When Byron persisted, his mother suggested that a visit with Father Vaughan, their pastor, might be in order, so the two could talk about Byron's burgeoning belief in the supernatural. The threat of having to spend additional time at church with the parish priest was enough to convince Byron to drop the issue, although it did nothing to discourage his belief he had just seen the late, great Babe Ruth.

Some years later, during his senior year at Cardinal Gibbons High School, Byron saw Ruth again. The school buildings and grounds had once been part of the St. Mary's Industrial School for Boys, an orphanage and reform school on the outskirts of Baltimore City. Ruth had spent the majority of his formative years there when his parents, out of desperation, signed the then eight-year-old Ruth over to the Xaverian Brothers. Some 70 years later, when Byron attended Cardinal Gibbons, Ruth's legend still loomed large within the halls of the former orphanage.

Byron played varsity baseball for his high school on the same field where Ruth once honed his skills. By then known as Babe Ruth Field, the ballpark was nothing fancy, just a dirt infield, cinder-block dugouts, and a rusty metal backstop. In the time since Ruth had attended St. Mary's, the field had been turned 180 degrees so home plate sat in place of centerfield. Byron didn't mind the ballpark's austere accommodations; he enjoyed playing on the historic field.

One Saturday morning, Byron arrived early to prepare for a noon game. It had rained the previous night and a light mist covered the ballfield. Byron noticed another game already underway, which, in and of itself, was not unusual, for other schools and amateur teams sometimes used the ballfield. What was unusual, however, was the arrangement of the field, with home plate situated in what was supposed to be centerfield.

At first, Byron figured the teams had rearranged the field so as not to play on the still-wet infield. But as he walked toward the relocated home plate, it occurred to him that the teams were using the old St. Mary's configuration. He looked across the field toward where the infield should have been and saw only grass, no dirt. The pitcher's mound and base paths were gone, as were the chainlink backstop and the cinder-block dugouts.

The players on the field wore flannel uniforms and three-fingered, over-stuffed baseball mitts that resembled some of the relics on display in the gym's athletic case. As Byron passed a scattering of spectators standing on a hill behind left field, he asked a young boy what teams were playing. The boy did not respond or even acknowledge Byron's presence. Approaching the players sitting along third base, he could see "St. Mary's" in block letters emblazoned across the front of their uniforms.

This can't be happening, he thought. *This can't be real.* A cold sweat coated his body. Feeling light-headed, he collapsed to the ground inches away from two spectators, neither of whom made any effort to move out of his way or to see if he was alright. No one around him seemed at all concerned about his welfare. After the warmth returned to his body, he sat up to watch the antique game, still annoyed that no one had paid any attention to his feeble condition.

"Let's go, George, hit it outta' here," yelled one of the players sitting along the third-base side of the field. At the plate, a gangly, left-handed batter lunged at the ball with a strong uppercut motion and the ball rose high into the air. Byron stood up to watch the ball's trajectory as it sailed out past right field, landing in a crowd of students who cheered and scrambled for the souvenir. The batter darted pigeon-toed around the bases and crossed home plate standing up, a home run. As the batter strutted past, Byron recognized him as a younger version of the same olive-skinned man he had seen outside St. Paul's Church seven years earlier. Ruth looked over at Byron and gestured, as if to say, "Did you see that?" and then looked away. *He saw me*, thought Byron. *No one else can, but he did.*

As soon as Ruth sat down on the bench, the mist covering the field grew thick as ballpark cotton candy, obscuring both teams and the infield. The ball game and the mist then faded, leaving Byron standing alone in left-center field. He looked around for the vanished game, still uncertain as to what, if anything, he had witnessed. Across the outfield in the direction of home plate, he saw the infield back in its usual spot. The backstop and dugouts had returned as well. Behind him, the batter's box where he had just seen Ruth hit a home run was once again a grassy outfield.

Some of Byron's teammates were sitting in the dugout, putting on their cleats, preparing to warm up. One teammate yelled over to Byron and asked what he had been doing in center-field. Byron feigned ignorance while his teammates insisted he appeared to be talking to someone who was not there. Byron made up some lie, fearing the ramifications were he to admit what he had seen. Byron's short stature already provided his teammates plenty of ammunition with which to tease him. He didn't need the added rounds that would have been inflicted upon him were he to say he had just seen George Herman Ruth hit a home run.

CHAPTER 4

Louie From Bowie

Ever since his first encounter with the Babe, Byron had developed a fondness for Ellicott City and the house on St. Paul Street. The Reutershans moved to Florida about the time Byron graduated from college and he was able to rent their house at a family-friendly discount. A Cape Cod of modest size with a single dormer above the center doorway, the dwelling suited Byron fine. One large, L-shaped room served as the kitchen, dining room, and living room. Byron kept the main room more or less picked up and occasionally vacuumed. However, with several laminated, particle board book shelves encircling the former antique store - each dipping ever so slightly in the middle from the baseball books and dust-covered memorabilia he had crammed onto the shelves – the place looked more like a thrift store than living space.

Off the main room was a small bedroom where Byron sometimes slept, although he often spent his nights in the main room sleeping on his La-Z-Boy. A second room he used as a study. More to the point, it is where he stored what seemed like a sea container's worth of baseball memorabilia – uniforms, bats and balls, hats and gloves, scrapbooks filled with newspaper clippings, programs, lineups, and scorecards. Some of the items were from his days in the minors; the rest was paraphernalia he had squirreled away from garage sales and swap meets.

The walls throughout the house were covered with framed

black-and-white photographs he had taken of every minor-league stadium in which he had ever played. It was part of his routine back then: when playing in a ballpark for the first time, he would stand at the top of the dugout steps and take pictures of the field, the crowd, and the dugout behind him. Byron hoped one day to publish a book of his baseball photographs, taken from his unique vantage point as a player. He knew some pictures might be a bit problematic, however, for many of his teammates followed their own routine of raising their middle finger toward the camera, showing Byron who they thought was number one.

⚾ ⚾ ⚾

On the morning following his Sunday trip to Baltimore, Byron woke up to find himself still in the La-Z-Boy, as *Sports Center* blared from the television. Pulling the recliner's lever forward, Byron propelled out of the seat and switched off the set. After a few perfunctory stretches, he rubbed his lower back in an attempt to repair the damage caused from having spent another night in the recliner.

Waiting for his coffee to brew, Byron thought about the events of the previous day. He examined the worn piece of metal, which, in the morning light, still looked nothing like the nickel he thought he had found in front of Murph's house. Byron aimed for the trash can next to the kitchen counter and flicked the metal piece across the room like a bottle cap, missing the rim by a good foot and a half. *Maybe I should keep it*, he thought, as he picked it up and tossed it on the counter. *A souvenir of my trip to Union Park.*

During the 40-minute drive from Ellicott City to his job with the Bowie Baysox at Prince George's Stadium, Byron fantasized about being able to go back in time and visit a place like Union Park – being able to watch a game between the National League Baltimore Orioles and Boston Beaneaters. He figured that most former players dreamed of going back and reliving their playing days. *There's nothing wrong with dreaming*, he thought.

In reality, Byron was just glad to be back in baseball, even if it were in the Baysox front office, literally and figuratively on the other side of the fence. Byron worked in signage – selling advertising space on the outfield wall, around the stadium concourse, in the restrooms above the urinals, and even on-air during games. "And now for the 'SprintVerizonAT&TCellularOne call to the bullpen!'"

While his official job title was Director of Sponsorship Sales, most of what he did at the stadium fell outside the official duties of his position. He worked on corporate accounts and season tickets. He sometimes helped run the scoreboard on game day, picking the songs they played or movie clips shown on the JumboTron during breaks in the action, during a pitching change, or when there was a conference on the mound. Byron played the Jeopardy theme song during opposing team mound conferences more times than he could remember and he still laughed every time he played it. His favorite movie clip was the scene from *Bull Durham* where the players converge for a mound conference and end up discussing what to give the left fielder for a wedding present.

Because of his size, Byron could, in a pinch, suit up as the Baysox's mascot, "Louie from Bowie." An oversized, animal-like creature costumed in green fur and purple feathers, Louie looked like the Philadelphia Phillies' Fanatic dressed in drag. Louie's actual gender remained a well-guarded secret within the Baysox front office, so much so not even Byron knew the answer. The irony of a former ballplayer suiting up to take the field as a mascot was not lost on Byron. In a perverse way, it provided him a uniformed connection to his past - not as a third baseman, but as Louie, from Bowie.

Over the years, Byron had met the challenge of being Louie with as much dignity as he could muster, paying strict adherence to the mascot code of conduct – "Be always courteous, do not behave in a rude or lascivious manner," and, most important of all, "never utter a word." Keeping the dial on mute proved to be the most difficult part of the code for Byron to honor, given the punching and prodding he endured from kids and adults alike while in uniform. Only once did he not stay true to the code. The unpleasantness that preceded the breach involved a marauding gang of unsupervised 10-year-olds that Byron sensed had no respect for the mascot or the man inside. After enduring a sustained assault and battery by the children, which involved, in no particular order, a souvenir bat, a box of mustard packets, three hot dogs, a baseball, a cup of soda, several foam fingers, and one well placed, excruciating shot to the groin, Byron broke the code. Although he was never certain the exact words he uttered, whatever they were, it was enough to ensure that his boss would think twice before asking Byron to don again the green fur and purple feathers.

⚾ ⚾ ⚾

Arriving for work at 10 a.m., Byron passed through the stadium's main gate, onto the concourse, and around to the third-base side of the ballpark for a quick view of the infield – his morning ritual. The Baysox were out of town, in the middle of a ten-day road trip, but there still was plenty of work to be done. Byron strolled over to his cubicle, passing the Baysox's general manager, Hank George, who already was at his desk in the team's administrative office, which doubled as the ticket booth.

"Good morning, Byron," said Hank. "Would you mind putting your stuff down and helping me in the outfield?"

"We gonna shag some flies?" asked Byron.

"No, we're replacing that section of outfield wall that caught on fire a couple of weeks ago."

"Whatever you need, Hank."

"Good."

"It may not have been much of a fire," said Byron, "but the crowd sure seemed to enjoy it. There were more ooh's and ah's for the burning fence than there were for the fireworks that started it."

"It did get a good response, didn't it? If it didn't cost so much money to replace each time, I might consider adding it as a promotion."

"I could work something up for you, if you'd like. 'Half-Price Burning-Down-The-House-Wednesdays.' We could play that old Talking Heads song between innings."

"Man, you and your lame puns. Do you ever stop?"

"No. It's in my DNA. My dad used to make them when I was a kid and it just kind of sunk in."

"Sounds like child abuse, if you ask me."

"To each his own. Hell, I even think of them in my sleep."

"What a nightmare."

"Ah - that's a good one, Hank."

"No, I didn't mean it. Stop it, okay? Come on, let's go."

The two left the office and headed toward the outfield fence.

"I'll bet I could get a fire extinguisher company to sponsor the burn, if you want."

Hank paused for a moment, considering Byron's suggestion. "No thanks," said Hank. "Even if I could find cheaper wall covering, I doubt we could get the insurance for it."

Hank's ability to think of every angle always impressed Byron. It was one reason he was a good general manager. A few years younger than Byron, Hank never played organized baseball; his interest in the game was strictly business. To Hank, minor-league baseball was just the first rung in the corporate ladder, and his Baysox general manager's gig was the first step. Hank figured he would make a name for himself in the minors and then catch on with a major-league club – similar to Byron's former career plans, except Hank would be wearing a suit, not a uniform.

Although well aware of Hank's single-minded acumen for the business of baseball, Byron still spoke to Hank as if he were a fan of the game.

"Hey, Hank," Byron called out as they took down the first of three charred sections of plastic. "Remember I was telling you about Union Park?"

"Yes," Hank yelled back.

"Well, I went to Baltimore yesterday to see where it used to be."

"Good for you," said Hank.

"And I found it."

"That's nice," said Hank, uninterested in Byron's story.

Byron debated whether to continue the conversation. Most often, Hank had little patience for Byron's ballpark banter and esoteric musings. However, Byron's sensible side lost the debate and he continued.

"I was in a restaurant down the street from where Union Park used to be and I met this old man named Mac who told me he could still see Union Park."

"That's great," said Hank. He was more interested in pulling down the plastic.

"Yeah, it is great. What's strange though is they tore down Union Park a hundred years ago."

"What's strange about it is you spending your weekend in Baltimore, talking to a crazy old man."

"I'm telling you what he told me. I'm not making it up."

"Did I say you were? Listen, maybe the old man's confused," said Hank, as he stopped what he was doing and looked over at Byron. "Maybe he's remembering something deep in his past. You get old and the mind plays tricks on you."

"Maybe, but just before that, I met another old man whose house is built on the land where the ballpark used to be. He told me he'd seen baseball players hanging around his yard."

"So you met two crazy old men."

"I had taken some pictures of his house and he told me I needed to give him my camera. When I tried to ask him a couple of questions, he told me to beat it."

"Maybe he's not so crazy after all," said Hank. "If I were him, I would have told you to beat it, too."

"Seriously, there's something going on. I'm just not sure what it is."

Hank stopped fiddling with the plastic sheeting for a moment and, after a long pause, looked over at Byron. "I hesitate to tell you this, and I'm probably going to regret it, but something like that happened here a couple of months ago."

"What?"

"This guy came by the stadium and told me he was looking for the entrance to 'Black Sox Park.'"

"What did you tell him?"

"I told him I'd never heard of Black Sox Park. He said he was looking for his teammates and wanted to know if I'd seen them playing here. I told him other than the Baysox and some college games, no one is allowed to play here. Then he said to me, 'I guess I asked the wrong guy.'"

"I know Black Sox Park," said Byron.

"Of course you do." Hank let out an exaggerated sigh.

"It was a Negro League park over on Mitchellville Road. The field where they played is part of the County recreation center there."

"If anyone knew that, it would be you," said Hank, unimpressed with Byron's obscure knowledge of the park.

"What did the guy look like?" asked Byron.

"Black guy, late sixties maybe. He looked like he was in good shape – like he took care of himself."

"What was he wearing?"

"I don't know, sweatpants, sweatshirt, maybe. He was carrying some kind of athletic bag. I figured he was in a senior league."

After installing the new outfield wall, Byron and Hank walked in silence back across the outfield's thick carpet of grass. When they reached the infield near the dugout, Byron cautiously stepped over the foul line, making sure his feet did not touch it. Hank looked at Byron and rolled his eyes. Byron didn't care, though. Some superstitions never died, even if he no longer was playing the game.

When they reached the stands, Hank broke the silence. "It doesn't surprise me someone would want to get back into the game. That guy was probably having some kind of mid-life crisis and was looking for a way to relive his past glories."

"Mid-life crisis? You said he was in his late sixties. If that's mid-life, then he's gonna be around until he's a hundred and forty."

"You know what I mean. He wants to go back to his youth."

"I don't think that's it," said Byron. "I think there's more to it."

"What do you think it is?" asked Hank.

"I don't know, maybe he's looking for something that you just can't see."

"What are you talking about? There's nothing more to see. That guy's like most of the players on this team, only a lot older, holding onto a dream he needs to let go of. You used to play. You remember that feeling. You can't tell me you don't wish you were still playing."

"And give up the privilege of selling advertising spots to Denny's? Not on your life."

"Yeah, right," said Hank.

"Well, if that guy comes back, let me know," said Byron, shaking his finger at Hank.

"Only if you promise to go with him and never return."

"And not see Louie again? You know I can't do that."

"Sure you can. In fact, I'll let you take Louie with you."

CHAPTER 5

A Modest Proposal

Searching the Internet for information about Union Park, Byron discovered he was not alone, that there were other like-minded people "out there" telegraphing through baseball websites their interest in lost ballparks. Byron's favorite site was *metaphysicalbaseball.com* – "Baseball Outside The Time And Space Continuum." Dedicated to preserving the memory of vanished ballparks, the site devoted much of its posts to the more recently departed ballparks, offering vintage pictures and postcards of those parks and descriptions and photos of what had been built in their place. Deadball-era lost ballparks - built during the later half of the 19th century - were discussed only in general terms, with a description of the parks, their former site, and the home teams that played there.

Byron toyed with the idea of sending *metaphysicalbaseball* some of the pictures he had taken in Baltimore, but he was reluctant to advertise to the world what he might have discovered. It also would have required him to develop the film, which was mixed in with 20 or so other rolls of film he kept in a coffee can on his dresser.

Another favorite of Byron's was *ballparkwatch.com*, which provided links to newspaper sites from around the country with articles discussing both major and minor-league stadiums. During the 1999 season, ballparkwatch posted stories from the *Detroit Free Press* about the unfolding final year of baseball at

Tiger Stadium. Since 1896, baseball had been played at the corner of Michigan and Trumbull, or as locals called it, "The Corner." With the closing of the stadium at the end of the 1999 season, baseball would lose its last continuous link between its modern era and baseball of the 19th century.

Checking the Tigers' upcoming home schedule, Byron received what he considered to be a sign – the Orioles were heading to Detroit that weekend for a three-game series and then to Cleveland. Given Cleveland's proximity to Detroit, Byron figured he could visit two stadiums in one trip - one stadium old and on its way out and Cleveland's Jacobs Field, new and on its way in. Over the years, Byron had met fans who "collected" baseball stadiums; now, it would be his turn to collect a few.

In hopes of finding a companion for the trip, Byron called his best friend, Charles Vincent (never Charlie, always Charles), who worked as an assistant curator at the Babe Ruth Museum in Baltimore. The two had met in Hagerstown, Maryland, during Byron's second year of professional ball. Ten years older than Byron, Charles worked then for the Hagerstown Suns as an assistant to the general manager. This made him a jack of all trades – groundskeeper, usher, ticket taker, souvenir seller, and bartender - kind of what Byron was for Bowie.

Byron knew from the moment he met Charles that he had found a kindred spirit. Charles was proud of working in Municipal Stadium, which, even then, was one of the oldest ballparks in the minor leagues. On the day they first met, Charles told Byron all about the history of baseball in Hagerstown, including the story of Willie Mays's professional debut there, when Mays was a player with the Trenton Giants, a Class B affiliate of the New York Giants. What should have been a moment of excitement and joy for Mays - his first professional game - was marred by racial slurs and derisive taunts by fans at the stadium. So bad was his treatment there that Mays swore he would never return to Hagerstown. As a life-long resident of that city, Charles remained embarrassed by the treatment Mays had received there in 1950.

I'm sure Charles will want to go to Detroit, thought Byron, as he punched the numbers on the telephone.

"Charles?"

"Hey, Bitty, what's up?"

"I'm offering you the chance of a lifetime," said Byron.

"I'm afraid to ask . . . . What is it?"

"I'm driving to Detroit this weekend and I want you to come with me."

"A weekend in Detroit? How's that the chance of a lifetime?"

"Because we're gonna see a game at Tiger Stadium."

"You're going all the way to Detroit for a baseball game? When did you decide this?"

"About five minutes ago. And I want you to go, too. I'll pay for the hotel and gas."

"I can't up and leave like that. Besides, we're opening a new exhibit this weekend and I have to work."

"I know I should've called sooner, but I only decided to go just now. Come on, can't you be spontaneous?"

"Sorry, man - besides, you're one to talk, 'Mr. Slave to his Routine.'"

"Charles - you do realize, don't you, that this is the Tigers' last season in Tiger Stadium. Once they're gone, they'll tear down the stadium and it will be nothing other than another lost ballpark."

"That's too bad. They shouldn't be moving."

"Well, they are and since I've never seen a game there, I'm going."

"You didn't go when you were a kid? I thought your dad was

from Detroit. Didn't he ever take you?"

"No, never did. But I'm going to correct that now. Someday, you'll be sorry you didn't see a game there, too."

"Oh, I've got that covered," said Charles. "I went to a game there years ago, when it was still called Briggs Stadium."

"Rats. Come on man. I need you to do this for me. Remember back in Hagerstown when you'd hit me fungoes?"

"I remember how crazy you drove everyone, coaches, players, grounds crew, anyone you saw, asking them to hit fungoes to you. Hell, the sight of you holding a fungo bat sent everyone fleeing like mice at the flick of a light switch."

"Yeah. But not you. You were there for me. Well, Charles, I need you to hit me some fungoes."

"Sorry, Bitty, I can't."

Byron took a deep breath. He hated being called Bitty, even by Charles. "You know, Charles, as I have told you countless times before, you can call me Byron. You don't have to call me Bitty."

"I know, Bitty."

Byron paused for a few seconds. "Maybe I should see if Maggie would like to go with me."

"You know she won't, so don't even bother asking her."

"Maybe she's never seen a game there, either."

"I doubt she has, but it's still a waste of time."

"You're probably right."

"We're still on for our trip to Fenway this summer, right?" asked Charles.

"We are, assuming I come back from Detroit. I might stay there and make some new friends."

"Good luck with that, Bitty. Whatever you do, don't tell them any stories about your days in the minors, or you'll find yourself alone there, too."

"What? You don't like my stories?"

"Not as much as I did the first couple hundred times I heard them. But if you get some new ones, maybe I'll listen."

"It's funny you should ask. I got one now."

"I didn't ask."

"Well, you're gonna want to hear this. You know how I've been researching Union Park?"

"Is that what you call your obsession? Research?"

"Yeah, research. And my research has uncovered something you boys at the Babe Ruth Museum should have found a long time ago, but didn't."

"What?"

"An actual sign from Union Park."

"What sign? Where?" asked Charles.

"In Baltimore, but I'm not telling you where."

"I don't believe you. You're not telling me because you're making it up."

"I'm not telling you because I don't want the sign to disappear while I'm gone. And, so you know, the guy who owns it told me he's not selling."

"And who, may I ask, is that?"

"Mac."

"Mac, who?"

"Just Mac. I don't know his last name."

"He's not another one of your imaginary friends, is he?"

"No, he's not, and besides, I don't have any imaginary friends."

"You haven't been seeing things again, have you? Don't tell me Babe Ruth paid you another visit."

"No," said Byron.

"So what does the sign look like?"

"It's kinda big - maybe eight feet across - made of wood."

"What does it say?"

"Union Park."

"Come on, Bitty, tell me where it is. You can trust me."

"Nope. I'll tell you when I get back, unless you want to come to Detroit with me, then maybe I'll tell you on the way."

"I can't go."

"Alright, suit yourself. I'll give you a call when I get back. Maybe we can have dinner there next week."

"Where is there?" asked Charles.

"Where the sign is."

"So, it's at a restaurant?"

"Damn. How did you know that?" asked Byron, proud Charles had picked up on his hint.

"You just said we'll eat there next week."

"I did, didn't I?"

"Give me a call when you get back."

Byron hung up the phone. *Man*, thought Byron, *I wish Charles would come with me to Detroit. At least I didn't tell him where the Union Park sign is. That should bother him until I return.*

Byron debated giving Maggie a call. He picked up the phone, but he put it down without dialing her number. Thinking about the day Charles had introduced him to her, he smiled a melancholy smile. Charles had known Maggie's family since she was a little girl and, when Byron learned this, he pestered Charles to introduce him to her. Charles acquiesced, figuring they might hit it off since they both were Catholic and loved baseball. He was right. The day they met, Maggie was working the turnstiles in the front of Municipal Stadium. Byron could still remember what she was wearing that day - gym shorts and an orange halter top with "Hagerstown Suns" emblazoned across her breasts.

What more could a man ask for? he remembered wondering. *A beautiful girl sitting at the entrance to a baseball park, wearing a baseball shirt and tearing tickets.*

Byron was already in his uniform and his cleats made a clicking sound along the concrete as he and Charles approached where Maggie was working. Byron held out his hand and she stood up from her stool to greet him. At a little over five feet tall, her diminutive size made Byron feel bigger than he actually was. She had long, wavy red hair and Irish-green eyes. He fell in love immediately and completely, in the all-consuming way only a 19-year-old can fall in love.

Whenever he thought about that day, his mind invariably would flash forward to other memories. He thought about the day Maggie told him she was pregnant, recalling the panic and the tears they both cried. He thought about the day, four months later, they were married at St. Mary's Catholic Church, recalling the ceremony's tempered happiness and the families' quiet embarrassment. He thought about the worst day of his life - the day, two months later, when Maggie went into premature labor, and the baby, a boy, died during delivery when the umbilical cord prolapsed. He could still feel the sense of loss, the grief, the guilt.

What he could not recall with any specificity was the subsequent fallout. It was left to his friends, like Charles and others who knew him well, to fill in the details of his life back then - his depression, his anger, and his excessive drinking. His season in Charlotte the following summer remained a blur. Whatever energy he could muster, he put into baseball, at the expense of his marriage. He could recall only one trip Maggie had made to Charlotte to visit him that summer. He was out of town the day she moved back in with her parents. He was out of town the day she called to tell him it was over.

Yet, through the years, even after the divorce and subsequent annulment, Byron and Maggie had remained friends. The common bond of a lost child brought them together on occasion, around the anniversary date, either over the phone or sometimes in person. He still cared for her and appreciated her willingness to listen whenever he called. She was sensitive to his eccentricities yet willing to tell him when he was acting stupid or making a bad decision. She, like Byron, had not remarried.

Maybe, I'll call her tomorrow, he thought, putting the telephone back on its stand. He put his hands in his face and rubbed his eyes. *After I see what happens tomorrow at work.*

⚾ ⚾ ⚾

The following day, Byron had the difficult task of convincing Hank he wasn't needed for the upcoming weekend series even though the Baysox would be back in town hosting the Akron Aeros. Byron tracked down Hank in the storage room on the third-base side of the stadium, "supervising" the beer inventory, counting the number of kegs on hand, making sure there was enough for the home stand.

"A little too early to be drinking, Hank," said Byron. "Don't you think?"

"What do you want, Byron?"

"I need the weekend off."

"Why, is there something wrong?"

"No, not really, although I have been feeling a bit run down, I guess." Byron considered telling Hank a white lie, something about a great-aunt from Saskatchewan dying, but his Catholic guilt kept him closer to the straight and narrow. "I need a couple days off so I can go to Detroit."

"You're feeling run down so you're going to Detroit?" Hank

asked. "Why? You planning to commiserate with the city? What's the matter with you?"

"Nothing more than usual. I want to see a game at Tiger Stadium. The Orioles are playing there this weekend, so it's the perfect time to go."

"It's not the perfect time to go. We have games this weekend."

"It's my one chance to see the Orioles play at Tiger Stadium this year. They're closing the stadium at the end of the season and I want to see a game there before it's gone."

"If the Baysox weren't in town this weekend, I'd have no problem with it."

"Please? Attendance is still pretty light. I really want to see the O's play in Detroit. Their only other trip there this year is the last week of August – during the Baysox's final home stand. I know you'll want me around here then."

Hank thought for a moment.

"Come on, Hank. Give me the weekend off. Please." Byron felt like a school kid asking his mother if he could go outside and play in a neighbor's yard.

"Okay," said Hank.

"Really? Thanks."

"You're welcome."

"What about you, you wanna come along?" asked Byron, emboldened by Hank's acquiescence. "On the way back, I'm gonna stop in Cleveland for a game. The Orioles are playing there, too. Then, I'll be home."

"Detroit, then Cleveland? That's even worse. If you're feeling so run down, why don't you take a real vacation? Go to Ocean City and sit on the beach or something."

"They're not closing the beach, Hank. It'll be around forever."

"Are you going with anyone?"

"That's the funny thing. No one else wants to go with me."

"Shocking," said Hank. "Maybe you should invite that man you met in Baltimore, old what's-his-name?"

"Mac?"

"Yeah – Mac. Why don't you ask Mac?"

Byron paused for a moment and considered Hank's suggestion.

"You know, that's not such a bad idea."

"Byron - I was kidding."

"In fact, it's a great idea. I could use the company. I'll bet his calendar is open."

CHAPTER 6

☉ ☉ ☉

Locked and Tied

Driving home that evening, Byron decided to invite Mac on the trip, figuring there was no harm in asking. The difficulty was, Byron had no way of reaching Mac, save another trip to Harwood, and even that was no sure thing. Byron checked the telephone book for the number of the Stone Tavern, but he found no listing. On the Internet he found the restaurant mentioned and a phone number, but no webpage for the Tavern itself. Byron called, but a recording came on saying the number had been disconnected. *That's strange*, he thought. *They must have changed the number. I guess I'm driving up there.* He grabbed his wallet and keys and his new good luck charm, the crusty piece of metal, which he stuck in his billfold so he would not lose it.

Taking Route 40 east, Byron caught most of the traffic lights and arrived in Harwood less than 20 minutes later. He slowed the car to a crawl on East 25th Street as he crossed Guilford, passing Murph's house on the right. No lights were on inside, although he thought he saw the outline of a person sitting on the front porch, talking to someone standing on the sidewalk.

While waiting for traffic to clear the intersection at 25th Street and Greenmount, Byron was startled to see sheets of plywood covering the front door and windows of the Stone Tavern. *What the hell? This can't be.*

Byron pulled into the lot and parked his car alongside the building. *Maybe there was a fire,* he thought, as he walked toward the entrance to the restaurant. Rusty nails held warped, water-stained plywood over the front door, suggesting the sheets had been there for some time. Byron saw no evidence of a fire or any other catastrophe that would have precipitated the restaurant's recent closing. Byron tried looking through the one side window not covered with plywood, but the small amount of daylight left did not reach inside. From all outward appearances, it looked as though the restaurant had been boarded up for years.

"This can't be," he said. "I was here last Sunday."

Byron left his car in the parking lot and headed across the street to a gas station at the corner of Greenmount and East 25th Street. The attendant inside the kiosk was focused on his Gameboy.

"Excuse me." Byron tapped on the window.

The young man looked up from his game.

"Do you know how long that restaurant across the street's been closed?" Byron pointed in the direction of the Stone Tavern.

"That place?" The man motioned in the direction of the Stone Tavern. "I've never seen it open."

"Never?"

"Not since I've been here."

"You don't know a guy who lives around here named Mac, do you?"

"Mac? No."

Byron left the gas station and walked across the street to Roland Billiards. "Sports Bar and Grill" proclaimed the establishment's green electric sign. With bars covering its windows, the one-story, 1950's-style red-brick building looked more like a small town prison than a bar and grill. Below the hours of operation posted on the thick glass double doors was a sign warning "Absolutely No One Under The Age Of 21 Admitted."

After what he had seen, or not seen, at the Stone Tavern, Byron felt the strong urge to have a drink - an urge he had never quite been able to lose. He hesitated a moment before entering the bar. *I can do this,* he thought, as he pulled open the door. The distinctive aroma of stale beer hit him as he walked inside. The Orioles-White Sox game flickered on a 1970's-era Sylvania T.V. suspended on a makeshift shelf above the Lucite-covered, plywood and naugahyde-padded bar. Byron watched the game for a moment before looking for a seat.

A patron at the bar, nursing a *Natty Boh,* turned around and gave Byron a quick look.

"This seat taken?" Byron asked, pointing to the stool next to the man. The man shook his head no.

Byron sat down and watched as the man took a long, slow drink. *Man, I used to love that beer,* thought Byron, his desire for a drink growing stronger. *Maybe I should leave.*

"Can I help you?" asked the man drinking the beer, who had noticed Byron's long, contemplative stare.

"Oh, sorry," said Byron. "That beer looks so damn good. Nothing like a cold frosty from the land of pleasant living."

"What?"

"You know - *Natty Boh* - 'From the Land of Pleasant Living,'" said Byron, referencing the beer's quaint slogan.

"I don't know, maybe," responded the man, uninterested in Byron's esoteric musings.

Byron watched the man gulp down half the bottle. He could almost feel the cold liquid on his lips, his throat opening up as the beer cascaded down. *I shouldn't be here,* he thought. *Not after what I saw at the Stone Tavern. Give me one and I'll drink four hundred.*

Byron stood up to leave as the bartender approached. "What'll you have?" the bartender asked, as he placed another beer in front of the man sitting next to Byron.

Byron sat back down, breathed a deep sigh, and replied, "Coffee, three creams." The bartender placed a napkin in front of Byron before walking away. Byron smiled.

"Excuse me," Byron said to the man sitting next to him. "Do you know if that restaurant across the street is closed?"

"What restaurant?"

"The Stone Tavern."

"You don't mean the old Little Tavern, do you? The one that's all boarded up."

"Yeah . . . I believe it's called the Stone Tavern."

"Well, whatever it's called - it sure looks closed to me," said the man, letting out a laughing grunt.

"I know it looks closed, but . . . ."

"Hey, Frank," said the man, turning to the patron on the other side of him. "You think that boarded up Little Tavern across the street is closed?" They both laughed.

"So it's been closed for a while?" Byron continued, undaunted by the man's sarcastic response.

"Long as I can remember."

"And it's not open only during the day or on weekends?"

"Son, it's never open."

"I see."

Sitting at the bar, watching the Orioles dismantle the White Sox, Byron didn't know what to believe. The Orioles were actually winning! No, that wasn't it. Could it be he had imagined his conversation with Mac at the Stone Tavern? That was one possible explanation, he thought, although the conversation seemed so real. If he did meet Mac there, then how was it the Tavern was now closed? Maybe Mac was like that player he had seen at the former site of Union Park - some type of apparition.

The bartender brought Byron a cup of coffee and a stainless steel creamer filled with milk. "One twenty-five," said the bartender.

Byron pulled a couple of dollars out of his wallet and handed the money to the bartender.

"Excuse me, do you know an old man who lives around here named Mac?"

"Mac? Mac who?" asked the bartender.

"I don't know his last name."

"No, can't say I do."

"What if I made that three dollars?" asked Byron, pointing to the two dollars.

"You can make it three hundred, but the answer would still be no."

Byron turned in the direction of his two new helpful friends. "Any of you gentlemen know a guy around here named Mac?"

They both gave Byron the same look, as if wondering why he was still talking to them.

"There's a 'Mac - Donald's up the street," said one of the men, laughing.

The other man joined in: "And I know that place ain't closed."

As Byron got up to leave, it occurred to him the two idiots at the bar, in their own way, had helped by reminding him how obnoxious a person can be after consuming too much alcohol. Byron was glad he wasn't sticking around for a beer.

Walking toward his car, he thought again about what had happened at the Stone Tavern and wondered whether the same thing might also be happening inside Roland's, so he headed back over to the bar for proof he had been there. Once inside, Byron asked the bartender for a receipt. The bartender responded with a "you've-got-to-be-kidding-me" look before punching some keys on the cash register, which kicked out a curled white slip of paper. He tore off the receipt and handed it to Byron.

"Business deduction," said Byron, trying to disguise his unorthodox request.

The bartender shrugged his shoulders and turned away. Byron pulled out his wallet and slipped the proof of his visit inside.

Instead of heading to his car, Byron walked west down East 25th Street in the direction of Guilford. A streetlight on the corner pierced the cool night air. Some kids playing on the corner ran past him and onto the darkened stoop of one of the row houses lining the street. Byron felt out of place, but he needed to find Mac and figured Murph might know where he lived.

Wait a second, he thought, as he headed toward Murph's house. *Since Mac told me Murph's name, all I gotta do is find Murph, confirm that's his name, and then I'll know Mac is for real and that we did meet.*

Murph's porch light was turned off; a trace of light escaped through the glass transom above the front door. The wooden stairs creaked with age as Byron walked up the front steps. Byron pushed the doorbell and, hearing no audible bell, opened the screen door, knocked, and let the screen door close. No one answered. After a minute, Byron knocked again, and, after two minutes, turned his back to the door. Before he could take his first step away from the entrance, the front door opened and the screen door slammed into his back, almost knocking him down the steps. A middle-aged woman came across the threshold, walking straight into Byron's back side.

The woman screamed, as did Byron.

"I'm sorry, ma'am," said Byron, his heart pounding. "I didn't mean to startle you."

"What the hell you doing here standing on my front porch?"

yelled the woman as she stepped back inside the house, closing the screen door between them.

"I'm sorry," said Byron. "I rang the bell, but no one answered. I'm looking for Murph. Is he here?"

"For who?"

"Murph."

"You mean the landlord?" asked the woman. "And you are?"

"My name's Byron Bennett. I met Murph a couple of days ago. I wanted to speak with him for a moment."

"Look, you guys gotta stop bothering that old man. He's not feelin' so good. I don't know what you're doing down there in the basement, shooting craps, whatever, but you can't be comin' 'round no more."

"Oh, I assure you ma'am, I'm not here to gamble. I just want to ask him a question."

"Well you can't talk to him now, so go away and leave him alone."

The woman slammed the front door shut.

What am I doing? wondered Byron, frustrated and embarrassed. *Begging to talk to some old man. This is stupid. Why on earth am I doing this?*

Walking down the front steps, Byron reached into his pocket.

"The sooner I get back to reality the better," he said.

He opened his wallet, intending to toss the crusty piece of metal back where he had found it.

Wait a second, he thought. The metal piece he found in his wallet was smooth to the touch, no longer rough around the edges. He stopped to examine it underneath a street lamp. "This can't be," he said. It was the nickel he had found the previous Sunday, once again in near-pristine condition.

Holding the nickel tight in his hand, Byron looked back at

Murph's house before turning and walking toward his car, picking up the pace with each step. As Byron crossed Barclay, leaving the confines of what used to be Union Park, the nickel grew hot and seemed to be moving in his hand. When he reached the other side of Barclay, the heat became unbearable and he dropped the nickel on the ground, letting out a yelp. Rubbing his right thumb over the palm of his left hand, Byron looked down at the sidewalk where the nickel lay – but all he saw was a crusty piece of metal, its surface once again corroded.

Byron reached down and picked up the piece of metal. Its surface was still warm. He looked around to see if anyone was watching, but saw no one. Spooked by the morphing nickel and the surrounding darkness, Byron ran the rest of the way back to his car, locking the doors as soon as he got inside.

Heading south on Greenmount, he drove as fast as traffic would allow. A mile or so out of Harwood, he pulled the piece of metal out of his pocket, turning it over and over in his hand as he drove. He tried to make sense out of what had just happened, but it made no sense. "Boy, my drinking must have done more damage than I thought," he said, trying to make light of the moment. But he knew what he had experienced was not something he could rationalize as a hallucination and be done with it. He had experienced things like this before, when he was younger, before he had ever started drinking. Except now it was more than visual. He felt the heat of the metal changing in his hand. It was tangible.

Byron switched on WBAL to catch the end of the Orioles game, although he paid no attention to the game itself, instead taking comfort in the familiar drone of the AM radio broadcast. Once back at his house, Byron collapsed into his recliner, exhausted from the events of the day, and soon was asleep.

Later that evening, the loud thump of the front door's brass mail slot closing awoke him from a sound sleep. Startled, Byron sprang up from his chair. "What was that?" he said out loud, looking around the room. He saw an envelope beneath the mail slot and walked over to pick it up. He opened the door but saw no one.

Returning to his chair, he examined the outside of the envelope. It appeared old, yellowish-brown, and fragile to the touch. Byron's name, hand-written in calligraphy, appeared on the envelope. There was no return address.

Inside the envelope, in handwriting similar to that on the front, was a note:

Dear Byron,

I heard you were looking for me this evening. Sorry you missed me. I cannot go to Detroit. When you are there, please say hello to Matty O'Boyle, an old friend. He used to work the grounds there. Last I heard he was selling souvenirs on Michigan Avenue down from the stadium. He'll know what you are looking for. When you are in Cleveland, stop by League Park. There is much there for you to learn. Also, Forbes Field in Pittsburgh.

Mac

What is this? thought Byron, almost annoyed. *The restaurant's closed so he comes all the way out here to give me the itinerary for my road trip? How the hell did he know I was even looking for him?* Byron read the note a second time, not believing what he was reading. *How did he know where I live? How did he know I was going to Detroit? And Cleveland? Why didn't he tell me he was here? Who the hell is Matty O'Boyle?* Byron pushed back into the La-Z-Boy and read the note again, this time admiring its exquisite penmanship.

The next morning, as he dressed for work, he remembered the note and, wanting to read it again, searched the area around his chair, but he could find neither the note nor the envelope. "Where is it?" he asked as he scoured the house. "It's got to be here someplace."

It was all to no avail. *I must have imagined it,* he thought. *I woke up when I heard the package fall through the door, but maybe it never happened. Was it a dream?*

⚾ ⚾ ⚾

At work that day, Byron kept to himself. He felt no need to share recent events with anyone, especially Hank. The two may have been friends, but Hank was still his boss and Byron did not want to provide Hank with additional evidence of his eccentricity.

That evening, he called Maggie.

"Maggie. Hey it's Byron. Have a minute? I need to talk to you about something."

"Well, hello Byron. It's been a while. How are you?"

"I'm fine, thanks. Listen, something's happened."

"How am I? I'm fine, too. Thanks for asking."

"Oh . . . I'm sorry. I didn't mean to be rude. So, how are you?"

"I'm doing okay, I guess."

"That's good. You wouldn't believe what happened to me a couple days ago in Baltimore."

"You're probably right, but that's never stopped you from

telling me before."

"Very funny. Maggie, I had another 'moment,' you know, like I used to have. In Baltimore - last Sunday."

"A 'moment?' I thought you stopped having those years ago."

"I did too. I was in this restaurant and I met this guy. He told me he could still see games being played at Union Park - where the Orioles used to play."

"So?"

"So? Union Park's been gone for over a hundred years."

"Oh, I see. So the guy's crazy."

"Yeah, maybe, except I think I saw the same thing - when I was standing in the alley where Union Park used to be. I saw a ballfield for a split second and then it was gone."

"Well, sounds like you're both crazy, then."

"There's more. When I went back yesterday to try and find the guy, I went to the restaurant where we met and it was all boarded up. I asked some people in the bar across the street about the restaurant and they told me the place hasn't been open for years."

"Wait. You're having these moments again and you go into a bar? That's a bad idea, Byron."

"I didn't drink anything but coffee."

"I still don't think you should be going to bars, period."

"After I got home last night, the guy dropped a letter in the mail slot, or at least I think he did."

"Did you talk to him?"

"No, I opened the door, but I didn't see anyone."

"What did the letter say?"

"I can't quite remember now, but it said that on my trip to Detroit I should look for one of his friends."

"Why don't you read it to me?"

"I can't."

"Why not?"

"It disappeared. I woke up this morning and couldn't find it."

"Byron, what do you want me to say? Yes, you're seeing ghosts - corresponding with them - and, yes, it's okay?"

"I know it sounds crazy, but it seems so real."

"I know it seems real to you, but listen to what you're saying."

"Believe me, I'm more than a little scared about all this. When I was just a kid, I figured it was some kind of childhood fantasy. And then that time on the train, I figured it was because I had just given up drinking and was upset because you wouldn't go with me. But, now . . . ."

"What do you want me to say?"

"Nothing - I just needed to tell somebody what was happening. And you're the only one I can tell this stuff to."

"What about Charles?"

"No. You know how he is. He always tells me to grow up. He may love baseball, but he's too straitlaced to believe anything like this. If it isn't in a book or on display in his museum, he won't believe it."

"You should talk to a professional about this, someone who can help you. What about Dr. Connor? Why don't you give him a call?"

"I don't need to talk to him. I already know what he would say."

After a short pause, Maggie asked, "So, you said you're going to Detroit? When? Why?"

"Friday morning. I'm going to see the Orioles play the Tigers. Then I'm following them to Cleveland."

"Oh - so you're finally going to see a game at Tiger Stadium."

"Yeah. I was hoping I could find someone to go with me, but

no one wants to. You don't want to go, do you?"

"Ah, no, Byron, thanks but, no. No, no, no."

"That's a 'no' then?"

"Yes. But, don't worry. You've never had any problem talking to strangers or making new friends."

"I didn't think you would go with me and that's not why I called. I just needed to talk to you."

"Well, you can always give me a call. I don't mind listening."

"Thanks."

"Let me know how your trip goes."

"I will. Goodnight."

"Goodnight, Byron."

⚾ ⚾ ⚾

At the end of the work day on Thursday, Byron was preparing to leave when Hank came over to his desk.

"So, you're still going?" asked Hank, knowing the answer.

"Tomorrow morning."

"You taking anyone with you?"

"I am. Babe Ruth agreed to come along, but I had to promise to pay for the hot dogs and beer."

"Well, tell the Babe I said 'hello.' In fact, let him know, if he's up for it, we'd love to have him do a personal appearance at a game this year."

"Sorry, but you'll have to ask him yourself. You can try him at the Babe Ruth Museum. I'll see you next Wednesday."

"Have fun. I hope it doesn't rain."

CHAPTER 7

❧ ❧ ❧

On the Road Again

There are two types of people in this world – those whose names appear in the *Official Encyclopedia of Baseball* and those whose names do not. The *Encyclopedia*, a proverbial Who's Who of baseball, contains the statistics of every big-league baseball player since before the advent of time. When Byron was young, he spent countless hours poring through it, memorizing stats of his favorite players and fantasizing that, one day, his name would be listed among them. Had things gone as planned, his name, "Bennett, Byron (Bitty)," would have been sandwiched between "Benners, Isaac B." and "Bennett, Charles Wesley," two players from the 1880's. Indeed, an earlier incarnation of Tiger Stadium, Bennett Park, was named after Charlie Bennett, a former Tigers' catcher and fan favorite whose career was permanently derailed when he lost both legs in a train accident.

Byron's copy of the *Encyclopedia* - the Fifth Revised Edition, published in 1970 - had a cracked spine and several pages that floated freely in the middle of the book. For Byron, it was the reading equivalent of comfort food. Whenever he needed a dose of nostalgia, he flipped through the book, rereading the dated stats of the dead and aging stars.

The night before he was to leave for Detroit, he grabbed the thick book from its place of honor on a bookshelf over his desk. The book included a section depicting seating charts of major league stadiums from the 1970's and he figured the antiquated information could prove useful in his quest to visualize any lost ballparks he visited. As a kid, Byron had dreamt of seeing games in those parks, seated somewhere along the third-base line. He tossed the *Encyclopedia* into his tattered duffel bag – a parting gift from the Rochester Red Wings – along with clothes for the trip. He also packed a copy of Ritter's *Lost Ballparks*. A more recent addition to his library, the book's photographs could be useful in helping him bring to life old ballparks such as Pittsburgh's Forbes Field and Cleveland's League Park.

Byron's anticipation for the trip kept him from a sound sleep and he was up and dressed by 4 a.m. A final burst of steam shot out the top of his vintage Mr. Coffee machine – endorsed by Joe DiMaggio! – signaling the coffee was ready. Byron remembered well the day he found the coffee maker at a garage sale, still in its original box, his euphoric reaction akin to a rare book dealer discovering some long-lost Mark Twain manuscript in a $5 used-book rack. He knew immediately the historical significance of the bargain he had uncovered the moment he caught a glimpse of Joltin' Joe's mug smiling at him from across the driveway, cup in hand, ready for a sip of joe.

The Mr. Coffee had cost Byron ten bucks – no haggling that day. Byron figured, why insult the seller? For several years he had kept the coffee maker in mint-in-the-box condition, not wanting to destroy its pristine state or its considerable financial value. One winter's morning, a momentary girlfriend shamed Byron into using the coffee maker when his old one gave out. Ultimately, Byron's magnanimous gesture was not enough to persuade the woman he was worth the cost of his baseball affliction, and she, like those before her, left him. He had no regrets, though, for he kept the box on display in his study, next to his Ted Williams Sears and Roebuck weight set, still mint-in-the-box.

Byron poured some coffee into his grandfather's glass-lined thermos – another gift from his estate – and made some sandwiches, using up all the bread. The pre-road-trip ritual of brewing coffee and making sandwiches dated back to his family's vacations when he was a child. In those days, everyone would be up by 4 a.m. and on the road by 5, the chirping of katydids outside the car's rolled down windows providing the pre-dawn soundtrack. His father's government salary did not allow for extravagant trips by airplane to exotic locations, so their trips most always were to New England to visit his mother's parents or to Michigan to visit his father's many sisters. Those were carefree times for Byron, sitting in the back seat of his family's BelAir station wagon, facing the rear, watching the ever-changing scenery disappear before him.

During his playing days, the countless bus rides through minor-league towns temporarily stripped the sheen of road trips to base metal. Still, he never lost the desire to hit the road and, as he prepared for his trip that morning, he felt the same anticipation and excitement he once had felt as a child.

It was still dark outside as Byron packed the car, a serenade of nocturnal sounds surrounding him. His car, a late 1970's Camaro he had bought with the meager bonus money paid him by the Orioles, had long since lost whatever respect it once engendered. Its bright orange paint was faded across the hood and trunk from years of exposure to the sun. Rust had devoured much of its rear quarter panels, which Byron kept patched with an assortment of fiberglass and body putty. The interior of the car looked as if it had once housed a small family of raccoons, although Byron recently had shelled out $150 to have a new headliner glued to the car's ceiling. It was the one thing he refused to put up with - driving around town with a decaying, polyester headliner draped over his head like a big, floppy hat. As for the rest of the car, he had learned to live with whatever embarrassment he felt about its appearance, focusing instead on the vague notion of one day having enough money to restore it.

The drive from Ellicott City to Detroit would take about eight hours, leaving plenty of time to make the game's 7:05 p.m. start time. Traveling west on I-70, Byron reached Breezewood in two hours. With no direct link between I-70 west and the Pennsylvania Turnpike, traffic crawled through the town's infamous stretch of tacky commerce. By 9 a.m., Byron reached the tail end of Pittsburgh's rush hour. Traffic moved at a moderate pace.

According to Mac's vanished itinerary, Byron's first stop was Forbes Field, former home of the National League Pittsburgh Pirates. Built by Pirates' owner Barney Dreyfuss in 1909, the ballpark was named in honor of British General John Forbes who, during the French and Indian War, captured the French outpost later known as Fort Pitt. Ritter's book mentioned a portion of the original outfield wall that remained at the site. Byron figured the wall alone would be worth the stop.

Passing a sign for Homestead, Byron thought about the famed Grays of the Negro National League, who played in that town and also at Forbes Field. Josh Gibson, "the Black Babe Ruth," as he sometimes was called, played for the Grays and the Pittsburgh Crawfords, another local team. Charles liked to turn that phrase around, referring to Ruth as "the White Josh Gibson," in recognition of Gibson's having hit more than 800 home runs during his baseball career. Byron had contemplated a stop in Homestead, as well, but learned that Municipal Field, where Gibson and the Grays once played, was long gone. He knew a portion of Ammons Field, where Gibson played the year he broke in with the semiprofessional league Crawfords in 1929, remained in Pittsburgh's Hill District, but decided against a stop there. It would have to be another ballpark, another day.

After clearing the Squirrel Hill Tunnel, Byron spotted the sign for Forbes Avenue/Oakland. Forbes Field, once located on what was now the campus of the University of Pittsburgh, was purchased by the University in the 1960's with the understanding it would tear down the ballpark and develop the land once the Pirates relocated to a new stadium.

After taking the exit, getting lost, and hoping not to have to stop for directions, Byron caught sight of Pitt's Cathedral of Learning at the corner of Forbes Avenue and Bigelow Boulevard. He knew then he was close, for he had seen in Ritter's book a picture of the cathedral, rising like a great, snow-capped mountain beyond the ballpark's left-field fence.

With classes at the university still in session, Byron parked five blocks away at a meter across the Schenley Drive Bridge and headed on foot for Forbes Field, his copy of *Lost Ballparks* tucked under his arm. Crossing the bridge, some 120 feet above Junction Hollow, where a branch line of the Baltimore and Ohio Railroad once ran, Byron admired the gently sloped, bucolic hills of Schenley Park and the nearby campuses of Carnegie Mellon University to the east and the University of Pittsburgh to the west.

Wesley Posvar Hall, a six-story, hulking, concrete, Brutalist monstrosity constructed by the University of Pittsburgh half a decade after the demise of Forbes Field, sat in the footprint of what was once the third-base side of the infield. It disappointed Byron to see that this building – which lacked any architectural *je ne sais quoi* – had supplanted the grand, historic ballpark.

Standing on the sidewalk in front of Posvar Hall, near the former entrance to the left-field bleachers, Byron was consumed by a sensation similar to what he had experienced the previous Sunday when visiting the site of Union Park – as if all that had happened before on that spot remained somehow frozen in time. Byron closed his eyes, trying to imagine Forbes Field rising before him. He remembered what Mac had told him about Union Park – *It comes and it goes.*

After a minute passed, Byron opened his eyes and, there, in front of him, perhaps six feet away, were two beautiful, young, female coeds, looking right at him, trying to hide the wide grins on their young, as yet unlined faces. Byron felt like a fool.

"Are you okay, mister?" asked one of the coeds.

"Oh, I'm fine. Thanks, though," said Byron, flustered.

"You look lost. You're sure you're okay?" asked the other.

Byron considered making up a story about this being the spot where his dog had died when she was hit by a car, but before he could gather the words for such a lie, the two coeds hurried by, still unsuccessful in their efforts to suppress their laughter. Byron watched the women cross the street and head inside the University library. Byron let out a deep sigh. *If only I were ten years younger*, he thought. *Of course, they must think I'm an idiot.*

With the coeds safely out of view, Byron turned his attention back to the matter at hand and opened Ritter's book to the chapter on Forbes Field, which included a photograph of home plate encased in glass on the first floor of Posvar Hall. Byron figured home plate was as good a place as any to start, so he entered the hall. A security guard, somewhere in his mid-50's, was sitting behind a metal, single-pedestal office desk covered with decidedly fake wood veneer. The guard's oversized, defensive-lineman frame dwarfed the tiny desk in front of him.

"Excuse me," said Byron. "I'm looking for the home plate from Forbes Field."

"Home plate?" asked the guard. "It's half way down the hall, next to that pillar." The guard pointed toward the middle of the building.

"Thanks," said Byron, walking past the guard's desk.

Although not invited, the guard stood up from behind his desk and began walking alongside Byron.

"You a baseball fan?" asked the guard, who stood at least a foot taller than Byron, making Byron feel as if he were a kid being escorted to class by a teacher.

"I am. How'd you know?"

"Your Orioles hat."

"Oh. How about you?"

"Not really," said the guard matter-of-factly. "I'm a Steelers fan. Baseball's too boring."

"That's the beauty of baseball," said Byron. "Watching the game unfold, unconstrained by time."

"I guess," said the guard in a noncommittal tone.

"I don't suppose you've ever seen Forbes Field?" Byron asked.

"Sure, years ago."

"Did you ever see the Pirates play there?"

"No, but I went to plenty of Steelers games. We played football there too, you know."

"We?"

"Well, you know, the Steelers. They've always been my team."

"Ah, of course . . . and I don't suppose you've seen Forbes Field recently?" asked Byron, half jokingly, although immediately wishing he hadn't.

"Seen what?" asked the guard.

"You know, pictures, have you seen pictures of the park?" asked Byron, recovering from his near gaffe.

"Yeah – there's one up there on the pillar."

The two approached the pillar as the guard pointed to the photograph. Taken from the vantage point of the "Crow's Nest,"

Forbes Field's press box perched on top of the grandstand behind home plate, the picture showed the entire outfield, as well as the Cathedral of Learning several blocks away. Next to the pillar, embedded in the floor and covered in glass, was a worn, pock-marked rubber home plate. Byron and the guard stood side by side, staring at the glassed-in plate as if it somehow held the keys to all the universe. Byron half expected light beams to shoot out of the enclosure, like something out of the climactic scene in *Raiders of the Lost Ark*. But nothing happened.

After Byron snapped a picture of home plate, the security guard leaned down toward him.

"You know," said the guard in a low whisper, "that ain't the precise location of home plate."

"Really?" asked Byron.

"Yeah, actually home plate was over there, in the ladies' room." The guard pointed to a door marked "Women." "But they couldn't put it there, 'cause, you know. So they put it here. They just don't tell you that."

"Sounds like a well-guarded secret," said Byron, proud of his pun. He waited a moment, hoping the guard might react to his play on words. Seeing no obvious response, Byron continued: "Do others know?"

"You're the first person I've told."

"Best keep it quiet, then," said Byron. The guard nodded in agreement at Byron's suggestion.

Byron considered asking the guard whether he could have a peek inside the ladies' room, but Byron's sensible side prevailed and he kept the request to himself.

"Well, I've got to finish making my rounds," said the guard. "Nice talking with you."

"You, too," said Byron.

Once the guard was out of view, Byron turned toward the entrance to Posvar Hall and paced 90 feet, stopping at the former location of third base. He was still well inside the building. An oil portrait of Wesley W. Posvar, the University's 15th chancellor, hung on the wall in the spot where the third-base stands would have been. The angle of his gaze suggested the good chancellor was fixated, in perpetuity, on action around second base.

Byron thought again about John McGraw. By the time Forbes Field was constructed, McGraw's playing days were over and he already was several years into managing the champion New York Giants. As was the custom back then, when his team was at bat, McGraw would stand in foul territory alongside third base. Byron imagined McGraw on that spot, yelling instructions to his players, giving signs to the batter, or arguing what he thought was a bad call.

After taking a picture of Chancellor Posvar and the area around third base, Byron exited the building and continued walking in the direction of left field. According to the *Encyclopedia's* schematic drawing of Forbes Field, the distance from home plate to the left-field corner was 360 feet. As he finished pacing off the final few feet, he noticed a line of bricks embedded in the sidewalk marking the left-field side of the outfield wall. The area where he was standing, in the left-field corner, used to house the scoreboard and, later, the bullpens. Known as "Greenberg Gardens" and, after that, "Kiner's Korner," the area was named in honor of two of the Pirates' more prolific sluggers who routinely deposited home runs over the left-field fence. A bronze plaque in the sidewalk marked the exact spot where Bill Mazeroski's ninth-inning home run cleared former Yankee catcher-turned-outfielder Yogi Berra and the left-field wall, clinching the 1960 World Series for the Pirates.

"Game over," said Byron to himself as he took a picture of the plaque.

Byron followed the line of bricks, crossing a narrow, two-lane street appropriately named Roberto Clemente Drive after the Pirates' former right fielder, to where the actual remnants of the outfield wall began. About 15 feet tall, and a little less than 200 feet long, the wall was constructed of red brick with concrete columns spaced every 12 feet. The columns were covered in faded green paint and the wall was capped with blocks of weathered, grey granite. Byron took several photographs of the extraordinary time-piece, including the original centerfield flag pole and two distance markers, still painted in white on the side of the wall - 457 to left center, 436 to right center.

The wall ended at what was once the right-field pavilion, leaving the remainder of the ballpark to the imagination. On the opposite side of the Forbes Field wall was a youth baseball diamond and the landing of a concrete stairway that long ago provided ballpark access for fans arriving from Joncaire Street in Panther Hollow. Named in honor of mountain lions that once roamed there, Panther Hollow was one of the more remote sections of Oakland. Byron took a picture of the stairway and its aqua-green pipe handrails, looking down toward Joncaire Street, which lay about 100 feet or more below, giving him a slight sense of vertigo.

Heading away from the platform, Byron was startled to hear the voice of a man arriving at the top steps, for Byron had seen no one there a moment earlier coming up the stairway.

"Good morning," said the man.

"Good morning," replied Byron.

The man wore long pants and a T-shirt and had a canvas gym bag slung over his shoulder. A black baseball cap emblazoned with a Pirates' gold "P" sat atop his full shock of white hair. "You must be in good shape," said Byron. "You don't seem a bit out of breath after walking up all those steps."

"It's my morning routine these days."

"That's great exercise."

"Nice day for a ball game, huh?" said the man.

"It is. I'm glad they left the outfield wall here. It helps give perspective for where the park used to be."

"It does that. Helps you envision the whole park, if you know what you're looking for. You're a player, I take it?"

"Used to be. How about you?"

"I played for the Pirates, on the other side of that wall," said the man, pointing toward the brick artifact.

"Really?" asked Byron, surprised. "It's a pleasure to meet you. I'm Byron Bennett." Byron held out his hand and the former Pirate reached out to shake it, but then pulled up short, offering instead a quick wave.

"My name's George Grantham. They call me 'Boots.'"

"George Grantham - like the drummer from Poco."

"Like what?"

"Poco - their original drummer's name was George Grantham."

"I'm not sure I know what you're saying - is it 'Poco?'"

"Yeah. Poco. They were a country rock band. I take it you're not a fan. That's okay." Byron wracked his brain, but could not recall having ever heard of a ballplayer named George Grantham. "Well, it must have been a great feeling playing in a place like Forbes Field," said Byron.

"It was. It's good to be back."

"So who was the greatest Pirate you ever played with?" asked Byron, still not wanting to let on that he didn't recognize the man's name.

"That would have to be Honus Wagner, although I didn't

play with him. But I knew him. He was one of my coaches."

"Honus Wagner! Wow!" said Byron, sounding like an excited schoolboy. "What a great player."

"Yeah. He was pretty old when I knew him."

"Did he talk much about his playing days?"

"Sure, he had lots of stories - about his days with the Pirates, about playing in the World Series. He had a hell of a memory - he could remember the smallest details about games he played back when he first broke into the league."

"You mean like when he played for the Louisville Colonels."

"Yeah. That's the team, the Colonels."

"Did he ever mention playing against the Orioles?"

"He did, in fact. Used to talk about John McGraw - how much he admired him. One time he told me I reminded him a bit of McGraw, because of how hard I played."

"That was quite a compliment he gave you. McGraw was a great player."

"He was, although I remember him more as a manager," said Boots. "So, you're here for the game, I take it?"

"No, just passing through. I'm heading up to Detroit for the weekend. The Tigers are playing the Orioles."

"So you're not here for the game against the Braves?" Boots asked in reply.

"Are the Pirates even in town? I thought they were playing in St. Louis this weekend."

Boots ignored Byron's question. The smile disappeared from his face. "Well, I hope you enjoy your game in Detroit," said Boots as he turned and headed in the direction of what would have been the right-field pavilion.

Byron wasn't sure what to make of Boots's changed demeanor, although he suspected he had missed an opportunity. He knew the Pirates weren't in town because he had checked the schedule before he left Ellicott City. Heading back toward Posvar Hall, Byron stopped before crossing Clemente Drive and looked back over his shoulder. He could see Boots standing at the end of the brick wall, on the side facing the youth baseball diamond. Boots appeared to be talking to somebody on the Forbes Field side of the wall, although Byron could not see who it was. Byron moved to his right several feet hoping to see who Boots was talking to, but, again, saw no one. When Byron moved back toward his left, Boots had vanished.

"Damn," he said. *How could I have been so stupid? I should have played along,* he thought, *or at least taken a picture of him.* Byron walked back over to the outfield wall and took another look around, but saw no one.

Glancing down at his watch, he realized he had spent almost an hour and a half on his detour to Forbes Field. He debated whether he should stay longer, in case something else happened, or in the event somebody else happened by, but decided against it. He picked up the pace as he headed back toward his car and an expired parking meter. A souvenir of his trip, courtesy of a university police officer, fluttered on Byron's windshield. *A ticket from Forbes Field,* he thought, laughing at his joke. *Something for the scrapbook.* He tossed the ticket inside his glove compartment, which hung open like a broken jaw, the latch having stopped working years ago.

Following Forbes Avenue back toward the highway, Byron thought about Boots's questions. *Am I a player? Was I here for the game?* These were the same questions Murph had asked the previous Sunday.

As Yogi Berra once said (although he denies it), it was "deja vu all over again."

CHAPTER 8

◎ ◎ ◎

Wagner's Ghost

Most people in the United States who have heard of John Peter "Honus" Wagner know him as the player whose name and image appeared on the legendary T-206 tobacco card, the most valuable baseball card ever printed. Some historians of the game consider Wagner to be the best shortstop of all time.

Born in Carnegie, Pennsylvania, in 1874, Wagner lived almost his entire life in that town. According to legend, long after his playing career ended, Wagner could be seen in his front yard on Beechwood Avenue playing baseball with neighborhood children. Some said after his death, his ghost made itself known at his old house from time to time, if you believed in such things. Byron decided to see for himself.

Following Route 376 west on the way to Carnegie, Byron passed Three Rivers Stadium, home to both the Pirates and the Steelers. The multipurpose stadium was located across the Allegheny River, where the river converged with the Monongahela River to form the Ohio River; hence the stadium's name. Byron shook his head at the thought of the Pirates having abandoned such a wonderful ballpark as Forbes Field for the generic and sterile confines of Three Rivers. Ironically, four blocks east of the stadium was the construction site of a new baseball park set to open in another two years, thereby rendering Three Rivers Stadium obsolete and, in time, another lost ballpark.

It was just a ten-mile drive from Forbes Field to Carnegie,

but even with his written directions, Byron had a hard time finding Beechwood Avenue once he entered the town. Driving through Carnegie's narrow, crisscrossing tangle of streets, Byron assumed he would simply stumble upon it. After 20 minutes of not stumbling upon it, Byron swallowed his pride and stopped at a gas station to ask for directions. There, he spotted a broad-shouldered man of an indeterminable, older age wearing a Pirates hat with flip-down sunglasses attached beneath the bill.

"Excuse me, sir," said Byron. "I'm looking for Beechwood Avenue. Do you know where it is?"

"Wagner's house, eh?" the man replied.

"Yeah. How did you know?"

"The Orioles hat you're wearing. Baseball fans come through here all the time looking for his house."

"Can you tell me how to get there from here?"

"That I can do. Make a right out of the station here onto Main," said the man, pointing toward the street. "Turn left on Broadway and then it's a quick jog and you make a soft right onto Beechwood. His house is near the corner of Beechwood and Christy, number 605." The man spoke with an ease and certainty, as if he had given the directions countless times before.

"Thanks very much," said Byron.

"You do know he's dead, don't you," said the man, laughing.

"That's what I've heard. Although I've also heard sometimes you can still see him playing catch in his front yard."

"Oh, you must be a ballplayer," said the man.

Oh, Lord, Byron thought. *Here we go again.*

"I played in the minors for a few years," said Byron.

"Minors, huh?"

"How about you?"

"I played for a few years, too," said the man.

"Pirates?" asked Byron, pointing to the man's hat.

"Pirates."

"This is amazing. I met another guy today who played for the Pirates - George Grantham - do you know him?"

"Boots Grantham? Sure. Good player, played hard."

Good player, played hard, thought Byron. *That's what Grantham told me Wagner said about him. Who is this guy?*

"So what's your name?" Byron asked.

The man stared down Byron before turning away without responding, no longer interested in the conversation.

The man's quick change in demeanor reminded Byron of the reaction Boots had had when he began asking specific questions about who the Pirates were playing. Byron followed the man as he walked toward the gas station.

"Excuse me, sir, I didn't catch your name."

"I didn't say my name." The man picked up his pace.

"Mine's Byron Bennett."

"I know who you are."

"You do?"

"Yes," said the man, stopping for a moment to look Byron in the eyes. "You're like an uninvited guest. Here's your hat, what's your hurry?" The man turned his back to Byron and continued walking toward the gas station.

Here's my hat? wondered Byron. *What is he talking about?*

Undaunted, Byron continued in pursuit. "Wait. Can I ask you one last question?"

"What?" asked the man, stopping at the door, his voice raised.

Flustered by the man's annoyed response and not wanting to upset him further, Byron asked: "I don't suppose you ever played at Union Park?"

The man paused to consider the question, still holding open

the gas station door. "You mean Recreation Park, where the Alleghenys used to play? Son, that was before my time so, no, I can't see it now, if that's what you're asking." The man slid inside the gas station, letting the door close behind him.

The Alleghenys? wondered Byron. *What does he mean he can't see it now?*

Byron opened the door and, once inside, found himself alone in a sparsely decorated room, with only a row of vinyl seats and a rack filled with engine oil and transmission fluid. An attendant sitting behind a wall of plexiglass looked up at Byron through the thick, scratched plastic. There was no door out of the room other than the one through which Byron had entered. *Unbelievable,* Byron thought. *He's gone. What is happening?*

"Did an old man with a Pirates hat walk in here a second ago?" Byron asked the clerk.

"Do you see anyone?" The clerk gave Byron a "what's-a-matter-with-you" look.

"Never mind," said Byron. "I think I know the answer. Twenty dollars on pump three, please."

After filling his tank, Byron followed the old man's directions, which took him past the Andrew Carnegie Free Library, situated on a hill two blocks north of Wagner's house on Beechwood. The library, a large, three-story mansion constructed of granite block and rust-colored brick, with tall arched windows and a pillared front entrance, was a testament to the neighborhood's once grand stature. Two blocks farther down, Byron reached the 600 block of Beechwood. Almost all the houses on Wagner's block appeared to date to the early 1900's and most were generally well-kept, although a 1960's-era apartment building loomed over the southern end of the street, stealing a good portion of the neighborhood's otherwise quaint ambiance.

Three houses from the corner of Beechwood and Christy, Byron spotted Wagner's former home, which he recognized from a picture of it he had seen on the Internet. Built for Wagner in 1917, his last year as a player, the house was a two-and-a-half story, tan-brick foursquare, with a central dormer and a front porch with matching tan-brick columns. Wagner lived there until his death in 1955. Four grey-painted concrete steps led from the sidewalk to a clay-tiled front porch and an ornate wood front door with leaded glass panels on either side of the door and in the transom above. To the left of the entrance was the house number "605" set inside a shield carved in granite, and to the right, a similar granite shield adorned with the initials "JW" framing the doorbell.

Having found Wagner's house, Byron wasn't certain what to do next. It looked as if no one was home, but Byron rang the doorbell anyway. Nobody answered. *At least I can tell my grandchildren I once rang Honus Wagner's bell*, he thought, amused by his feeble joke. As he stood next to the front door, Byron noticed two older men sitting on nylon mesh lawn chairs in the driveway across the street, watching him. *I've heard of this before,* he thought. *It's a "Pittsburgh patio."* Byron gave the men a nervous wave, hoping to assure them of his good intentions. Neither man waved back, acting instead as if they had not seen him.

After taking some pictures of the house number and the unique doorbell, Byron walked back down the front steps and around to the side yard. The smell of recently cut grass from the yard next door hung in the air. Wagner's yard had been cut recently as well, although not so meticulously. *A house this famous should be a museum*, he thought. *I'd pay to have a look inside.*

To the left of the house, a wooden staircase led to an entrance on the second floor, suggesting the house had been divided into apartments. The backyard, overgrown with shrubs and trees, sloped away from the house, hiding what looked like a large garage. Byron was tempted to take a walk around back, but with the men still watching him from across the street, he could not muster the nerve and, instead, returned to the front of the house. After taking a few more photographs, Byron headed across the street to chat up the neighbors and see what they knew. One man was wearing shorts and a sleeveless T-shirt, the other jeans and a flannel shirt.

"Good afternoon, gentleman," said Byron.

Both men nodded.

"Didn't that house across the street belong to Honus Wagner?"

"It did," said the man wearing the T-shirt.

"I don't suppose either of you knew him when he lived here?"

"I did," said the other man. "I was a kid when he died, but I knew him."

"Wow. Do you remember anything about him?"

"Yeah. He was a nice old guy - used to see him out and around. I even played catch with him in his front yard there."

"That's cool."

"Yeah. Wish I'd kept the ball he signed. I played with the one he gave me. I didn't know it would be worth a fortune one day."

"That's a sad story."

"I guess."

"Do you know who lives there now?"

"No, I don't."

"I think some renters," said the man with the flannel shirt.

"Do you mind if I ask you kind of a crazy question? And don't take this the wrong way, but, have either of you heard any stories about Wagner's ghost hanging around his house?"

The men looked at each other. "Oh, he's one of them, huh?"

said the man wearing the flannel shirt.

"One of them crazies," said the other man who had once known Wagner.

"No, I'm not crazy," said Byron. "I heard something about that and was wondering . . . ."

"I knew he was one of them crazy people when I saw him," the man with the flannel shirt said to his friend.

"You can spot 'em a mile away," said the other man. "Look at that piece-of-crap car he drives."

"Hey, guys, I'm right here," said Byron. The men looked up at Byron, but didn't say another word.

Jerks, thought Byron, as he headed toward his car. *They think I'm crazy? At least I didn't play with a thousand-dollar baseball and ruin it.*

Byron got back in his car and waited a moment before turning the ignition, although he wasn't sure what it was he was waiting for. Byron saw no baseball players milling about, no ghost of the great Honus Wagner, or anyone else, not even that old man from the gas station. With the exception of the men across the street, the place seemed exceedingly quiet and normal.

Move along, people, show's over, nothing to see here, thought Byron, starting his car. Byron looked over at the two men sitting in the driveway who were likewise watching him. Byron rolled down his window in contemplation of saying something he might later regret. *Nah, why bring myself down to their level*, he thought, before driving away.

Leaving Carnegie and merging onto the highway, he thought about the old ballplayer he met at the gas station and wondered who or what he was. He thought about Union Park, the one in Pittsburgh, the one the old man mentioned.

Another ballpark for another day, thought Byron.

CHAPTER 9

❀❀❀

Mud Hens

During Byron's days in the minors, every time he passed through Toledo, Ohio, or even thought of Toledo, the lyrics to the song "Lucille" would get stuck in his head. All he could hear was Kenny Rogers's rough tenor lamenting his dark encounter in a Toledo bar with Lucille where she removed her wedding ring. As Byron aimed straight toward Toledo on I-80, years removed from his days in the minors, he had two-and-a-half hours to completely overanalyze the song.

While the songwriters who penned "Lucille" wrote of love lost, to Byron, the words captured perfectly the way he felt about baseball and the bad times he experienced his first year out of organized ball and the hurt that never seemed to heal. Byron wondered if Lucille's ex-husband remained bitter the rest of his life. He wondered if Lucille ended up coming home, allowing the hurting to heal. Somehow, he doubted it.

When not dissecting the meaning of "Lucille," he thought about mud hens. Since the early 1900's, baseball teams named for this short-winged, long-legged bird had inhabited the area in and around Toledo, long after the city's once thriving swamps and marshland had disappeared. Mud Hens – an ignominious name. Many former Mud Hens went on to achieve major-league fame, including, appropriately enough, the once ignominious Casey Stengel, manager of the Toledo Mud Hens from 1926 to 1931.

Byron had first heard of the International League Toledo Mud

Hens watching reruns of the 1970's television show *M*A*S*H**. His favorite character, Corporal Klinger, often sported a Mud Hens hat when he wasn't dressed in women's clothes. As a kid, the hat with the Mud Hens logo made more of an impression on Byron than the fact that there was a man on television dressed in drag. Years later at a Mud Hens game, Byron met Jamie Farr, the actor who played Corporal Klinger, and asked him to sign a Mud Hens hat he had acquired from the opposing team.

During his two seasons in the International League, Byron traveled to Toledo with some regularity. Feeling nostalgic, Byron changed his plans and continued west on I-80, past the exit for I-75, which would have taken him north to Detroit, and headed in the direction of Ned Skeldon Field, home of the Toledo Mud Hens. Situated at the intersection of Key Street and Dussel Drive in Maumee, a suburb south of Toledo, the stadium was part of a larger athletic complex with several youth baseball and softball diamonds. Byron knew all about the history of the ballpark. In its former life, Skeldon Field was a race track, converted to baseball in 1965. Ned Skeldon, a Maumee county commissioner, helped bring minor-league baseball back to Toledo after a nine-year absence, and the town fathers thanked him by naming the former race track turned ballfield after him.

Driving south on Key Street, past the third-base side of Skeldon Field, Byron pulled into the parking lot and could tell the team was out of town. It was past 3:00 p.m. and the players' parking lot was filled with an assortment of cars and pick-up trucks, but no players were out on the field, suggesting the players had left their cars in the stadium lot when they caught the team bus out of town. A man walking from the parking lot toward the entrance to the Mud Hens' front office came within ear shot and, when asked, confirmed the Mud Hens were playing in Scranton and would not be back until the following week.

Byron walked around the stadium to a parking lot behind left field. An open gate in the chainlink fence allowed him access to the area behind the tall, wooden outfield wall, still painted a faded ocean blue - just as Byron had remembered it. Approaching the outfield fence, Byron was flooded with memories of his playing days. Images of teammates and players from other teams he had not thought of in years swept past him like debris in a flooded river.

Peering through a break in the fence, Byron smiled as he realized the stadium had changed little since his playing days. Aluminum seats, their slat backs painted bright orange, dotted the entire lower seating bowl. In the uppermost reaches of the stadium along the third-base side were rows of metal bleachers underneath what was once was the race track's covered grandstand. The grandstand area was taller than the remainder of the covered seating area behind home plate and along the first-base line.

Man, it sure feels good to be back, he thought, *although a little weird to be outside, looking in.* He considered jumping the fence to have a look around, but instead, stayed where he was, staring through the fence at the area around third base, thinking about plays he had made there, as well as plays he had not. *Good times,* he thought, *at least for the most part.*

As he walked back to his car, Byron thought about a friend and former teammate who had worked at a nearby bar. *I wonder if Rob's still there? Maybe I'll check out the Parkway.* Byron turned the ignition and headed north to the Parkway Lounge, a local hangout wedged into a 1950's strip mall. The Parkway was a true neighborhood bar – a place the locals loved and out-of-towners knew nothing about, unless a local had tipped them off. Byron fondly recalled the lounge's unassuming ambiance or, more to the point, its complete lack of ambiance.

The drive from Skeldon Field to the Parkway took Byron north on Anthony Wayne Trail. As a history buff, Byron knew well the legend behind the name. In 1794, "Mad Anthony" Wayne, a former Revolutionary War Brigadier General, was called into service by George Washington to fight Native Americans in the Ohio Territory. General Wayne won the decisive victory at the Battle of Fallen Timbers in an area that later became the town of Maumee, although Byron could never determine whether any lives were lost on the land that made up Skeldon Field. As a way of saying thanks, the residents of the town immortalized Wayne's name, sticking it on just about any surface not covered in feathers, fur, or skin. In addition to the road, Wayne's name adorned businesses throughout Maumee, including, Anthony Wayne Family Practice, Anthony Wayne Animal Hospital, Anthony Wayne Dental Group, Anthony Wayne Barbershop, and Anthony Wayne Tire & Auto Repair. Of all Maumee's local tributes, Byron wondered if Wayne's descendants would have found the most gratifying the tire shop named in his honor.

As Byron approached the shopping center on Detroit Street, the sight of the familiar red "Parkway" sign glimmering above the bar's facade brought back memories of nights he had spent there with his teammates - good nights, but some bad nights, too: nights when he could not remember what he had said or how much he had had to drink, nights when he had no recollection of when or how he had made it back to the team hotel. *That was 10 years ago*, he thought, getting out of his car. *Those days are long gone.*

Byron grabbed his copy of the *Official Encyclopedia of Baseball* from the back seat of his car and headed across the parking lot toward the lounge. To the left of the Parkway was a photography studio Byron remembered, although the tack shop to the right was gone, as was the Fanny Farmer candy store on the corner, which was now an office supply store. Walking through the front door, Byron smiled, for much like Skeldon Field, it seemed as if little had changed at the Parkway in the past decade. Apparently, time stood still in Maumee, which, for Byron, was a good thing.

It's like going back in time, this place, he thought. *Nothing's changed. It even smells the same, spilled beer and greasy french fries.* Inside was a long, narrow room with a sunken cocktail bar on the left and small round tables and chairs on the right. The area behind the bar was lowered several feet so patrons sitting at the shortened, table-height bar were at eye level with the bartender. Although unintentional, Byron was well aware of the benefits of such a design, as it helped ensure inebriated patrons had less of a fall to the floor off the short bar stools.

Byron recognized a waitress standing behind the bar.

"Doris!" he called out.

Doris waved back and pointed toward an open table. Byron took a seat facing the television above the bar. He watched Doris glide around the back of the lounge, picking up dirty dishes and placing them in grey plastic tubs next to the waitress station. *I can't believe she's still here*, he thought.

Doris was an institution and a throwback. Even ten years earlier, she seemingly had worked at the Parkway Lounge forever. At five foot eight, not including her foot-high beehived hair, she was hard to miss or forget.

Byron looked up at the television. "Luke Spencer?" he said, surprised to see the soap opera *General Hospital* playing on the television over the bar. *Boy, this place is a time capsule. I didn't know that show was still on.*

"So, what will it be, Byron?" asked Doris, placing on the

table a glass of water and silverware wrapped in a napkin.

"You remember my name!"

"Of course I do. I know the names of all my regular customers."

"I'm impressed."

"So, what'll it be?" asked Doris, guest check book in hand.

"Hamburger, medium well."

"In case you're wondering, we still don't carry National Bohemian. Budweiser draft alright?"

"Boy, you do have a good memory, but no thanks. Those days are over. Coffee and three creams, please."

"Good for you, Byron."

Doris returned with a cup of coffee, dropping a handful of creamers on the table alongside the cup.

"So, how've you been?" asked Byron.

"No complaints, but the day's still young," Doris said with a chuckle.

"Looks as if not much has changed around here."

"Not much new here, except that god-awful karaoke machine." Doris pointed to a back room where a man in his mid-forties was killing Eddie Money's 1980's lament "I Wanna Go Back" as his female companion looked on in bemused silence.

"Karaoke?" asked Byron. "In the middle of the afternoon?"

"It brings them in – all types - which is good."

"Speaking of 'all types,' does Rob White still work here?"

"He does. In fact he's working tonight. Doris looked down at her watch. He'll be here in about 20 minutes. His shift starts at 4:30."

"Four-thirty? Perfect."

While waiting for his food, Byron flipped through the *Encyclopedia*, looking for the name of the Pirates' player he had met at Forbes Field earlier in the day.

What was the guy's name? he wondered. *George Grantham, "Boots," that's it.*

On page 186, between "Grant, James Ronald," who played two games for the National League Philadelphia Phillies in 1923, and "Grasmick, Louis Junior," who also played two games for the Phillies, in 1948, was a player listing for "Grantham, George Farley (Boots)." According to the *Encyclopedia*, Boots played both infield and outfield for the Pirates from 1925 to 1931. During his 13 year career, he played also for the Cubs, the Reds, and the Giants, a total of 1,444 games, batting an impressive .302. Also, according to the *Encyclopedia*, Boots was dead, at least as of March 16, 1954.

"Damn," said Byron in a voice just above a whisper. "I knew it, I knew I shouldn't have let him leave." Byron realized he was talking to himself and looked around the bar, hoping no one had heard him. *Damn, I was talking to a dead man.*

A knot formed in his stomach. At first, the thought of dead ballplayers coming back to play in long-lost ballparks had been nothing more than a vague, almost romantic notion. Having now come face-to-face with an actual, presumably deceased, ballplayer unsettled Byron. It challenged what he had been told his whole life, by his parents, by his friends, by Maggie, by his pastor, and by a psychologist who got paid a lot of money to tell Byron what he already knew – you live and you die, plain and simple. With the exception of perhaps Elvis, human beings only came back from the dead in books and in the movies, not in real life.

Waiting for his food, Byron tried applying logic to the moment. Maybe the man claiming to be Boots was some nut, or someone playing Byron for a fool. Maybe it was all an elaborate hoax, although he couldn't think of anyone who would be willing to go to such efforts just to put one over on him.

Or perhaps, he thought, his encounter with Boots was another case of "José Pilotosia" – the phenomenon whereby an old baseball player, reportedly deceased, is discovered alive and well and still loving baseball. The namesake of this phenomenon – José Piloto – was a Negro League player for the Memphis Red Sox in the late 1940's. According to the *Biographical Encyclopedia of the Negro Baseball Leagues*, Piloto died in Mexico from blows he received during an "argument." As it turned out, the report of Mr. Piloto's demise was greatly exaggerated, as Mr. Piloto was alive and well, and living in Prince George's County, Maryland.

Byron knew this because Mr. Piloto had attended Bowie Baysox games, signing autographs during its annual Negro League Night. During one such celebration, Mr. Piloto graciously signed Byron's copy of the Negro Leagues encyclopedia, without objection, signing it above his name, and death notice, on page 628.

So, maybe, the *Official Encyclopedia of Baseball*, like the *Biographical Encyclopedia of the Negro Baseball Leagues*, was wrong. Maybe Boots was alive and well and hanging around Forbes Field, hoping to catch a Pirates game. Or maybe he was deceased and still hanging around Forbes Field hoping to catch a Pirates game.

Doris returned to the table, waiting for Byron to close his book before placing the food in front of him.

"What's the matter, Byron?" asked Doris, sounding concerned. "You're awfully pale. You look like you've seen a . . . ."

"Don't say it," said Byron, cutting her off. "I'm just not feeling well. I've been driving since early this morning and haven't had enough to eat, I guess."

"Well, let me know if you need anything else."

As Byron picked at his food, his stomach still unsettled, into the Parkway strolled Rob White, wearing a cowboy hat, jeans, and a well-worn "Property of Toledo Mud Hens" T-shirt. His boastful yet somewhat hesitant stride reminded Byron of a rodeo rider who had dismounted in pain from a bull. Not quite 5'10," Rob was not physically imposing. Still, he could fill a room with his charisma alone. He and Byron were teammates on the Charlotte O's for one season, and they became fast friends. After signing with another organization, Rob ended up playing first base for the Mud Hens. The two played against each other Rob's final year in professional ball. During Byron's final season with Rochester, Rob was out of baseball and working at the Parkway Lounge, which also helped explain why Byron spent his free time there whenever he was in Toledo.

Byron called across the bar: "Hey, Rob, where's your glove?" Byron never let Rob forget the time he ran from the dugout to his position at first base without his glove, having left it on the bench in the dugout. It wasn't that he had taken the field without his glove; rather, it was that he hadn't realized his error even after he tossed a ball to warm up his fellow infielders. Not until the second baseman threw a rocket back toward Rob did he realize he had forgotten his glove. Byron tried bestowing on Rob a new nickname, but "Gloveless Rob" never quite caught on.

Rob looked over at Byron and shook his head. "Itty Bitty Byron Bennett, you back in town to give it another try? The Mud Hens could use a third baseman who knows how to boot grounders back toward the catcher."

"I guess that's fair, 'Gloveless,'" said Byron.

Rob plopped himself down in the seat across the table from Byron and leaned back in the chair.

"What are you doing in Toledo?"

"I'm on my way to Detroit to see the Tigers. They're closing the stadium, you know."

"That's what I've heard."

"Man, it's good to see you."

"You too, Bitty."

"So you're still here at the Parkway? I mean . . . that's good."

"It's good because I'm part owner now. I figure another few years and I'll be able to buy the place outright, once Mr. 'H' retires."

"Sounds like a plan," said Byron, nodding his head with approval. "How's Lily? You guys still happily married?"

"We're still married, let's put it that way. How's about you? No ring on your finger, I see."

"Still single, though not for lack of trying."

"Still scaring them away with your endless tales of life in the minors, huh?"

"That and all the crap in my house."

"Do you ever hear from Maggie?"

"Sometimes. She'll call me once in a blue moon, but mostly when we talk it's because I call her. I tried to get her to come with me to Detroit, but she said 'no.'"

"And that came as a surprise to you?"

"No, not really."

"Still sober, I see," said Rob, pointing to Byron's cup of coffee.

"I am and I have you to thank."

"I was just one of many."

"Yeah, but you forced the issue. That first summer out of baseball I was pretty messed up."

"Well, you're better now."

"I'm recovering - always recovering, everyday. If it wasn't for

AA - I don't know where I'd be. I'm eight years sober."

"Good for you. Still with the Baysox?"

"Yup, it keeps me in the game, sort of, at least."

"Nothing wrong with that. So, what game are you going to see in Detroit?"

"The O's. All three games this weekend, starting tonight."

"You know, I've lived in Toledo more than twelve years now and I've never once made it up to Detroit to see a game."

"You're welcome to come with me."

"Man, that would be great, but I can't. Gotta work," said Rob, disappointed. "Otherwise, I would."

"What about tomorrow? You can meet me there."

"I don't know."

Byron wanted to tell Rob about his encounter with Boots Grantham in Pittsburgh, but was hesitant at first, knowing how ridiculous the story sounded.

"You still go to Mud Hen games, don't you?" asked Byron.

"Sure, when I can. Sometimes I go see games in Akron, too. Lily's parents are still there."

"Do you ever hear stories about old players coming back to the ballpark for a game?"

"You ARE here for a comeback!" Rob said, laughing.

"No, I'm not talking about me, I'm talking about old ballplayers."

"Dude, in case you hadn't noticed, we both fall into that category."

"No. What I'm talking about is guys who look to be in their sixties or seventies hanging around the ballpark."

"Like for an old timers' game?" asked Rob.

"No, nothing formal like that, just old guys looking to play."

"Can't say I have. Have you?"

"Yeah, I have."

"Where? Bowie?"

"No, not Bowie - Pittsburgh. I stopped there this morning on the campus of Pitt to see where Forbes Field used to be. They left part of the outfield wall there and when I was taking some pictures, this old guy came over and started asking me questions. He told me he used to play for the Pirates and that he was there for a game."

"Yeah?" asked Rob. "So what?"

"So what? The Pirates are in St. Louis this weekend."

"Hmm," said Rob, nodding his head. "Guess he was confused. So, what did you tell him?"

"I told him I was going to Detroit for a game. When I said that, he lost interest and walked away."

"Did he say what his name was?"

"Yeah - George Grantham."

"Like the drummer from Poco?"

"Same name, different guy - he said they called him 'Boots.'"

"Never heard of him."

"I hadn't either, but look at this." Byron grabbed the *Encyclopedia*, turned to page 186, and placed it on the table in front of Rob. "Look." Byron pointed to Boots's stats in the middle of the page.

Rob scanned the page and glanced up at Byron. "A career .302 hitter - that's decent."

"No Rob, look at this." Byron pointed to his vital statistics.

"What?"

"Boots is dead," said Byron.

"Boots is dead?"

"Look here."

"He is dead."

"That's what it says."

"Maybe you got his name wrong," said Rob.

"I don't think so."

"Maybe he's lying. Maybe he's not Boots."

"Maybe."

"Or maybe," said Rob, his voice tapering off.

"What?"

Rob paused for a moment, laying his hands in front of him on the table. "Now that you mention it, something like this did happen to me a few years back - you know, old guys like this – not at the Ned, but at Swayne Field - or at least where it used to be."

"You mean where the Mud Hens used to play? It's Swayne Field Shopping Center now. I remember the sign in the parking lot."

"Right."

"Did you know," added Byron, "after they tore down Swayne Field in the 1950's, they built the largest Kroger store in the country there?"

"I didn't know that. Kroger's is long gone, it's a Food Town now. But back to my story . . . I used to volunteer at the Boys and Girls Club across the street and sometimes, when I went to Food Town to buy lunch, I'd see these old guys hanging out in front of the store. There's a 'No Loitering' sign next to the front door and I always thought it was funny how they hung around all day in front of that sign and no one ever said anything."

"Scofflaws," said Byron.

"Yeah, except one day I got the feeling no one else could see them except me."

"What do you mean?"

"I never saw them talk to anyone who wasn't in their group. No one else ever seemed to notice them standing there either and Food Town never did anything about it. This one guy in particular, he'd always ask me the same thing."

"What?"

"If I knew how to get inside the ballpark. The first few times, I tried explaining to him the Swayne Field sign was for the shopping center and there was no ballpark anymore. After a while, I just ignored him."

"You know there's a section of the old outfield wall behind the shopping center. It's in pretty bad shape though - keeps getting tagged."

"There is? How the hell do you know that?"

"I read about it on the Internet."

"Man, you have way too much free time on your hands."

"Hey, it's baseball history - at least I'm not surfing the net for porn."

"I think baseball history is like porn to you."

"You know, speaking of porn, did you see the latest issue of Baseball Digest? Man, that pullout picture of Brady . . . ."

"Don't even go there," said Rob, stopping Byron in mid-sentence.

"Do you think those old guys knew about the wall?"

"Why would that matter?"

"I don't know. Maybe it's like the outfield wall in Pittsburgh, where Forbes Field used to be. Maybe it means something to those old players."

"I have no idea. All I know is one day they weren't hanging around anymore and then I never saw them again."

"They must have found the wall," said Byron.

Rob thought for a moment. "You know, I never put this together before, but a friend of mine in Minneapolis, he experienced something like this too."

"Who?" asked Byron.

"Eric Mann – a buddy of mine from high school. He played a couple of years in Florence for the Blue Jays."

"Eric Mann? Is that a real name? I don't remember you ever mentioning him."

"Yeah, well, we kind of lost track of each other, but a few years back he called me up and we started talking again. Then, when I was in Minnesota, I went to see him. He works at a bank built where the Millers used to play."

"Nicollet Park," said Byron.

"That sounds right."

"It's mentioned in this book I've been reading. Ted Williams was a Miller. He played there."

"Really? I didn't know that."

"And Babe Ruth, too - he'd barnstorm there after the Yankees' season was over."

"Huh," said Rob.

"And Lou Gehrig as well."

"Bitty, enough with the factoids, alright?" Rob raised both hands in the air as if to signal "stop." "Can I finish, please?"

"Sorry."

"Well, there's nothing left of the ballpark now, not even the outfield wall."

"There's a plaque," said Byron. "I saw a picture of it on the Internet."

"Yeah, I saw the plaque, too. Anyway, Eric told me about these old guys who'd come into the bank and ask him where the players entrance was. He said they'd talk to him and nobody else."

"Because he used to play ball?" asked Byron, guessing.

"I don't know - maybe. When I was there, we stopped by the

bank and Eric showed me around."

"Did you see any old players?"

"No, not that I could tell," replied Rob.

"Well, there's something going on at these old ballparks. I'm just not sure what it is."

"It's weird, huh?"

"Yeah, it is weird. I wish there was some way to tell if they're really ghosts."

"Ghosts?" asked Rob. "Who said anything about ghosts?"

"You did. You said only you could see those guys in front of Food Town."

"I said it seemed that way, but I don't know that for certain. And I sure as hell don't believe in ghosts."

"Okay, you don't believe in ghosts." Byron held his hands out in front of him. "Still, it is hard to explain."

"You don't believe in ghosts, do you?" asked Rob.

"I don't know."

"Well, I don't," said Rob. "And don't be telling me you do."

"Alright, I won't."

"I'm sure there's a logical explanation. We're just not smart enough to think of it."

"I guess," said Byron, discouraged by Rob's reaction.

"Well, I better get to work."

"And, I better be on my way."

"Yeah, you should be going. And if you brought any ghosts in here with you, make sure you take them when you leave."

"Don't worry, I left them in the car."

"Good."

"I'll be in Detroit all weekend if you want to come up – tomorrow or Sunday – they're both day games."

"I'll think about it. Maybe Sunday, if I can get someone

to cover my shift."

"Of course you can get someone to cover your shift. You're the owner."

"Part owner."

"Give me your telephone number and I'll call you tomorrow," said Byron.

"Call me here tomorrow night. Here's the number." Rob picked up a Parkway Lounge matchbook sitting in an ash tray in the next table over and handed it to Byron.

"If you don't hear from me, give me a call," said Byron. "I'm staying at the Renaissance."

"I will. It's been great seeing you, buddy – assuming this is you and not some ghost," said Rob, laughing.

"I'll give you a call tomorrow night."

"Okay, if I can make it Sunday, maybe you can tell me some more of your ghost stories."

"Maybe. Hope to see you Sunday."

As Rob walked toward the bar, Byron could hear him singing the theme to the movie *Ghost Busters*. Rob punctuated the song's title for emphasis as he sang the refrain, making sure Byron heard him. Rob laughed all the way into the kitchen.

After Rob departed, Doris walked over to the table and handed Byron his check. He looked at the $10 check and handed Doris a $20 bill. "Keep the change."

"Thank you," Doris said, stashing the bill in the front pocket of her apron.

"Good seeing you," said Byron. "And thanks for remembering me. It's nice to be remembered."

Pulling out of the parking lot, he thought about driving the six or so miles up Detroit Avenue to Swayne Field Shopping Center, maybe having a look around and taking some pictures of the old outfield wall. But it was already well past 5, and with rush hour picking up, he decided to continue northeast on Mad Anthony's trail. Swayne Field would have to wait, another ballpark for another day. Ten minutes later, Byron was on I-75 heading north toward Detroit.

CHAPTER 10

❀ ❀ ❀

Michigan and Trumbull

With its considerable north-south expanse, I-75 had the distinction of providing travelers direct access to five major-league baseball stadiums. Beginning in Florida, northwest of Miami, and stretching almost 1,800 miles through Georgia, Tennessee, Kentucky, Ohio, and into Michigan's Upper Peninsula, the homes of the Florida Marlins, the Tampa Bay Devil Rays, the Atlanta Braves, the Cincinnati Reds, and the Detroit Tigers all dotted its route. Four of the stadiums were within three miles of the interstate. The fifth stadium, Tropicana Field, was located in St. Petersburg, 20 miles from I-75 on I-275.

Byron had traversed the stretch of I-75 from Toledo to Detroit with his family on their many trips from Baltimore to his dad's family in Port Huron. Even back then, I-75 was an imposing stretch of highway, whether facing frontwards or backwards.

Byron's trip to Tiger Stadium took him along that same stretch of I-75 during the evening's rush hour. Traffic was heavy, spread across all four northbound lanes, with semi-trailer trucks making up half the volume. A light rain was falling, which did not bode well for Byron's efforts to make it to Michigan and Trumbull on time, unless, of course, the rain delayed the start of the game.

Traffic slowed 25 miles south of Detroit, near the exit for Rockwood. Ten miles and half an hour later, Byron switched on the radio, flipping the dial until he picked up Ernie Harwell's voice on WJR coming over the airways. The rain eased off and traffic moved better once Byron passed Lincoln Park. When he reached the exit for Michigan Avenue, he heard Harwell report the game's score in the bottom of the first, Baltimore 1, Detroit 0.

Traveling east on Michigan Avenue, Byron passed several blocks of empty lots and shuttered buildings, remnants of Detroit's more prosperous times. After a mile, the rather bleak landscape gave way to a most extraordinary sight. Rising above the low roofs of the narrow brick buildings that stood like war-weary soldiers along Michigan Avenue, Byron could see the light stanchions of Tiger Stadium piercing the damp spring evening. With night fast approaching, the stadium lights glowed in the moist air like a trio of full moons.

Byron drove past fans wearing blue, orange, and black who were making their way along Michigan Avenue a couple of blocks west of the stadium. Cars were parked in vacant lots and in the front yards of the houses and businesses along both sides of the street. A man waving a white rag motioned for Byron to park in his make-shift lot. Byron waved back, gave the man an appreciative nod, and continued along Michigan until he crossed Cochrane Street, still west of the stadium.

At the corner of Michigan and Trumbull, a red traffic light brought Byron's car to a stop; he was glad for the opportunity to take a look around. To his left was the stadium's main entrance, with people milling about, taking in all the stadium had to offer. The fans seemed in no rush to enter through the gates even though the game already had begun. It was as if the game itself was secondary to the anticipation and nostalgia of entering Tiger Stadium.

Once the light turned green, the car behind Byron honked twice, admonishing Byron to move along. Byron continued east on Michigan another two miles to the Renaissance Hotel. When the Renaissance was built in the mid-1970's, it was the world's largest private development project and considered a marvel of urban renewal. The seven shiny glass towers that encompassed the Renaissance Center stood in stark contrast to the distinctly older buildings and empty lots scattered around much of downtown Detroit.

After a few wrong turns, Byron negotiated his car through the maze of buildings to the front entrance of the hotel. Byron gave his keys to the valet and made his way across the hotel's cavernous, uninviting lobby. The exposed concrete walls and pillars dominating the hotel lobby appeared no less dated than the older, time-worn buildings hovering outside in the shadow of the Renaissance Center's skyline.

Once inside his room on the 31st floor, Byron dropped his bags on the bed and hurried back down the elevator and outside the hotel into the cool Detroit night air to catch a cab back to the stadium. The drone of the game playing on AM radio escaped from the rolled down window of a taxi idling in front of the hotel.

"Tiger Stadium, please," said Byron, as he opened the back door of the cab.

"The game's well underway, you know," said the cabby as he lowered the radio's volume and pulled down the arm on the taximeter.

"What inning is it?" Byron asked.

"Bottom of the third," said the cabby as he pulled out of the hotel's circular drive.

"This is my first time going to the stadium."

"First time, eh? You're in for a treat, then, that is, if you like old stadiums. This is it, you know, the Tigers' last year there."

"That's why I'm here."

The cab turned the corner onto Michigan Avenue, and Tiger Stadium once again came into view. The approach from the east was more picturesque than the trip from the west off I-75. The main entrance provided a glowing neon gateway to the stadium rising beyond the corner of Michigan and Trumbull. The final, glimmering rays of the evening's sunset had disappeared behind the stadium, an appropriate metaphor not lost on Byron.

"It's too bad they're closing it," said Byron.

"Yeah, I'll be sad to see her go. I'll tell you what, though, that stadium is the only reason most people come down to Corktown anymore. There's a lot of people who won't come downtown at all because they don't like the area."

"Do you think that will change once the new park opens?"

"We'll see," said the cabby. "The new stadium's only about a mile from here, but there's gonna be a lot more going on there. They got the Fox Theater, and they're building the new football stadium there, too. So, we'll see."

The cab pulled up to the curb along Michigan west of Trumbull and Byron got out, handing the cabby $10. "Keep the change," said Byron, closing the door with a resounding thud.

The cabby turned up the radio before pulling away and Byron heard Harwell announce the score at the top of the fourth inning, Baltimore 3, Detroit 0.

Although the game was almost an hour old, Byron was not alone buying his ticket at the main ticket booth. As a young couple in front of him debated where to sit, Byron considered purchasing a ticket along third base, but, with the game almost half over, decided to save his money and buy a cheaper seat. The couple in front of him settled on $5 centerfield upper-bleacher seats. The price and location sounded good to Byron and he purchased a $5 ticket as well. Heading toward the main gate,

Byron handed his ticket to an elderly man wearing an orange and blue usher's vest, standing next to a row of blue and chrome turnstiles.

"Sorry," said the man, handing Byron his ticket back. "You can't come in through this gate with a bleachers ticket. You have to go down to the entrance to my left almost to the corner."

The man pointed north down Trumbull toward the West Fisher Freeway.

"Oh," said Byron, looking again at his ticket.

Walking toward the bleachers entrance, Byron passed a group of Tiger fans huddled around two bronze plaques attached to the stadium's light-blue, glazed-brick facade. Further down Trumbull, Byron looked up at the stadium, which was cantilevered over the sidewalk. The sound of the crowd rose high above the stadium lights before cascading down onto the sidewalk below. Underneath the cantilever near the end of the block was a weathered blue sign with white-block lettering announcing "BLEACHER ENTRANCE - Boxes - Reserves - General Adm. Grand Stand Tickets Corner Cochrane & Kaline Drive."

Byron approached the gate underneath the sign and handed his ticket to another elderly man who smiled and nodded, noting Byron's Orioles cap.

"Orioles fans are always welcome here at Tiger Stadium," said the usher.

"Thank you," said Byron, appreciating the gesture. "I'll be sure to tell to the folks around me you said that, in case the score gets ugly for the Tigers."

"Enjoy the game," said the man.

Inside the stadium, Byron stopped at a stand selling programs and scorecards and bought one of each. The vendor handed him his purchases, along with a short orange pencil with "Tiger

Stadium" imprinted on the side in block letters. Byron hadn't kept score in years but figured they'd make good souvenirs of his trip to Detroit.

Heading up the ramp, he realized that, in addition to a separate entrance, the bleachers section had separate concessions stands and restrooms as well and allowed no access to the rest of the ballpark. Although he had hoped to explore the entire stadium, with the game almost half over, and two more games yet to see, Byron decided to stay where he was, so he continued his climb up the concrete ramp toward the top of the stadium.

Approaching the upper-level concourse, Byron recalled his first trip to a major-league ballpark. He was no more than seven years old when his Cub Scout pack attended an Orioles doubleheader against the Oakland Athletics at Memorial Stadium. He remembered making his way to the stadium's upper deck, the steep walk up the ramp set between two tall concrete walls. He remembered looking beyond the entrance to the seating area and seeing, for the first time, the field's vivid green expanse below him.

As Byron reached the top of the ramp and stepped out into the open air of Tiger Stadium, he felt as if he had been transported back in time. He stared out at an island of grass surrounded by a sea of blue and orange seats.

His momentary solitude was cut short. "Can't stand there," said a man behind him, sounding annoyed. "You're blocking the entrance, you've got to move along."

Byron turned around and faced the man, who was wearing a dingy orange vest and a soiled, dark blue usher's hat. Byron saw no one standing behind the man waiting to come in, causing him to wonder why, at that particular moment, the usher felt compelled to flex the limited authority granted to him by the

Detroit Tigers Baseball Club. Byron shook his head as he made his way past rows of long metal benches.

Seating in the bleachers section was general admission and that evening there were plenty of seats from which to choose. Byron sat down on a bench at the top of the section. A chainlink fence at either end of the bleachers separated him and the rest of the riffraff from the higher-priced, reserve seats in a clear demarcation of the Tiger Stadium pecking order.

Fewer than 200 fans sat scattered throughout the bleachers. Byron's chosen perch, high above the stadium in dead centerfield, provided a terrific vantage point from which to view the entire field and the surrounding stadium, as well as a portion of the Detroit skyline. The one downside of his vista was that he could not see the centerfielder, who, presumably, stood somewhere on the field below.

The stadium was enclosed on all four sides, its shape resembling a square cigar box. Byron was struck by how much smaller the stadium appeared on the inside than he had expected. The rows of seats in the reserved upper and lower decks did not reach as far back as those in more modern ballparks. Steel girders supporting the upper deck and the roof over the upper-reserved grandstand obstructed the view of spectators sitting near them in both the upper and lower seating bowls. But fans such as Byron, sitting in the cheap seats, had a view of the field unobstructed by girders: there was no roof above the bleachers and, therefore, no girders were in the way. In earlier times, ballpark bleachers were constructed of wood and, with no covering over the benches, the sun would bleach the wood; hence the name. On Saturday, Byron planned to buy a seat closer to one of those riveted beauties; a seat that also, hopefully, would provide a view of the centerfielder.

Byron struck up a conversation with a man two rows in front of him who was sitting with his teenage son.

"Great night for a game," said Byron.

"Any night here is a great night for a game," replied the man.

"Do you come to a lot of games?"

"A dozen or so a year. My son's a fan, too, so we come as much as we can."

"Sitting in this section makes it affordable."

"Oh, I could afford more expensive seats, but we rarely sit anywhere else. People up here are true baseball fans - here to watch the game, not to see and be seen."

"The people down below don't know what they're missing."

"You're an Orioles fan, I take it?" asked the man, pointing to Byron's hat.

"Born and raised."

"I remember the Orioles from when I was a kid. What a great team they were. Brooks Robinson and Frank Robinson."

"Yup, Boog and Belanger, Palmer and Cuellar. Paul Blair - best centerfielder I ever saw."

"And the second baseman, Davey Johnson. He managed the Mets, too, and then the O's."

"And of course," said Byron, "Earl Weaver, the Earl of Baltimore."

"My son was hoping to see Cal Ripken, Jr., play tonight, but I guess he's still injured."

"It's his back. He's getting old."

"Aren't we all?"

"Speaking of old, this place is priceless. I can't believe the fans here haven't put up more of a fight to keep it. It's historic. They should fix it up."

"There's a lot of us who don't want to leave, but, what can

we do? The owners see a worn-out stadium getting in the way of their dollar signs. A new ballpark means a greater revenue stream. That's what speaks to them."

"I doubt Red Sox fans would ever allow the team's owners to tear down Fenway Park and replace it with a new stadium. The same with Cubs fans and Wrigley."

"Yeah, but those teams sell out almost all of their games. Look around you. We'll be lucky if we pull in fifteen thousand tonight."

"Those places are no more baseball shrines than Tiger Stadium," said Byron. "And they've been playing baseball here longer than they have in those parks - at least twenty years longer."

"It doesn't matter now. Once the Tigers leave, it's only a matter of time before this place meets the wrecking ball. The city doesn't have the foresight or the money to do anything other than tear it down - just like they've done with so many other places that used to make this city great."

As the game progressed, Byron watched the father and son, lost in their casual conversation, and thought of his own son, who would have been about the age of the young teenager sitting with his father. Byron often found himself thinking about his child, trying to imagine what he would have looked like had he lived, comparing that uncertain image to the children he saw who would have been about his son's age. Although he never knew his son, he felt as if he knew what he would have been like, believing he would have shared his own passion for baseball. He liked to think that his son would have come with him on this trip to Detroit and the two of them would have shared in their own casual conversation - a ritual as much a part of baseball as the game itself.

As the evening's contest unfolded, Byron tried to remember the name of the person mentioned in Mac's vanished itinerary.

Still uncertain whether he had imagined the note, Byron recalled that the man sold souvenirs in front of the stadium and that his name was Marty, or something like that.

With one inning of the game remaining, Byron decided to take some pictures of the ballpark but discovered that, in his haste to make it to the stadium, he had left his camera in the hotel room. This turned out to be a blessing in disguise. Because he had no camera, he felt no compulsion to take pictures or capture anything for posterity.

That night, nobody had asked Byron if he was a player or if he knew the location of the ballpark entrance, or made him feel as if he were an outsider or an uninvited guest. For one night, at least, there was no mystery to unravel and he was able to sit in his $5 seat and enjoy the game, taking it all in with the exception of the centerfielder. For the first time in a long time, Byron didn't obsess about not being down on the field, playing baseball. For one night, Byron was just a fan of the game.

Chapter 11

Ee-Yah

The next morning, Byron returned to Tiger Stadium, stopping first at the main gate near Michigan and Trumbull to take a picture of a plaque honoring Tyrus Raymond "Ty" Cobb. The plaque made brief mention of Cobb's baseball accomplishments: Ty Cobb, the "Greatest Tiger Of All, A Genius In Spikes." Byron figured the reference to Cobb's spikes was a cleverly disguised acknowledgment of Cobb's volatile nature: he was notorious for showing hostility toward anyone who dared cross his path, including spiking opposing team players in the legs when he slid into a base.

After taking the picture, Byron walked around the exterior of the stadium, snapping more photos as he headed north on Trumbull, west on Fisher, south on Cochrane, and east on Michigan. Still early, it was wonderfully empty and quiet around the stadium, allowing Byron to take unencumbered shots of the facade from almost every vantage point. After twice walking the perimeter of the stadium, Byron still had time to kill before the gates opened. He watched the increase in activity outside the stadium, with vendors claiming premium space on the sidewalks along Michigan Avenue and a trickle of fans beginning to arrive.

Hoping to find Mac's friend, Byron approached one vendor setting up a food stand outside the main gate.

"Soda, water, one dollar," the vendor barked in Byron's direction.

"No thanks," said Byron. "I'm looking for a guy named Marty who sells souvenirs around here. Do you know him?"

"Marty? Never heard of him."

Byron approached a second vendor, this one selling pretzels and sodas out of a shopping cart farther west on Michigan.

"Pretzels $2," stated a makeshift cardboard sign attached to the vendor's cart.

"I'm looking for a souvenir vendor named Marty. Do you know him?"

"Nope, don't know him."

"Pretzels, two dollars," the man said as Byron walked away.

Byron approached each of the dozen or so vendors up and down Michigan and Trumbull, but none of them claimed ever to have heard of the elusive souvenir vendor Marty. *I must have imagined the note*, he thought.

Crossing Trumbull heading away from the stadium, Byron continued east on Michigan and stopped in front of Sportsland USA, a souvenir store that took up two adjoining storefronts in the middle of the block. The large picture windows on the store's first-floor facade were covered with weathered and water-stained beaded board. On the second floor were two bay windows centered above the first-floor picture windows. Stacks of boxes and papers in front of the bay windows blocked whatever view there might have been of the street below or the stadium to the right. In between the two merged storefronts, a large V-shaped electric sign above the sidewalk announced, in faded blue and red lettering, "Sportsland USA, Sports Souvenirs, All Pro Teams, Open Year Round."

Another sign taped to the door informed Byron that Sportsland did not open until 10 a.m., although there appeared to be customers already inside the store. After pulling on the locked door, Byron knocked and a rumpled man wearing a navy blue, satin Tigers jacket and a trucker-style Tigers hat lumbered over, unlocking the door. "We open at ten o'clock," said the man.

"I know. I'm looking for someone," said Byron. "I thought you might know him - Marty - he sells souvenirs."

"Don't know a Marty, but I know a Matty."

"Matty. That's it," said Byron, correcting himself as he recalled the man's last name. "Matty O'Boyle. Do you know where he is?"

"Sure, he works here on weekends - he'll be in about 10:30."

"Thanks."

"He's probably down at Casey's having breakfast if you want to see him now."

"Casey's? Where's that?"

"Couple blocks down Michigan past the stadium." The man pointed in the direction of Tiger Stadium. "It'll be on your right, just past Harrison."

Matty O'Boyle, thought Byron, heading in the direction of the stadium. *No wonder no one had ever heard of "Marty the vendor."*

Between Cochrane and Harrison on Michigan, Byron passed two other souvenir stores and a restaurant, Corktown Tavern. The colorful signs on the side of one building - festive, yellow-and-green-painted advertising - resembled the type of signs that long ago might have adorned Tiger Stadium's outfield wall. An assortment of two-story brick buildings, all of different vintage, lined Michigan Avenue past Harrison. On the corner, Oblivion's Corktown Cafe - a 1960's-era two-story plain brick box of a building - seemed out of place alongside its older neighbors. A lighted box sign in front of Oblivion's advertised "Detroit's Best Lunch, Salsa Saturdays, Free Disco Dance Lessons 9PM."

Next to Oblivion's was Casey's Pub Corktown. The entrance

to the building, with its circa-1800's brick facade and curved shamrock-green awning above wooden double doors, was a pub crawler's visual siren call, especially when juxtaposed next to Oblivion's and its "Free Disco Dance Lessons."

Business was brisk at Casey's that Saturday morning, the tables and booths filled with stadium workers wearing team-issued uniforms and fans wearing assorted Tigers paraphernalia. To the left of the front doors, an older gentleman sat alone at the bar. *That must be him*, thought Byron, walking toward the bar.

"Is this seat taken?" Byron asked the man.

"No, it's all yours."

"Thanks." Byron sat down, two stools over from the man.

The bartender glanced over at Byron. "Coffee?"

"Yes, thanks. And three creams."

The bartender poured Byron a cup and handed him a menu.

"You hardly touched your food," said the bartender to the old man. "Do you want me to wrap it to go?"

"No, thanks though." The old man handed the bartender some money.

"Excuse me, sir," said Byron to the old man. "Can I ask you a question?"

"You just did."

"Oh, yeah, I did. Then can I ask you another one? Wait, make that two."

"Shoot."

"Are you Matty O'Boyle?"

"I am," he said, as he stood up to leave.

"Wait . . . ."

"You asked your two questions, you have more?"

"Yes. A friend of mine, Mac, he said he's a friend of yours. He asked me to find you. Do you know him? He lives in Baltimore."

"What's his last name?" Matty asked.

"I don't know. I just know him as Mac."

"You don't know his last name?"

"No. He used to be a groundskeeper for the Orioles, though. He heard I was coming to Detroit and he wanted me to look you up. He told me to tell you he's doing fine."

"And you are?"

"Byron, Byron Bennett." He held out his hand, but Matty gave him a quick wave. *Why doesn't anyone want to shake hands anymore?* Byron wondered. *The cold and flu season's over.*

"Mac told me you used to be a groundskeeper at Tiger Stadium," said Byron.

"Me? No. Sorry."

"That's strange. I wonder why he'd tell me that?"

"You'd have to ask your friend Mac."

"He's your friend, too, right?"

"Never heard of him."

"You haven't? But your name is Matty O'Boyle?"

"'Tis that, Byron Bennett."

Matty pushed in his stool, grabbed his jacket, and headed for the door.

Byron watched Matty leave, wondering why Mac had told him to look for Matty O'Boyle, yet Matty claimed never to have heard of Mac. *Maybe it's a coincidence*, he thought. *Maybe I did imagine the note. I never did find it.* Byron decided not to follow Matty out of the restaurant, having grown tired of pestering old men with questions they had no interest in answering. Besides, he was hungry and needed to eat, and he knew where Matty worked in the event he changed his mind and wanted to pester him some more.

"Do you know Matty very well?" Byron asked the bartender.

"You know, the man who just left?"

"Sure. Everyone knows him. He's been here forever - he works up at Sportsland. It's the funniest thing, though, he comes in here most Saturday mornings, but he never seems to eat anything he orders and I end up throwing it away."

"Maybe it's the food," said Byron.

"The food here is fine, thank you very much. Look around. Everybody else is eating it."

"Looks good to me."

"So, I take it you're from out of town?" The bartender pointed to Byron's Orioles cap.

"Yup. Ellicott City, Maryland, outside Baltimore. My name's Byron Bennett."

"Name's Paul. Welcome to Corktown. You heading to the game?"

"I'm here for the weekend - my first time. I wanted to see Tiger Stadium before they closed it."

"Did you go last night?"

"I did, although I got there late."

"So, what did you think?"

"It's a great old place. I can't believe they're closing it - there's so much baseball history there."

"There's baseball history everywhere in this town. Even this bar - it's historic."

"How?"

"Well, from what I've heard, Lou Gehrig came in here the day his consecutive game streak came to an end."

"Wow." It was the type of baseball tidbit Byron enjoyed hearing.

"May 2, 1939," said Paul, "the Yankees were playing the Tigers." Byron did the math with his fingers. "That's sixty years ago this week."

"It is. Another historic spot is the lobby of the Cadillac Hotel, a mile past the stadium on Michigan," continued Paul. "That's where Gehrig met the Yankees' manager before the game to tell him he wanted out of the lineup. When the game was over, Gehrig came here and had a cup of coffee sitting at the bar."

"He sat at this bar?" Byron asked.

"This bar. Well, not this exact one - it's newer, I think. But he did come here for coffee."

"But not *this* coffee," said Byron, pointing to his cup.

"No, a different pot. That I *do* know."

"Mind if I take a picture?"

"Be my guest."

Byron pulled out his camera and took a picture of Paul standing behind the bar, his arms crossed, and then took a shot of the dining room.

After finishing his food and paying his tab, Byron walked back toward the stadium. The sidewalks were crowded with fans and vendors. A souvenir stand at the corner of Michigan and Harrison offered Tiger Stadium commemorative souvenirs and Byron stopped to have a look. A vendor was rummaging through some boxes stacked on a chair behind a wood screen covered with pennants. As Byron picked through some lapel pins in a basket on the table, the vendor walked around from the back side of the stand.

"Hello, Byron," said the vendor.

Byron looked up. It was Matty.

"Mr. O'Boyle?" Byron asked, surprised to see him.

"Call me Matty."

"Alright. Matty."

"Look, I'm sorry I was short with you back there. I didn't

want to say anything in front of Paul - the bartender. He listens to everyone's conversations and I didn't want him hearing ours."

"So, then, you *do* know Mac."

"I do."

"And you *were* a groundskeeper at Tiger Stadium."

"Not Tiger Stadium - Bennett Park."

"Bennett Park?" asked Byron, the confusion evident in his voice. "That's impossible."

"No, it's not."

"But they tore down Bennett Park a hundred years ago to make way for Tiger Stadium."

"No, you've got it wrong," said Matty. "Tiger Stadium didn't replace Bennett Park. Navin Field did. And it was ninety years ago, not one hundred."

"Navin Field," said Byron. "But whether it was ninety or a hundred years ago, it's still impossible."

"In 1938 they changed the name to Briggs Stadium in honor of the new owner," said Matty, ignoring Byron's mathematical calculations. "They didn't start calling it Tiger Stadium until 1961."

"So you're telling me you used to be the groundskeeper at Bennett Park."

"Yup."

"Assuming you were ten when you started working there, that would make you at least one hundred. You don't look that old."

"Looks can be deceiving," said Matty.

Byron stared at Matty, pondering his outrageous claim.

"Did you ever play baseball, you know, professionally?" Byron asked, breaking the momentary, awkward silence.

"Not professionally, no. I played when I was a kid with friends in the neighborhood."

"So you're not a player."

"No. I'm a vendor."

"A vendor who used to be a groundskeeper at Navin Field one hundred years ago."

"Bennett Park," said Matty, now annoyed. "Looks like Mac misjudged you."

"I'm sorry, Matty. I don't mean to be flip. It's just that ever since I met Mac, things like this keep happening to me."

"That's alright. I guess it's to be expected. If Mac is letting you in, as you say, you need to open your mind and be more receptive."

"That's why I'm here. I'm being receptive. Let me in."

"It doesn't work that way. First, you've got to believe before you have any chance of getting in."

"I have to believe? Believe what?"

"It's something you won't be able to understand until you believe it."

"That makes no sense. It sounds like something out of Dr. Seuss."

"Yeah, well, that's not surprising. Theodor was a man in the know."

"Theodor?"

"Theodor Geisel, you know, Dr. Seuss."

"You mean he . . . ."

"Let's not get into that right now," said Matty. "All I can tell you is don't be constrained by reason or rational thought. That doesn't apply to what you're going through. If you try to apply reason to what's going on, you'll never believe it, and then you'll never know."

"Well, let me ask you this. If you were a groundskeeper at Bennett Park, how is it that you're still alive?"

"Again, if you insist on being constrained by rational thought, you'll never understand."

"But, before I understand, I have to believe, at least according to you."

"To understand, first you have to believe."

Okay, I'll play along, thought Byron.

"Since you worked at Bennett Park, then you must have known Hughie Jennings when he managed the Tigers."

"He hired me in 1910, the year after they won their third straight pennant. I knew him until Ty Cobb took over as manager eleven years later."

"You knew him in 1910? That's incredible. So, what was he like?"

"Very religious, a little high strung, but a great baseball man, really understood the game. You know he still holds the record for being hit by a pitch - 51 times in one season?"

"I knew he held the record. That's an awful lot of taking one for the team."

"It is, indeed."

"How was he with Ty Cobb?"

"He's the one guy who knew how to keep him in line."

"What about that 'Ee-Yah' thing he used to do? What was that?"

"You mean when he was coaching? Sometimes he'd get a little too excited and start jumping up and down with his hands above his head, yelling 'Ee-Yah, Ee-Yah.' It was pretty funny. We always figured it meant something like 'here we are.' It became his nickname."

"Well, since we're suspending rational thought, have you seen him lately?" Byron asked, half joking, but half serious. "Is he here now?"

"If I told you he was, would you believe me?"

"You're the one who said I should suspend reason. So, I'm asking. Have you seen him lately?"

"I'm not at liberty to say. In fact, I've already said too much."

Byron looked surprised. "I didn't realize there was a protocol to all this."

Matty raised his eyebrows and pursed his lips. He waved his hand, palms open, like a practiced magician. "Oh, there is, you wouldn't believe the rules they make us follow. But that's enough. No more questions."

Byron gave Matty a long look. There were so many questions he wanted to ask, but apparently he already had used up his quota.

"Say, how much are the pins?" Byron pointed to the lapel pins displayed on the table. "You can answer that question, right?"

"Take one. Consider it a gift."

"Thanks, Matty, I think I will." Byron picked out a round blue and orange pin depicting the stadium at the corner of Michigan and Trumbull, encircled with the words "Tiger Stadium, 1912 - 1999." He stuck the pin on his hat.

"So, why the souvenir stand? I thought you worked at Sportsland?"

"I do, this is something I do on the side, when necessary."

"You mind if I take your picture?" Byron asked.

"Go ahead, you can give it a try," said Matty.

Matty put his hands on his hips and posed for the picture. As Byron readied his camera, he half expected Matty to blink and disappear, à la Barbara Eden in *I Dream of Jeannie*. Byron framed the shot, making sure Tiger Stadium was visible in the background.

"Well, you better be on your way, Byron. You came to see a game, didn't you?"

"I did - but I also came to see you. Maybe I'll see you later."

"Start believing and you might," said Matty.

"Oh, by the way, is there anything you want me to tell Mac for you?"

"Yeah, tell him I'm looking forward to seeing him next year."

"What? Mac's coming here next year?" asked Byron.

"That's the plan."

Byron crossed Harrison, stopped for a moment, and turned around, half expecting Matty to be gone. And, sure enough, he was. Matty and his entire souvenir stand had disappeared. Byron felt flushed, as if he were about to faint. He took a few more steps and, upon reaching the stadium, sat down on the sidewalk with his back against the stadium wall.

Byron closed his eyes, ignoring the people walking past him toward the corner of Michigan and Trumbull. *Yesterday Boots, and now Matty*, he thought. *What is wrong with me? Why is this happening again, why after all these years?*

Once he felt better, he stood up and stretched his legs. Pulling his hat off his head, he examined the Tiger Stadium pin Matty had given him. *So, I didn't imagine him*, he thought. *He just disappeared. Now I know how Major Nelson must have felt.*

"Ee-yah."

CHAPTER 12

◎ ◎ ◎

Suspending Rational Thought

It was a beautiful day for a baseball game. The previous evening, the Orioles had defeated the Tigers 9-4, behind what had become a typical outing from Mike Mussina, nine hits, three earned runs in six innings pitched. Mussina would be a free agent after the season and rumor had it that if the Orioles didn't offer him a six-year, bajillion-dollar deal, he would test free agency. Byron wondered how much money a person truly needed for playing a kid's game.

That Saturday afternoon, Byron needed only $20 to buy a lower-box ticket in the right-field corner, section 144, row 4, seat 3. The first few rows of section 144 were directly inside the right-field corner, at ground level. Byron felt as if he were sitting right on the field.

The visiting team bullpen was 20 feet away, in front and to the left of where Byron sat. The Orioles took batting practice while pitchers ran sprints between the right-field corner and centerfield. Orioles' shortstop Cal Ripken, Jr., although on the disabled list, took batting practice. Fans watching him hit were hoping to see home runs, but none of the balls he connected with cleared the outfield fence.

The stadium loudspeakers boomed late 1970's-era guitar-synth rock by the Cars, appropriate, he thought, given Detroit's distinction as the Motor City. Once the pitchers finished their sprints, Orioles' relievers Mike Timlin and Jesse Orosco stopped to chat with a group of fans and sign autographs for some kids wearing Orioles Dugout Club T-shirts. Bullpen coach Elrod Hendricks caught the eye of one of the kids and tossed him some bubble gum. Another child wore a hat with the emblem of the Negro National League Baltimore Elite Giants, a Baltimore Negro League team from the 1930's and 1940's. Byron wondered if the girl appreciated the significance of the hat she was wearing.

Ripken, standing next to the batting cage, chatted with Eddie Murray, the former Orioles' star and current first-base coach. Once batting practice ended, the grounds crew rolled the batting cage toward left field. The players on the field jogged toward the visiting team dugout along the first-base side of the field. Cal and Eddie strolled side by side toward the dugout, while a crowd of fans tried in vain to capture the attention of the two future Hall of Famers.

As the players disappeared inside the dugout, Byron rose from his seat and took a walk around the ballpark. In the course of 20 minutes, he went through three rolls of film, taking photographs of the field from every conceivable angle, again, for posterity.

The game itself was a proverbial home-run derby, with the Orioles smashing four off Detroit's hurlers and the home team hitting two. The game was not well-attended and the announced crowd of 18,068 seemed even smaller when spread throughout the park. An usher told Byron the team expected bigger crowds once school let out and summer began. The Tigers' final home stand against the Kansas City Royals in September already was sold out.

The teams did all their scoring by the fifth inning, with five of Detroit's seven runs coming in the second inning off Scott Kamieniecki, who did not make it out of the inning. In the later innings, with the players' bats silenced, the game took on the air of a more casual affair. The sun's rays burst through the clouds moving west to east, lending a dramatic backdrop to the rather mundane proceedings on the field below. The sunlight cast irregular shadows on the playing field. Ghostly outlines of the stadium's light stanchions appeared along the third-base line, stretching farther across the field as the afternoon sun slid toward the west.

With the game winding down, Byron looked around the stadium from section to section. Looming behind home plate at the top of the ballpark, facing toward Michigan and Cochrane, were giant letters that spelled out "TIGER STADIUM." For fans sitting inside the stadium, the lettering appeared in reverse. As shadows crept farther onto the field, the lettering cast an image of the sign onto the grass along third base. Byron took a photograph of the shadowy "TIGER STADIUM" lettering on the field just before it vanished as the sun disappeared behind a cloud.

The Tigers won 7-6. When the game was over, Byron remained in his seat watching the grounds crew tend to the infield as fans filed out of the stadium. As a player, Byron was almost always the last to leave, lingering on the bench and looking out on the field once the game ended. On this day, long after the lines to exit the stadium had cleared out, the lower seating bowl was still dotted with people sitting in their seats or walking in the aisles.

A man stood patiently as his son picked up discarded plastic souvenir drinking cups. A group of children crowded around the Tigers' dugout, waiting in vain for one of their heroes to return. Byron thought back to his last game in the minors, sitting in the home team dugout watching the grounds crew cover the field with a tarp. He remembered giving his bat away and wondered whatever happened to the kid he gave it to, whether the kid went on to play high-school or college ball or maybe was himself in the minors now. Then he thought about his last hit. *If only Dulin had followed coach's signal and stopped at third base, I might have scored and we might have won that game.*

An usher approached Byron and told him it was time to leave. Unlike the usher he had encountered the previous evening, this one seemed almost apologetic for having bothered him.

After exiting through Gate 1, Byron stood alongside other fans crowding the sidewalk at "The Corner," including those lining up to take turns posing for photographs next to Cobb's plaque. To the right of the plaque, a state historical marker summed up Tiger Stadium's history and its significance to the people of Detroit:

> *TIGER STADIUM*
>
> *Baseball has been played on this site since before 1900 and it has been the home of the Detroit Tigers from their start as a charter member of the American League in 1901. Standing on the location of an early haymarket, the stadium has been enlarged and renamed several times. Once called Bennett Park with wooden stands for 10,000, it became Navin Field in 1912 when seating was increased to 23,000 and home plate was moved from what is now right field to its present location. Major alterations later expanded its capacity to more than 54,000 and in 1938 the structure became Briggs Stadium. Lights were installed in 1948 and in 1961 the name was changed to Tiger Stadium. The site of many championship sporting events, the evolution of this stadium is a tribute to Detroit's support of professional athletics.*

And now, the stadium was being abandoned by Detroit, just as Baltimore had abandoned Union Park and Memorial Stadium, and just as almost every other major-league city had abandoned their earlier, historic ballparks. At least the people of Detroit could take some comfort in knowing that Tiger Stadium and its earlier incarnations had lasted over 100 years - longer than any other ballpark.

Byron asked a fellow dawdler to take his photograph standing next to the stadium plaque. The dawdler obliged and a handful of Tiger fans gathered near the plaque let out a good-natured chorus of boos, taunting Byron about his Orioles hat.

Eventually, the crowd dispersed and stadium workers locked the main gate. Byron was still in no hurry to leave. Lights behind the main gate darkened and a "CLOSED" sign appeared in the ticket window. With few fans still milling about, an eerie silence engulfed the stadium. It was a silence that would be, in coming years, all too familiar at the corner of Michigan and Trumbull.

Byron caught a cab back to the hotel and arrived in his room at 6 p.m. He searched through his duffel bag and found the matchbook Rob had given him from the Parkway Lounge. Sitting down on the edge of the bed next to the night stand, Byron reached for the phone and dialed the number for the Parkway.

A woman answered the phone.

"Hello, is Rob White there?" asked Byron.

"I'm sorry, who?"

"Rob White."

"I don't know who that is. Is he a customer?" asked the woman.

"No, he works there. He's a bartender. He's supposed to be working tonight."

"There's no one here by that name, sir," said the woman.

"You must be mistaken," Byron said. "Let me talk to the manager."

"Just a minute."

A man's voice came on the line. "May I help you?"

"I'm looking for Rob White. He should be working there tonight."

"He used to work here, but not anymore."

"What? I saw him there yesterday. Did he quit today or something?"

"No. He's been gone for years."

"He has? What about Doris - the waitress? Is she there?"

"Sorry, Doris? She's gone, too. She died several years ago."

"What? Oh, no . . . that can't be," said Byron.

Byron hung up the telephone and fell back onto the bed. *Not again*, he thought. Byron felt sick to his stomach.

After a minute or two passed, Byron sat up. He picked up the matchbook from the bedside table and twirled it through his fingers like a magician twirling a coin. *This makes no sense. I was there yesterday. I have the matches to prove it. I spoke to both of them.* He thought about what Matty had told him, that he couldn't apply reason or rational thought to what he was experiencing.

Then, the telephone rang, startling Byron. He reached across the bed to answer it. "Hello?"

"Hello, Bitty?" asked a man on the other end.

"Yes?"

"It's Rob, Rob White."

"Rob!" said Byron. "I just called the Parkway. They said you weren't there any more."

"I know. I was yanking your chain. I told the cashier if someone called for me, don't admit to knowing me. I thought you could use a good *Twilight Zone* moment. You certainly fell for it."

"You jerk," said Byron, stopping before he said anything else.

"Man, I got you."

"Yes, you did."

"Who's leaving their glove in the dugout now, Bitty?"

"Very funny," said Byron. "So Doris, she's not dead?"

"She's fine," said Rob. "Her hair's never been higher. So, how many ghosts have you met in Detroit?"

"Well, since you don't believe in ghosts, I'll just say that I met one very old man who claims he was a groundskeeper at Tiger Stadium almost a hundred years ago."

"And you believed him?"

"I don't know. He disappeared after we finished talking. I turned around and he was gone."

"And you haven't been drinking, have you?" asked Rob.

"No."

"You've been getting plenty of sleep?"

"Yes. I've been sleeping fine."

"Well, tell you what, I found someone to cover my shift tomorrow, so I'm coming up in the morning. I've always wanted to meet a real ghost."

"Great!" said Byron, excited Rob would be joining him for the game. "But, I'll warn you now, turns out this guy is pretty selective about who he talks to. Don't blame me if he doesn't want to talk to you."

"Don't worry, I can get him to talk. So, where should we meet?"

"What time can you be here?"

"Eleven a.m. good?"

"Yeah. Let's meet at the corner of Michigan and Trumbull. Do you know how to get here?"

"I know where the stadium is. I drove passed it a couple of

years ago. See you tomorrow, 11 o'clock."

"See you then."

Hanging up the telephone, Byron lay back down on the bed, breathing a deep sigh of relief. *Boy*, thought Byron. *He sure got me.* Byron was glad Rob was coming up. He needed someone to share the craziness with, even if he wasn't certain introducing Rob to Matty was a good idea.

Byron imagined the introduction: *Matty, this is my friend, Rob. We used to play minor-league ball together. Rob, this is Matty. He's a ghost. Don't bother trying to shake his hand.*

After his long day at the park, Byron was too tired to venture outside for dinner and instead took the elevator to the Summit Restaurant at the top of the Renaissance Hotel. The revolving restaurant provided an impressive view of Detroit and Windsor, Ontario, and then Detroit, and then Windsor, a complete rotation every 20 minutes.

As night drew near, the lights of Windsor's casinos beckoned Americans from across the Detroit River. In the United States, the sun was beginning to set. To the west, the light stanchions of Tiger Stadium remained on, glowing in the night sky, like ghosts against a darkened orange sunset. A mile or so to the east of Tiger Stadium, the construction site of Detroit's new baseball stadium was barely visible in the fading twilight.

Out with the old, in with the new.

Chapter 13

●●●

Sportsland U.S.A.

After a night of intermittent sleep, Byron was wide awake at 5:00 the next morning. Too many thoughts were racing through his mind. It had been one week since his trip to Baltimore, where he met both Murph and Mac, and he thought about all that had happened since then – his encounter with Boots during his stop in Pittsburgh, the old man in Carnegie who disappeared inside the gas station, his meeting with Matty at Tiger Stadium. Although it was several hours before he was supposed to meet Rob, Byron was dressed and ready to leave the hotel by 6 a.m.

Walking through the Renaissance Center lobby, Byron spotted a lone janitor wearing a dark blue Tigers hat with a white "D" in royal lettering. He was buffing the floor near one of the elevator banks. *Maybe he's an old ballplayer?* Byron wondered as he walked by. Byron waved hello, but the two never made eye contact as the janitor remained focused on his assigned task, leaving the question unanswered.

Byron headed outside as dawn broke. A thin orange strip of daylight was visible on the horizon beyond Windsor. Byron walked past a cabby leaning against the hood of his taxi.

"Need a ride?" asked the cabby.

"No thanks," said Byron. "I'm heading over to Tiger Stadium."

"Suit yourself, although I sure wouldn't want to walk it alone this time of day."

Byron headed northwest up Griswold Street to Michigan

Avenue. Two blocks ahead, he spotted the silhouette of the once regal Cadillac Hotel, now a dilapidated relic of the old, automobile-driven Detroit. In the early dawn light the edifice loomed like an apparition over the intersection of Michigan Avenue and Washington Boulevard. Byron half expected the hotel to disappear as soon as the first direct rays of sunlight fell upon it.

But, as morning broke, the thirty-story, Italian Renaissance skyscraper remained. The lobby entrance on Washington Boulevard was boarded with plywood shellacked with peeling hip hop posters. Although he could not see inside the hotel, Byron knew it was through those doors that Lou Gehrig and his manager, Joe McCarthy, had met that morning in 1939, the day Gehrig took himself out of the Yankees' lineup. Byron waited for a moment, half expecting Gehrig to come walking out the lobby doors. Other than a homeless man asking Byron for spare change, nothing happened.

Byron took a picture of the lobby doors and their incongruous coverings and continued north on Washington, walking a half mile to the construction site of the new ballpark. The walk itself was uneventful, a surprisingly peaceful stroll past darkened buildings that long ago must have seemed to have had endless possibilities. *And the cab driver said this area was unsafe*, thought Byron.

It being a Sunday morning, there was no construction activity at the new ballpark site. Byron walked around the perimeter of the site, trying to imagine how the ballpark would look when completed. Feeling as if his being around the new ballpark site was somehow cheating on Tiger Stadium, he didn't stay long and took no pictures.

On his way to Tiger Stadium, he passed the boarded-up shell of the once statuesque Madison-Lenox Hotel at the corner of

Madison and Grand River Avenues. The hotel was an apparition of smaller stature than the Cadillac. The city already had stripped away most of the hotel's front entrance and it appeared as if the remaining structure soon would be razed. Byron wondered if visiting ball clubs like the Orioles ever stayed in the Madison-Lenox when they were in town to play the Tigers. Byron tried imagining how the hotel would have looked. He imagined players like John McGraw and Wilbert Robinson coming out the front door, dressed in suits and ties, looking to catch a Detroit United Line trolley to the ballpark.

Byron knew there wasn't much chance that morning of finding McGraw's ghost lurking there, or at the corner of Michigan and Trumbull, for that matter. According to his research, during the 100-plus seasons of baseball at the Corner, McGraw had played only four games in Detroit, all during the American League Orioles' first western trip in 1901. McGraw played third base in a doubleheader on May 30th that year, which the teams split 10-7 and 1-4, at what was then Bennett Park. The following day, the teams played to a 5-5 tie, and on the final day, June 1st, the Orioles beat the Tigers 3-1. By the time the Orioles headed west in June the following season, McGraw had departed for his new job with the New York Giants. Thus, fate limited McGraw's playing career at the Corner to one game more than the number of games Byron would attend at the stadium that weekend.

After reaching Tiger Stadium, Byron walked two more blocks to Casey's for breakfast.

"Good morning, Paul," Byron said to the bartender as he sat down at the bar.

"Byron, right? You're here early."

"Have you seen Matty O'Boyle today?"

"No, not this morning. He usually doesn't come in on

Sundays. If he does, it's after church for a cup of coffee."

"Does he ever finish his coffee?"

"Now that you mention it, I don't know. Sundays are pretty busy, so I really haven't noticed."

"I went by the Cadillac Hotel this morning, on the way over here," said Byron.

"What did you think? Pretty sad, huh?"

"Yeah. I hope they find someone to buy it and fix it up."

"If they do, they should give the guy a statue and stick it in front of the hotel."

"Or at least give him free Cadillacs for life."

Byron ordered breakfast and, with two hours to kill before he was to meet Rob, had time to read the entire Sunday edition of the *Detroit Free Press*, including the comics, the circulars, and the obituaries. After finishing breakfast and the paper, Byron left Casey's and walked over to Tiger Stadium's main gate, where he found Rob holding court with the ushers waiting to open the ballpark.

Rob spotted Byron and waved him over.

"How was the drive?" asked Byron.

"Great. It took me no time to get here. Seventy-Five was clear sailing."

"Good. Glad you could make it."

"These fine men have told me the gates open at eleven and that we'd better get our seats ASAP because they're expecting a sellout," said Rob.

"Fat chance of that," said Byron. "There were only 18,000 here yesterday. We can get our tickets after we meet Matty."

"Well, then, let's go meet that dead friend of yours," said Rob.

"He works up the block at a souvenir store," said Byron.

The two crossed Trumbull heading east on Michigan. In front

of Sportsland USA, an A-frame sidewalk sign painted Tigers' orange beckoned fans to stop and shop. "OPEN Detroit's Original Home for Ballpark Souvenirs Sportsland USA," stated the sign.

"Sportsland USA,' huh?" asked Rob. "Are you sure it's safe for you to go in there?"

"What do you mean?"

"Look at the place - it's got baseball crap everywhere. You may get lost in there and never leave."

"I'm an adult. I can handle it."

Byron held the door open for Rob. As Byron crossed the threshold into the vast sea of memorabilia, his head began throbbing from sensory overload. Hats and pennants, miniature baseball bats and programs, autographed photographs and player posters lined the walls and the counters of the store's main room. Merchandise was crammed haphazardly inside glass cases underneath counters. Rows of clothing carousels packed with T-shirts, sweatshirts, and jackets lined the expansive middle portion of the room like ballroom dancers twirling on the dance floor. On a shelf above the front entrance, 40 or so bobblehead dolls stood at attention, nodding ever so gently in agreement each time the front door opened or closed.

"Man," said Byron, "this place has enough stuff to make even the Collyer brothers claustrophobic."

"Who?"

"The Collyer brothers. You never heard of them?"

"Nope," said Rob.

"Homer and Langley - they were compulsive hoarders who lived in New York City. They were crushed to death by all the junk in their apartment."

"Well, I hope you've learned a valuable lesson from their misfortune."

"I have. I never stack boxes in my house any higher than my chin."

Byron could have spent hours rummaging through the store's overwhelming maze of baseball souvenirs, but, coming to his senses, focused instead on the task at hand.

"Do you see him?" asked Rob.

"I don't."

"Excuse me," said Byron to the man he had spoken with the day before. "Is Matty here today?"

"Yeah. He's in the back." The man pointed to a storage room at the far end of the store.

Byron pushed his way past racks of T-shirts and jerseys, the clothes seemingly grabbing at him, imploring him to take a closer look. He walked around the back counter and through the entrance to the storage room. Matty was pulling Tigers hats out of a large cardboard box and placing them in stacks on the counter.

"Good morning, Matty!" said Byron.

Matty turned toward Byron and nodded. "Hello, Byron."

"Do you have a minute?" asked Byron. "I wanted you to meet a friend of mine."

"Sure," said Matty, looking around. "But, you haven't told him anything, have you?"

Before Byron could answer, Rob came into the room.

"Matty, this is Rob; Rob, this is Matty." Rob, standing at the threshold, gave Matty a wave.

"Nice to meet you, Rob," said Matty. "A friend of Byron's is a friend of mine."

"I'm not sure I'd call us friends," said Rob, laughing. "Bitty and I played ball together, years ago."

"Did you say 'Bitty?'"

"I did. That's Byron's nickname," said Rob. "Everybody

called him that."

"And I couldn't stand it, either," said Byron.

"All the more reason to call you Bitty," said Rob.

"Where were you guy teammates?" asked Matty.

"Charlotte O's," said Rob.

"An Orioles' affiliate," said Matty.

"Bitty here tells me you used to be a groundskeeper at Tiger Stadium."

"A groundskeeper?" asked Matty, annoyed. "He must be confused. I've worked here twenty years. Before that, I worked for Ford up in Dearborn making Mustangs."

"Really? Well, I've known Bitty a long time and I can vouch for the fact that he's often confused."

Matty forced a smile in response to Rob's joke. Then he gave Byron a stern look.

"You boys heading over to the game?" Matty asked.

"We are," said Byron. "I guess we better be going."

"Nice to meet you, Matty," said Rob.

"Nice meeting you. Enjoy the game."

Rob headed out toward the main room. Byron stayed back for a moment, allowing some distance between himself and Rob.

"Byron," whispered Matty.

Byron looked at Matty, who motioned with his hand to come closer.

"Sorry about that," said Byron.

"It's not for me to tell you what you can or can't do, but if I were you, I'd keep details of our conversation yesterday between us."

"Why?" Byron asked.

"Let's just say you need to be more discreet about all this. If you start telling others, you might find the door's been shut and it won't open again, ever. This isn't for everyone to know. Very few people in your position ever find out about it."

"What do you mean, people in my 'position?'"

"You're what is known as, in the parlance, a 'lifer.'"

"You mean, I'm alive?"

"That's one word for it," said Matty.

"So, what are you?" asked Byron.

"A souvenir vendor."

"Hey, Bitty," called out Rob. "You coming?"

"Be there in a minute."

"You better go, Byron. And remember 'Discretion is the better part of valor.'"

"Shakespeare, right?" asked Byron.

"Yup."

"He also said 'A little bit of knowledge is a dangerous thing!'"

"Actually, that was Alexander Pope, not Shakespeare," said Matty.

"I had no idea, I was just guessing."

As Byron made his way back through the swarm of T-shirts, he noticed Rob standing at the cash register, paying for some souvenirs.

Back on Michigan Avenue, Rob reached into his plastic shopping bag and tossed Byron a T-shirt. "Here you go, Bitty. Something to remember the day by."

Byron examined the T-shirt. On the front was a picture of Tiger Stadium and on the back was a list of the Tigers' 1999 home series.

"You shouldn't have," said Byron.

"Don't worry," said Rob. "You're buying the hot dogs today."

"Fair enough."

Foot traffic along Michigan had picked up and the sidewalk

was crowded with fans migrating toward "The Corner."

"So what happened back there?" asked Rob. "Why didn't he let on about him being a groundskeeper?"

"Like you said, I must be confused," said Byron.

"I'll tell you, Byron, he didn't look like a ghost to me. What did he say to you after I left?"

"He said I shouldn't be telling people about this."

"You better tell me," said Rob.

"Let's get to the game, okay."

"You're not taking this seriously, are you?"

"No, of course not," said Byron, lying to avoid seeming foolish.

After crossing Trumbull, they stood in the ticket line and listened to the family in front of them debate where to sit. "Section 144 in the right-field corner has good seats," Byron offered to the father, unsolicited.

"Oh. How much are those?" he asked.

"Twenty bucks each."

The father purchased five tickets in section 144 and Byron and Rob purchased two $20 lower-box tickets in section 108, along the third-base line.

Byron and Rob entered through the main gate and proceeded through the concourse to the entrance to the lower-box seats.

"Ready for a dog?" Byron asked. "It's almost noon now, so it's okay."

"Ready as I'll ever be," said Rob.

They stopped at a concession stand around the corner from their section and purchased four hot dogs and two sodas. The two then made their way through the entrance to section 108, stopping so Rob could see the field.

"It's smaller than I thought it would be," said Rob.

"I had the same reaction the other day. You know, looks

can be deceiving."

"You should know," said Rob. "So when are you gonna tell me what Matty said?"

"Let me put it this way. I think I may have blown it with him when I told you his secret. He became very defensive, saying I shouldn't be telling other people about it. Who knows? Maybe he can hear us now. So, if you don't mind, I think it's better if I don't say anything else."

"Boy, you really are Rod Serling."

"It's nothing personal."

"A paranoid paranormal who prefers to preserve his privacy," said Rob in a creepy Serlingesque voice.

"Very clever."

Byron and Rob rose for the national anthem. They both shouted out a healthy "O" for Orioles when the singer reached the line "O say, does that Star Spangled Banner yet wave." After doing so, they smiled at each other approvingly.

Before the crowd had time to settle back into the seats, Brady Anderson, the Orioles' lead-off hitter, smacked a home run off Detroit starting pitcher Dave Mlicki.

"Boy, Anderson sure got a hold of that one," said Rob.

"Nice swing," said Byron.

"You played with him in Rochester, didn't you?" asked Rob.

"Yeah, in 1988, although I never figured him to be much of a home run hitter. Shows what I know."

"Do you ever talk to him now?"

"Nah, I haven't spoken to him in years. He wasn't with Rochester that long. He spent most of that year with Baltimore."

"Do you ever wonder how different things would have been if you had gotten the call and he didn't?"

"There wasn't much chance of that. Besides, he was an

outfielder and I was an infielder."

"You know what I mean. Don't you ever wonder how it would have been?"

"Of course I do. Don't you?"

"Sure, but I wasn't as good a player as you. You should have gotten the call. It was bad luck you didn't."

"I'm not sure how much luck had to do with it. There were plenty of players better than me. Besides, Anderson was a true prospect. They traded Mike Boddicker to the Boston Red Sox to get him."

"The O's got Curt Schilling, too, don't forget," said Rob.

"I know. My point is the Orioles considered Anderson a prospect. They never considered me one. I was picked late on the second day of the draft."

"On the day I was drafted, I was glad I got chosen at all," said Rob.

"Me, too. But, in the end, I was filler - filling out the roster while the Orioles developed their true prospects. They were going to do everything they could to justify the bonus money they paid those guys."

"At least we made it as far as we did - triple A," said Rob. "Most players don't even get that far."

"I know."

"Maybe this stuff about us thinking we see old ballplayers happens to us because we miss the game and want to play again so badly. We start seeing things that really aren't there. I saw a TV show once where they talked about something like this - where people had what they called 'shared delusions.'"

"I'm not under any delusion about what I've seen," said Byron.

"Sure you are. You think you see an old ballplayer at the University of Pittsburgh, where Forbes Field used to be. You think some guy stocking hats at a souvenir stand is a hundred-plus-year-old groundskeeper. If that's not delusional, I don't know what is. My friend in Minneapolis thinks he sees old ballplayers at the bank where he works - where the Millers used to play. I think I see them at the grocery store where the Mud Hens used to play. You start thinking about all the games that were played there and the mind plays tricks on you. Before you know it you're seeing things when actually there is a completely rational explanation that you don't want to see because you're delusional."

"Again, I don't like the idea that you think I'm delusional."

"I didn't say just you."

"Yeah, but you told me earlier you didn't believe those guys you saw at Food Town were ghosts."

"I did say that and I don't think they're ghosts. They were a bunch of old guys hanging out at a shopping center. To be honest, this whole ghost thing kinda creeps me out. I'd rather baseball was just a game and nothing more. It is just a game, you know."

"It is," said Byron. "One that gets inside your head and never leaves."

The friends were quiet for a while but settled slowly back into concentrating on the game. After two innings, the Orioles were up 2-0. The game moved quickly and, during the top of the seventh the Orioles tacked on three more runs, making the score 5-0.

During the seventh-inning stretch, Byron asked a man sitting behind them to take a picture of him and Rob. After the man handed the camera back, Rob turned to Byron and said, "Well, I hate to leave before the Tigers' big rally, but I gotta be heading back to Toledo."

"Are you sure you can't stay for the rest of the game?"

"No, I told Lily I'd be home in time for supper."

"Well, thanks for coming out."

"You're heading to Cleveland tomorrow?" asked Rob.

"I am."

"Don't forget your EMF meter."

"My what?"

"You know - your electromagnetic whatever it's called, to detect ghosts. You do have one, don't you?"

"Funny," said Byron. "That's okay. I'm fair game, I guess."

"That you are, Bitty, that you are. Some things never change."

The two shook hands and Rob left.

Byron sat back down in his seat and watched the last two innings of the game. The Tigers' rally never materialized. After watching the other fans around him leave, Byron stood up and took one last photograph of the field, although his heart was no longer in it. He had hoped to find comfort in sharing his experience with Rob, but it had the opposite effect. The way Rob had bolted before the game was over, Byron knew that he was just being kind, not telling Byron to his face he thought he had lost it. It would be Rob's only game at Tiger Stadium, and he left after seven innings.

⚾ ⚾ ⚾

That night, Byron could not sleep. He was bothered by Rob's reaction earlier in the day and needed to talk to someone. So, he called Maggie.

"Hey, Maggie, did I wake you?"

"What time is it?"

"Eleven-thirty."

"It's late, Byron."

"I know. I'm sorry. I couldn't sleep and needed to talk to you."

"Where are you?"

"Detroit."

"Let me guess, baseball and ghosts?"

"You know me so well."

"Too well."

"Remember I told you I thought it was happening again? You know, me seeing things."

"How could I forget?"

"Well, it happened again yesterday, in Detroit. But the guy I met told me I shouldn't tell anybody else what I've seen."

"Then why are you telling me?"

"Because I've got to tell someone and you're the only one who will listen."

"So, who's this guy you're talking about?"

"Promise not to repeat what I tell you?"

"Byron, who on earth would I tell? I'd be too embarrassed."

"Okay. The guy's name is Matty O'Boyle. He sells souvenirs at Tiger Stadium, except I think that's a cover."

"Why?"

"Because he pretty much told me so. He said he used to be a groundskeeper at Tiger Stadium - back in 1910."

"Okay. Well, that's impossible."

"That's what I told him. But, see, I think he's a ghost."

"The guy makes an outrageous claim so you automatically assume he's ghost?"

"How else do you explain it?"

"Easy - he's lying to you."

"No, he's not."

"How can you be so sure?"

"Because Matty is the guy that Mac told me to look for."

"Mac?"

"Yeah - the guy in Baltimore - who told me he could see Union Park."

"Maybe Mac's pulling your leg and enlisted Matty to help."

"Why would some guy I hardly know want to put one over on me?"

"Maybe he's crazy. Maybe someone you know put him up to it. Charles, maybe. I don't know."

"No, that's not it. See, what I didn't tell you was after Matty and I finished talking, he disappeared into thin air, along with his souvenir stand."

"He disappeared? As in vanished?"

"Yes."

"Okay. I've heard enough. I told you last week how I feel about this. I may not be your wife anymore, but I'm telling you - call Dr. Connor."

"I'm not calling Dr. Connor. I need to figure this out on my own."

"You haven't been to any bars up there, have you?"

"One, but I didn't have a drink, if that's what you're asking."

"It is."

"Maggie - I can handle that now. When I was in Toledo, I went to the Parkway Lounge and didn't even think about having a drink."

"Well, that's good, I guess."

"You'll never guess who I ran into at the Parkway."

"George Washington."

"Good guess, but no. Rob White - you remember him, don't you?"

"I remember the name."

"He's the guy who left his glove in the dugout."

"Oh yeah 'Gloveless Rob.'"

"Well, I convinced him to come up to Detroit for a game. I told him what was happening because I thought he would understand. He seemed to at first. I even introduced him to Matty. But then he freaked out once I started talking about ghosts."

"I thought you told me that souvenir guy disappeared."

"He did, but, see, I know where he works."

"This definitely sounds like something you should be telling Dr. Connor, not me."

"I guess it wouldn't surprise you to learn Rob now thinks I'm nuts."

"I'm sorry, but I think you're gonna get that reaction from anybody you tell this stuff to."

"Even you?" asked Byron.

Maggie paused for a moment. "I've known you a long time and I know how consumed you can get. But, just because you think you're seeing ghosts again, doesn't mean I should believe it, too."

"Fair enough."

"But, do I think you're crazy? No. I don't. And that's the crazy part . . . I don't."

CHAPTER 14

Oberlin Yeomen

The following morning, leaving Detroit, Byron eased off the accelerator as he passed Tiger Stadium, taking one long, last look at what one day would be another lost ballpark. Continuing west on Michigan Avenue toward Clark Street, he glanced occasionally in his rearview mirror, watching as Tiger Stadium grew smaller with each passing city block. Less than a half mile from the stadium, only the unlit light stanchions rising above Michigan Avenue remained visible. Then, the stadium disappeared altogether.

Driving south on I-75 toward Toledo, Byron thought about Rob, wondering whether he had told his wife about the trip – whether he had mentioned Byron's paranormal leanings or his encounter with Matty. Byron knew Lily as a pleasant, no-nonsense person who had been drawn to Rob by his gregarious, larger-than-life personality. Back when he and Rob were still teammates, Byron sensed Lily had little use for baseball and that she looked forward to the day when her future husband no longer made his living playing a child's game. Byron was certain his recent musing to Rob about Matty and his description of old ball players hanging around abandoned ballfields would confirm Lily's belief that grown men should not concern themselves with matters such as baseball.

Still, Byron admired Rob and Lily, for they somehow had found common ground and had kept their relationship together. The same couldn't be said for Byron. As he approached Toledo, albeit from a different direction, he found himself thinking not about the song "Lucille," but about Maggie.

Even after his divorce, Byron had a hard time letting go, especially since, it seemed, Maggie had no interest in dating again. When he was a couple of years out of baseball and no longer drinking, Byron went looking for a second chance. He had not spoken with Maggie for several months and called her up once he knew he could handle seeing her again. She agreed to meet him in Cumberland, Maryland, at a vintage train station where they ran two-hour excursion trains on an old branch line. Byron had taken Maggie there when they were still together. That first train ride had been one of the good times and Byron was going to surprise her with a second ride on that train.

Maggie met Byron at the station about 20 minutes before the train was set to depart. He still remembered every word of their conversation.

"Hello, Maggie." Byron tried to give Maggie a hug and she gave him a quick, awkward embrace. "You look great," he said. "It's good to see you."

"Thanks, Byron. You too."

"How's the job going? Charles told me you're working at the *Morning Herald* now."

"I'm enjoying it - covering high school sports and the like."

"I'm back in school, you know," said Byron.

"Charles told me. The University of Maryland."

"Yup. I've been trying to get myself straightened out. After I graduate, I'll look for a job teaching history at a high school where I can coach baseball."

"That's a great plan."

Byron searched for more to say. Maggie wasn't helping. "How's your mom doing? She okay?"

"It's been hard the last year or so. But she's doing better. I know she never told you, but she appreciated your coming to Dad's funeral. After all that happened, it took a lot for you to be there."

"I liked your Dad. I can understand why he wasn't happy with me. I would have felt the same way if I was him."

"I appreciated your being there, too. You've got a great shoulder to cry on. You're a good friend, Byron."

"I'm still not drinking, you know."

"I'm glad to hear it."

Byron took a deep breath. "Maggie, I want to get back together. I was an idiot, but I've changed."

"Byron." Maggie paused for a moment. "Don't do this, not now."

"What do you mean?"

"I'm happy you're getting yourself together, but I've moved on. I'm seeing somebody now. He works at the paper. I thought Charles must have told you. We've been dating almost six months. I like him."

"But what about you and me?"

"Please, don't do this. You and me? There is no more you and me. We used to be married, but we're not anymore."

"But I've changed . . . ."

"I'm sorry, Byron. I can't do this."

With nothing more to say, Maggie turned to leave. Byron watched her walk away, trying not to let his emotions show. There would be no second chance.

Byron remained on the platform, his eyes fixated on the spot where her diminutive frame had disappeared from view. A voice coming from the other end of the platform startled him out of his vacant stare. "All aboard," yelled a phony conductor wearing a phony conductor's hat and looking down at his phony conductor's pocket watch.

Byron looked up at the costumed conductor and then down at the two $38 tickets he was holding in his hand. Then he looked at the train, which had pulled into the station, steam billowing from its engine, and thought, *what the hell.* He boarded the train for the 32-mile excursion run through the hills of Cumberland.

His tickets included lunch in a 1930's-era dining car. A porter seated him at a table for two at the far end of the car. "Are we dining alone?" asked the porter.

"Yes, we are."

Byron watched as the porter removed a set of china and cutlery from the table.

"That makes it even worse, you taking away her plates."

"Would you like me to leave them here?"

"Well, I did pay for two lunches."

"I can leave them if you'd like."

"No, I'm not really that hungry. Just take them."

Byron looked around the dining car. A family, with parents and grandparents, sat at two tables along the windows to the left of Byron. In front of him was a young couple sitting way too close together. *Oh great,* thought Byron as the couple began exploring their immediate surroundings, *just what I need.*

The train lurched to a start. Trying to ignore the young couple's consensual groping, Byron looked out the window as downtown Cumberland passed by at three miles an hour. The train crossed a branch of the Potomac River and rumbled northwest through a spectacular water gap known as the Narrows and into the Allegheny Front ("America's First Gateway to the West," according to the train's brochure). After passing through Helmstett Curve, the train approached Brush Tunnel, which was carved through the side of a mountain. Inside the tunnel, the train's lights flickered, then cut off, leaving the dining car in total darkness. Once the train cleared the tunnel, daylight filled the windows and the lights came back on inside the car. Byron looked around the car. The young couple and the family were gone. In their place sat three groups of men dressed in suits, their ties loosened, playing cards, and drinking beer, their voices raised.

Byron rubbed his eyes, thinking it was all in his head, blaming it on his mood. But, when he opened his eyes again, the men were still there. *At least that horny couple's gone*, he thought.

The scenery outside his window no longer resembled the vistas pictured in the brochure. The train clipped along at speeds of 60 or 70 miles per hour, much faster than the plodding speed of the Western Scenic Railroad. Mile after mile of treeless farmland, the type one would expect to see further west in Pennsylvania, replaced the lush green, rolling hills of the Allegheny mountains.

The porter returned with Byron's meal, although Byron did not recall ever placing his order.

"You a rookie?" asked the porter. "I noticed you're not sitting with the others."

Byron stared at the porter, not certain at first what to say. "Yes, sir," said Byron, finally, nodding his head in agreement. "I'm a rookie. So, when's our next stop?"

"Won't be until Pittsburgh," said the porter. "Another hour or so."

"Is Pittsburgh our final stop?"

"Son, you *are* a rookie. This train is heading to Cleveland. Your team's playing the Indians tomorrow."

"You're right," agreed Byron, thinking it best to go along.

Byron listened to the men as they played cards, their voices growing louder with each downed beer. They were talking baseball, pitchers and pitching, hitters and hitting. Byron figured they must be members of the Washington Senators, traveling to Cleveland for a series against the Indians. He did not recognize any of their faces. At various times, he tried talking with some of the men closest to him, but they did not respond to his questions - perhaps because he was a rookie or, more likely, because they couldn't hear him. All during the ride, the porter was his lone source of conversation.

The train slowed down as Byron finished his lunch. He stared out the window as his dining car passed through another tunnel. Once out of the tunnel, the sign hanging on the station platform announced the train's arrival in Frostburg, Maryland. *I thought he said Pittsburgh*, Byron wondered.

As the locomotive rolled to a stop, Byron gazed away from the window and back toward his fellow travelers. The ballplayers were gone. The family and the couple were back, gathering their belongings and heading toward the front of the train. *What is wrong with me?* he wondered. *I must be losing it. This thing with Maggie has really messed me up.*

The porter came over to his table and cleared his dishes.

"Pittsburgh already?" Byron asked the porter, anxious about what the man might say.

"Frostburg," said the porter, giving Byron a wink. "Welcome back."

"What happened to the players?"

"They made it to Cleveland a long time ago, son," said the porter.

"What about you?"

"It wasn't my time. I was born too early. I hope you enjoyed the ride, though."

❧ ❧ ❧

Byron wondered how different his life would have been had Maggie boarded the train with him on that day. Would he have seen only her and no ghostly ballplayers during the ride through the hills of western Maryland? Would he and Maggie have remarried? Maybe he would have found a job teaching high school history where he could coach baseball. Maybe he would not now be alone, driving to Cleveland, looking for old ballplayers and lost ballparks.

❧ ❧ ❧

A beautiful day had dawned in the Heartland. The Ohio Turnpike was wide open with few semis making their way east. Flat was the landscape. Byron noted his progress by counting the mile markers between rest stops and highway exits, searching in the distance for their sky-high advertising signs selling food and gas. The even terrain accentuated the deep blue sky dotted with rolling cumulus clouds. Cresting the occasional highway overpass offered Byron panoramic views of the green farmland of north central Ohio. *This is great*, thought Byron. *The heat, the road, the sun shining down, nothing but time*. Although the stretch of highway from Fremont to Elyria paralleled the shores of Lake Erie, there was no vantage point from which to view the lake, which lay perhaps five or so miles to the north.

The rich fabric of baseball history is woven throughout the Midwest, but perhaps nowhere more so than in Ohio. Many of the state's villages, towns, and cities boasted stories of baseball's grand past. Traveling the turnpike, 20 miles west of Cleveland, Byron spotted a sign for one such city - Oberlin - and the college that bore its name. Byron knew Oberlin's significance in the annals of baseball history. Moses Fleetwood Walker and his brother Welday, two African-American students at liberal

Oberlin in the early 1880's, played baseball for the school for two seasons, unusual enough at that time. More rare was that they played professional ball in 1884 when they joined the then-major-league American Association Toledo Blue Stockings - during the team's one season in existence. Soon after that season, blacks were banned from playing in the major leagues until 1947, when Jackie Robinson broke the color line.

The opportunity for a baseball excursion pushed Byron off the turnpike and south onto Highway 58. Oberlin's campus, nestled within the town, seemed larger than Byron would have expected for a college of fewer than 3,000 students.

Oberlin's athletic fields were in the northwest quadrant of campus, off Union Street. The John Herbert Nichols Gateway, erected in honor of a former athletic director, marked the entrance to the athletic complex. A plaque attached to the gateway noted that Mr. Nichols "lived, taught, and fostered for over forty-five years the ideal of a wholesome athletic program for all Oberlin men."

All Oberlin men? wondered Byron as he read the plaque. *I thought this place was started as a women's college, too. What about their wholesome athletic program?*

Once through the Nichols Gateway, Byron passed a faded poster announcing Oberlin's already-completed 1998 North Coast Athletic Conference football schedule. Byron parked his car in the lot adjacent to Savage Field, home of Oberlin's football team since 1925, and walked underneath the stadium's antique brick and concrete grandstand toward a dirt path that brought him to Dill Field, the school's baseball diamond.

The Yeomen's ballpark was of modest size, with a chainlink backstop and ten rows of metal bleachers on either side of cinder-block dugouts. *Baseball at its best*, he thought. *Just like*

Cardinal Gibbons. Pure and simple - no frills.

There was no activity on the field other than a middle-aged black man on a riding lawnmower. Byron sat down in the bleachers along the third-base line and watched for about ten minutes as the man rode back and forth, creating an elaborate checkerboard in the grass surface. *Well, here I am in the middle of northern Ohio watching a guy cut grass. How pathetic. At least I'm not watching the grass grow.*

When he had seen enough, Byron stepped down off the bleachers, stopping for a drink of water from a small, stainless steel fountain perched atop a painted green pipe. As he left the field, the man cutting grass guided the tractor alongside a fence, parking it close to where Byron was walking.

"You gave it quite the yeoman's effort out there," said Byron, proud of his pun. "I'm surprised you're not sweating," he said, pointing to the man's "Property of Yeomen Athletics Department" shirt.

"I'm sorry, what'd ya' say?" asked the man as he walked along the fence.

"I said I'm surprised you're not sweating. It's getting pretty hot out here."

"Getting there."

"So, this is Oberlin's baseball field?" asked Byron.

"This is it, Dill Field."

"Do you know how long the team has played here?"

"Since the 1920's, when they finished Savage Field."

"How did they do this year?"

"Better. We won six games, it's the most we've won in years."

"Not an NCAC powerhouse, I take it," said Byron.

"I don't think we've won more than thirty games in the past 10 years."

"I'm looking for the field where an Oberlin player named Fleetwood Walker would have played, back in the 1880's." The question seemed strange to Byron as soon as he asked it, given its obscure subject matter.

"You're talking about Moses Fleetwood Walker, the first black major-league ballplayer."

"That's him," said Byron, realizing perhaps the question wasn't so obscure. "So, this isn't the field where he played, right?"

"It's not," said the man. "During Fleet's time, the team played over in Tappan Square."

"Where's that?"

"On the east side of campus, next to downtown." The man pointed in the direction of the Nichols Gateway.

"Great. I think I'll check it out."

"You driving?"

"I am."

"Then you're gonna wanna take Union Street to North Professor. It will take you past the square. It's the large park just before town. There's a bandstand in the middle and a stone arch on the east side of the square."

"Thanks."

Driving south on North Professor Street, Byron approached Tappan Square on his left. He drove past the square and turned left onto East College Street, where he parked his car at a meter.

If there ever was a ballfield in Tappan Square, it was long gone, replaced by a mix of mature shade trees, green space, and bricked pathways. In the northeast quadrant of the square was an open bandstand with an oversized roof and decorative concrete wheels that seemed like a cross between a Chinese rickshaw and a Japanese pagoda. Southwest of the bandstand was a stone memorial arch commemorating Oberlin student missionaries killed during the Boxer uprising in China in 1900.

The bandstand and the memorial arch were the only architectural additions to the square. Several large boulders scattered around the square were covered with spray paint, suggesting perhaps a lax attitude by campus officials toward graffiti artists.

Byron sat on the ground, leaning his back against a boulder that offered spray-painted congratulations to the class of 1999. He watched some students playing frisbee in the mid-afternoon sun.

"The ballfield was over there," said a voice behind him.

Byron turned around, looking up in the direction of the voice. The groundskeeper he had met at Dill Field was standing behind him, pointing toward the center of the square.

"Well, hello again," said Byron, standing up. "Did campus security ask you to keep an eye on me or something?"

"Nah. Just passing through. I'm done for the day."

"So, where was the ballfield?" asked Byron.

"It used to be there, across from the old College Chapel." The man pointed in the direction southeast of the memorial arch. "It was still there when the chapel burned down in the early 1900's. It was nothing more than a grass field with some worn dirt paths between the bases, nothing special."

"You know your history. I'm Byron Bennett."

"Jim Walters."

Byron held out his hand. "Better not shake," said Jim, holding up his hands which were covered with tractor grease. "Damn thing broke down twice while I was riding it."

"Oh. Okay."

"There's a lot of history buried beneath this square," said Jim. "A hundred years ago, the college had buildings scattered everywhere here."

"What happened to them?"

"Many of them burned down. Those that didn't, they tore down to make room for this park."

"And the baseball field, was it torn down, too?" Byron asked.

"Like I said, it wasn't much more than a grass field."

"They should put a plaque in Tappan Square marking where the field used to be. It's historic."

"It is. Hey, I'm heading over to grab a beer. Care to join me?"

"Sure, I could go for a cup of coffee."

"We'll go to Feve's. It's one of the few places in this town where you can get a beer. They got sandwiches, too, if you're hungry."

"Feve? Why do they call it that?" asked Byron.

"Something to do with coffee beans, I think, although I'm not quite sure."

"Maybe it was supposed to be 'Fever' but the 'r' fell off the sign," said Byron.

"I don't think so."

"'Fever' doesn't sound like a very healthy place to eat, if you ask me."

The two headed south on North Main Street. The Feve was a two-story brick building located mid-block, with two entrances, one on either side of the building. "We're going in here," said Jim as he opened the door on the right. Byron followed him into a long, narrow room with a bar on the left and an open kitchen in the back. The rest of the room contained a scattering of tables and chairs easily moved to accommodate the large number of undergraduates who undoubtedly packed the place on weekends. An exposed brick wall on the right side of the room gave the place a rustic feel.

A bartender standing near the back kitchen waved to Jim.

"Hey, Patty," called Jim.

"The usual?" she asked.

"The usual."

Jim and Byron took seats at the bar.

"Byron, this is Patty, best bartender in Oberlin. Patty, this is Byron."

"We only got two bars in this town, so it ain't saying much that I'm the best."

"Nice to meet you, Patty."

"What can I get for you?"

"Coffee, three creams."

Patty grabbed a bottle of beer from the cooler and popped the cap before handing Jim the bottle.

"'Burning River?'" asked Byron, looking at the label.

"You're probably too young to remember," said Jim. There was a river in Cleveland that caught fire once - the Cuyahoga."

"I remember reading something about that."

"The river was so full of garbage that sparks from a train ignited oil floating in the river. It helped shame Congress into passing the Clean Water Act."

"Good to know the garbage didn't burn in vain."

"Yeah, and it's a clever name for a beer, too."

Byron picked up a laminated menu off the bar and called over to the bartender.

"Kitchen open?" asked Byron.

"Always," said Patty.

"I'll have a tuna sandwich, rye bread," said Byron.

"Nothing for you, right Jim?" asked Patty.

"I got what I need right here."

As the bartender headed toward the kitchen, Byron thought

about Jim's response and recalled how drinking beer once made him feel the same way. *Those days are long gone*, he told himself.

"So, I take it you're a baseball fan?" asked Jim.

"Yeah, more like an addict."

"Well, you're not the first person who's come here looking for where Fleetwood Walker used to play. A couple of years ago, we had this one dude who brought with him a psychic who claimed she could channel Fleet's spirit. He asked me if I knew where the team used to play, so I figured 'what the heck,' and we went over to Tappan Square. That psychic was out there for who knows how long, floating around, feeling the air, taking measurements with some kind of contraption."

"An EMF meter?" asked Byron.

"I don't know what it was."

"So did they find Fleet's spirit?"

"No. They were wasting their time. Most people I meet here seem normal, like you. They're interested in the history of the game. But every so often we get some damn lifer who thinks he can see Fleet's ghost playing baseball on the square."

Lifer? wondered Byron. "What do you mean 'lifer?'"

"Oh . . . well, you know, someone who's living who's looking for the dead."

"So I take it you're not one of them?"

"Me? No. Why do you ask?"

"You're the one who mentioned Fleetwood Walker's ghost. I was just wondering."

"Well, the answer's 'no.'"

"But you are Oberlin's resident baseball historian," said Byron.

"Nah, I just cut the grass."

The bartender brought Byron his food.

"So what do you do when you're not feeding your baseball addiction?" asked Jim.

"I work for the Bowie Baysox. They're a minor-league team in Maryland."

"I've been to Bowie. They got an old Negro League park near there."

"Yeah. Black Sox Park." *Who is this guy?* Byron wondered, surprised that Jim had heard of what was a rather obscure ballfield.

"Right."

"How do you know about that place?"

"I played some ball in my day," said Jim.

"For who?"

"Oh, mostly semi-pro teams. No place in particular, anywhere we could find a game. A bunch of teammates and I organized a tour a few years back, playing old Negro League parks."

"Wish I'd heard about it. I would have come and watched. It sounds like a great idea."

"How about you, did you ever play?"

"I played in the minors for a while," said Byron. "A bunch of Orioles' affiliates, but I never made it to the majors."

"Who'd you play for?"

"Let's see, Bluefield, Hagerstown, Charlotte, and Rochester."

"And now Bowie," said Jim.

"I sell advertising. It doesn't pay much, but it keeps me in the game, I guess."

"Guess I'm keeping myself in the game too, cutting grass that is."

"Good lawnstriping back there. I was impressed with the effort you gave it, since the season is over."

"Just making sure the field stays in shape for next season," said Jim.

"Or, in case Fleet shows up and wants to play," said Byron. Jim raised an eyebrow and gave Byron a long look.

"Anything else for you two?" asked Patty.

"Nothing for me," said Jim. "I've got a game this afternoon."

"You still play?"

"Senior league, nothing fancy."

Patty placed the check on the bar.

"So where you heading from here?" Jim asked.

"I'm going to the Jake tonight, and tomorrow, League Park. Then I head home."

"I play there sometimes, it's a public park, now, you know, although it's in pretty bad shape."

"That's what I've heard."

"You'll meet some characters there."

"Like who?" Byron asked.

"Characters," said Jim, smiling, "like you. Well, I'd better be on my way." Jim dropped three dollars on the bar to cover his Burning River.

"If you're ever in Bowie, give me a call," said Byron.

"You never know," said Jim, walking out the door.

As Byron finished his food, he picked up Jim's bottle of Burning River, noticing that it still looked full.

"You going to drink that, Byron?" asked Patty. "It's a shame to waste it."

"No. I was wondering why Jim didn't drink it."

"Can you keep a secret?"

"Sure."

"He never drinks the beer he orders when he comes in here after work."

"Does he ever order food?"

"No. Just beer."

"Why doesn't he order something cheaper, like a soda?"

"I've never asked him 'cause I figure it's none of my business, but, between you and me, I think he used to have a problem, so now he orders a beer and he uses it as some kind of test, to see if he's cured."

"Well I can appreciate that, although I'll tell you, you're never cured. I haven't had a drop in eight years. I drink coffee instead."

"As long as he pays for it, I don't care what he does with it."

Heading back to his car, Byron spotted a parking ticket fluttering on his windshield, as if waving hello. *Great, "One Hour Parking,"* thought Byron, reading the sign posted in front of his car. *Another souvenir for the scrapbook.* He stuffed the ticket inside the glove compartment.

CHAPTER 15

◎ ◎ ◎

Hello, Cleveland!

Approaching Cleveland from the west, Byron merged onto the stretch of the highway that crossed the Cuyahoga River. The Cuyahoga, meaning "crooked river," snaked through downtown Cleveland, flowing north into Lake Erie. As Byron drove over the bridge, Jacobs Field's distinctive upper deck and light stanchions came into view.

Since June 1995, the Indians had sold out every home game at Jacobs Field, so Byron's hopes of attending a game that evening meant buying a ticket from a scalper. After checking into the Radisson Hotel on Huron Street, Byron approached the concierge desk, where stood a nattily dressed clerk wearing a maroon polyester suit with a Radisson patch and a uniform tag with his name, "Jim Colbert," centered below the left breast pocket.

"May I help you?" asked the concierge.

"Hello, Mr. Colbert," said Byron, looking at the man's name plate. "I don't suppose you know of anyone selling tickets to tonight's game."

Colbert smiled. "You're the third person to ask me tonight."

"Tough ticket, huh?"

"Not if you know where to look. Your best bet is to head out the front doors and walk down East 6th Street toward the ballpark. There's people selling tickets outside of Gate A."

"Gate A - thanks very much."

"If no one's there, you can try in front of the stadium on Ontario Street."

"Thanks again," said Byron.

After crossing Huron, Byron heard the calls of scalpers on East 6th.

"Who needs tickets?" "Got two here." "Who's buying?"

Byron approached a bearded, heavy-set man wearing baggy shorts and a Chief Wahoo T-shirt.

"I just need one," said Byron to the man.

"Sorry, can't sell just one. I'll sell you two, though."

"No, thanks."

Further down the street, Byron approached a second man waving four tickets in his right hand.

"I need one ticket," said Byron.

"Can't break 'em up. But I'll sell you two for forty."

"Where are they?"

"Left field, upper deck."

"Can I see the tickets?"

The man held two tickets out in front of him, in such a way as to suggest he did not want Byron to touch them. The face value was $6 each. "No thanks," said Byron.

Determined not to get taken too badly, Byron headed toward the main box office at the corner of Ontario and West Eagle Avenue, where another group of men stood huddled together, some with tickets raised in the air, unconcerned they might be observed by one of Cleveland's finest.

"Who's selling?" asked one of the men standing with the group.

"Just need one," said Byron.

"I'll sell you one," said another man who looked to be in his late forties.

"How much?"

"Fifteen dollars. Upper reserved, Section 533, good seat."

"Sold," said Byron, handing the man fifteen dollars. *A six dollar nosebleed ticket for fifteen dollars,* he thought. *At least I didn't get stuck buying two for forty dollars.*

After completing the transaction, Byron addressed the group of men. "Do you think it's politically correct to scalp tickets at an Indian's game?"

"What?" responded one of the scalpers, as the rest of the group ignored Byron's inquiry.

"You know, scalping tickets at an Indian's game, is that politically correct?"

"What are you? A cop?"

"No, I'm not a cop. I didn't ask if it was illegal. I asked if it was politically correct."

"Politically correct?" asked the man. "You want to know what I think of politically correct? Here." The man gave Byron the finger.

Byron shook his head, disappointed. "Can't anyone take a joke anymore?" he asked, walking away. *I should have taken a picture of that idiot to stick in my book of ballparks.*

The sidewalk along Ontario Street was crowded with people – more than twice as many as he had seen the day before in Detroit. A Monday night in May, yet the game was on its way to being a sellout, luring more than 42,000 fans to the ballpark. Sunday's game in Detroit the previous day had brought a mere 16,000 fans to that dying ballpark.

Jacobs Field's design was asymmetrical, the result of having to fit the stadium into the surrounding neighborhood, much the way ballparks were designed 100 years earlier. A combination of granite, limestone, and tan-colored brick gave the stadium's facade an updated, yet classic look. The curved face of the main entrance reminded Byron of pictures he had seen of the entrance to Brooklyn's Ebbets Field at the corner of Sullivan and McKeever Place. A one-story-tall neon sign, proclaiming "Jacobs Field, Home of the Cleveland Indians" evoked the simple, white-block lettering of "Ebbets Field."

Byron entered the stadium through Gate D at the corner of Ontario and Carnegie. As was becoming his modus operandi, Byron took pictures of the stadium concourses and walkways, the concession stands, the seating bowl, and the playing field before he found his seat.

The Orioles were taking batting practice in the cool evening air. Ushers lined the entrance to each of the walkways leading down to the reserved field-box seats, dissuading those with cheaper tickets from congregating with the fans in the higher-priced seats.

While an usher was helping another ticket holder, Byron slipped past the entrance to section 146 and headed down the aisle to take some pictures at field level.

Watching the Orioles alternate turns in the batting cage, Byron imagined himself standing in the cage, taking a few swings. Had his baseball career gone the way he had hoped, he would have been a seasoned veteran out there, playing his final year or two of pro ball. Byron spotted a couple of players he knew from his days in the minors, but he had no interest in calling over to them.

Byron imagined how the conversation would have played out:

Hey, Brady, Byron would have called, knowing it would have taken several attempts before the player acknowledged his existence. Players are good at ignoring cat calls from fans in the stands.

Bitty? Is that you? Brady would have asked, assuming he even remembered Byron.

It's me.

What are you doing here?

Just catching a game.

You work around here?

No, I work in Maryland, for the Baysox.

Oh, what are you, a scout?

No, I work in the front office - I sell advertising, that kind of thing.

Oh, I see, well that's good, I guess.

Byron was certain any conversation with the millionaire ballplayer would have reached that awkward phase, with Byron having to make excuses for why he wasn't doing more with his life. To avoid such embarrassment, Byron kept to himself, preferring anonymity, which wasn't hard to come by. Other than Mac and a few friends, no one had recognized him as Bitty Byron Bennett in almost ten years.

After batting practice ended, Byron made his way up the ramp behind home plate to the 500 level, occasionally looking down at the field through the lower-level concourse. Section 533 and the surrounding sections of the upper deck were already half filled with fans interspersed throughout. Byron took his seat in row W, close to the top of the stadium. From his spot high above the lawn-striped outfield, the players in their white uniforms looked like albino ants scurrying for crumbs across green linoleum. For Byron, the $5 bleacher seat at Tiger Stadium was a much better deal, even if he couldn't see the centerfielder.

With the game almost underway, a man who looked to be about the same age as Byron sat down in the seat next to him.

"So how much did you pay for your six-dollar seat?" Byron asked the man.

"Ten bucks."

"Damn," said Byron. "I paid fifteen."

"I usually wait until game time to buy mine. The scalpers don't want to get stuck with tickets, so they slash their prices."

Byron noticed the man's use of the word "slash," which, when said in conjunction with the word "scalpers" seemed even more politically incorrect, but decided to keep the observation to himself.

"My name's Byron Bennett. What's yours?"

"Steve Quinn, nice to meet you."

"So I take it you've been to Jacobs Field before?" asked Byron.

"The Jake? Sure. First time this season, though."

"This is my first time ever. It's a nice ballpark."

"Yup, nothing like 'the Mistake by the Lake.' What a dump that place was. If you went to a game this early in the season, you'd freeze your chops off from the cold wind coming off the lake."

"Hence the nickname, I guess," said Byron.

"Yeah, that, and its enormous size. It was built as part of the effort to lure the 1932 Olympics to Cleveland. When that failed, the Indians moved in, although they still played some games at League Park. When the crowds were small it was cheaper to play in the old park rather than open up Municipal Stadium."

"I'm going to League Park tomorrow morning, on my way out of town."

"It's worth a stop. The neighborhood's not that great, but you should be fine."

"That's what I've heard. I'm amazed the place is still there."

"Yeah. It's because of the neighborhood it's in. Once it went downhill, the demand for land there tanked. Of course, that's what saved League Park. If a developer had wanted the land, League Park would have been wiped away clean."

"So I take it you don't miss Municipal Stadium?" asked Byron.

"What's to miss? Pretty much everything's better here, except you can't just walk up to the box office and buy a ticket to the game."

"The same thing happened at Camden Yards. You never used to have a problem buying a ticket when the Orioles still played at Memorial Stadium."

"You sure never had a problem getting tickets to Municipal Stadium. Most people couldn't care less about the stadium or the Indians back then. The place held seventy-thousand people, but they were lucky if they got ten thousand. I'd sit in the upper deck and there'd be nobody else around me. If you wanted a foul ball, you'd get one. They'd land where no one was sitting. Sometimes those foul balls would sit there for a couple innings until some kid came along and picked 'em up."

"And now Cleveland sells out every one of its games," said Byron.

"It helps that the team doesn't stink, either. Tonight should be sellout number 305."

Rising for the national anthem, Byron stood with his hat to his chest as a local country singer belted out a twanged version of the song. Repeating what he and Rob had done the previous day, Byron shouted out "O" when the anthem reached the appropriate line. An older couple in the row in front of him turned and gave him an annoyed look.

"It's something we do in Baltimore," Byron said to Steve when the anthem was over.

"I know. I heard it when I was at Camden Yards a couple of years ago for a playoff game - that and 'Thank God I'm A Country Boy' during the seventh inning stretch."

"It's a tradition they couldn't get rid of even if they wanted to," said Byron.

Byron's seat provided a spectacular view of downtown Cleveland. As evening gave way to night, the lights of the Federal Courthouse Tower and surrounding buildings provided a striking backdrop for the stadium and the game being played on the field below.

Almost every seat was filled. There were few casual fans. Most watched the game fixated on every pitch, every runner, every out. It was in stark contrast to the games in Detroit, where the stadium was less than half filled with fans who seemed more interested in the past than the present. Of course, it doesn't matter where the game of baseball is played, nostalgia is an essential component - a place where the past and the present exist side by side, commingled amongst the fans with the memories of their youth and the athletes playing in the shadow of those who came before them.

Witnessing Cleveland's success with Jacobs Field first hand, Byron could see why Detroit's owners wanted a new ballpark. Still, Byron knew that one day Jacobs Field would be like Tiger Stadium - another tired, worn-out ballpark whose best days were long past. Then it would be only a matter of time before another, shinier, more elaborate ballpark with even higher profit margins arose along the shores of Lake Erie, relegating the Jake to the history books, removed from the landscape like the "Mistake by the Lake."

That night, the Indians beat the Orioles 3-1. After the game, Byron felt no compulsion to linger. As he stood to leave, Steve turned to him and said, "Since you're making the effort to go to League Park, you may want to bring some change with you."

"Why, to feed the meters? I do get my share of parking tickets."

"No, you just might find it useful to have some change in

your pocket - pennies, the older the better."

"Oh, because of people coming up and asking me for money?"

The man nodded. "Just bring some change. Trust me."

Byron made his way along the crowded stairway to the concourse below. Heading down the ramp, Byron was trapped in an exodus of fans oozing toward the exits.

Byron made a fist and raised his hand above his head. "Hello, Cleveland!" he said to no one in particular. A man walking next to him turned and laughed.

"Spinal Tap," said the man.

"Derek Smalls," said Byron.

"Bass player," said the man.

"Right again," said Byron.

"Cleveland's Xanadu Star Theater," said the man.

Now that, Byron didn't know.

CHAPTER 16

◎ ◎ ◎

Lexington and East 66th

League Park was home to the National League Cleveland Spiders from 1891 until 1899, when, like Baltimore, the city lost its National League franchise. Unlike Union Park, however, baseball returned to League Park in 1901 when Cleveland joined the newly formed American League along with Baltimore, Detroit, Chicago, Boston, Washington, Philadelphia, and Milwaukee.

Inaugurated on May 1, 1891, League Park opened ten days before the Orioles began play at Union Park on May 11th of that same year, and just five years before Detroit began play at the corner of Michigan and Trumbull in 1896. All three ballparks originated during the deadball era, when baseballs were not as tightly wound so the ball did not travel as far when hit, and home runs were fewer. Byron thought about the word – "deadball" – and wondered if there was now a second deadball era with games once again being played in lost ballparks. If nothing else, Byron enjoyed the pun.

Three miles east of Jacobs Field were the remnants of League Park. Byron headed east on Carnegie Avenue and the sites soon came to resemble what he had seen on the stretch of Michigan Avenue west of Tiger Stadium. Boarded up houses and empty lots littered the landscape. The few buildings still occupied seemed tired and frail. Turning left on East 65th Street, Byron traveled north in the direction of Lexington Avenue past a run-down commercial district and several blocks of once dignified houses whose collective fate now seemed uncertain at best. One block east, at the corner of Lexington and East 66th Street, stood League Park, or what was left of it.

The site was anchored by a two-and-a-half story, gabled, stucco and brick building which once housed the team's administrative offices. A sign above the entrance identified the building as "League Park Center, 6401 Lexington Ave." Byron parked his car and grabbed his copy of *Lost Ballparks*. Standing in front of the building, he opened the book and flipped through the pages. "Here it is," he said, admiring the book's reproduction of a League Park postcard, circa 1910, which included in the foreground a picture of the building.

Byron took several pictures of the intricate brickwork adorning the building fronting Lexington Avenue. The first floor was partitioned by four concrete, octagonal columns, which long ago separated the ballpark's ticket windows. A wall of glazed yellow bricks topped with four rows of four-inch-square glass windows cordoned off the old ticket windows and the standing area in front.

Three distinctive, brick archways rose above the second-floor windows facing Lexington. Two similar archways graced the building's second floor facing East 66th Street. To the right of the building, facing East 70th Street, Byron noticed several weathered doors, all of which once opened into the now demolished right-field grandstand. With that structure long gone, the single oak door on the second floor and the double oak doors on the third floor beneath the gable's peak were, literally, doors to nowhere – time pieces that Byron felt deserved a better fate, or at least a fresh coat of varnish.

He took a picture of the Ohio historical marker noting the significance of the site:

LEAGUE PARK

League Park opened on May 1, 1891, with the legendary Cy Young pitching for the Cleveland Spiders in their win over the Cincinnati Red Legs. The park remained the home of Cleveland's professional baseball and football teams until 1946. In 1920 the Cleveland Indians' Elmer Smith hit the first grand slam home run, and Bill Wamby executed the only unassisted triple play in World Series history. Babe Ruth hit his 500th home run over the park's short right field wall in 1929. With the park as home field, the Cleveland Buckeyes won the Negro World Series in 1945.

Byron walked around behind League Park Center in the direction of home plate, which remained in its original location near the corner of Linwood Avenue and East 66th Street. Connected to the back side of the building paralleling East 66th Street was a red-brick wall with two archways that once provided entrance to the park between the ticket office and the first-base grandstand. As a preservation measure, the archways were enclosed with additional brick.

Next to the brick archways, further north on East 66th toward Linwood, was a section of the lower grandstand enclosed by a chainlink fence to keep people from sitting on the deteriorated concrete risers. Byron picked up a small piece of concrete that had fallen outside the fence – a souvenir of League Park.

They won't be wanting this, he thought, justifying his acquisition. *If they ever cleaned this place up they'd just toss it away anyway.*

In front of the stands, underneath some weathered sheets of plywood, Byron could see a portion of the dugout steps and a walkway that would have led to the clubhouse. He thought about climbing the fence and prying loose some of the wood for a better look inside the walkway, but he didn't want to do anything that might encourage further deterioration of the ball-park's structural remains.

After taking some pictures of the brick wall and crumbling concrete stands, Byron made his way back to East 66th Street, heading in the direction of League Park Center. As he rounded the corner onto Lexington, he was startled to see a large group of people standing next to the former ticket office as if waiting to buy tickets. The men were dressed in three-piece suits and bowler hats, and some wore spats above their shoes. The women wore long puffed dresses with high neck collars and opulent hats. Byron looked around for a tour bus, wondering for a moment how the costumed visitors had arrived at League Park.

Wait a second, he thought. *The building looks different. It's changed.* Gone was the yellow-brick and glass wall along the ground floor of League Park Center, replaced by what looked like the original ticket windows between each of the concrete columns. Gone, too, was the large "League Park Center" sign, replaced with smaller signs announcing various ticket prices. "Box and Reserve 55¢, 40¢ Tax Paid" stated a sign above the ticket window to his far left. "Pavilion 15¢, Tax Paid" stated another sign above the ticket window to the right of the first window. A metal gate closed off the two remaining, unmanned grandstand ticket windows further to the right.

The ballpark's change in appearance left Byron feeling disoriented - as if he had awoken from a deep sleep and was uncertain where he was. It was similar to what he experienced in Baltimore at the former site of Union Park. However, unlike there, the image of League Park did not immediately vanish.

The crowd around him continued to grow and lines formed in front of the building. Once he was able to comprehend the circumstances in which he found himself, he adapted, doing what anyone else in his position would have done – he got in line. It was human nature, really - see a line, get in it, and then sort out later what the line was for.

Behind him, hundreds of people were making their way to League Park. To the right of the ticket office, the three-story, right-field pavilion made of brick and wood towered over the building. An outfield fence constructed of concrete, wood, and metal replaced the chainlink fence that, moments before, had run along Lexington Avenue. The Ohio historical marker was gone.

I've seen this before, he thought. *It's that postcard in Ritter's book.* He opened *Lost Ballparks* and flipped to page 102. The grandstand to his right and the outfield fence along Lexington appeared as they did in the postcard. So did the ballpark's ticket office.

Beyond the fence, the sound of batting practice rose above the clamor of the crowd, although Byron could not see the field from his vantage point. A gaggle of children jockeying for position took turns peeking through an opening in the right-field fence, hoping for a glimpse of their heroes.

Byron could not believe the scene around him. Scared and excited at the prospect of buying a ticket and entering the ballpark, he tried to remain calm, his body shaking ever so slightly. The line he was in - for box and reserve tickets - moved slowly, people talking amongst themselves. Byron looked down at his Orioles T-shirt, shorts, and sandals, self-conscious of the just arrived, nattily attired compatriots standing next to him. Byron turned to a man standing behind him and smiled a scared, uneasy smile, but the man made no eye contact with him. Byron asked the man if he knew who Cleveland was playing, but the man did not answer, as if he could neither see nor hear Byron. When his attempts to converse with others standing in line failed as well, Byron knew he was standing in a sea of apparitions. His body shook ever more slightly and a tingling sensation surged across his back.

Keep cool, he thought. *I've got to stay cool.*

He stuffed the piece of League Park concrete into his pocket and pulled some money out of his wallet to be ready when the time came for him to buy his ticket. As he reached the front of the line, he looked at the woman behind the window and said, "One box seat, please, third-base side." He placed a one-dollar bill on the ledge below the opening in the ticket window.

The woman looked down at the money and then up at Byron. Startled, she pushed Byron's money back toward him.

Oh no, he thought. *What are you doing, lady?* He looked down at the new, crisp dollar bill. *It must be the money,* he thought, and he grabbed the dollar back, stuffing it inside his pocket and trying to find some change to give the woman. It was too late.

The woman pulled down the shade and placed a "CLOSED" sign in the window. Silence engulfed the crowd and the ballpark, Byron's presence having caused a ripple in the once calm sea of people. Those behind Byron, and those in line to his left, drifted away, including several who sailed right through Byron, although he felt nothing. As the crowd dispersed, their images faded, like mist evaporating in the morning sun.

Once the apparitions disappeared, Byron found himself alone, his heart still racing. The ticket windows once again were walled off by brick and glass. "Damn," he said. "I was so close. How could I be so stupid?" *This must be why that guy told me to bring some change with me. Lincoln wheat backs would have worked, I guess. Who was that guy, anyway? He seemed so normal.*

Byron looked down Lexington and noticed an oddly dressed, heavy-set, middle-aged man watching from across the street.

"Hey, you!" Byron called out to the man.

The man did not respond.

"Did you see that?" yelled Byron.

The man said nothing and turned to walk away.

"Hey!" Byron yelled. "Can you hear me? Hello."

Byron ran across the street. The man looked back before quickening his pace. Byron lengthened his stride and caught up to the man half way down the block.

"Excuse me," said Byron, stepping in front of him. "I wanted to know if you saw what just happened?"

"I didn't see anything," replied the man.

Byron stared for a moment at the man's unusual outfit - a sweatshirt emblazoned with the words "Cleveland Spiders" across the chest and what appeared to be a vintage usher's cap much too small for the man's inordinately large head.

Would you look at this guy, thought Byron. *It's me in twenty years if I don't get a life.*

"Look, I don't want any trouble," said the man.

"I don't want any trouble either. I just want to know if you saw anything unusual?" *Other than yourself, that is*, thought Byron.

The man in the usher's hat took two steps backwards and stroked his beard as he looked Byron up and down.

"Well," he said, finally. "I did see you waiting to buy a ticket at a building with no ticket windows, that's rather unusual."

"I'll give you that. What about the lines of people, though? Did you see them?"

"No."

"What about the crowd, the ballpark?"

"No, although it looked like *you* were experiencing something like that – inching toward the front of the building, grinning and talking to yourself."

"I guess I looked kind of moronic, huh?" asked Byron, softening his tone.

"Far be it from me to judge."

"My name's Byron Bennett." Byron extended his hand to see if the man would reciprocate – the ritual Byron now used as his manual EMF meter - but the man sneezed and Byron jerked his hand back.

"Excuse me."

"Bless you."

The man wiped his hands on a cloth handkerchief he pulled out of his back pocket. "Thanks," he said.

"So, what's your name?"

"Peter Cronin."

"Nice to meet you, Peter. I see you're a Cleveland Spiders fan." Byron pointed to his decidedly homemade sweatshirt.

"I am. They're my favorite team."

"Your favorite team? They played 100 years ago."

"Did you know exactly one hundred years ago today, May 11, 1899, the Spiders played the St. Louis Perfectos here at League Park? The Spiders lost 8-6, dropping their record to three wins and seventeen losses."

"Wow, I had no idea. Three and seventeen to start the season? That's 1988 Orioles bad."

"Actually, the 1988 Orioles started off 0-21, so at this point in the season, the Orioles had a worse record than the Spiders."

"That's true, but how many games did the Spiders win that season?"

"They won twenty games that year – still baseball's record for futility."

"And they're your favorite team."

"Yup."

"The O's won 54 games in '88," said Byron.

"And I take it they're your team." Peter pointed to Byron's hat.

"The Orioles are - not necessarily the 1988 team."

"Did you know that the Spiders' seventh win of the 1899 season came here at League Park on May 25th at the expense of your Orioles, also by a score of 8-6?"

"I did not know that, either." *Good grief,* thought Byron, *I hope I don't sound like this guy when I talk baseball.*

"The following day, the Orioles evened the series, beating the Spiders by the same score," said Peter. "Those were the only two games played here between your Orioles and my Spiders that year. In fact, they were the last games ever between the two clubs at League Park."

"Again, wow," said Byron. "Hey, I'm sorry if I seemed a bit off-putting at first. I saw something and I was hoping maybe you saw it, too."

"If it's any consolation, I know how you feel," said Peter.

"You do?"

"Sure - ghost hunting can be very frustrating."

Peter's comment startled Byron even more than the man's encyclopedic knowledge of the historically inept Cleveland Spiders. Byron did not consider himself a ghost hunter and did not like the label. Ghost hunting was for flakes. Sure, Byron knew he had his moments, but he never thought of himself as a flake.

"Ghost hunting?" asked Byron.

"Yeah. You *are* looking for ghosts, aren't you? You're not just here taking pictures. If you were, what just happened, wouldn't have."

"Look," said Byron, "I'm no ghost hunter – that's crazy."

Byron shook his head.

"Still can't accept it, huh?" Peter nodded his head up and down. "It took me a while, too."

"So, you're saying you are a ghost hunter?"

"I'm not saying that or anything else to you because you'll tell me I'm crazy. Man - I hate it when people call me crazy."

"I won't call you crazy. I won't call you anything. I promise."

Peter thought for a moment, stroking his beard and adjusting his usher's cap. "Okay, since you've promised. A year ago, I was walking down Lexington over there," Peter pointed down the street toward centerfield, "and I saw the original outfield wall appear out of nowhere. I saw kids lying on the sidewalk, pressing their faces up against the opening between the sidewalk and the right-field gates, trying to see into the ballpark."

"I saw something like that, too," said Byron, excited. "There were kids over there trying to look through a crack in the right-field fence." Byron pointed toward the right-field fence.

"Yeah, but that's all I saw," said Peter. "From the way you were acting, I take it you saw the team offices and the ticket windows that used to be there."

"I did."

"I didn't see that. And, when it happened to me, it was over in a flash. I ran down Lexington as fast as my bad knees would take me toward the grandstand entrance to try and get in, but as I did, the ballpark was disappearing right beside me. It was as if the wind I was kicking up running along Lexington was sweeping away the outfield wall as I passed. When I reached the entrance to the grandstand, everything behind me was gone. Then everything in front of me disappeared too, and I was back standing in front of that chainlink fence."

"Yeah, the same thing happened to me, kind of," said Byron.

"As soon as I tried to buy a ticket, everything changed back to the way it is now."

"I saw you pull some money out of your wallet - you should have used change - old coins, if you have them."

"I should have."

"It's too bad, too, sounds like you were real close."

"Crazy, huh?"

"There you go using that word again."

"Oh, no, sorry," said Byron, shaking his head. "I didn't mean you."

Peter started walking across the street toward League Park Center and Byron followed suit.

"Look, you should be honored. From what happened – I'd say someone out there is trying to let you in."

"Like who?"

"I don't know, an old ballplayer, maybe. Do you have any deceased relatives who played professionally?"

"No. Not that I know of."

"Did you ever play?"

"I played in the minors."

"Well, you've gotten somebody's attention because this kind of thing doesn't just happen."

"Do you think there are old ballplayers inside there now?" asked Byron, pointing toward the right-field fence.

"Do you promise not to call me crazy again?"

"Yes, I promise."

Peter paused, as if trying to find the right words. "It's almost like there's this subculture of baseball players who come back to these abandoned ballparks and, as long as there's still some piece of the ballpark there, a fence, home plate, the playing field, whatever, the players can enter through that spot and play baseball again."

Byron stared at Peter, amazed by his theory, for it meshed with what Mac had told him about Union Park, although, from what he had seen, no part of Union Park remained at the site.

Peter glanced down at the copy of *Lost Ballparks* Byron was holding in his hand.

"Open the book to the chapter on League Park, page 101," said Peter.

Byron found the page and held out the book so they both could see it. "I was looking at this page a few minutes ago," he said.

"See the grandstand?" asked Peter, pointing to the picture. "We're standing here. With that picture, standing here, I can visualize the entire ballpark."

Byron looked at the picture and then at the remains of League Park. "I can see it in the picture, and I can figure where it used to be," said Byron. "But, I can't see it."

"You saw it a few minutes ago. It's still here, you just need to concentrate."

"The ballpark's still here?"

"Well, I think so. At least that's the theory. Like I said, I haven't made it inside to see for myself. But the old ballplayers, I bet they can see it. They remember how the place used to look when they played here."

"Kind of like going back to the house you grew up in and seeing your old bedroom, just as it used to be, even though it's all changed now."

The two passed through a gate in the right-field fence and started walking toward the infield and the cordoned-off portion of the grandstand.

"I'm sure it's the same for these players, except it's a ballpark. You're damn lucky to have gotten a glimpse of it."

Lucky? Byron thought. He had never considered himself lucky.

"When I was a kid, my being able to see the past - I hid it from my friends because I knew they wouldn't believe me. They would've called me a freak."

"Would've said you were crazy."

"You have to admit, though, this whole thing, it is a bit out of the ordinary."

"Being out of the ordinary doesn't make it crazy."

"I guess. When I was a kid, I told my folks what I'd seen once and they didn't believe me. The few friends I've told don't believe it either. They give me a hard time and tell me to grow up."

"It's a gift and you should use it to find a way inside that ballpark."

"And how do I do that?"

"That's the sixty-four-thousand-dollar question, isn't it? If I knew the answer, I sure wouldn't be here talking to you, I'd be watching the game."

As they reached home plate, Peter looked down and pointed at Byron's hand, in which he was holding the piece of concrete from the grandstand. "Souvenir?"

"Yeah. I figure it's trash that the city hasn't thrown away yet."

"I hear they're going to tear out this section anyway and just leave he wall behind it. So I think you're safe."

"What teams do you think are playing here right now?" Byron pointed to the infield.

"The Indians, maybe, or the Spiders, or maybe the Blues, or the Bronchos, or the Naps - it could be any of the old Cleveland teams. If they're playing a game from a hundred years ago, then it's the game I told you about - the Spiders versus the Perfectos."

"If that's the case, boy, I'd love to put some money on the Perfectos. What did you say the score was?"

"Eight to six, but good luck trying to collect any winnings."

"Do you know any other ballparks like this, where this kind of thing happens?" asked Byron.

"Nothing confirmed. Forbes Field in Pittsburgh, maybe. The outfield wall is still there. Braves Field in Boston - Boston University uses what's left of it as a soccer stadium. Sportsman Park in St. Louis - it's the Herbert Hoover Boys & Girls Club now. They've got an athletic field where left field used to be, so maybe something's happening there."

"How about Chicago?"

"Old Comiskey Park is gone, although I haven't seen it since they tore it down. It's a parking lot."

"Like that Joni Mitchell song about turning paradise into a parking lot," said Byron.

"Exactly, they didn't know what they had until it was gone."

"At least the Cubs were smart enough to keep what they've got," said Byron.

"Wrigley Field - you've gotta give them credit for that."

"True."

"South Side Park, where the White Sox played before Comiskey, is a housing project now," said Peter. "It was a few blocks from Comiskey, although I doubt there's anything there, either. Rube Foster lived down the street - his Chicago American Giants played at South Side once the White Sox left. They put up a historical marker for Rube there, but not much else."

"What about where the Cubs played the last time they won the World Series?" asked Byron.

"West Side Park? That's a hospital now - University of Illinois Medical Center. I haven't seen it, but I doubt there's any original buildings left at the site."

"So, what have you seen at Forbes Field?" asked Byron.

"Well, the outfield wall and home plate."

"Anything else - like what's not there now?"

"No, nothing."

"When I was there, I met this guy who claimed to have played for the Pirates – George Grantham."

"The drummer from Poco."

"That's what I said. But, no, different guy. They used to call him 'Boots.' Ever heard of him?"

"Oh, yeah, I've heard of Boots, but, I never met him. A friend of mine did. He's a fellow believer."

"Boots is dead you know," said Byron.

"Boots is dead, yes, although I'm not sure the guy my friend met was *the* Boots."

"Why not?"

"I have my suspicions. My friend told me he thinks he saw Boots get in his car and drive away. I'm not sure ghosts can drive, although I could be wrong."

"Are you suggesting someone is impersonating these old ballplayers? Why would they do something like that?"

"Maybe they're trying to get inside, just like you and me."

"When I first saw Boots, he came up the stairway behind the Forbes Field wall. There was no car."

"He came up from Panther Hollow," said Peter, stroking his beard. "Interesting."

"So you've met other people like us, who, you know, can see what we see?"

"Sure, I've met a few over the years, but the problem is we don't stay this way forever."

"What do you mean?"

"Eventually, we stop believing. Everyone I've met who once believed or thought they believed has stopped believing."

"You mean like with Santa Claus - you reach a certain age and you realize it simply isn't possible?"

"No, it's more like they've forgotten what they've seen, as if someone erased their memories clean. Like my friend who saw Boots – I called him after I hadn't heard from him in a while and asked if he'd seen anything new. He told me he had no idea what I was talking about. I asked him about Boots and he said he'd never heard of the guy."

"But *you* still believe," said Byron, pointing to Peter.

"I do, at least for now."

"So what's with the usher's hat?" asked Byron, pointing to the vintage hat perched atop Peter's large head.

"Oh, this?" he asked, taking the hat off. "I bought it on eBay because I thought I'd have better luck getting inside if I wore something authentic, but I'm starting to think now it's not even from League Park. The label on the rim says it was made in Cincinnati, so I think maybe it's from Crosley Field."

"Have you seen anything there?"

"No, not yet. There's nothing left of the ballpark and the playing field is gone – covered with office buildings and a parking lot. Someone put some seats from Crosley in front of one of the new buildings, and there's a plaque in the lobby of another, but nothing in its original location."

"So, no one can get in," offered Byron, following Peter's logic.

"Right. There's one original building still there, next to the site on York Road, behind where the left-field grandstand used to be. Here, I'll show you." Peter reached again for the book. "Page 43," said Peter, turning to the page. "See that white brick building with the smoke stack?" Peter pointed to a postcard reprinted on the page. "That building's still there. If there's a link to Crosley, it's through that building."

"I read somewhere that they moved part of Crosley Field to Kentucky," said Byron.

"Yeah. A man bought a bunch of stuff from the ballpark and stuck it on his farm, but that's gone now, too. There's a replica of Crosley up in Blue Ash, including the original ticket booth and some seats they moved there from the farm."

"What about Tiger Stadium? Have you been there?"

"Once," said Peter.

"Seen anything unusual?"

"You mean other than Mark Fidrych? No. But I wouldn't expect to – the Tigers still play there."

"Why does that matter?"

"Well, I figure if the place isn't abandoned, the old ballplayers can't play there. Once the Tigers leave the stadium, it'll be fair game, so to speak."

"So, all those ghosts who haunt Yankee Stadium, they're out of luck, huh?" asked Byron.

"Yup. And there's no way they'd ever tear down Yankee Stadium."

"I'm an Orioles fan and even I'd hate to see it go."

"Yeah. Too much history there."

"So, how do you know all this?" asked Byron.

"A bit of research, and a lot of supposition, and it makes sense."

"It makes sense if you're crazy."

"There you go with that word again," said Peter. "I like to think of it as suspending reason. Some things you've got to take on faith."

"Like religion."

"The church of baseball."

"I was at Tiger Stadium last weekend."

"And you didn't see any activity there, did you?" asked Peter.

"I'm not sure I should tell you."

"Why not?"

"I got the distinct impression I should keep my mouth shut about what I saw."

"So someone gave you a hard time, eh?"

"You could say that."

"Who, that guy at Sportsland?" asked Peter.

"Matty O'Boyle?"

"Yeah, that's the guy."

"How do you know Matty O'Boyle?" asked Byron.

"I met him when I was there, although I don't think he's a ghost, if that's what you're wondering. I suspect he's another likeminded fellow, like us, only older. Once Tiger Stadium closes, I think he hopes to take over as a 'groundskeeper,' if you will. When Detroit tears down Tiger Stadium, it'll be Matty's job to make sure some portion remains."

"What about Union Park in Baltimore - where the old National League Orioles used to play? Have you been there?"

"No, but I haven't heard of anything going on there, either."

"What about Oberlin College?"

"You mean because of Fleetwood Walker?"

"Exactly."

"Save your energy. I spent a good chunk of time and money there a couple years back and came up with nothing – even brought in a psychic to try and conjure up some spirits of dead players."

"Was the psychic a woman?"

"Yeah, how did you know?"

"Just a guess - most women I know are psychic."

"I think about all we did was piss off any spirits who might have been lurking about," said Peter. "I've come to realize ghosts can be very sensitive. They don't like us snooping around where we're not invited."

"Well, this is all very fascinating, but I've got to be hitting the road."

"Nice to have met you."

"You too. And, thanks. You've convinced me I'm either lucky or insane."

"Well, maybe you're a little bit of both. Either way, I'm glad I could help. Here, let me give you my card."

Peter opened his wallet and handed Byron a crinkled, decidedly homemade business card. "President, Cleveland Spiders Historical Society," said Byron, reading the title from the front of the card. "President, huh? Who's your vice president?"

"That position is currently vacant. Interested?"

"Sorry, I'm an Orioles fan."

"Oh yeah, you are. Best way to reach me is by email. My address is on the card."

"Thanks. If you don't mind, can I take your picture?"

"Sure."

"Move to your right so I can get the ticket office in the background," said Byron.

Peter posed for his picture, standing as if he were holding an imaginary bat, waiting for the pitch.

"I'll send you a copy."

Byron headed back to his car as Peter stayed behind, giving Byron a quick flick of a wave as Byron drove off.

Heading south on East 66th Street, Byron tossed Peter's card inside the glove compartment, glad to have some proof that he had, in fact, met Peter Cronin.

"Take it on faith," Peter had told Byron. *I have no problem taking things on faith,* thought Byron, *but it's good to have some hard evidence, as well.*

CHAPTER 17

◎◎◎

The Temperance Tavern

Byron headed south on I-77 out of Cleveland. One hundred miles down the interstate, as he approached I-70, he spotted a sign for Newcomerstown - another Ohio village in which the rich fabric of baseball history was woven. Byron recognized the name, for he knew Denton True "Cy" Young was from the area around Newcomerstown. Byron couldn't remember how or why he knew this. It was one of the thousands of otherwise useless, inane facts that had made their way into the recesses of his subconscious.

Situated in the rolling hills of Tuscarawas County, Newcomerstown was a short detour off the highway on the drive home. Byron thought it appropriate to stop, since Young was the Cleveland Spider who pitched the inaugural game at League Park in 1891.

Byron exited the highway and drove straight into Newcomerstown on Canal Street, although he had no idea what he was looking for. In the center of town, he spotted a historical marker for the Erie and Ohio Canal, which once traversed north of where he was driving. The marker, however, made no mention of Cy Young.

Continuing west on Canal Street, Byron spotted a sign for the "Temperance Tavern Museum" next to a white, colonial-style, clapboard house. Byron figured it a good bet that someone in the museum would know something about Newcomerstown's favorite son.

Wide wooden steps led from the sidewalk to the museum's front porch. Byron pulled on the locked door and then rang the bell. A moment later, the door opened and a woman who looked to be in her late 60's greeted Byron. She was wearing a pair of glasses that looked as if they might once have belonged to Granny on *The Beverly Hillbillies.*

"Hello, young man, come on in. Welcome to the Temperance Tavern Museum." A wide smile graced the woman's face.

From the front hall, the place looked more like a residence than a museum, and Byron felt as if he were paying a visit to a long-lost aunt in Saskatchewan.

"Yes, welcome," said a second, nearly identical woman with a nearly identical grin, the one readily apparent distinguishing characteristic being that the second woman wore no glasses.

"Thank you, ladies," said Byron.

"And what brings you to Newcomerstown today?" asked the woman with glasses.

"I'm interested in Cy Young. Do you have anything in the museum about him?"

"Well, yes, we do," she said. "Are you interested *only* in baseball? There's much to see in addition to baseball."

Sensing the disappointment in their voices were he to choose only baseball, Byron told the women he would be happy to visit the entire museum.

"Wonderful," said the bespectacled woman.

For the next 45 minutes the women regaled Byron with the history of Newcomerstown, which was named in honor of the Indian King Newcomer and was at one time the capital of the Delaware Indian Nation. "The Temperance Tavern itself was built in 1841 and served as a stopover for those traveling the Erie and Ohio Canal," said the woman without glasses. In the basement of the tavern, the women showed Byron a crawl space above the kitchen hearth believed once to have served as a hiding place for those traveling the Underground Railroad.

"We haven't been able to document the tavern as an official stop yet, but we're working on it," said the woman wearing glasses, a look of both disappointment and determination on her face.

"Yes," said the other woman, looking equally disappointed yet determined. "There's a lot of Amish in the area, you know."

"I figured as much. I saw evidence of their transportation dotting the side of the road."

"You mean you saw their horse and buggies?"

"Yeah, well, the gifts their horses leave behind."

"Oh," said the women in unison.

"So did they call this place the 'Temperance Tavern' because they didn't serve alcohol to tavern guests?" asked Byron, thinking the answer obvious from the name of the establishment.

Both women looked at Byron with almost identical, blank stares.

"You know, like the Temperance Tavern in *Tom Sawyer*," Byron added. "Where Tom finds Injun Joe passed out."

"I don't know why they picked that name," said the woman with glasses.

"You know, 'temperance,' meaning abstaining from alcohol," said Byron, "and this being once called the 'Temperance Tavern,' maybe they didn't serve alcohol here."

"Sorry, we're not sure why they named it Temperance Tavern," said the woman without glasses, shaking her head. "No one's ever asked us that question." Both women shook their heads in unison before nodding in agreement.

Regardless of its derivation, Byron took solace in the name.

"Well, you came to see baseball, so let's go upstairs to the

Cy Young room," said the woman wearing glasses.

The women escorted Byron up a narrow staircase to the second floor hallway where they were greeted by an oversize portrait of Newcomerstown's other favorite son - Woody Hayes - hovering above a display case filled with yellowing newspaper articles and what looked like pre-industrial-revolution football memorabilia. The women stopped alongside the display case, one on each end. Byron had no choice but to review the case's contents.

"Woody Hayes was a great man," said the woman wearing glasses. "Did you know he was from Newcomerstown, too?"

"I do now," said Byron.

After discussing where Woody Hayes attended high school (he was three years ahead of the bespectacled woman's oldest sister at Newcomerstown High), his service in the United States Navy during World War II, his five national titles with Ohio State, his 13 Big Ten conference titles, his 205-61-10 head coaching record, and many other Woody Hayes fun facts, Byron was shown a small room facing the back of the tavern. The tiny room, which once must have been used for the most diminutive of tavern guests, held an exceptional display dedicated to the life and times of Cy Young, including personal mementos from Cy Young's baseball career, as well as from his life after baseball in Newcomerstown.

"Mr. Young was born in Gilmore, about ten mile east of here, just after the end of the Civil War," said the woman wearing glasses. "He quit school in the sixth grade to work on his daddy's farm."

"The first professional team he played for was up in Canton," said Byron. "I passed through there on the way here."

A glass case along the right side of the room displayed several of Young's well-maintained scrapbooks from his playing days, a frayed-at-the-edges grey wool fedora, and a pair of black, high-button shoes - "The last hat and pair of shoes ever worn by Cy Young," announced the placard inside the display case.

"So he must have been buried barefoot if these are the last shoes he ever wore," said Byron to the women who were standing at the room's threshold.

"Oh, I don't know about that," said the woman wearing glasses.

The display case included a reproduction of Young's 1937 Hall of Fame plaque. "Young was elected on the Hall's second ballot, along with John McGraw," said Byron, not sure whether the women standing in the doorway were still listening to him.

"He won 511 games during his major-league career," said the woman wearing glasses, still listening. "That was 221 games in the American League and 290 in the National League."

"A major-league record," added the woman not wearing glasses, "along with his 316 losses, also a record, both of which probably never will be broken."

The women nodded in agreement. Byron nodded as well, impressed with the ladies' mutual knowledge of Young's baseball accomplishments.

In the far right corner of the room was a worn, leather-upholstered rocking chair, with magnificent, oversized, curved wooden arms worn at the edges from years of use.

"Cy used to sit in that rocker on the front porch of his home and wave to people passing by," said the woman wearing glasses. "Toward the end of his life he had all types of visitors – because of his baseball career. People would come by to visit, take his picture, or ask for an autograph. Whenever a car stopped in front of the house, his dog would run over to the porch. If the visitor brought a camera, the dog would jump up on the porch and stand next to the rocker, as if posing for the picture alongside Mr. Young."

"Did either of you ever meet Cy Young?" Byron asked.

"I did, when I was young," said the woman wearing glasses. "He was old even then."

"Did you ask him for his autograph?"

"Oh, heavens, no. I had no idea how important a man he was until I was much older, long after he passed."

The *piece de resistance* of the Temperance Tavern Museum's Cy Young display was his complete 1906 Boston Red Sox baseball uniform, with its distinctive emblem of a single red sock stitched across the front of the jersey. In 1903, then with Boston, Young started the first game of the first World Series. Honus Wagner, playing for Pittsburgh, went 1 for 3 against Young that day, with a double, a run batted in, and run scored.

"This is amazing," said Byron, pointing to the uniform hanging in the display case on the wall.

"Mr. Young gave this uniform to a friend years ago," explained the woman not wearing glasses. "His friend was a blacksmith and kept it locked in a trunk in his shop. After the blacksmith died, his daughter inherited the house and the trunk. Years later, she opened the trunk and discovered Mr. Young's uniform, which she donated to the museum."

"Had that uniform been discovered in any other town, I'll bet it would have landed in an auction house and sold for tens of thousands of dollars," said Byron.

The ladies beamed with pride at Byron's enthusiasm. "Well, we're glad we have it here in the museum," said the woman not wearing glasses.

"You mentioned Cy Young's house," said Byron. "Is it still standing?"

"He lived in two different houses over the years," said the woman wearing glasses. "First, on a farm in Peoli. After his wife died, he sold the farm and moved in with the Benedums who had a farm down the road. He lived there the rest of his life. He died in that house."

"Is that house still standing?" asked Byron.

"It was last time I was out there, but that was some time ago. I heard some Amish people bought the land it's on and were going to tear the house down, if they haven't already."

"Do you have directions to the house?"

"Nothing written down, but I could draw you a map."

Both women left the Cy Young room, allowing Byron to linger by himself for a moment. He took photographs of the uniform hanging on the wall as well as some of the items on display in the case.

Walking back down the stairs, he was greeted by the woman wearing glasses, who came out of her office with a hand-drawn map showing the location of the house where Young died.

"Take Canal Street out of town and follow the signs for Route 258," offered the woman, pointing to her map depicting a crooked road, drawn with equally crooked writing. "After a few miles, you'll see a farmhouse by the road on your right, followed by a church. The house is where Mr. Young lived. He's buried in the cemetery next to the church."

"What's the name of the church?" Byron asked.

"It's a Methodist church - Peoli Methodist Church, I think."

"I've marked where his grave is, too, if you want to see it," said the woman, pointing again to her map.

"Thanks very much," said Byron.

"We also have a little-league field named after him," said the woman not wearing glasses. "There's a monument next to the ballfield up on North College Street. If you want to see that, head back down Canal Street and turn left past the Huntington National Bank. The field is at the top of the hill. You can't miss it."

"Thanks very much," said Byron. "You've been very helpful. This is a fine museum you have."

Before leaving, Byron dropped a $5 donation in the jar by the front door and signed his name in the guest book.

Byron headed up North College in the direction of the little-league field. A sign announcing "Cy Young Park Newcomerstown, Ohio" with a drawing of Cy Young in mid-windup greeted park visitors. To the right of the park was the Cy Young Memorial Swimming Pool, an odd choice for a memorial, thought Byron, as he never figured the rotund Young to be much of a swimmer. *The town fathers knew him better than I do, I guess.*

To the left of the parking lot was a more appropriate memorial to Young - a little-league field complete with outfield fences, dugouts, and a chainlink backstop. In front of the field was a white granite monument honoring the former pitcher. A ghostly looking granite bust of Young, his eyes sunken, his face expressionless, peered out from the monument's 12-foot center section. The monument's considerable size – more than 20 feet across – was an obvious testimonial to Newcomerstown's esteem for its native son. Unfortunately, the granite head faced the parking lot, not the baseball diamond, rendering Young's image unable to view any action on the field.

A flyer tacked on a telephone pole next to the ballfield advertised the upcoming "Cy Young Days Festival – June 25-26, 1999 – A weekend of baseball, in memory of Newcomerstown's own, the Great Cy Young." Leaving Cy Young Park, Byron tipped his hat to Cy's ghostly granite head. True to his form when pitching, Young's expression did not change – not even a wink.

Byron drove back through Newcomerstown and out to the highway in search of Young's former home. After a few miles, the asphalt road turned to gravel, then to dirt, and then back to gravel. Byron felt every bump and pothole between Newcomerstown and Peoli. After several miles of not seeing any sign for Route 258 and with the road surface now more dirt than gravel, Byron knew he was lost. He pulled his car over to the side of the very narrow road and opened up the complementary Ohio Turnpike state map he had picked up at a rest stop. As he looked in vain for the tiny town of Peoli, an Amish man wearing black pants with suspenders looped over a white shirt, a straw hat covering his curly blond locks, and a full ZZ Top-style beard, minus the mustache, approached him on foot.

"Excuse me, sir," said Byron before the man passed by his window, "but I'm afraid I'm lost. Could you help me please?"

"I can give it a try," said the man.

"I'm looking for the town of Peoli. Am I anywhere close?"

"You're pretty much in Peoli now, but there is no town to speak of. It's mainly farmland."

"I'm looking for the house where Cy Young used to live - he was a baseball player."

"I don't know much about baseball, but I can tell you where they've put a sign that says Peoli. Maybe you could start there. Would you like me to tell you how to find it?"

"Sure, that'd be great."

"Turn around here and follow this same road until you see another road that heads off to the left. Take that road and you'll reach Peoli Road. Turn right and you'll see the sign."

"Peoli Road. Thanks very much."

The man tipped his hat and flashed Byron a wide smile, revealing his exquisitely white teeth.

Byron followed the man's directions and ended up once again on Route 258, still lost. After passing several miles of farms, he came across a sign that proclaimed, simply, "Peoli." True to the man's words, Byron saw no actual town, only farmhouses and farmland. Byron continued on the road another half mile, where it curved sharply to the left. After making his way around a blind corner, he saw on his right a small cemetery and a simple, red-brick church with a modest, wood steeple housing a large, bronze bell. Along the side of the road was a stand-alone brick marquee sign identifying the place as "Peoli Church." In the bottom right corner of the sign was a rather primitive-looking, hand-painted depiction of an old-style baseball glove and baseball with a facsimile signature of "Cy Young" painted on the sweet spot between the seams. "This is it," he said.

Clear skies and occasional meandering cumulus clouds topped the green grass and white-specked marble-and-granite landscape. Young's headstone, one of the largest markers in the cemetery, was nestled amongst perhaps two hundred other graves set on a hill alongside the road. An oversized, carved granite baseball with eagle's wings on either side graced Young's gravestone and that of his wife, Roba. Byron read Young's vital statistics: "Denton T. 'Cy' Young, Mar - 29 - 1867, Nov - 4 - 1955." *He beat Honus Wagner to the grave by a month*, thought Byron, recalling Wagner had died in December that same year.

Byron took a picture of the winged baseball and the accom-panying inscription on the gravestone: "From 1890 to 1911 'Cy' Young pitched 874 major league base ball games. He won 511 games, three no hit games, and one perfect game in which no man reached first base." What the gravestone did not mention was that a year after Young died, Major League Baseball post-humously inaugurated the "Cy Young Award," at first presented annually to the best pitcher in baseball and, since 1967, given to the top pitcher in each league. Byron figured Young qualified as a top pitcher in both leagues, having won over two hundred games in each.

Deposited in front of Young's gravesite were several baseballs and a faded Cleveland Indian's rally towel, offerings left by fans or perhaps by an aspiring player or two. When Byron was a player, it never occurred to him to seek intervention by leaving baseballs at a Hall-of-Famer's gravesite. Had he known then what he recently had learned, Byron would have done so. He dared not touch the towel or any of the balls, for fear of what might happen – something along the lines of Dorothy and the talking apple trees in *The Wizard of Oz*, perhaps.

Byron took a stroll around the other gravesites. *I bet Fred D. Miller must feel pretty damn proud about being buried next to baseball's winningest pitcher*, thought Byron, referring to the man who was interred to Young's left. *That is, assuming he's a fan of the game.* Reading Miller's vital statistics, Byron noticed Miller was born the same year as Young and predeceased Young by a year. *Peoli's a small town*, he thought. *They must have known each other.*

As it turned out, all was quiet at the cemetery. *If anyone here has something to say, they ain't talking*, thought Byron, a quip he found exceptionally funny. Byron paid his respects to Young and headed back to his car. There had been no "activity," as Peter would say.

Byron rummaged around the front seat of his car and found the map the woman at the museum had drawn for him. He drove back down Route 258 and, after passing the sign for Peoli, spotted a farmhouse less than 30 feet back from the road. He had not noticed the house on his way to the church and was surprised by its sudden appearance as he rounded the corner. A Midwestern, two-story, white, clapboard "I house" with eaves and a gabled roof, its front porch ran the length of the house, supported by four round, wooden pillars. Its center front door was framed by two double-hung windows on either side and three similar sets of windows spaced evenly on the second floor.

This must be it, he thought, pulling onto the side of the road in front of the house's shallow, gravel driveway. The house looked well kept, with a tidy front lawn, nothing like he had expected based upon the description of the house offered to him by the woman at the Temperance Tavern Museum. Byron searched the back seat of his car looking for his camera, which he found hidden amongst an array of empty coffee cups and fast-food wrappers. Getting out of the car, he looked back over at the house and noticed an old man whom he had not seen when he pulled up sitting in a wooden rocking chair on the front porch, just to the right of the front door. Startled, Byron stopped in his tracks alongside his car, still about 25 feet from the front porch. Byron could not make out the old man's face at first, but he recognized the chair the man was sitting in. With its oversized wooden arms, it was identical to the rocker he had seen at the museum. Gradually, the man's features came into focus.

Wait a second, thought Byron. *That's Cy Young – cue the dog.*

Without fail, Young's dog came running around the house from the side yard and jumped up onto the front porch, just as the woman in the museum had described it. Young rocked back and forth in his chair, a pipe in his mouth. He reached down and patted the dog on its head. Young appeared to Byron much thinner - and older - than he did in the photographs Byron had seen of Young during his playing days.

As the significance of the spectacle sunk in, the excitement of seeing the Hall of Fame pitcher's ghost sent blood pulsating through Byron's body, making it hard for him to do anything other than stand where he was, in awe of what was before him. Byron opened his mouth to speak, but no words came out. He tried waving at Young, but his arm grew heavy and he had to lower it to his side. Young motioned for Byron to come closer. He tried taking a step forward but he no longer was able to move his legs, which felt as if they were encased in a block of cement. Byron tried snapping a photograph, but he couldn't lift his arms high enough up to take the picture. Young's dog gave Byron a puzzled, disappointed look, as if wondering why Byron hadn't taken the shot. Unable to move, Byron stared at baseball's greatest pitcher, a stupid grin plastered on Byron's anxious face.

Young pulled himself out of his rocker, his ancient hands gripping the rocker's curved, wooden arms. After straightening his body and gingerly arching his back, Young opened his mouth to speak. Byron, still unable to move, strained to hear what wisdom the great Cy Young was about to impart.

"Son, your headlights are on." Young pointed to Byron's car. Byron let out a sigh through his frozen grin as his shoulders slumped. Young waved goodbye and headed inside the house, accompanied by his dog. Byron could sense the dog's continued disappointment as the screen door swung haltingly shut. Once Young was gone, Byron's muscles loosened and he was able to move his arms and legs. *Damn*, he thought. *What is wrong with me? I choked. No picture and no autograph, either.*

His muscles no longer tense, Byron took a step toward the house, but he froze again as he noticed the structure's appearance begin to change, aging before his very eyes. It was as if he were watching time-lapse photography. No more than a minute later, everything stopped and all that was left standing in front of Byron was a rundown shell of a house. He stared in disbelief at the building. Gone was the white clapboard, replaced by a hodgepodge of weathered wood, metal slats, and a patchwork of decaying, brownish-red-asphalt siding. Gone was the original front porch with its round, wooden pillars, replaced by a shingled, plywood overhang propped up by six 4x4 wood posts.

Discarded oak flooring and plaster lath removed from inside the house sat with other debris in a trash pile to the right of where Byron was standing. The original front door remained in place, although it, too, was weather-beaten and in need of patching and painting. An assortment of farming implements and odd pieces of furniture in varying degrees of disrepair and rust sat strewn across the front of the house in such disarray that even Fred Sanford would have been embarrassed by the yard's disheveled appearance. Next to Byron's car appeared a white, hand-painted sign in simple black lettering which stated "Brown Eggs For Sale, Not Over a Week Old, No Sunday Sale, 1.25 a dozen." The Amish were selling eggs out of the famous pitcher's former home.

Spooked by the house's sudden change, Byron did not reflect for long on the building's sad, neglected state, or its dim future. After taking a couple hurried photographs and grabbing a piece of rotted oak flooring from the scrap pile, Byron jumped in his car, rolled up the windows, and locked the doors. *What is happening to me?* he wondered, pulling out onto the state road. *This isn't a matter of suspending reason, this is nuts.*

Several miles out of Peoli, a smile crept across his face. *That house just about turned to dust,* he thought. *How frickin' cool was that?*

Before reaching the main highway, Byron pulled his car onto the shoulder of the road, debating for a moment whether to return to Young's house and grab some additional souvenirs from the scrap pile or perhaps even buy a dozen brown eggs. His reasonable side prevailed and, instead of acting on his impulse, he made his way onto Highway 36. Byron looked over at the piece of flooring he had snatched from Young's front yard. *That board is the perfect accent piece for my mantle. Right next to my chunk of League Park concrete.*

○ ○ ○

Driving home, he replayed in his mind all that had happened on the trip. Peter's warning about other believers who had forgotten everything they had experienced concerned him. *That's not gonna happen to me*, he thought. *Not if I can help it.*

○ ○ ○

Byron arrived home a little after 10 Tuesday evening. Pushing open his front door, he stepped over several days' worth of mail deposited beneath the door slot. He dropped his duffel bag on the floor and scooped up the usual assortment of junk mail, catalogs, and bills, placing it on the kitchen table.

Exhausted from the drive home but still too creeped out by all that had happened to simply go to bed, he picked through the mail. A large, stiff, manila envelope stuck out from the pile. All that was written on it was Byron's name - no stamps, no return address, no postmark. He thought he recognized the handwriting, however.

Byron opened the package and pulled out what was an extraordinary, engraved invitation, browned and brittle from age. At the top of the invitation was a drawing of a baseball pennant flying from a flag pole. The pennant stated: "Champion Baseball Club United States, Baltimore 1894-5-6." Below the pennant was a picture of a ballplayer holding a bat, with the letter "B" positioned on either side of the player.

The invitation stated:

The President and Directors
of the
Baltimore Base Ball & Exhibition Co.
sincerely trust to have the pleasure
of the company of yourself and Lady
at the
Inaugural Game
of the Base Ball Championship Season
of 1899
Union Park, Huntingdon Ave.
with the
New York Club
Saturday, April 15th 1899

The enclosed card will admit only to grounds and Grand Stand.

Nothing else was inside the envelope. However, a note written in pencil on the reverse side of the invitation stated: "Welcome back. Found this in my travels – knew you would appreciate having it. Take care. Mac."

Man, this is cool, he thought. *Written proof Mac exists.* Byron stared at the wonderful artifact, grateful Mac had sent it to him. Before heading to bed, Byron made a photocopy of the invitation using the printer attached to his computer. This time, Byron wasn't taking any chances.

CHAPTER 18

@ @ @

Coogan's Bluff

A few days after returning home from his trip, Byron and Charles met in Bowie for a Baysox game. Afterwards, they went to dinner at Rips, a local hangout down the street from the ballpark.

Thinking about Matty's admonishment, Byron was concerned others might be observing his actions. "Paranormal paranoia" as Rob had called it, albeit mockingly. Byron struck an internal compromise, deciding not to mention anything about Matty or what Matty had told him.

"You're telling me you *saw* League Park?" asked Charles. "Not just what's there now, but the whole ballpark?"

"Yes."

"So it's happening again - you think you're seeing ghosts."

"Not ghosts, necessarily, it's more like I'm seeing the past."

"You realize what you're saying is impossible, don't you?"

"I'm just telling you what happened. And, it's not only me. There was another guy there, Peter, who told me he'd seen it, too."

"And who is Peter?"

"A fellow believer, unlike you."

"Well, I may not have met him personally, but having worked at the Babe Ruth Museum for almost fifteen years now, I can say with some certainty that I've met people just like him. Those people seem normal at first."

"Actually, Peter seemed anything but normal when I first met him."

"Well, when people like that open their mouths, you realize they've spent way too much time in their basements gluing together model airplanes. I don't believe their stories and neither should you. It's not healthy."

"Regardless of what you think - I *saw* League Park."

"Can you prove it?"

"I have Peter's business card."

"His business card? That's not proof. What is he? Wait, let me guess . . . a professional plasma donor."

"No, he's President of the Cleveland Spiders Historical Society."

"Oh, man, that's even better. I rest my case."

Byron stared at Charles, annoyed.

"You didn't happen to take a picture of what you saw, did you?" asked Charles.

"No. It happened so fast. I didn't have time. But I do have an invitation to opening day Mac sent me."

"That's not proof you saw League Park. Look, I know you *think* you saw it, but that was all in your head. You must've got caught up in the moment."

"Can't you suspend reason, even for a moment?"

"No. I can't."

"I should have known better than to tell you all this."

Charles paused for a moment. "You haven't been drinking again, have you?"

"No. And why does everyone ask me that damn question every time I mention something like this?"

"Drinking wouldn't solve anything, Byron."

"I'm not drinking."

"Well, whatever it is that's making you see these things, it isn't healthy. Living in the past isn't healthy."

Growing weary of Charles's plaintive sermon, Byron sought to change the tone of the conversation, make it more philosophical. "You know what they say, don't you? - 'Those who ignore the past are destined to repeat it.'"

Charles thought for a moment. "But doesn't that mean if you *want* to repeat the past, you should ignore it, not embrace it?"

"I don't know. It was a joke. I don't want to talk about it anymore."

"You know, Bitty, if you weren't so obsessed with baseball, maybe you'd have a more normal life. Maybe you and Maggie would still be together."

Okay, thought Byron. *Here comes the sermon about Maggie.* "You think I don't know I blew it with Maggie? Of course, I know it. The sadness I feel never goes away. But what happened, happened. I can't change the past."

"No, you can't, so stop trying. All this bullshit about lost ballparks, that's just what it is - bullshit. You should forget it and move on with your life."

"Enough already." Byron raised his hands, palms facing toward Charles.

Charles stared down at the floor, not saying a word. "Byron, I'm just trying to help," he said, eventually, before looking back up at Byron.

"I know and I should know better than to tell you any of this crap."

"You know, Maggie called me the other day."

"She did? Good."

"That's it? You don't want to know what we talked about? You always want to know what we talked about."

"Okay. What did you guys talk about?"

"You. She asked if I had spoken to you recently."

"What did you tell her?"

"I said 'Yes.' I told her about your new obsession, although she seemed to know all about it. She's concerned about you."

"Yeah, I called her when I was in Detroit and she said the same thing. Although, she was able to listen to me without calling me names. Unlike you."

"Oh, I listen. You just don't like to hear what I have to say."

After another brief pause, Charles asked, "So, when are you gonna show me the Union Park sign? I thought we were supposed to have dinner there."

Byron thought for a moment, realizing his dilemma. "You know, I *should* move on. There's nothing to see at that restaurant."

"I knew it," said Charles. "I knew you were making it up."

"I wasn't making it up. I saw the sign. The place is closed now, that's all. I went by there before I left for Detroit and the restaurant was boarded up. Looks like it's closed for good."

"Okay, well, I'd still like to see where Union Park used to be, if you don't mind showing me."

"As long as you don't start preaching to me while we're there."

"Deal."

⚾ ⚾ ⚾

The following weekend, they drove to Harwood. Byron showed Charles pictures of Union Park and explained how it once fit into the neighborhood, facts Charles found logical and interesting. He also showed him Murph's house, where he thought home plate once sat, but said nothing to him about Murph - or Mac. The Stone Tavern remained shuttered. They tried looking through the one window not covered with plywood, but they could not see the Union Park sign.

On the way home, they talked about the modern-day Orioles, saying nothing more about the team of McGraw, Jennings, and Keeler. Byron switched on the Orioles game. Mike Mussina was making easy work of the Anaheim Angels, holding them to one run through seven innings.

"Enjoy having Mussina now," said Charles. "Next year he'll be playing somewhere else."

"If he doesn't feel any allegiance to the Orioles after all these years, who needs him?"

⚾ ⚾ ⚾

As the minor-league baseball season gained momentum, Byron found he had little time for deadball. His job with the Baysox kept him at the ballpark day and night whenever the team was in town. Once school was out for the summer, Byron knew attendance at Baysox games would double; so, too, would his tasks around the ballpark. Whatever time he had for research was limited to weekends when the Baysox were out of town.

Believing Byron didn't already have enough to do, Hank put him in charge of "Heavy Hitters," the Baysox's new promotional program that "rewarded" fans' attendance at Baysox games. Fans earned a point for every game they attended.

Rather than running the scoreboard, Byron was forced to spend the first several innings of each game hawking plastic "Heavy Hitters" cards to the teeming masses streaming through the turnstiles. One point earned fans a free soft drink. Three points, awarded for attending three games, earned them a small popcorn. Twenty points earned them a "behind-the-scenes" stadium tour, "including Clubhouse!" - the highlights of which included cinder-block walls and plywood lockers strewn with players' sweaty clothes, half-eaten food, and grimy baseball equipment. *Look kids! That's real indoor-outdoor carpet!*

The last Sunday in May, the Baysox were wrapping up their home series against the Binghamton Mets. As he did during the seventh inning of every home game, Byron packed up the "Heavy

Hitters" promotions table and placed it in a storage room beneath the upper-deck grandstand. With nothing left to do until the end of the game, Byron watched the last couple of innings from an upper-deck Baysox "Luxury Sky Suite." The suite was luxury in name only – and minor-league at that – a painted, cinder-block room with a refrigerator and sink, a couple of laminated tables, four armchairs, and five stools placed along a wall of glass over-looking the field below.

Byron locked the door behind him and sat down on one of the stools at the counter facing the field to watch the game's penultimate inning.

"Byron," called Hank. "Open up. I know you're in there. I saw you through the glass from the stands."

"Go away," Byron yelled back. "Louie and I want to be left *ALONE.*"

Hank opened the door using one of the hundreds of keys hanging from his key chain – the man loved his keys, a symbol of his authority, perhaps. "What have I told you about watching the game from up here?" asked Hank.

"Come on, Hank. I'm just killing time waiting for the game to end."

"I've been looking for you. A coach for Binghamton wants to see you. He said you guys used to play together and you've been avoiding him all weekend."

"Who, Chuck Stevens?"

"I don't know – he said his name so fast, I didn't quite catch it."

"Yeah, that's Chuck. He's a fast talker. Did he say what he wants? I'm not in the mood to see him."

"He didn't say, but as a member of the Baysox front office, you have an obligation to be cordial to the management of the opposing team."

"Okay, okay, I'll talk to him."

"You know, I don't understand why you don't keep in touch with your old teammates – especially the ones who are still in baseball. It certainly wouldn't hurt your career."

"You mean my career as a pitch man for 'Heavy Hitters?'"

"You know what I mean. Promise me you'll go down to the visitors' locker room as soon as the game ends. If you don't, you're fired."

"Yes, sir," said Byron, giving Hank a lazy, Bill Murray-in-the-movie-*Stripes*-style salute.

After Hank left, Byron returned to his seat. He was in no hurry to see Chuck Stevens. Two years earlier, Chuck had given Byron a hard time about not doing more with his life, believing that an ex-player – even a former minor-league player – should not be working at an entry-level baseball position as long as Byron had.

When the game ended, Byron took his time heading down to the visiting team's locker room out beyond left field. By the time Byron arrived, many of the Mets players were already showered, dressed, and seeking solace on the team bus, eating their buffet dinners off Styrofoam plates. Chuck and the other coaches were in the visiting manager's office, still in their uniforms. Bowie had beaten the Mets 5 to 1, taking two out of the three games in the series, and the Mets' coaches looked less than ecstatic.

Byron knocked on the office door. The coaches all looked up at him in unison, like spectators at a tennis match following the volley. Chuck excused himself and walked out of the office, closing the door behind him.

"Hey, Bitty, thanks for seeing me. How have you been?" The two shook hands.

"Been fine, thanks. You?"

"No complaints. You know me. I love baseball, although not as much on nights like tonight."

"Tough game," said Byron.

"Your boy, de la Hoya, sure pitched a gem."

"He did. So, you wanted to see me, coach?" Byron asked, sounding like a scared rookie called into the manager's office.

"Yeah. There's something I wanted to talk to you about. Let's go outside."

They left the clubhouse and walked toward the outfield fence. The stadium lights had dimmed and the pyrotechnicians had begun the first round of the evening's fireworks display.

"Best not stand too close to the field," said Byron, over the sound of the exploding fireworks. "Sometimes errant fireworks make their way over here. That wall over there already caught fire once this year." Byron pointed toward the wall he and Hank had replaced earlier in the spring. They walked away from the noise, to where the team bus sat idling.

"You seem nervous, Chuck. You okay?"

"Yeah, I'm fine."

"You know, if it's about my job, I'm quite happy working here."

"I'm sure you are, Bitty. But that's not why I wanted to see you – although I still think you could do better." Chuck took off his baseball hat, rolling and twisting the bill with his hands.

"What is it, then?"

"I saw Rob White at an Aeros game. He told me about your trip to Detroit."

"He did? What did he say?"

"Well, he told me about some of the interesting people you've met."

"Like who?"

"Like that souvenir vendor in Detroit. The old ball player

in Pittsburgh."

"Did he happen to mention anything about shared delusions?"

"Shared what?"

"Delusions. Never mind."

"I didn't ask to see you so I could give you a hard time," said Chuck. "I wanted to talk to you about something that happened to me last year."

"You're not jerking my chain, are you? Did Rob put you up to this?"

"No, he didn't. Something happened to me and it sounds like the same thing might have happened to you."

"What?"

"Last September, I was in New York visiting a friend. I took my boy with me and we went to see a game at Yankee Stadium. It was a day game and when it ended there was still plenty of daylight left so my friend – who's a bit of a baseball nut, like you – took us to see where the Polo Grounds used to be. It was across the river from Yankee Stadium."

"Across the Macomb Dam Bridge."

"We parked our car near a park called Coogan's Bluff. There's a beat-up chainlink fence around it with some woods below so we squeezed through an opening in the fence and followed this dirt path down to an old stairway left over from the Polo Grounds. My friend said they built the stairway so fans could get from the subway to the Polo Grounds. Half way down the stairs is a platform with a plaque dedicated to John Brush, the Giants' former owner."

Although Byron had read plenty of books mentioning the Polo Grounds and Coogan's Bluff, he had never heard of the Brush memorial stairway. Byron listened intently to Chuck's story.

"We stood there on the platform looking across Harlem River

Drive. There's a housing complex built where the Polo Grounds used to be. You could barely see through the trees, but I swear to you, Byron, as I was standing there I saw the Polo Grounds. I saw the back of the ballpark and ramps leading to the upper deck. I saw a sign above the ramps that said 'Giants vs. Cubs, 1:05 Today.' There were people heading to the park dressed in these old-style clothes - some of them walked past me on the stairway. Then, after about a minute, it all disappeared. It happened so quick, I figured it was just my imagination, but it all seemed so real. I asked my friend if he'd seen anything and he said 'no.' He thought I was kidding – but I wasn't. I didn't say anything to my boy, though. I didn't want him to think his old man had lost it."

"That's an amazing story," said Byron.

"I know what I saw," said Chuck, "but I didn't believe it until Rob told me what happened to you."

"Did you tell Rob what you told me - about the Polo Grounds?"

"Heck, no – he'd think I was crazy."

"But you had no problem telling me about it."

"Yeah, but you're already . . . I mean . . . . Hell, maybe we're both crazy."

"And you're sure you weren't simply imagining it?" Byron asked.

"I'm sure. When I got back home, I found some pictures of the Polo Grounds on the Internet. They matched what I'd seen, and I'd never seen those pictures before. I had no idea what the Polo Grounds even looked like until I saw it that day."

"That's amazing," said Byron.

"How's about you? What have you seen?"

Byron was reluctant to tell Chuck much about anything he

had seen, for fear of who - or what - might be listening to their conversation. "You know, I'm not sure I've seen anything. I think it was all in my mind."

"Come on, Bitty," said Chuck. "When we played together, you were always talking about old time baseball, about the towns we were playing in. You'd bore me to death sometimes. But, I'd always listen. What do you think this means? Tell me what you told Rob."

"Well, it sounds like Rob already told you everything."

"What about that guy in Pittsburgh - who was he?"

"George Grantham - like the drummer from Poco."

"The drummer from Poco?" asked Chuck.

"Yup, same name. They called him 'Boots.'"

"What did he say to you?"

"He asked me if I was going to the game – you know, the Pirates game. But, you see, the Pirates were playing in St. Louis, so I didn't know what he was talking about. I told him I was going to Detroit to see the Orioles play. That's about it."

"Do you think he was a ghost?"

"I don't know what he was, although Boots is dead."

"He's dead? The guy you were talking to?"

"The real Boots is dead, yes. But who knows if the guy I was talking to was really Boots? He could've been pulling my leg."

"What about the guy you met in Detroit? Rob said you thought he was a ghost, but he wouldn't own up to it."

"I don't think he was a ghost," replied Byron, not wanting to say anything to him about Matty O'Boyle. "I think he was just some crazy guy who knew a lot about baseball."

"Hmm, kinda like you."

"In a way, yeah, I guess, although you're one to talk, 'Mr. I can see the Polo Grounds.'"

"You know Clint Eastwood made a movie called *Coogan's Bluff*," said Chuck.

"He did, didn't he? I'd forgotten that."

"I rented it after what I saw there. It had nothing to do with baseball. In fact, Eastwood's character - Walt Coogan - never made it anywhere near Coogan's Bluff or the Polo Grounds."

"Too bad. Who knows what he might've seen?"

"Yeah, who knows?"

"Well, Chuck, I've gotta go. The fireworks should be over soon and I need to be up by the front gates when they're done."

"I gotta go too. The bus will be leaving soon."

"Hey, next time you see Rob, ask him about the guys he used to hang out with in front of the Toledo Food Town."

"What guys? Would I know them?"

"I doubt it, but ask Rob."

"I will," said Chuck, shaking Byron's hand.

At least I know he's not a ghost, Byron thought as he watched Chuck walk away.

Heading back toward the visitors' dugout, Byron stopped to watch the tail end of the grand finale. It was a good-size crowd for a Sunday night and most of the fans had stayed for the fireworks. A good night, overall, for the Baysox, and a good night for Byron, who was emboldened by Chuck's story, although he felt somewhat guilty for not telling Chuck more or what he had seen at League Park.

Coogan's Bluff, huh? Byron wondered. *Sounds like it's time for another road trip.*

As the pyrotechnicians fired off the final shots, Byron thought about Rob, wondering about the context in which he had told Chuck about the trip to Detroit. Byron wondered whether Rob suspected he was drinking again and had told Chuck about his concerns.

After the fireworks ended, the stadium lights came back on, encouraging those who had stayed in their seats to make their way to the concourse. Byron walked into the ticket office. Hank was sitting at his desk, putting the day's take into a zippered night deposit bag.

"So, how's coach?" asked Hank.

"He hasn't changed a bit. Just being nosey."

"What did he want?"

"Nothing, just wanted to know how I was doing."

"How *are* you doing, Byron?" asked Hank.

"I'm fine."

"Are you still looking for old ballplayers in old ballparks?"

"If I said 'yes,' would you be willing to come with me? I may be heading to New York soon."

"Ah, thanks, but no."

"Suit yourself."

"Don't you ever think about finding yourself a woman and settling down?"

"I did once," said Byron. "It didn't work out."

"That was a long time ago. Isn't it time you tried again?"

"Sure, not now. Soon, maybe."

"Well, let me know when you're ready. I can fix you up with some pretty nice specimens."

"Specimens? What are you, a biologist?"

"Yeah, a love biologist."

"That's disgusting. No thanks, doc."

"You know, you're not getting any younger."

"I know."

○ ○ ○

It was past midnight by the time Byron arrived home. He

switched on the computer and searched the Internet for sites mentioning the Polo Grounds and the Brush memorial stairway. Sure enough, *metaphysicalbaseball.com* had several references to the stairs, whose inscription stated "The John T. Brush Stairway Presented by the New York Giants." Dedicated in 1913 to the former Giants' owner - the same owner who hired John McGraw as manager in 1902 - the stairway at 157th Street and Edgecombe Avenue in Harlem once led to ticket booths behind home plate, allowing subway riders who departed the 155th Street station more direct access to the ballpark. According to the website, the Brush stairway was the sole baseball relic remaining at Coogan's Bluff, although a plaque commemorating the Polo Grounds had been placed on one of the support columns in the housing complex at the site.

Byron knew Chuck was on to something and was thankful for the tip. He thought about other famous, former New York ballparks he could visit – Ebbets Field and Washington Park, both in Brooklyn, and Hilltop Park in Washington Heights. It was now a matter of finding the time.

CHAPTER 19

◎◎◎

Byrdland
July 1999

As spring gave way to summer, the mundane routine of each day replaced the excitement Byron had felt earlier in the season. For Byron, spring was like a hitting streak where he could see the ball well and hit just about anything thrown at him. Once summer crept in, the streak ended, leaving Byron searching, hoping for something, anything, to happen.

On days off, Byron returned time and again to Harwood, the place Mac referred to as the "center" of Baltimore baseball. Byron spent hours researching Harwood's many former baseball venues. With Charles's help, he gained access to the extensive archival collections at the Babe Ruth Museum.

According to Byron's research, five ballparks once graced Harwood or its immediate vicinity, with two on the same site. In addition to Union Park, there was Huntington Park, located across the street from Union Park at the southeast corner of East 25th Street and Barclay, and home to the American Association Orioles from 1883 to 1889. The original Oriole Park, located four blocks north and one block east of Union Park at the southwest corner of East 29th Street and Greenmount, was home to the American Association Orioles in 1890 and 1891. American League Park, built on the former site of the original Oriole Park, was home to the American League Orioles in 1901 and 1902. Terrapin Park, located catty-corner to American League Park at the northwest corner of East 29th Street and Greenmount, was home to the Federal League Baltimore Terrapins in 1914 and 1915 and the Negro American League Baltimore Elite Giants from 1938 to 1944.

Byron took turns visiting each of the sites, looking for clues, hoping to find remnants of the old ballparks. One Sunday afternoon in mid-July, while the Baysox were on the road, Byron visited the former site of American League Park. It was a melancholy affair, for American League Park represented the end of major league baseball in Baltimore 100 years earlier. Half way through the Orioles' 1902 campaign, John McGraw jumped leagues and cities, joining the National League New York Giants as player-manager. McGraw was wise to leave. At the end of the season, the American League relocated the Baltimore franchise to New York, leaving Baltimore without a team for the ensuing 52 seasons. Baltimore's former franchise became the New York Yankees, the most successful franchise in baseball history. That fact was foremost of the many reasons Byron could not stand the Yankees.

Byron's calculations suggested home plate was once located in the southeast corner of East 29th Street and Barclay, with the first-base line running parallel to Barclay and the third-base line running parallel to East 29th Street. A McDonald's now stood at the site, its restaurant and drive-through covering the left-field corner and its parking lot covering home plate and most of the infield. Two-story row houses fronting both sides of Llchester Road, constructed after the demise of American League Park, covered the remaining portion of the ballpark site.

Byron twice circled the perimeter of the park, walking north on Greenmount, west on East 29th Street, south on Barclay, and east on East 28th Street. Nothing seemed out of the ordinary and it appeared nothing remained of the old ballpark. After his second circuit, Byron stopped inside the McDonald's, hoping perhaps to spot an old ballplayer or two. Not only did Byron *not* see any ballplayers, but, based upon his unscientific survey, was disappointed to learn that none of the McDonald's employees he met had any clue the fast-food joint was built atop a historic ballpark site.

Byron found particular irony in a customer wearing a traditional, dark-blue New York Yankees hat with overlapping, white stitched "N" and "Y" lettering, sitting in one of the booths along the third-base line. When asked, the man seemed unaware that the team whose hat he wore once played where he now sat eating french fries. The man told Byron he wasn't even a Yankees fan and that he just liked the hat. Byron wondered if the man was lying – trying to hide his obvious embarrassment for not knowing such an elementary baseball fact - for Byron could not imagine anyone voluntarily wearing such a fatuous hat unless he was a player for or a fan of the team.

On the southeast corner of East 28th Street and Greenmount, across the street from the former ballparks site, was "Byrdland," a carry-out Byron suspected was named in honor of Orioles' mascot and the many ballparks of Harwood. A one-story, red-brick building of perhaps 1930's vintage, the carry-out was an appendage to the front of a larger, two-story Victorian-era duplex. A metal sign with painted red lettering above the front entrance announced to everyone within sight that the carry-out had it all: "Byrdland Grill, Deli & Grocery – Sea Food, Sub, Cold & Hot Sandwiches, Ice, Cold Soda, Ice Cream, Medicine, Beauty Supply & General Merchandise." As if that were not enough, a second sign on the wall to the right of the front windows expanded Byrdland's extensive menu, advertising additional offerings of "Fried Chicken" and "Lake Trout."

Byron figured it a good bet the proprietor of such an appropriately named establishment would have some knowledge of the ballparks that once graced the area, and he headed across the street to find out.

Black-metal grates covered the two windows and the thick glass front door of the depression-era exterior. Inside, a wall of plexiglass protected the store's employees from its customers, reflecting the owner's apparent concern for security. A white-painted tin ceiling was the sole architectural feature reflecting the building's true age, the remainder of the room's decor being post-1968 urban unrest. Everything sold at Byrdland, the lake trout, the submarine sandwiches, the soda, the beauty supplies, had to pass from behind the plexiglass wall through an opening in one of two plexiglass cylinders. An advertising sign taped above one of the cylinders invited customers to enjoy "Ice Cold Coca Cola Inside." *They should change that to read 'outside,'* thought Byron, *'cause they sure don't want you inside.*

One object left unprotected in the customer standing area was a 1980's Ms. Pacman video arcade game sided with fake-wood veneer. *I'm surprised it's not bolted to the floor,* thought Byron as he dropped 50 cents through the coin slot. Byron played a game while waiting for several customers to place their orders or pick up food.

Once the last of the customers departed, Byron struck up a conversation with the oversized gentleman standing behind the plexiglass wall. The man claimed no knowledge of the former, resident ballparks and was unwilling even to conjecture about the origin of the name "Byrdland." The most he would say was that the current owner's name was Francis and they would be changing the name of the store to "Frank's Carry Out" as soon as the new signs arrived. Disappointed and deflated, Byron took a picture of the Byrdland sign - captured, of course, for posterity - and left the store.

Still desperate for a dose of baseball karma, Byron drove four blocks north and east to the site of Memorial Stadium. Although no longer in use, Memorial Stadium remained, abandoned but largely intact, while the city debated its future. A chainlink fence enclosed the parking lot ringing the stadium, but Byron was able to drive his car into the lot through one of the gates city workers had left unlocked. He parked north of the stadium, near where Frank Robinson's famous home run had landed after clearing the left-field fence on Mother's Day 1966.

Memorial Stadium was quiet as a cemetery. From Byron's vantage point, looking south through another chainlink fence beyond centerfield, he could see the playing field, the seating bowl, and the expansive upper deck. It appeared as if some of the metal bleachers in the upper deck already had been removed. Twenty thousand blue and grey stadium seats remained, stoical, spread throughout the inanimate silence of the lower seating bowl.

With its manicured grass long gone, overtaken by a vast array of tall weeds and short scrub trees, the outfield looked more like the California Low Desert, minus the mountains, than a ballfield. The infield, too, was consumed by clumps of weedy vegetation. Five years after the Orioles departed, the Baltimore Ravens had played their first two seasons of football at Memorial Stadium, but had moved the previous year to a new home built next to Oriole Park at Camden Yards. Large rolls of astroturf, once the gridiron of the Ravens, sat in piles outside the gate, discarded. Byron grabbed a slice of the fake grass for his collection, but tossed it back onto the pile since the astroturf had no connection to baseball.

Witnessing firsthand the once proud stadium waiting in eerie silence for the wrecking ball was depressing, not the positive baseball karma Byron had sought that Sunday afternoon. A stiff wind, the type that would have favored long-ball hitters like Robinson, ripped along the lower seating bowl, across the now wretched outfield, and into the parking lot, hitting Byron squarely in the chest. Like Mac and his memories of Union Park, Byron had seen games at Memorial Stadium and could still visualize how the stadium once looked. He could see the crowds in the stands, the players on the field, the impeccable carpet of grass, the electronic glow of the scoreboard beyond the outfield, and the brick, oval-shaped stadium structure, which was once the pride of Baltimore.

Before the Major League Orioles arrived at Memorial Stadium in 1954, the International League Orioles had played from 1944 to 1953 in an earlier incarnation of the ballpark, known then as Municipal Stadium. Byron wondered whether any old ballplayers from that team might appear. However, other than a man walking his dog around the northern edge of the parking lot, Byron saw no one there that day.

As he stared at the seating bowl, he remembered one game in particular. He was young, sitting with his Cub Scout troop in the left-field bleachers, throwing ice in the direction of Oakland Athletics' outfielder Joe Rudi. Years later, Byron was certain he had paid his penance for his earlier, youthful indiscretion, when a fan in Rochester dumped beer on him as they both tried to catch a pop foul along the third-base box seats. Jogging back to his position, the beer-soaked ball still in Byron's glove, he heard someone who was sitting next to the fan call out, "Nice try, Joe." Byron glanced back at the fan: he looked like an older version of Joe Rudi - the same long, scraggly mustache and stringy hair, but more grey than brown.

Returning to his car, Byron stopped to pick up a golf-ball-size piece of cedar, with its bark still attached, lying next to the fence. Long ago, a line of cedar trees stood behind centerfield, providing a bucolic barrier between the ballfield and the asphalt parking lot. The city had removed the trees in preparation for the beginning of the stadium's end game. Byron placed the chunk of cedar on his dashboard before driving out of the parking lot.

On his way home, he stopped at Royal Books, a used-book store on East 25th Street six blocks west of the former site of Union Park. He had discovered the book store on a previous trip to Baltimore and was surprised not to have seen it before, given how well he thought he knew the area. Located in a row house mid-block, the building's once ornate brick and carved-stone facade was hidden beneath sheets of yellowing whitewash. Marble steps, concave from a century of foot traffic, led to a small landing at the entrance to the shop. A sign to the right of the front door instructed customers to ring the bell for entry. Byron did as instructed and a buzzer soon sounded, unlocking the door.

Shelves of used books in Mylar dust jackets lined what was clearly a high-end book store. Byron browsed the neatly arranged titles, mostly modern literature, crime fiction, and books made into movies – nothing concerning baseball or any other sports, at least that he could see.

A woman sitting at a desk in the middle of what was once the front parlor asked Byron if he needed help. Little did she know.

"Do you have any books on baseball?"

"A few," she said. "It's not our specialty. They're upstairs in the back room."

"Keeping them hidden, huh? Kind of like ham at a Kosher-style deli," said Byron. "It's not on the menu, but the locals know to ask."

"I guess," said the woman, unimpressed with his analogy. "This will go quicker if I show you where they are."

Byron followed the woman up a less-than-plumb side staircase to a second-floor hallway packed floor to ceiling with more Mylar-covered books on neatly arranged shelves. In a small back room facing the rear of the building were several shelves crammed full of books lying every which way - in stark contrast to the books shelved elsewhere in the store.

"I haven't had time to organize these," she said. "Baseball books could be anywhere on this shelf, but mainly here." The woman pointed to the top two rows.

"This is a pretty good selection of books," said Byron, looking through the titles.

"The owner tries to keep books of local interest on hand, including the Orioles. Feel free to look around."

In front of him at eye level was a long-out-of-print book entitled *The Home Team, A Full Century of Baseball in Baltimore, 1859 to 1959,* by James Bready. The one copy of this book Byron previously had seen was in McKeldin Hall's rare book room at the University of Maryland.

A chair across from the bookshelf invited Byron to take a seat. He turned each page, handling the book as if it were a frail, ancient manuscript. The price of $60 seemed a bit steep for his wallet, although he knew he had no choice but to buy it. The book was signed by the author on the title page and dedicated to "the only person I know who has seen more Orioles games than me." The person's name was illegible, having been crossed out in a different color ink.

Inside the front cover was a reproduction of the famous Union Park photograph taken during the Orioles' championship game with Boston in September 1897. On another page was a photograph taken literally down the street, showing Union Park's entrance on East 25th Street. The painted sign above the entrance looked identical to the one Byron had seen hanging in the Stone Tavern.

Soon, Byron was lost in the details of the book, intrigued by the chapter on Thomas J. Murphy – a groundskeeper at Union Park. The book described Murphy's handy work, which provided a distinct home-field advantage for the Orioles. This included grading the third-base line with a slight incline so bunts rolled fair, placing hardened clay in front of home plate to help effectuate the Baltimore chop (whereby the batter strikes at the ball with a downward motion of the bat, sending the ball bouncing over the infielder's head), and mixing soap shavings in the dirt around the pitcher's mound, thus making it difficult for visiting hurlers to grip the ball after rubbing dirt into their hands.

Byron wondered whether Murph, the man who lived at 313 East 25th Street, could be Thomas Murphy, or maybe a descendent. According to Mac, Murph was once a groundskeeper at Memorial Stadium. Could it be Murph worked at Union Park, as well, just as Matty worked at Bennett Park? If so, that would make him a ghost.

A chapter on the 1901 American League Orioles included a picture of an engraved invitation similar to the one Byron had received from Mac a few weeks earlier. The invitation pictured in the book celebrated the inaugural game of the 1901 season at American League Park, also once located near Royal Books, a few blocks north and east.

Byron tucked the book under his arm and browsed the remaining titles on the shelf. He found several volumes about Cal Ripken, Jr., and autobiographies of Brooks Robinson, Jim Palmer, and Earl Weaver, but nothing else on the old Baltimore

Orioles. Byron headed downstairs and handed the book to the woman at the front desk.

"Great store you have here," said Byron.

"Thanks, it's not mine."

"I've been looking for a copy of this book for years."

The woman examined the cover of the book. "This one came in the other day."

"Do you know who brought it in?"

"No. I paid him outright for it so he didn't start an account, but I remember him because this was the only book he brought in."

"What did he look like?"

"He was an older man, white hair, not quite your height."

"Was he wearing a Giants cap?" asked Byron.

"Oh, I don't remember that."

The woman handed Byron his receipt. He thanked her and left.

Standing on the sidewalk in front of the store, Byron flipped through the book and reread the inscription. *I wonder how many Orioles games Mac has seen.*

CHAPTER 20

🏀🏀🏀

Old Friends

The last weekend of July, the Baysox were playing the Seawolves in Erie, Pennsylvania, giving Byron a chance to return to Baltimore, this time with a different angle. His visit to Cy Young's grave back in May had him thinking, for he had heard that some of the old Orioles were interred in local cemeteries.

During his earlier trip to Byrdland, he overheard two customers who worked at Greenmount Cemetery talking about some of the more notable residents buried there, including John Wilkes Booth, who was interred next to his parents in a grave marked by a simple, granite stone. Given Greenmount Cemetery's proximity to the "center" of Baltimore baseball, maybe a few old Orioles were buried there as well. And, maybe, something would happen if he went there. So Byron decided to check it out for himself.

It was a beautiful day to visit Greenmount - the birds were singing, not a cloud in the sky. It did not escape Byron's notice that his excitement about visiting a cemetery was sad commentary on his life.

From his research, Byron knew Willie Keeler was the first of the old Orioles' Hall of Famers to pass away, dying in 1923. Hughie Jennings died in 1928, while John McGraw and Wilbert Robinson both died in 1934. Ned Hanlon passed in 1937 and Joe Kelley, the last of the old Orioles' Hall of Famers, died six years later in 1943. Each of the old Orioles were elected post-humously to the Hall of Fame. McGraw was elected to the Hall in 1937, Keeler in 1939. Both Jennings and Robertson were elected in 1945. Kelley was elected in 1971, some 28 years after his death. Hanlon had to wait the longest, not gaining election to the Hall of Fame until 1996, some 59 years after his death.

An ornate, castle-like structure with stone archways and a copper roof served as the main entrance to the cemetery at the corner of Greenmount Avenue and East Oliver Street. The entry-way befitted the cemetery's stature as Baltimore's largest final resting place. Byron parked his car in the lot next to a building marked, appropriately, "office."

Sitting in the office at a desk behind the front counter was a frail, old man who looked as if he might soon be joining the ranks of those already registered at Greenmount.

"Excuse me," said Byron. "Do you know if there are any former baseball players buried here?"

"There's a couple. I could look 'em up for you if you'd like. We've got 'em sorted by profession."

"Great, thanks. I'm looking for any Orioles buried here."

The man had difficulty opening the desk drawer, which appeared stuck, so Byron offered his help. As Byron came around the counter, the drawer loosened, sending the man and his chair wheeling back several feet into Byron. The man extracted from the drawer a three-inch-thick computer printout which he placed on the counter with a resounding thud. Leafing through the pages listing the names of the dearly departed interred at Greenmount, the man stopped in the middle of the printout, pointing his finger at an entry on the page.

"Here's one – Richard Prime Brown. 'Stub' was his nick-name. Says here he was a pitcher for the Orioles from 1893 to 1894 – born in Baltimore on August 3, 1870, and died here March 11, 1948."

"Stub Brown. I remember reading about him. He quit the Orioles half way through the year they won their first pennant."

"Bad move on his part."

"Any other Orioles?" asked Byron. "Like John McGraw or Hughie Jennings?"

"No. No one like that. Let's see, 'Arthur Vincent Campbell' – Vin Campbell, played for the Cubs, Pirates, and Braves in the early 1900's. He died in 1969."

"No other ballplayers?"

"Not according to my list. You mentioned McGraw, though. If you want to see his grave, it's over at New Cathedral Cemetery."

"It is? Where's that?"

"It's northwest of here, maybe four or five miles."

"What's the name again?"

"New Cathedral. I used to work there. They've got a bunch of old ballplayers – several Hall of Famers."

"Great - thanks," said Byron.

"If you're heading over there, use the entrance on Frederick. The other gates are closed."

"Frederick. Thanks."

Byron decided to skip the gravesites of former Oriole Stub Brown and Vin Campbell and instead visit New Cathedral Cemetery. Once back in his car, he headed northwest out of the city but soon was lost. He checked his map – something he was starting to do with more regularity - and identified two different roads on the outskirts of Baltimore named "Frederick" – "Frederick Avenue" and "Old Frederick Road." Both had cemeteries.

Byron drove to Frederick Avenue and the closer of the two cemeteries. Houses surrounding the cemetery suggested the neighborhood, though once prosperous, was now, sadly, another of the "down and going" areas of Baltimore. He entered the cemetery through a 15-foot-tall wrought-iron gate, but saw no sign identifying where he was. He pulled his car up alongside a man sitting in a pickup truck. From the contents of the truck bed, it looked as if the man had been doing some digging.

"Excuse me, is this New Cathedral Cemetery?"

"No, this is Loudon Park," said the man. "New Cathedral is north of here, up on Old Frederick Road."

"So I take it John McGraw's not buried here?"

"Who?"

"John McGraw, the baseball player."

"I don't think so," replied the man. "I can check my list, though."

The man leaned around behind his seat and pulled a stack of papers up off the floor.

What is it with these people and their lists of the dead? Byron wondered.

"Let's see, McGraw . . . . Nope, no McGraw. We've got plenty of other ballplayers though," said the man, showing Byron a section entitled "Baseball Players."

"Who've you got?" Byron asked.

"Let's see – Harry 'Chub' Aubrey, Clarence 'Cupid' Childs, Lewis 'Buttercup' Dickerson, Fernandas 'Ferd' Eunick, Clarence 'Slats' Jordan, George 'Dummy' Leitner, Allan 'Rubberarm' Russell, and Milton 'Mikado Milk' Scott. Let's see, Bill Keister - they called him 'Wagon Tongue' - he might have played with McGraw. He was an Oriole."

"I think Keister played for the American League Orioles, but I'm not positive." Byron didn't recognize any of the other players as former Orioles.

"We've also got H.L. Mencken and Samuel Seymore," said the man, "if you're interested."

Byron recognized the journalist H.L. Mencken. "Who's Seymore?" asked Byron.

"He was the oldest surviving witness to Lincoln's assassination. He was five years old when he saw it. He died in 1956."

"Did he play baseball?"

"I don't know," said the man.

The man gave Byron directions to New Cathedral Cemetery, which was on the other side of Loudon Park. Byron decided to leave a visit to the gravesites of Wagon Tongue, Chub, Cupid, Buttercup, and the others for another day.

Ten minutes later, he found the entrance to New Cathedral Cemetery. *I should have known*, thought Byron as he passed between two large stone pillars marking the entrance to New Cathedral. *I pass this place on my way to Camden Yards.*

To the left of the gates was a white, colonial-style clapboard house with an arrow-shaped sign pointing visitors toward the office. "Please Ring Bell For Service" stated a sign on the front door. Ringing the bell, he thought of Zuzu, Jimmy Stewart's daughter in the movie *It's A Wonderful Life*, and wondered whether another resident of New Cathedral had received a pair of angel's wings.

No one answered, so Byron rang the bell a second time. *More wings*, he thought.

An elderly woman opened the door. "Sorry," said the woman. "It takes me a minute to get over here from my desk. Come on in." The woman took her place behind the front counter. "And what can I do for you today?"

Byron took off his Orioles cap as he walked inside. "I'm looking for John McGraw - that is, where he's buried," said Byron, placing his hands on the counter's yellow Formica top. "Is he here?"

"He is," said the woman, sounding as if she expected McGraw to come walking around the corner any second. The woman handed Byron an 8 inch by 14 inch sheet of paper entitled "Baseball Hall of Famers." The paper included a map of the cemetery showing the location of several former players.

"Wow, sort of a Hollywood map of the stars, except it's a cemetery," said Byron. "I guess I'm not the first person to come here looking for his grave."

"No, you're not. As you can see, we have several Hall of Fame players here, including John McGraw, and they all were Orioles." The woman pointed to Byron's Orioles cap, which he had placed on the counter.

The list was impressive. In addition to McGraw, three other Orioles were buried at New Cathedral – right fielder Joe Kelley, catcher Wilbert Robinson, and manager Ned Hanlon.

"Amazing," said Byron. "All four here at New Cathedral."

"We get quite a few Orioles fans. You'll see some orange and black wreaths out there left over from Christmas."

Byron thanked the woman. As he was leaving, he put on his Orioles hat and tipped the bill in the direction of the woman.

The graveyard was divided into sections single A through triple V, like minor-league baseball, except the cemetery had more leagues. The map's legend included symbols for identifying the final resting place of each Hall of Famer.

Walking back to his car, Byron noticed the day's earlier clear skies had thickened with clouds and it looked as if it might rain. Wasting little time, he made his way to the first grave on the list - John McGraw. A meandering, single-lane road took him past tidy rows of marble and granite headstones toward "Lot 197, Section L." McGraw's final resting place was hard to miss – a stately granite mausoleum, with an oxidized, green copper roof. About the size of a two-room summer cottage, the structure was set into the side of one of the more prominent hills in the cemetery. The names "J.J. McGraw – S.J. Van Lill, Jr." were carved in granite above the entrance to the mausoleum. Four stone pillars stood like centurions guarding the copper-faced door. McGraw's grave, ostentatious when compared to the mid-west sensibility of Cy Young's winged baseball, seemed to capture, as Young's had, the nature of the man entombed within.

Byron parked his car around the side of the hill where the road widened and walked back toward McGraw's gravesite. He tried pulling on the door leading into the mausoleum, but, not surprisingly, it was locked.

"You can't go in there," said a voice behind him. Byron looked to his right and saw a man wearing grey overalls, with a shovel slung over his shoulder, walking toward him from around the side of McGraw's mausoleum.

"Oh, sorry," said Byron. "I'm not even sure why I did that."

"You're not the first person who's tried to get in there. I take it you're an Orioles fan?" The man pointed to Byron's hat.

"I am. I hear you get a good number of fans visiting his grave."

"Maybe two or three a month, sometimes more. There are other Orioles buried here as well – Ned Hanlon, Joe Kelley, Wilbert Robinson. People come to visit them, too."

"That's what they told me up at the office," said Byron, holding up his map of the dead stars.

"We've even got a damn Yankee, here."

"Who?" asked Byron.

"Walt Smallwood."

Byron didn't recognize his name. "A Yankee buried in Baltimore," said Byron. "That's ironic."

"He was from Baltimore. Besides, he played only a handful

of games for the Yanks."

"Did you know him?" asked Byron, half joking.

"Nah. Our paths haven't crossed. So, why are you here?" asked the cemetery worker, looking serious.

"What do you mean?"

"Well, you're not a relative."

"Nope, just a fan of the Orioles."

"You out here trying to communicate with the dead?"

"Me? No." Byron still couldn't bring himself to admit otherwise.

"The reason I ask, see, is sometimes we get people out here who think they can talk to the dead – especially them dead Hall of Famers. You wouldn't believe the people who ask me about that."

"And what do you tell them?"

"I tell them they're wasting their time. It's a bit taboo, don't you think, someone that famous, haunting the place where they're buried. Kind of depressing, too, let me tell you."

"I see your point."

"Besides, them Hall of Famers got better places to be."

"Like where?"

"Like the ballpark," said the cemetery worker, looking Byron straight in the eye, in a tone suggesting the answer should have been obvious.

Byron's ears picked up. "You mean like Union Park?" he asked.

The cemetery worker smiled. "I knew you were a player."

"I used to be . . . . I played for the Orioles in the minors."

"I played, too," said the cemetery worker.

"For who?"

"The Orioles."

"Amazing. My name's Byron Bennett."

Byron held out his hand, but then pulled it back realizing

the man probably had no interest shaking his hand.

"Jimmy Mathison. Pleased to meet you."

Byron thought he recognized Mathison's name, but he couldn't remember anything about him.

"You played infield," Byron guessed, hoping he was right.

"Third base."

"That was my position, too," said Byron, glad his guess proved correct. "I wish I'd made it to the majors."

"I played there for about a month," said Mathison. "It was the best month of my life."

"You're lucky you made it. For me, there was always some other player ahead of me in the pecking order, no matter how hard I tried."

"Sometimes it's better to be lucky than good. I was in the right place at the right time. Sometimes that's all it takes."

"You've still got to be able to play the game."

"True," said Mathison, shaking his head in agreement.

"So, how many players do you get coming through here?"

"We had three or four here last April. Other than that, not too many."

"Who were they?"

"Can't say for sure, just a bunch of old men. We don't look the same anymore. In fact, you look pretty good for your age, you've held up well."

"Thanks," said Byron, not sure what to make of Mathison's reference to his age. "How did you know they were players?"

"The same way I knew you were – I just *knew*."

This guy thinks I'm a ghost! thought Byron. He could feel his heart starting to pound. *I should be careful what I say.*

"Do you know why they were here?" Byron asked.

"A reunion of sorts. They come up here once every couple of

years to celebrate the start of the season."

Not wanting to seem too inquisitive about the old ballplayers, Byron changed the subject. "Say, who is S.J. Van Lill, Jr.?" asked Byron, pointing to the frieze above McGraw's mausoleum door.

"You'd think I'd know that, working here and all, but I don't. There used to be a company in Baltimore called Van Lill, so maybe he worked for them. You can ask one of the ladies in the front office, they might know."

"I will, thanks."

"Well, I've got some digging to do. Nice meeting you."

"You too."

Byron watched Mathison walk toward the bottom of the hill, dragging his shovel behind him.

An old ballplayer working in a grave yard – Byron knew there was something Mathison wasn't telling him. Although Byron figured Mathison was a ghost, he hadn't been able to muster the nerve to ask.

Byron popped the trunk of his car and pulled out a Wilson Sporting Goods bag in which he kept the foul balls he found in the parking lot after Baysox games. Inspired by what he had seen at Cy Young's gravesite, he grabbed a Rawlings Official Eastern League baseball, with scrape marks where the ball struck the asphalt, and returned to McGraw's mausoleum. He placed the ball in front of the copper door. Afterwards, he said a short, awkward prayer. Words of thanks, really.

According to his map, Byron's next stop on the New Cathedral Cemetery Tour 1999 was Joe Kelley's grave, a long fly ball over the hill from McGraw's mausoleum. Byron parked his car next to a set of marble stairs at the base of a small hill. Grabbing another asphalt-scraped baseball from his Wilson bag, he walked up the hill to Kelley's grave. Kelley was buried alongside his wife and son. Byron placed the baseball next to Kelley's headstone. "Joseph J. Kelley, Husband, 1871 - 1943," stated the headstone. Byron returned to his car, took the last baseball out of the bag, and walked the short distance to Ned Hanlon's grave.

"Edward Hanlon, August 22, 1857, April 14, 1937," stated Foxy Ned's headstone. A matching block of granite to the right honored the memory of his son: "Joseph Thomas Hanlon, Born March 3, 1893, Died July 31, 1918, Killed In Action, Buried At Thiaucourt, France." Byron placed the baseball between the two blocks of granite.

Wilbert Robinson's grave was situated in the northeast section on the opposite side of the cemetery. A large chunk of black granite was missing from the corner of Robinson's headstone, which Byron attributed to the work of an overzealous Brooklyn Dodgers fan, the team Robinson once managed. Row houses on West Saratoga Street, beyond the cemetery's wrought iron fence, overlooked Robinson's grave. Glancing at the houses, Byron wondered whether any of the residents knew the identity of their famous neighbor. Byron apologized to Robinson's gravestone, for he had run out of baseballs, but he vowed to bring another one, should he ever return to the cemetery.

On his way back toward the cemetery's front gate, Byron stopped again at the office.

"I hope it's okay," said Byron to the woman, "but I left a few baseballs down at the gravesites."

"That's fine," said the woman. "I'll tell the workers to leave them there."

"Also, I had a question – Mr. Mathison told me you might know the answer."

"Mr. Mathison?" asked the woman.

"Yes, Jimmy Mathison – I saw him over by John McGraw's

mausoleum. He said he worked here."

"We don't have anyone working here by that name," said the woman.

"He's about my age and height. A little heavy set."

"You must mean West Consin. He's about your height. He's working here today. You must have spoken with him."

A second woman, who was sitting behind the desk and had been listening to their conversation, stood up, list in hand, and approached the counter. "You know, we have a James Mathison who's *buried* here. He was an Oriole. Maybe you saw his name on the headstone and confused the two."

The woman handed Byron the paper from which she had been reading, listing the names and occupations of other famous, or near-famous, people interred in the cemetery. The woman pointed to the second page. "See? Lot forty-eight, section K – Mathison, James."

"That must be it, I must have seen his name and confused the two. Well, thanks very much," said Byron, after a short, awkward pause. "You've both been a big help."

"Go, Orioles!" said the second woman as Byron walked out the door.

As he climbed into his car, Byron realized he had forgotten to ask the identity of S.J. Van Lill. *I guess it really doesn't matter*, he thought.

Turning right onto Old Frederick Road, Byron saw Mathison standing next to the graveyard fence, pulling weeds. Byron slowed his car to a crawl and rolled down the passenger-side window.

"Excuse me, Jimmy."

Mathison looked over at Byron and walked toward his car. "What is it?" he asked.

"Your name is Mathison, right?" asked Byron, pulling

up to the curb.

"Yes."

"The woman in the office said your name was West Consin."

"That's the name I go by now. I thought you being a player yourself, you'd want to know my real name."

"Oh, yeah, that's what I figured," said Byron, trying to cover his flub. "Say, what year did you play for the Orioles?"

"1902 – late August through September. After that, my major-league career was over."

"You said you played third base."

"Mostly third, sometimes short."

"Did you ever play with McGraw?"

"No, he'd left for New York by then."

"Oh, yes, he had."

"I owe him, though," said Mathison. "If he hadn't quit the Orioles, I might never have made it to the bigs."

"Right place, right time," said Byron.

"Yup."

"If you don't mind me asking, what are you doing hanging around here now? Why don't you join the other players down at Union Park?"

"I never played at Union Park. I played at Oriole Park. It's a McDonald's now. There's nothing left of it, at least from what we've seen so far, so none of us can get in."

"You mean you and your teammates?"

"My teammates – anyone who played for the Orioles in 1901 and 1902, including McGraw, we can't get in there. Even after Andy died, we couldn't get in."

"Andy? Who's Andy?"

"Andy Oyler. He played third base after McGraw left and before I got there. He was the last of us to go. He died in 1970."

"Andy Oyler." Byron thought for a moment. "Isn't he the guy who hit that two-foot home run at Nicollet Park?"

"The one that got stuck in the mud by home plate? That's him."

Byron was amazed by all he was hearing, for Mathison had confirmed Pete's theory. As the conversation continued, Byron could feel his heart once again pounding, from both the excitement and the fear of knowing he was talking to an actual old ballplayer. He gripped the steering wheel so Mathison would not see his hands shaking.

"But there *is* something left of Union Park," said Byron.

"I guess. I hear they play games there, but I've never seen it. If you didn't play there, you can't see it. And, they won't tell you, believe me."

"How about Memorial Stadium?" asked Byron. "It's still there." Byron was excited by the prospect of games being played there once again.

"Well, as you know, you can't play there until the entire team is dead."

"Oh, yeah," said Byron. "Guess I'm getting ahead of myself." *Keep cool, Byron*, he thought. *Don't blow this.* The longer the conversation continued, the more tied up in knots his stomach felt.

"The Orioles started playing there in 1954."

"They did."

"As long as there's still one member of the '54 Orioles alive, the team can't go back and play until he dies, assuming something's left of the park when he does."

"That's pretty morbid, don't you think."

"I think it's just the opposite - life after death."

"What about League Park – in Cleveland?" asked Byron. "You played there, right?"

"I did, we played them there in September '02."

"Have you ever gone back to Cleveland for a game?"

"I was there a couple of times, but it wasn't worth the trip."

"Why not?"

"The manager never put me in. You know how managers are."

"That I do."

"Maybe I'll head up to Detroit after the Tigers move out. Otherwise, I'm just biding my time waiting for someone to unearth something from Oriole Park."

"I hope someone does. Good luck, Jimmy. Maybe we'll meet again."

"You never know."

"Oh, Jimmy, by the way, 'West Consin?'"

"Funny, huh? I played for a mill team near Milwaukee one summer."

"I see."

"Say, Byron, where'd you get the car? I thought we couldn't drive."

"It's 'cause I'm younger. You'll see more of it now with guys my age." Byron didn't know how to respond to Mathison's question and the lie he gave was the best he could do. As he sped away from the curb hoping to avoid any more questions, Byron's hands continued shaking as he clutched the steering wheel. *Another conversation with another ghost,* he thought. *Man this is stressful. My stomach feels like crap.* A block past the cemetery, he pulled over and waited for his stomach to settle.

After calming down, he pulled away from the curb and headed northwest on Old Frederick Road. He watched the cemetery disappear in his rear-view mirror. He thought about what Mathison had told him, about games being played at Union Park, and how, for players to get back in, there had to be some portion of the park remaining at the site, just like Peter had conjectured. But what portion of Union Park remained? There was nothing now, at least not that he had seen.

Driving home, Byron turned on the radio but couldn't find the Orioles game. Switching the dial, the Simon and Garfunkel song "Old Friends" came floating over the airwaves. *How apropos*, he thought, wondering if Mac was now controlling the airwaves. Byron sang overtop Paul Simon's voice to the song's final lines about holding onto photographs and memories. As the guitar's last measure hung in the air, Byron turned off the radio, humming the melodic, melancholy tune the rest of the ride home.

CHAPTER 21

@ @ @

The Summer Game

In the weeks following Byron's trip to New Cathedral Cemetery, the Baysox's summer season entered full stride, leaving little time for Byron's research. When possible, he took trips to Union Park or one of the other Baltimore baseball sites, all to no avail. No Mac, no Murph, no old ballplayers. It seemed Murph was never home and nothing ever was out of the ordinary, just rows of houses, empty lots, mom-and-pop restaurants, and liquor stores.

On his trips to Baltimore, Byron also made a habit of driving by former homes of the old Orioles, at least those he was able to find that were still standing. One such residence was a former boarding house at 12 West 24th Street, where McGraw and his teammate Hughie Jennings lived during the baseball season. The house was a narrow, Federal-style, three-story brick row house with double-hung windows on the second and third floors. Six granite steps led to a plain wood door fronted with an iron gate. To the left of the door was a pair of windows, also covered with iron bars. Byron marveled at the idea of McGraw and Jennings sitting on those same steps, talking with neighbors in the evening about the game that day or the next day's contest.

Seven blocks east and one block south of Union Park, the building was less than a ten-minute walk to the ballpark's former site. Byron imagined McGraw and Jennings leaving the boarding house on a summer's morning for Union Park. Perhaps children sitting on the stoops of the row houses along the route recognized the two Orioles and called out to them, maybe asking for their autographs. Byron spoke once with the current occupant of the modest house who, on one trip, he saw standing at the front door talking on the phone. The woman had no idea who John McGraw was but seemed excited to learn that someone "famous" once lived in her home.

Two blocks north and four blocks east of Union Park was another of McGraw's former residences, 2738 St. Paul Street, where he lived with his first wife, Minnie, from 1898 until her death a year and a half later. McGraw's neighbor on St. Paul Street was Wilbert Robinson, who lived with his family next door at 2740. Both buildings were three-story, Queen-Anne-style row houses with glazed-brick fronts, stone trim, and tile roofs. Unlike the former boarding house on West 24th Street, McGraw's home on St. Paul better fitted the stature of the future Hall of Famer. Byron tried on several occasions to meet the owners of McGraw's former home for a possible tour of the home, but the opportunity never presented itself.

Other dead stars' former homes included Hughie Jennings' house at 529 East 23rd Street and Joe Kelley's homes at 530 East 22nd Street and 2826 North Calvert Street. Jennings' home, a brick two-story row house with a curved front, was uninhabited. Plywood covered the front door and windows, as well as the houses attached on either side, the city having taken possession of the properties as part of an urban-renewal project. Kelley's home on East 22nd Street, a three-story, tan-brick row house with a first-floor stone front, was next door to the rectory of St. Ann's Catholic Church, where John McGraw and his second wife, Blanche Sindall, were married in 1902. Kelley's home on North Calvert Street, a three-story Queen Anne row house with tan bricks, was where he died in 1943.

Despite the connections of these dwellings to the old Orioles, Byron neither witnessed nor sensed an other-worldly presence of old ballplayers haunting their former homes. This did not deter Byron, however, from occasionally visiting the sites in the off chance that one day he might find himself in the right place at the right time.

◊ ◊ ◊

On one trip to Baltimore, Byron drove south on North Howard Street to an old brownstone north of Franklin Street near the Maryland Historical Society, two miles south of the players' homes on St. Paul Street. "Five-Nineteen," he said. "There it is." The three-story townhouse long ago had been the Diamond Cafe, owned by McGraw and Robinson. Believed to have been the first sports bar in the country, the cafe included a dining room, reading room, gymnasium, and locker room, as well as space for indoor sports such as duckpin bowling and billiards. An electronic scoreboard displayed the progress of Orioles away games, as well as the results of other baseball contests. When not playing and not on the road, McGraw and Robinson often could be found holding court at the bar with their adoring, paying cranks. Had Baltimore not lost its major-league franchise, McGraw might have remained in Baltimore for his entire career and continued his outside business pursuits there once his playing days were over.

The windows of the brownstone were covered with plywood. Any architectural flourishes that once adorned the building had been ripped from the facade, suggesting the building and the others alongside it were slated for demolition. Byron pulled on plywood covering the front door, hoping perhaps it was loose enough to allow him entry, but it was nailed shut. He walked through an alley mid-block and around to the back side of the Diamond, but he saw no way to gain access to the building without breaking and entering. Not yet desperate enough to risk such a charge, Byron returned to his car.

On the way home that evening, Byron stopped by a local drugstore to pick up some film he had dropped off for developing. Among the 30 rolls he had taken on his various baseball trips were pictures of East 25th Street and Guilford shot on various dates from various angles, pictures of Forbes Field and Honus Wagner's house, Tiger Stadium and Oberlin College, League Park and Cy Young's house. The printed pictures offered Byron few new insights or clues.

Most significant was the picture he thought he had taken of Matty O'Boyle in front of Tiger Stadium. The photograph showed Tiger Stadium, but no Matty, proving either that Matty was a ghost - assuming the old adage that you can't photograph a ghost was true - or that Byron was a lousy photographer.

Byron's picture of Peter Cronin, however, confirmed he wasn't a ghost, again assuming the correctness of the old adage. There was Peter, standing in front of League Park, imaginary bat in hand. It was a great shot, but disheartening nonetheless. When the two had met, Peter told Byron about other believers he had befriended over the years who, eventually, had lost their faith.

Since their meeting, the two had spoken over the phone a few times, but as the weeks passed, their conversations became somewhat strained. To Byron, Peter seemed almost jealous whenever Byron would recount details of his experiences.

The last time they spoke, Peter seemed even more detached. Byron had sent Peter a copy of the picture he had taken and called him a few days later. Their conversation confirmed Byron's worst fears.

"Hey, Peter, it's Byron."

"Byron?"

"Yeah. Byron Bennett. We met at League Park a couple months back."

"We did?"

"Yeah. I was there in May."

"What are you talking about?"

"I'm the Orioles fan. You were wearing that Cleveland Spiders sweatshirt. We talked about League Park and what you had seen there."

"I'm sorry. I don't remember any of this."

"But I sent you a picture in the mail last week. Didn't you get it? It shows you standing next to the ballpark."

"Oh, yeah. I got that picture. I was wondering who took it. I've been to League Park before, but I don't remember anyone taking my picture."

"You don't remember meeting me, telling me about the old ballplayers who play at League Park?"

"I don't remember you, so how could I remember what you say we talked about?"

"And the picture - it doesn't jog your memory?"

"I don't like strangers taking my picture."

"But you posed for the shot - like you were batting."

"Listen. You're the second person who's called me asking questions like this. It's not funny and I don't appreciate it. Don't call again."

"Wait, somebody else called you, too? Who?"

Byron heard Peter hang up the phone without answering.

It's happened, thought Byron. *He doesn't remember a damn thing. What should I do now? I could be next.*

◍ ◍ ◍

Byron had not spoken with Maggie since returning from Detroit. He did not feel right calling her just to tell her more stories she was uninterested in hearing, but what happened to Peter had forced the issue. Gathering his nerve, he called her, asking if she wanted to go with him to a night game at Hagerstown's Municipal Stadium, the first Monday in August. He figured she would have a hard time saying no since she lived near the stadium. He was right.

It had been almost a year since they had seen each other and Maggie surprised Byron with a prolonged hug when they met at the stadium in front of the ticket booth.

"I figured this would be a good place to meet since this is where we first met," said Byron, smiling as they passed through the turnstile. "Remember?"

"I remember."

"Whatever happened to that Suns shirt you were wearing that day?"

"Which one was it?"

"It was orange, sleeveless, said 'Suns' across your . . . you know, the front."

"Oh, I'm sure I got rid of it years ago," said Maggie.

"That's too bad. It looked great on you."

Maggie smiled.

They sat in the second row of box seats behind home plate. The short distance between the grandstand and the batter's box meant they were close enough to tell if the umpire needed deodorant. Whenever a player fouled a ball back toward the protective screen, Maggie flinched while Byron instinctively held out his hands as if to catch it.

"You know, this is a great spot to watch a game," said Byron. "The view here's not much different than the one from the dugout."

"I like that the stadium hasn't changed much since they built it in the 1930's," said Maggie. "It's got a great feel to it."

"You know, you say that kind of stuff and I think, are we all that different?"

"Okay, Byron. Enough of that. So, why did you want to see me, anyway? Still chasing ghosts?"

"I just wanted to see you."

"Oh. Then, we're on a date? There's no ulterior motive?"

"No . . . well, boy, that's a loaded question. There is something I need to talk to you about, but I also wanted to see you."

Maggie sighed. "So, what is it?" she asked.

"When I was in Cleveland, I met someone. Someone who, it turns out, is a lot like me."

"Really? What's her name?"

"Stop it, Maggie - it's a guy."

"Sorry. I couldn't resist. So who's the lucky guy?"

"His name is Peter. I met him when I was at this old ballpark site. We started talking and it turns out he's seen what I've seen, you know, things from the past."

"A kindred spirit."

"Yeah."

"And he was just hanging out there, huh? Does this guy work for a living?"

"I don't know. I guess he does. He gave me his business card. He's President of the Cleveland Spiders Historical Society."

"He must be a very busy man."

"The thing is, I called him a few days ago and he acted like he had no idea what I was talking about - like he had forgotten everything he knows - everything he told me about these lost ballparks."

"Maybe he was making it all up to begin with."

"I don't think so. When I first met him, he told me this might happen."

"What might happen?"

"That he could lose his memory about all this stuff - about what he had seen. He said it happens to everyone after a while and could happen to me, too."

"So there's still hope for you," said Maggie.

"Come on Maggie, I'm serious."

"So am I. It could be the best thing that ever happened to you."

"I probably shouldn't say anything else."

"There's more?"

"Yeah, well, there was this other guy I wanted to tell you about, but I think I better quit while I'm behind."

"You can't say that and expect me not to want to hear what you were going to tell me. Who's your other new friend?"

"Okay, since you asked, but you're not going to like it. His name is James Mathison. I met him at a cemetery in Baltimore."

"A cemetery? Please tell me you were there because somebody died."

"Well, no one recently. I was there visiting John McGraw's grave site."

"So now you're visiting cemeteries of dead ballplayers?"

"Yes. Just let me tell you about Mathison and I won't say anything else."

"Proceed."

"Alright. Mathison - I'm 99 percent certain he's a ghost. He played for the Orioles back in 1902 and works at the cemetery now. He goes by the name of West Consin."

"West Consin?" Maggie asked.

"Yeah. Funny, huh?"

"No, not 'funny, huh?' Listen to what you are saying,

Byron - you met a ghost who works at a cemetery who used to be an Oriole. This is more out there than the guy who forgot what he used to believe."

"I know it sounds a bit crazy."

"A 'bit crazy'? How can you be sure this guy is dead?"

"Well, we didn't shake hands."

"What? You didn't shake hands? What's that supposed to mean?"

"I don't think ghosts can shake real people's hands, or if they can, maybe they're ice cold or something. I don't know."

"Was there anything else that made you think he was dead - like his arm falling off or you could see his bones poking through his shirt?"

"No. It's not like that at all. He looks normal, just old, although he didn't look quite as old as others I've seen. But he knew all about what's happening in these old ballparks - that there are games still being played there. Peter told me the same thing."

Maggie stared out at left field, following the trajectory of a fly ball hit to the Macon Braves' left fielder. "What was that story you told me a long time ago?" she asked. "The one about Babe Ruth, back when you were in high school?"

"Oh, the one where I saw him playing a game at Cardinal Gibbons, on the field where he used to play."

"What do you remember about that game?"

"Well, I saw him hit a home run. I could see the game, the field, the fans. After he rounded the bases, he ran past me and looked right at me. Then he disappeared along with the rest of the game."

"Did you see anything like that on your trip?"

"Kind of, yeah. In Cleveland, I saw League Park as it used to be, but only for a couple minutes. I never actually saw the game, just the stadium and fans waiting in line to get in."

"You really believe all this, don't you?" asked Maggie.

"I do."

"I mean, you're certain."

"I am."

"Okay. Well, okay."

Maggie shifted in her seat to watch the game. Neither one said anything more about what Byron had seen. When the game was over, Byron walked Maggie to her car and gave her a kiss on the cheek. She gave him a hug, although not as prolonged as when she arrived, and when she pulled away, he noticed tears in her eyes.

"You okay?" he asked.

"I'm fine," she said, wiping her eye. "I'll see you, Byron."

Maggie got into her car and Byron closed the door for her.

When he reached his car on the other side of the parking lot, Maggie pulled up beside him.

"Still driving that old Camaro, I see."

"Yup. It's gonna be an antique soon, you know. Wanna' go for a ride?"

"No thanks, Byron. I've already been."

As Maggie pulled away, Byron watched her drive out of the parking lot. He waited until her car disappeared from view before getting into his almost-antique Camaro for the trip home.

CHAPTER 22

@ @ @

The Boys of Summer

During the first week of August, with Bowie playing the Senators in Harrisburg, Pennsylvania, Byron toyed with the idea of taking a quick trip to Philadelphia to visit the former sites of that city's famed lost ballparks: Baker Bowl, home to the Phillies from 1887 to 1938, and Shibe Park (also known as Connie Mack Park), home to the Phillies from 1938 to 1970 and the Athletics from 1909 to 1954. From what he read on the Internet, he knew that the former site of the Baker Bowl was occupied by a gas station with an adjoining empty lot and a two-story International-style industrial building. Several buildings that once surrounded the ballpark remained, including the former Brooks Brothers warehouse on West Leigh Avenue, its distinctive, v-shaped front visible in pictures of the old ballpark, and the Broad Street train station.

On the former site of Shibe Park was the Deliverance Evangelistic Church. Surrounding the mega-church were many of the same row houses that once caused Connie Mack to build a spite fence in right field along North 29th Street to keep fans sitting on rooftops across the street from watching the games for free. A granite statue of Mr. Mack that once sat in a park on Leigh Avenue across from the ballpark long ago had been relocated to a plaza outside Veterans Stadium.

Remembering the time he and a friend were mugged near the Vet after a Bruce Springsteen concert at the Spectrum, Byron decided instead of taking a trip to the City of Brotherly Love, he would head further north to New York City. He had mixed feelings about visiting New York, given that two New York teams had stolen both the Orioles and John McGraw. In many ways the thefts had signaled the death knell of Baltimore baseball 100 years earlier. But Byron hoped his trip might provide a way to bring some of that history back to Baltimore. And his last conversation with Peter had heightened the urgency he felt about making the drive and finding something - anything - hidden within the ruins of the summer game in New York.

Arising early in the morning, Byron made it to New York City in four hours. His first stop was Harlem, the former site of the Polo Grounds, home to three different teams: the National League New York Giants from 1891 to 1957, the New York Yankees from 1913 to 1922, and the New York Mets in 1962 and 1963. Byron drove to Coogan's Bluff at 155th Street and Edgecombe Avenue. The Polo Grounds once were located below the bluff in an area known as Coogan's Hollow. Some of the more famous photographs of the Polo Grounds were taken from the vantage point of the bluff, looking down on the field. Examining the photographs in Ritter's book, Byron recognized several of the white-brick and tan-brick apartment buildings fronting Edgecombe at the top of the bluff.

The park was cordoned off by a dilapidated chainlink fence, exactly as Chuck Stevens had described it. As Byron scaled the enclosure, the interlocking metal mesh wobbled like a flag in a stiff breeze. It collapsed as he reached the top, sending him to the ground on the other side, narrowly avoiding the 40-foot drop into the woods below.

"Dammit," he said as he lay on the ground, examining a gash on his arm and a rip in his t-shirt. *That would have been hard to explain*, he thought, standing up. *I can see the headline now: "Man Plunges To Death Heading To Vanished Polo Grounds."*

Byron followed a dirt path along the fence into the woods where he found the top landing of the John T. Brush Memorial Stairway and made his way down 36 crumpled concrete steps - he counted each one - to the center platform bearing the former owner's name. He was surprised no one had stolen any of the inscription's bronze lettering, given the concrete's deteriorated condition. Desperate for a glimpse of anything paranormal, Byron stood frozen on the platform and stared through a thick maze of trees at the Polo Grounds Towers, a high-rise public-housing complex built on the ballpark's former site. *Chuck said it appeared when he was standing here*, he thought.

After a while, Byron sat down on the stairs. *Why can't I see it? He wasn't even looking for it.* His mind wandered to thoughts about John McGraw, then the Giants, then the Yankees, only to be startled by the voices of several men who were coming up the steps from Harlem River Drive. Byron stood up and three men came into view about 15 steps down the stairway. The men's boisterous talk and rather unkempt appearance suggested to Byron they had nothing to do with baseball or the Polo Grounds and that it was time for him to make his way up the stairway and out of the woods rather than hang around to find out if they had ever seen the Polo Grounds.

As he climbed the stairway toward Coogan's Bluff, he turned around and noticed one of the men had spotted him and was continuing his way up the stairs behind Byron. Uncomfortable with the prospect of being alone on the stairway with the man, Byron quickened his pace.

"Hey, you," yelled the man, his voice agitated. "What the hell you doing sitting in the woods, here? This is our spot."

Byron turned and looked at the man as he continued his climb. *There but for the grace of God go I*, he thought. "I was looking for the Polo Grounds," he said.

"What are you, crazy? You can't see the Polo Grounds. They're gone - 35 years this April."

Byron did the math in his head. *It was 35 years ago.* As he reached the top of the landing, he turned to look at the man, who was making his way back down the steps. "Hey, how'd you know it was 35 years ago?" Byron called to the man.

The man stopped and looked up at Byron. "Because I was a Giants fan and I was there when they tore it down. I got paid to pick up concrete after the demolition and load it into dump trucks. You never forget something like that."

The man turned and continued his descent. Byron realized he had misjudged the man and wished he had made more of an effort to talk to him. Stepping back over the chainlink fence he had knocked down, Byron thought about what the man had said, agreeing with his insightful analysis. *He's right. I am crazy.*

With the locals having retreated to their sanctuary, Byron stood at the top of Coogan's Bluff, looking past Harlem River Drive toward the Polo Grounds Towers and Yankee Stadium, off in the distance, east of the Harlem River.

Byron went back to his car and headed south on 155th Street, taking Harlem River Drive to 8th Avenue and the entrance to the Polo Grounds Towers complex. On his right, he spotted a faded blue sign resting on top of a one-story, flat-roofed brick building fronting 8th Avenue. "Welcome to Polo Grounds Towers," stated the sign. Byron parked his car at a meter, grabbed his copy of *Lost Ballparks*, and proceeded through the black metal gates into the apartment complex. A stolid 30-story, red-brick apartment building now desecrated the site of the demolished ballpark, stealing any sense of the national pastime or of its having once been played there.

A sign for "Willie Mays Field" marked the former location of centerfield, now a recreation area consisting of six asphalt basketball courts. Byron opened *Lost Ballparks* to page 164 to look at the picture of Willie Mays's famous basket catch of Vic Wertz's line drive, taken at the Polo Grounds during the 1954 World Series. *Basket catch, basketball,* he thought. *Maybe that's why they built these courts here.*

Byron took a picture of the sign and the basketball courts before heading in the direction of home plate. He knew what to look for, having seen on the Internet a picture of a bronze plaque marking home plate's approximate location attached to the base of one of the apartment building's concrete pillars. Byron flipped through the pages of *Lost Ballparks,* studying various pictures of the Polo Grounds, trying to determine the boundaries of the old infield. If the placard was correct, it appeared the apartment building sat squarely atop the infield. In hopes of finding third base, Byron checked several outside doors, but they all were locked. He watched two women enter the building through one of the side doors but decided against following them in. From the current lay of the land, third base would have sat within one of the first floor apartments and Byron did not like the implications of asking residents who resided nearby whether he could have a look around.

With nothing left to see and apparently no ballplayers to be found, Byron departed Coogan's Hollow in search of his next stop, Hilltop Park. As he turned onto Broadway in the direction of Washington Heights, he thought about the Drifter's hit song about that famous boulevard. The stretch of Broadway on which he was driving, some 120 blocks north of Times Square, offered little in the way of neon lights or magic in the air. Ninety years earlier, however, the area was magical, even without any neon, for perched on a hill overlooking the Hudson River at the southwest corner of Broadway and 168th Street was Hilltop Park, where the New York Baltimore Orioles - *a.k.a.* the New York Highlanders and later renamed the Yankees - played from 1903 to 1912.

Byron left his car double-parked next to a meter on 165th Street and ran across the street to the New York Presbyterian/ Columbia Medical Center. *Why did it have to be a hospital?* he wondered, as he studied the buildings and tried to get his bearings. Byron had never felt comfortable around hospitals and it had nothing to do with the food. His grandfather, to whom he was very close, had spent his last few weeks tied with tubes to a hospital bed. This left a lasting impression on Byron. The birth and loss of his son at Washington County Hospital in Hagerstown only added to the sadness he felt around hospitals.

His unease had kept him from making the one-hour drive from Ellicott City to Howard University Hospital in Washington, D.C., the former site of Griffith Stadium, home of the Washington Senators from 1911 to 1961. Although home plate was once located in what was now the hospital's emergency room, he had no interest in seeing it. Given his proclivity for visiting cemeteries in search of ghosts, however, Byron's continued uneasiness around hospitals seemed a bit arbitrary, even to him.

Walking the grounds of Columbia Presbyterian, it was clear to Byron nothing remained of Hilltop Park. Erected in the 1920's, the medical center engulfed the entire site. Flipping through the pages of *Lost Ballparks*, he recognized in one photo-graph a trio of brick, walk-up apartment buildings beyond what was once left field. Those six-story buildings remained at the corner of 168th and Broadway, housing offices, a restaurant, and Melbran's Pharmacy.

South of 168th Street, a garden in the middle of the medical center included a bronze plaque noting the approximate location of home plate. The New York Yankees donated the plaque to the hospital, unveiling it in 1993 during a dedication attended by former Highlanders' pitcher Chet Hoff, who was then 102 years old. Mr. Hoff went on to become the oldest ex-major-leaguer ever before his death five years later.

The medical center's chapel was constructed on what once was the right side of the ballpark's infield. *A true "church of baseball,"* Byron thought. He considered this to be glorious use of the land, in stark contrast to the garages and parking lot covering Union Park's former ballfield. Although it pained him to admit it, Byron was impressed the Yankees had seen fit to memorialize the location of the franchise's second home. He wondered whether the team would be willing to place a similar marker in Baltimore at the McDonald's parking lot at East 29th Street and Greenmount – the franchise's first home.

There being nothing left of the old ballpark, Byron had little interest in determining whether any old ballplayers were hanging about, even though he saw several candidates being pushed around the hospital courtyard in wheelchairs. Before departing Columbia Presbyterian, Byron took pictures of the bronze marker and the church.

Returning to his car on 165th Street, Byron was relieved to find that New York's finest had left no souvenir of his visit to Hilltop Park on his windshield. As he made his way out of Manhattan, heading southeast on 155th Street, he again spied Yankee Stadium looming in the distance. Once across the

Macomb Dam Bridge, which brought him into the Bronx, he found himself face-to-face with the House that Ruth Built. *They sure named that bridge right*, thought Byron. *Damn Yankees - Dam Bridge*. Byron gave the stadium several long looks as he eased onto the Major Deegan Expressway. As the stadium receded from view, he hummed a solemn version of "(You've Gotta Have) Heart."

Approaching the Triborough Bridge, stuck in slow-moving traffic, Byron pondered his trip to New York, wondering why so little of New York's baseball past had revealed itself to him. He wondered why Chuck Stevens had seen the Polo Grounds when he wasn't even looking for it, yet Byron had seen nothing at all. As traffic crept along the Brooklyn-Queens Expressway, Byron thought about how much the city of Brooklyn once loved its Dodgers. He hoped for better baseball karma as he arrived in New York City's most populous borough.

After a few wrong turns put him in one of the more deflated-looking sections of Bedford Stuyvesant, Byron headed south to Park Slope, where he found the remains of Washington Park – a spectacular (at least to Byron) 20-foot-high, white-washed brick wall on Third Avenue, between First and Third Streets. Built by team owner Charles Ebbets, Washington Park was, from 1898 to 1912, home to the borough's National League franchise, known as the Bridegrooms, later as the Superbas, and then as the Trolley Dodgers.

In 1899, former Baltimore Orioles Willie Keeler, Joe Kelley, and Hughie Jennings played for the home team in Washington Park. Orioles' owner Harry Von Der Horst had sent the three players, along with manager Ned Hanlon, to Brooklyn at the end of the 1898 season. At the time, Von Der Horst was part owner of both the Baltimore and Brooklyn franchises and decided the time had come for his Brooklyn team to win a championship – at the expense of his Baltimore franchise. His scheme worked, and Brooklyn won the National League pennant in 1899 and 1900, due largely to the superior play of those three Orioles and the skills of their ex-Orioles' skipper.

No historic marker noted the significance of Washington Park's brick wall, even though the relic was believed by some to be the oldest baseball structure still standing in its original location. To the untrained eye, the wall itself seemed rather pedestrian and was easily missed. To Byron, however, the unimposing wall was a priceless artifact. As with his visit to the Polo Grounds, Byron saw no old ballplayers loitering along Third Avenue, although he did make contact with a security guard sitting inside a small shack in the Con-Edison yard occupying the site. Byron was disappointed to learn the man had no clue he was guarding the former site of a major-league ballpark or that he was sitting in the approximate location of left field. The guard also had no interest in Byron providing him additional fun facts about Washington Park. He did, however, offer to take Byron's camera from him if he didn't stop photographing the Con-Edison yard. Apparently, Byron's obsession had made him a security risk.

Sensing the need to move on, and with the afternoon sun beginning to soften, Byron made his way three miles southeast to Brooklyn's Flatbush section. Ebbets Field Apartments, a public-housing project rising some 22 stories above the former playing field, now occupied the former site of famed Ebbets Field, home of the Brooklyn Dodgers from 1913 to 1957. Byron was certain that of all the famous, lost baseball palaces, Ebbets Field was the one park most likely to be teeming with old ballplayers. Again, he was mistaken.

A sign in the courtyard of the housing complex perhaps said it best:

Please NO
Ball Playing
Dogs Allowed
Bicycle Riding
This Area For Tenants Of Ebbets Field Apts Only

No ball playing, indeed, thought Byron.

Byron walked the perimeter of the site – Sullivan Place to Bedford Avenue to Montgomery Street to McKeever Place. Opposite the ballpark site on McKeever were Jackie Robinson Elementary School and Ebbets Field Middle School, both built in the 1960's. Several buildings that once surrounded the ballpark remained. From a picture of Ebbets Field in *Lost Ballparks*, Byron recognized a four-story walk-up with an attached one-story pharmacy that sat just beyond the right-field fence. He likewise recognized a one-story building housing a Firestone tire store and several other single-story buildings farther down Bedford, all remaining from the era of Ebbets Field.

Byron's half-hour stroll around Ebbets Field rendered nothing other than some photographs and a five-minute chat with one of Brooklyn's finest as to why Byron was circling the block of a public-housing project, taking pictures. Byron kept his composure the entire five minutes, never once uttering the words "ghost" or "old ballplayer," talking instead about his love of baseball and the old Brooklyn Dodgers.

Before departing for the trip home, Byron had one last stop in Brooklyn – the famed, if elusive, Ebbets Field flagpole. Famed because, according to *metaphysicalbaseball.com*, when Ebbets Field was torn down in February 1960, the centerfield flagpole was preserved and relocated to a Veterans of Foreign Wars Hall somewhere in Brooklyn. Elusive because none of the borough's several VFW halls made any mention of the flag pole or its location on their respective websites, leaving its whereabouts unknown.

Byron spent the final hour and a half of his trip driving the claustrophobic streets of Brooklyn, visiting as many VFW halls as he could find. Byron had assumed the location of the famed Ebbets Field flagpole would be common knowledge amongst any and all veterans he might meet within the VFW halls of Brooklyn. It wasn't. None of the veterans he spoke with had any idea what he was talking about. With daylight disappearing more quickly than parents dropping their kids at daycare, Byron did something against his nature. He gave up. Tired and frustrated, he checked his map and found the most direct route out of Brooklyn.

On his way out of town, however, the baseball gods, perhaps sensing Byron's disappointment, smiled down upon him. Driving south on Utica Street toward the Belt Parkway, Byron caught glimpse of a flagpole in front of a one-story, red-brick building. He pulled his car over to the curb for a closer look. A plastic banner hanging from the roof identified the building's current occupants – the Canarsie Casket Company. The banner partially obscured another sign, carved in granite and set into the building's brick wall.

Getting out of his car, Byron spotted the letters "VFW" to the left of the banner. At the base of the flag pole, also carved in granite, was the following inscription:

Center Field Flag Pole
of
Ebbets Field
Donated By
Kratter Corp.

With the famed Ebbets Field flagpole elusive no more, Byron did little to hide his elation. A woman who appeared to be in her late fifties stopped on the sidewalk in front of Canarsie Casket Company so as not to block Byron's shot as he took several photographs of the famed Ebbets Field flag pole.

"Would ya' like me to take your picture next to the flag pole, mister?" asked the woman in her thick Brooklyn accent.

"That'd be great," said Byron. "This flag pole used to be at Ebbets Field, you know."

"Really? I had no idea," said the woman. "I walk by here every day and I never once paid that flag pole any attention."

Byron stood next to the flag pole, making sure not to block the granite inscription as the woman took his picture.

"You know my father used to take me to Ebbets Field when I was a little girl. He loved the Dodgers."

"You went to Ebbets Field? You're lucky."

"My father was a police officer. Sometimes the Dodgers would pay him to stand on the field to keep an eye on the crowd. That's when he'd take me. He'd find me an empty seat close to where he was standing and stick me in it. That way I'd get to watch my dad and the game."

"Do you remember seeing Jackie Robinson?"

"I do. Jackie, Pee Wee, the Duke, Campy, Gil Hodges. I saw 'em all."

The woman read the inscription at the base of the famed Ebbets Field flag pole. "You know, I remember Mr. Kratter," said the woman, pointing to the words "Kratter Corp." encased in the granite inscription.

"Who was he?" asked Byron.

"Marvin Kratter - he's the guy who tore down Ebbets Field. He was in real estate. My mother worked a year or two for him."

"I take it Mr. Kratter wasn't well-liked in Brooklyn?" asked Byron.

"Nah, he was okay. It wasn't his fault the Dodgers left. It was O'Malley's fault. At least Mr. Kratter left us the flag pole."

"Gotta give him credit for that," said Byron.

"Well, better be on my way, nice talkin' with ya," said the woman.

Byron gave a short wave goodbye as the woman made her way down Utica Street. Before heading back to his car, Byron took a picture of the Canarsie Casket sign.

Sadly, the future of the famed Ebbets Field flag pole appeared uncertain, for next to the sidewalk, in front of the flag pole, was a "Building For Sale" sign.

Brooklyn baseball fans never could catch a break (with the exception of 1955). A sign hanging in the courtyard of the Ebbets Field Apartments taunted that ball playing there was not allowed. Likewise, the famed Ebbets Field flagpole – the one piece of Ebbets Field remaining in Brooklyn – resided in front of a building that manufactured caskets, at least for the moment. Life is full of irony, much of which goes undetected. Not so for Brooklyn, Ebbets Field, and its famed flagpole.

CHAPTER 23

Rounding Third and Heading for Home

During the Baysox's final home stand, Hank asked Byron to join him for a late dinner at Rips. Although Hank clearly had something he needed to say, Byron dominated the conversation, talking about his favorite subject.

"Did you know McGraw and Jennings were best friends, on and off the field?"

"I think you've told me that before."

"They roomed together when they were players. In fact, Jennings was McGraw's best man at his wedding, and Keeler and Kelley were his groomsmen."

"That's great."

"Did you know both McGraw and Jennings attended Allegany College in New York, although neither graduated?"

"I've never even heard of Allegany College."

"That's because it's now St. Bonaventure University. Did you know they established the school's winter baseball program?"

"I did not."

"And the school's baseball complex? It's named in honor of their famous alumni."

"If they didn't graduate, are they still alumni?"

"They're alumni even if they didn't earn a degree."

"I think you're wrong."

"I bet I could have made that team," said Byron.

"St. Bonaventure's?"

"No, the Orioles, the National League Orioles."

"I'll bet you could have, Bitty," said Hank.

"I'm just as tall as any one of them old Orioles."

"I'm sure you are, Bitty."

"Man, you know I hate it when you call me Bitty."

"I know, Bitty."

"What about you, do you think you could have made that team?"

"You know I never played much baseball and, besides, I could never hit a curve ball," said Hank.

"Couldn't hit the ol' curve, eh? Now Keeler, there's a guy who knew how to hit just about anything they threw at him. If you were an infielder, you had to know where to play him. Either back, to catch any ball he might try to slap over your head, or up, in case he tried to bunt."

"Keeler was an Oriole?" asked Hank.

"One of the best."

"You know, Byron, you've got to stop obsessing about the past."

"I'm not obsessing about the past. I'm a historian! That's what we do. If you loved baseball like I do, I'm sure you'd feel the same way."

"I doubt it. Anyway, there's something I need to tell you." Hank pulled his chair closer to the table, suggesting to Byron the import of what he was about to say. "I'm not sure you've heard yet, but the Baysox are for sale and it looks like they've found a new ownership group who'll be coming in this winter."

"I heard rumors about that."

"If that does happens, I'll be out the door."

"Are you sure?"

"Yes, I hear the new owners are bringing in their own people. But that means the same thing could happen to you."

"This isn't good," said Byron.

"You should be okay for at least a couple of months. It's going to take them a while to figure out the lay of the land. But, if I were you, I'd keep all this talk about the old Orioles to yourself. You don't want to give them a reason to let you go."

"Is there a problem?"

"No, not as far as I'm concerned. You're a great worker. But I'm not sure another GM would have the patience to put up with all your idiosyncrasies."

"'Idiosyncrasies,' huh? Oh, I get your point, 'idiots and crazies.'"

"That's not what I meant."

"I know. I was joking. I tend to do that when I'm nervous."

"You must be nervous all the time, then."

"I heard rumblings about a sale, but I hear stuff like that every year," said Byron.

"This time, I think it's for real."

"Well, if you do end up leaving, I know you'll land somewhere else," said Byron. "Hell, you'll probably have something lined up by the end of the winter meetings."

"Let me know if there's anything I can do. I'd be glad to give you a reference. Depending on where I end up, maybe I can find a spot for you, too."

"Thanks, Hank."

They both sat quietly for a few awkward moments. Then Hank slid his chair out and pushed himself away from the table. "Listen - I have to get back."

"Well, I'll see you."

"Goodnight, Byron."

Byron stayed behind and finished his coffee. He thought about what he could do if he lost his job. It was inertia, plain and simple, that kept him at Bowie. He already had been through one change of ownership and survived. But he sensed things could be different this time.

Walking across the gravel parking lot behind Rips, Byron noticed someone had written "Go O's" in the dust on his car windshield. Byron recognized it as Hank's handy work.

On the way home, Byron turned on WBAL to listen to the Orioles-Indians game. The Birds' once promising season had turned sour with their record at 60 wins and 73 losses. Orioles' relief pitcher Jose Reyes gave up three runs in the top of the seventh and the O's were losing 7-6. Byron figured the Orioles would reach 74 losses by the time he made it home. Already depressed at the thought of being unemployed, he turned off the radio. He had a hard time listening to Orioles games when his team was losing.

After arriving home, Byron picked up his copy of the *Baltimore Sun*, which had been lying on the sidewalk the entire day and was faded from the sun.

Once inside, he dropped the paper on the kitchen table and sat down to look through the classifieds. *Guess I need to get serious about finding a job this winter.*

After scanning the want ads, he turned to the obituaries, a section he perused whenever he read the paper.

Amongst the listings of former teachers, county workers, volunteers, and homemakers, one obituary stood out:

"Tim Murphy, 87, Noted Baltimore Groundskeeper."

There was no mistaking the picture. "Oh God!" said Byron. "It's Murph. He's dead!"

Murph's obituary stated:

> *Timothy J. Murphy, 87, a former groundskeeper for the Baltimore Orioles during the 1950's and 1960's, died August 30 at his home in Baltimore. He had kidney failure.*

Beginning in the 1930's, Mr. Murphy worked for the City of Baltimore performing maintenance for what is now the Department of Recreation and Parks. In 1947, he was assigned as one of three groundskeepers responsible for maintaining the city's Municipal Stadium. He assisted in the city's renovation and expansion of the stadium, renamed Memorial Stadium, and oversaw its transition to a major-league facility in 1954.

Mr. Murphy was appointed head groundskeeper of Memorial Stadium in 1958, a position in which he served until his retirement in 1969. He earned much praise as groundskeeper, not only for his excellence in maintaining Memorial Stadium's ballfield, but also for his beautification of the stadium surroundings through the planting of flower gardens and flowering bushes and trees.

With his appointment as head groundskeeper for the Orioles, Mr. Murphy followed in the footsteps of his great-uncle Thomas Murphy, a groundskeeper for the champion National League Baltimore Orioles of the 1890's.

Mr. Murphy was a lifelong resident of Baltimore. Upon his retirement, he volunteered for the City of Baltimore, helping with maintenance of the city's youth baseball parks, as well as sponsoring a youth baseball team for some 20 years in the Harwood section of the city. Even long after his retirement as groundskeeper, it was common to see former ballplayers, professionals and little leaguers alike, visiting Mr. Murphy at his home in Harwood.

Murph's death notice appeared on the opposite page. It made no mention of any living relatives or decedents:

Viewing at James E. Lincoln Funeral Home, 108 W. North Ave, Baltimore, September 3 from 5 to 6 p.m. Services will be held at St. Ann's Roman Catholic Church, 528 E. 22nd Street, Baltimore, September 4 at 10 a.m. Interment New Cathedral Cemetery, Baltimore.

Byron's eyes filled with tears. For reasons he found hard to explain, he cried for several minutes. He wondered why Murph's death made him feel so sad, for he barely knew the man. They'd met just once, talking briefly. Perhaps it was because, with Murph gone, he feared he had lost his one, last chance of uncovering the mystery surrounding Union Park. Having been unable to locate Mac, Byron saw Murph as his last tangible link to that era.

Getting up from his chair, he paced back and forth through the living room. As he thought about Murph, Byron realized Murph's death answered several questions. He knew now Murph was a lifer, like him, not a ghost. He also knew Murph was a grounds-keeper at Memorial Stadium, just as Mac had told him. He knew Murph was a relative of Tom Murphy, the former groundskeeper at Union Park, living in a house built on the ground where his great uncle once worked. He wondered whether the ballplayers that hung around Murph's house were ghosts at all or, instead, as mentioned in his obituary, were former, living players or little leaguers who'd come by to pay him a visit.

Byron clipped Murph's death notice from the paper and slipped it inside his wallet. Byron's mood brightened as he realized that Murph's death, while sad, may have provided a new opening for him. Maybe he would see Mac at the wake. Maybe others, too, would come.

⚾ ⚾ ⚾

Byron arrived 20 minutes before Murph's wake was set to begin. The parking lot next to the Lincoln Funeral Home on West North Avenue was almost empty, giving him his pick of spaces. Byron parked his car in a far corner of the lot, away from the building, and waited with the motor and air-conditioner running. He watched other people enter and, at 5 p.m., got out of his car and walked across the mostly deserted parking lot to the front of the funeral home.

He passed a man and a woman smoking cigarettes outside the entrance to the funeral home, presumably mourners taking a break from paying their respects. *Nothing like tempting fate*, thought Byron, as he waved away a cloud of smoke that had gathered around the front steps.

A man in a dark-blue, three-piece pinstriped suit greeted Byron as he came through the threshold. With a greying black Afro and mutton chop whiskers, the man looked as if he could have been Eddie Murray's uncle. The man's wide lapels suggested he was stuck in the 1970's.

"Good afternoon," said the man in a soft, low voice.

"Good afternoon," said Byron in an equally soft, equally low voice. "I'm here for Murph's viewing."

"You mean Mr. Murphy?"

"Yes, sorry, Mr. Murphy."

"Yes, sir, parlor number two on your right."

"Are any of Mr. Murphy's relatives here?" asked Byron.

"I'm not certain he had any, sir. I believe his viewing was arranged by an acquaintance."

"Who?"

"I'm not at liberty to say, sir, sorry."

Byron walked into the parlor and there, to his left, was Murph. Byron never felt at ease attending open-casket viewings, staring down at the deceased's lifeless body, the face caked in pasty makeup. The whole ritual seemed to him a bit odd – people making small talk about the deceased while the corpse remained on display a few feet from the chit-chatting mourners.

Murph's viewing was a quiet affair. Byron thought back to the wake he had attended for Maggie's father - the hundreds of people crammed inside the tiny Hagerstown funeral home, Maggie and her mother standing nearby, greeting mourners and accepting their condolences, Maggie crying on Byron's shoulder in the sitting room off the main parlor.

For Murph, there was no receiving line or anyone to speak with as Byron approached to pay his respects. It was one of the downsides of dying at such an advanced age: by outliving most of his peers, few were left to see him off.

An elderly couple Byron did not recognize stood next to the casket with their heads bowed. After the couple departed, Byron knelt on the padded kneeler next to the casket. He stared at Murph's large, ancient hands folded across his body, not knowing what to say. Given recent events, he figured he should have no trouble talking to dead people. However, looking down at Murph's lifeless body, he was at a loss for words.

"Well, Murph, you're in a better place now," Byron mumbled, sounding perfunctory. "You lived a long life and I'm sure you'll be missed. Rest in peace."

As he stood up, Byron made the sign of the cross and walked back toward the entrance to the parlor. Expecting more people to be coming through the parlor door any minute, and hoping to see someone he recognized, Byron sat down in an embroidered arm chair inside the parlor next to the entrance. Byron waited, hoping for Mac to come walking into the parlor, but he never did.

During the next half hour or so, 17 people – Byron counted each one - filed through Murph's parlor in the Lincoln Funeral Home. It would have been 19, but one couple entered the wrong parlor and left after realizing their mistake. Byron recognized no one. Where was Mac? Where were all those grateful ballplayers mentioned in the *Baltimore Sun?*

By six o'clock, Byron had been alone in the parlor for over 20 minutes. Just him and Murph. Eddie Murray's uncle walked into the parlor and stood behind Byron to his left. Byron sensed it was time to leave, so he stood up. As he walked toward the exit, the woman he had run into at Murph's house the previous May hurried by.

"Hello," said Byron, as she passed. "Sorry about your loss."

The woman stopped and looked at Byron. "Thanks," she said. "Do I know you?"

"We met a few months back, at your house. I was looking for Murph. You came through the front door and ran into me."

"Oh, you. Yes, I remember. Well, if you'll excuse me, I've got to pay my respects."

After leaving the funeral home, Byron drove the six blocks up Charles Street, turning right onto East 25th Street. As Byron passed Murph's house, he wondered what secrets Murph took with him to his grave. Who were those ballplayers mentioned in the *Baltimore Sun?* Where were they now?

Byron pulled into the parking lot of the still-closed Stone Tavern, made a U-turn, and headed west on East 25th Street. Driving back to Ellicott City, he was thoroughly depressed. He thought about Murph and how he had lived his whole life, and yet, in the end, only a handful of people had shown up to see him off. Feeling macabre, Byron thought about his own life and how he had nothing to show for it. He feared he would end up the same way – no wife, no children, no grandchildren, alone in a rented house surrounded by mountains of baseball crip crap.

Lying in bed, awaiting sleep, Byron dreaded the idea of attending Murph's funeral the next day. If more people had come to the viewing, Byron might not have felt compelled to attend; however, given the circumstances, Byron knew it was the least he could do. Inasmuch as Mac hadn't bothered to show up at Murph's viewing, he doubted Mac would be at the funeral, either.

⚾ ⚾ ⚾

Byron arrived at St. Ann's Catholic Church half an hour before the service was set to begin. The church was located at East 22nd Street and Greenmount Avenue, next door to Joe Kelley's former row house and three blocks south and two blocks west of the former site of Union Park. It was a fitting place for Murph's funeral service, given its proximity to the old park and its old Orioles connection as the sight of McGraw's second marriage.

The gothic-revival church, constructed of grey stone and white marble, had two steeples, one soaring high above the church to the right of the front entrance and a second, of lesser height, behind and to the left of the entrance. A pointed stone archway made of alternating blocks of marble and stone framed a set of red-painted doors decorated with ornate iron hinges. A simple yet elegant rose window, framed by a similar stone archway centered above the entrance, added an understated flourish to the front of the church.

"Anchored In Faith" announced the white plastic lettering of the church's marquee sign next to the sidewalk. The reference to "anchored" was a pun, for resting alongside the cornerstone to the right of the entranceway was a large, gold-painted, allegorical anchor once belonging to Captain William Kennedy, Commander of the Baltimore clipper ship *The Wanderer*. Kennedy prayed for safe return when caught in a storm off the coast of Vera Cruz and had promised to build a church should his prayers be answered. They were, and Kennedy kept his promise, providing the land and money to build St. Ann's.

The good Captain was buried beneath the main floor of the church, along with his wife, both of whom died in 1873, the year the church was built. Byron stepped lightly overtop Captain Kennedy's marble grave marker in the floor and took a seat in one of the tall, stiff wooden pews located underneath the many arched columns bracing the church's vaulted ceiling.

Other people trickled in, taking seats in the front half of the church - more than had attended Murph's viewing the previous night, although not as many as Byron had hoped for. Other than the woman who lived in Murph's house, Byron recognized no one at the service. Byron overheard two elderly gentlemen sitting in the pew behind him talking about Murph. Byron asked them how they knew Murph and was told they worked with him at Memorial Stadium. Byron asked if they knew Mac, remembering Mac's claim to have worked there as well, but neither man recognized Mac's name.

After the reading about Lazarus's emergence from his tomb,

Byron listened to the priest's standard life and death homily, his words suggesting he did not know Murph very well, if at all. The service included Liturgy of the Eucharist. In bemused silence, Byron watched the confused faces of those sitting around him who clearly were unfamiliar with the Order of the Mass. After the service ended, the 40 or so in attendance waited as Eddie Murray's uncle and another pallbearer from the funeral home wheeled Murph's pall-covered casket up the aisle. A cool, stiff breeze hit everyone as they filed slowly out of the church, an early warning of the impending change in seasons.

The paltry procession of cars following the hearse to New Cathedral Cemetery made its way through the entrance on Old Frederick Road, pausing for a moment in front of the white clapboard house. Starting up again, the vehicles followed in orderly fashion as the hearse slowed approaching John McGraw's mausoleum. Although the decrease in speed was due to the narrow right turn beyond the mausoleum, Byron liked to think it was because the lead driver knew the significance of the gravesite to his right.

After winding back around the other side of the hill, the procession stopped in front of marble steps leading to Joe Kelley's grave. Byron waited in his car as Murph's casket was removed from the hearse, then he joined the procession once it proceeded on foot up the marble steps. A freshly dug grave underneath a white, pop-up canopy awaited Murph's arrival, five plots from Joe Kelley.

How fitting, thought Byron. He looked around at the others gathered next to Murph's grave, but he saw no one with whom he felt he could share the coincidence.

A cool wind swept across the cemetery as the priest read from the book of Genesis:

*By the sweat of your face shall you get bread
to eat, until you return to the ground, from
which you were taken; For you are dirt, and
to dirt you shall return.*

Byron thought about these words, certain that Murph, himself a groundskeeper, would have appreciated the biblical passage. His sadness at Murph's passing and at the small number of people who had stopped to notice again brought tears to his eyes as the priest finished the final prayer.

Once Murph's remains were lowered into the ground, those gathered around took turns tossing handfuls of dirt on top of his casket. Byron imagined, in contrast, the throngs of people who must have attended McGraw's burial at New Cathedral. He turned away from Murph's gravesite and looked up across the hill toward where McGraw was interred and was surprised to see perhaps 100 men at the top of the hill, looking solemnly toward Murph's grave. Many in the group were wearing baseball uniforms – not the tight fitting, polyester uniforms worn by modern-day players, but, rather, the baggy, wool uniforms of yesteryear.

"Oh, my Lord," he said. He looked around at the others in attendance to see if anyone had heard him.

"It's okay," said a woman standing next to him. "He's in a better place."

Byron nodded at the woman and then looked up again at the top of the hill.

That's amazing, he thought, *look at them all.* Byron took a deep breath, finally contented at the scene before him.

As the priest concluded the service, the sound of bagpipes lilted over the hill, emanating from somewhere within the group of men. Byron recognized the tune, "When Irish Eyes Are Smiling." It brought a smile across his face, for he knew Murph was not forgotten and those who perhaps knew him best had returned to pay their respects. Byron was certain that, among those standing beside Murph's casket, only he could hear the sound of the bagpipes, for no one there gave any notice to the music or to the men in the distance.

The priest turned away from the grave and those gathered around him followed him back toward their cars. As the bagpipe's final refrains faded, Byron took a few steps in the direction of the players. Before he could make his way very far, the players faded too. Byron continued his climb anyway. When he reached the top, he was alone amongst the headstones. Looking down on the other side of the hill, Byron could see the green copper roof of McGraw's mausoleum.

Byron walked back down the hill, stopping for a moment at Murph's grave.

Byron heard someone behind him. "Thanks for coming." It was Jimmy Mathison, or West Consin, depending upon your frame of reference, ready to complete his work. "I know Murph appreciated your being here."

"I wanted to come."

"You're not an old ballplayer, are you?" Jimmy asked.

Byron, startled by Jimmy's question, responded: "No, not yet. I'm just a fan."

Mathison nodded and then slowly offered a slight smile.

Passing Joe Kelley's grave, Byron noticed the baseball he had left there earlier that summer and realized he had forgotten to bring a ball for Wilbert Robinson's headstone. Byron promised himself that, next time, he would be certain to bring two baseballs, one for Robinson and one for Murph.

CHAPTER 24

Boston Bean Eaters

The last weekend in September, with the regular season drawing to a close, the Orioles were scheduled to play a four-game series against the Boston Red Sox at Fenway Park. Although Byron had purchased tickets for him and Charles when they first went on sale back in January, all he was able to buy for that Saturday game were two obstructed-view seats. Such was the fervor for baseball in Boston.

In preparation for the trip, Byron had researched Boston's many lost ballparks, identifying three sites he wanted to visit – the Huntington Avenue Grounds, the South End Grounds, and Braves Field. However, as the day of the trip drew near, Byron abandoned his plans to visit those sites, not wanting to hear any more lectures from Charles about how he was living in the past or how he had screwed up his life.

Byron and Charles left for Boston on a Thursday morning, the last full week of September. The trip would take eight hours by car. Along the way, Charles sensed a change in Byron and was surprised to learn he had brought none of his research about any of Boston's lost ballparks.

"What do you mean we're not stopping at Braves Field?" demanded Charles somewhere between exits one and two on the New Jersey Turnpike. "I want to see those old ballpark sites and so do you."

"You tell me all the time I need to stop living in the past," said Byron, "that baseball should be a hobby, not an obsession."

"I know I do," said Charles. "It should be, but that doesn't mean you should abandon your interest in baseball history altogether. Look at me, I'm just as fascinated by it as you. I'm just not gullible enough to think that if I squint my eyes real hard and click my heels three times, I can see the past."

"And that's why I didn't bring anything with me," said Byron. "I don't want you making fun of me, especially if something should happen."

"Listen to me! You're Bitty Byron Bennett! You've been planning this trip for months. You're *going* to visit those old ballparks. It's what you *do*. Besides, with me there, nothing's gonna happen."

"Okay," said Byron. "If you promise not to give me a hard time."

"I promise."

The two drove another 10 miles, each not saying a word. Charles flipped through a Boston area guide book while Byron stared straight ahead, his hands gripping the steering wheel. As they passed exit three on the turnpike, Byron noticed a sign for Camden and started thinking again about the Orioles.

"You know, there is something I haven't told you," said Byron, breaking the silence. "Now that you're not being judgmental. Wanna hear it?"

"Be my guest. It's a long way to Boston."

"I went to Tim Murphy's funeral last week."

"Who?"

"The old groundskeeper at Memorial Stadium."

"Oh, yeah, I saw in the paper he died. He came to the museum once and gave a talk a few years back. Nice guy."

"Nice guy? Not to speak ill of the dead, but he was a jerk

when I met him."

"When did you meet him?"

"That first day I went to Union Park. He told me to get the hell off his property."

"His property?"

"Yeah. Remember that house I showed you where I thought Union Park's home plate used to be?"

"I do."

"Well, that was his house."

"Huh, that's funny. You know, his uncle used to be the groundskeeper at Union Park."

"I didn't know that until I read it in the paper. Anyway, I went to his burial at New Cathedral Cemetery and I saw the most amazing thing: all these old ballplayers in uniform standing at the top of the hill looking down as his casket was lowered into the ground."

"I hadn't heard about that. Did you recognize anyone?"

"No. When I started to head up the hill, they all disappeared."

"Disappeared?"

"Yeah. They vanished into thin air."

"Oh, man. Not again."

"Remember - no passing judgment. Be like Maggie, just listen."

"You haven't told Maggie any of this, have you?"

"No, I haven't spoken to her since before Murph's funeral."

"Well, you must have told her something. She was pretty upset when she called me last week."

"She did seem a little sad the last time I saw her."

"When was that?"

"A couple of months ago - we went to a game in Hagerstown. We talked about what she was doing and I told her about my trip to Detroit. Everything seemed fine until we were leaving."

"I take it you told her about League Park?"

"Yeah. I told her even more than I've told you, since you don't seem to want to hear it. Maggie may not believe it, either, but at least she listens *without* passing judgment."

"From the conversation I had with her, I'd say she's passed some judgment now," said Charles.

"What do you mean?"

"She told me she wishes things were different between you and her."

"Different? How?"

"You know, different. As in the way it was when you guys first met. But she knows that's not realistic because it would require you to change."

"Come on. She's not interested in me like that, not anymore. We're just friends." Byron paused a moment. "We are just friends, right?"

"I didn't get that feeling from her this time. She seemed more than just concerned about you."

"Wait . . . I'm the one who wished things could be different, not her," Byron said, pointing to himself. "She moved on a long time ago."

"Sometimes people move back."

"Wow. You mean after all these years, she wants *me* back?"

"That's the impression I got."

"Well, what should I do?"

"Maybe it's time for you to stop all this nonsense."

Byron sighed. "I can't. Not now. I'm getting too close. Besides, she's right. I can't change who I am."

"Of course you can. You stopped drinking, didn't you? That was an addiction, too. Like baseball is now."

"It's not the same thing at all. I've been seeing things like this since I was a kid. There's stuff I've never told you. I can't stop seeing what I see. And even if I could just walk away, I know I'd end up regretting it."

"You've spent the last fifteen years regretting what happened between you and Maggie. Now you have the chance to fix it, but you can't have both."

"I've got to see this through."

"It's your decision, but I think you're making the wrong one."

They arrived in Boston late in the afternoon and checked into a hotel in Dorchester, five miles south of downtown. Friday morning, they caught the subway, or "the T" as the locals called it, to Northeastern University, arriving at the corner of Huntington Avenue and Opera Place, the former site of the Huntington Avenue Grounds. From 1901 to 1911, the ballpark was home to the American League Boston Americans, later to be named the Red Sox.

Not sure what it was they were looking for, Byron stopped a student sporting a Boston Celtics hat, figuring he might know the location of the former Huntington Avenue Grounds.

"You mean the statue of that pitcher?" asked the student.

"Yes, Cy Young," said Byron.

"That's on the other side of the building across the street."

After crossing Huntington Avenue, Byron stopped a second student who guided them to the Cabot Physical Education Center. A memorial plaque posted on the side of the building noted the location of the left-field foul pole. In the plaza in front of the athletic center stood Young's bronze statue, placed in the approximate location of the pitcher's mound, staring toward his nonexistent battery mate. For Byron, it was like seeing an old friend.

The former ballpark grounds were demarcated by

Northeastern University as "World Series Way." The school's decision to commemorate the site with a statue of Young seemed appropriate to Byron, because Young was the first pitcher to take the mound when Boston inaugurated the Huntington Avenue Grounds in 1901 – just as he had taken the mound for Cleveland in the inaugural game at League Park ten years earlier. Huntington Avenue Grounds was the site of several other baseball "firsts" involving Young, including in 1903, when he pitched the first game of the first World Series ever played, and in 1904, when he pitched the first perfect game of the modern era.

"You do know why they called him 'Cy' Young, don't you?" Byron asked Charles.

"Something to do with a cyclone, perhaps?"

"Kind of. His nickname started out as 'the Canton Cyclone.' 'Canton,' because that was the team he played for when he first broke into baseball with the Tri-State League, and 'Cyclone,' which was later shortened to 'Cy,' because of his unhittable fastball."

"So, I was right," said Charles.

"Yeah, somewhat, although I doubt you knew his original, longer nickname."

"No, I didn't, but now that I do, I'll probably forget it. My head's not big enough to store as much useless information as yours."

"Useless information? If you're a fan of the game, you crave information like that."

"Maybe, if you're an obsessive-compulsive fan of the game."

"That's right, attack the man, not his principles."

"No, I *am* attacking your principles. If I wanted to attack you, I would have called you a 'stupid little obsessive-compulsive fan of the game.'"

"Now you're being mean."

Byron asked Charles to take his picture standing next to Young. Up close, the statue looked nothing like his apparition in Newcomerstown.

After examining Young's statue, Charles looked over at Byron. "Cy seems pretty tight-lipped. You think he's gonna say anything to you?"

"Not with your mocking attitude," said Byron.

"What if I turn around? Will he say something then?" Charles turned away from the statue.

"He winked at me!" gasped Byron.

"What?" asked Charles, turning back around.

"Forget it, you missed it."

"Did he say anything about his nickname - like how you're wrong about the original, longer version?"

"No, but he told me he would've attacked your principles, but he could tell you didn't have any."

After taking a few pictures of the surrounding buildings, Byron turned to Charles. "Okay," he said. "Let's go."

"That's it?" asked Charles. "I thought you had a whole routine."

"I do, but not today. I don't have any of my research. I don't have any pictures of the ballpark, so there's nothing to compare this place to."

It seemed to Byron as if nothing of the Huntington Avenue Grounds remained at the site, and he doubted there was any way old players could gain access to the ballpark. The same appeared true for the South End Grounds, located adjacent to the Huntington Avenue Grounds. The former home of various Boston teams from 1871 to 1914, including both the National League Boston Bean Eaters and Boston Braves, the South End Grounds was separated from the Huntington Avenue Grounds by the New York, New Haven, and Hartford railroad tracks.

The tracks remained but were cordoned off by a chainlink fence. Byron recalled that the subway station at Ruggles and Tremont Streets, south of Northeastern University, was constructed on the site of the South End Grounds, so they returned to the T, hoping to take the train one stop to Ruggles Station.

Once inside the station, they realized the two stops were on different lines. The ensuing 30-minute ride, with two line changes, was hardly worth the trip, as there was nothing of the South End Grounds left to see other than a plaque at the station commemorating its former incarnation. As Byron took a picture of the plaque, a station attendant pointed out a parking garage constructed in the former outfield. After taking a picture of the garage, Byron departed with Charles via the T for Braves Field.

Home of the National League Braves from 1915 to 1952, Braves Field was located a mile west of Fenway Park on Commonwealth Avenue. The ballpark, or what was left of it, resided on the campus of Boston University. After the Braves abandoned Boston for Milwaukee in 1953, the University took over the ballpark, demolished a portion of the field and grandstand to construct a gymnasium, and converted the rest of the grandstand and most of the outfield to a modest-sized football stadium. When Boston University disbanded its football program, the stadium, renamed Nickerson Field, was converted for use as a soccer venue.

As soon as Byron alighted the train on Pleasant Street, he spotted the distinctive tan-colored, stucco, Mission-Revival-style building that once housed the Brave's administrative offices and was now the University's police station. Beyond the building, Byron could see the back side of the former right-field bleachers.

In the concrete plaza between the police station and the bleachers, a plaque commemorating Braves Field told the story of the longest game in major-league history, played there on May 1, 1920. For 26 innings, the Braves battled the Brooklyn Dodgers to a 1-1 tie, with both pitchers throwing complete games.

"Do know who the manager for the Dodgers was that day?" Byron asked Charles.

"Of course I do. Wilbert Robinson."

"Good, good. See how the plaque says that the 1915 World Series was played here, even though the Braves weren't in the series that year. Do you know why that is?"

"Sure, the Red Sox played here because Braves Field seated more people than Fenway. The Sox's owner wanted to sell more tickets. See? I know as much as you."

"Very good," said Byron. "One last question. Babe Ruth was a Red Sox in 1915, right?"

"Of course," said Charles.

"How many games did he pitch for the Sox in that World Series?"
"One."

"Nope - Ruth didn't pitch any games in the 1915 World Series."

Charles threw up his hands, palms spread and out. "What? Wait, that's not fair," he said.

Byron clasped his hands to his cheek in mock horror. "And to think you work at the Babe Ruth Museum!"

"It was a trick question."

"He pitched one game in 1916 and two in 1918."

"I know. But it still wasn't fair."

An open gate between the police station and the right-field bleachers provided access to the playing field where some students were kicking a soccer ball on the artificial turf. Charles sat in the stands and watched the action while Byron strolled around Nickerson Field, taking pictures.

The seating area was comprised of what once was Braves

Field's right-field bleachers section. The original concrete-and-stucco wall surrounding the perimeter of the bleachers remained intact. Aluminum benches had replaced the original wood bleachers, with the exception of four rows of red plastic stadium seats incongruously placed in the middle section. Byron stood in the back row farthest from the field, trying to determine how the bleachers would have fit within the confines of Braves Field, but, without any pictures, he was unable to conjure up any images of the ballpark.

The concourse and concession stands underneath the bleachers dated back to Braves Field. Byron closed his eyes, imagining the scene under the stands some 50 years earlier: the concession area alive with people, the sounds of vendors hawking their wares, and the smell of grilled hot dogs and onions.

At the end of the concourse under the stands, a separate walkway led from the Braves' former offices to what was once right centerfield. Byron leaned over the rounded metal railing separating the concourse from the walkway, and, peering to his left in the direction of the field, heard the sound of cleats clicking along the concrete walkway. Looking to his right, Byron saw three players wearing old Boston Braves uniforms walking on the pathway below. *Oh boy*, he thought. *It's happening again. Where's Charles?* Byron's heart started racing as the adrenaline kicked in.

Byron yelled to the players as they passed, but they didn't acknowledge him, which, of course, in and of itself, was not unusual for a ballplayer. As they headed toward the field, Byron kept his eyes on them until, from his vantage point, he no longer could see them from underneath the grandstand. Byron jumped the rail, landing on the walkway some six feet below. The players were about to enter the field, but as soon as Byron caught up to them, they disappeared.

"Who you looking for, Bitty?" yelled Charles from his seat in the bleachers as Byron walked out onto the field.

Byron looked up at Charles but did not say a word.

"What is it?" asked Charles, who was now standing up in the bleachers, looking concerned.

"You didn't see that?" asked Byron, as he walked toward Charles in the bleachers.

"I didn't see anything, except you come running out that tunnel. What happened?"

"Nothing," Byron lied. "It was just my imagination."

"I don't believe you."

"You're the one who tells me it's all in my head. Well, everything's fine now. Everything's back to normal."

"Normal? Nothing's ever normal with you."

The following afternoon, Byron and Charles took a tour of Fenway Park and later that evening attended the Red Sox game. They sat ten rows behind a steel girder, which blocked their view of left-handed batters standing at home plate. To Charles, the pole was a huge nuisance. Byron, however, didn't mind the obstruction at all. To him, it was part of the ancient ballpark's charm. The Red Sox beat the Orioles 4-1, behind seven strong innings of four-hit ball by Pedro Martinez. Watching the game, Byron was glad the Red Sox still played baseball at Fenway Park. He took comfort in knowing there was at least one historic, old ballpark not in imminent danger of becoming lost. It meant he could enjoy the game and, for one night, not worry about old ballplayers haunting the ballpark - or him.

CHAPTER 25

❍ ❍ ❍

The Ghost of Union Park
October 1999

A century had passed since the old Orioles played their final few home games at Union Park. The players did not know it then, but those games in early October 1899 would be Union Park's last professional games ever. The Orioles' final four games that season were played on the road in Brooklyn, at Washington Park. Brooklyn already had clinched the pennant, thanks in part to four former Baltimore Orioles. In contrast, the 1899 Orioles had been out of serious contention for the pennant for more than a month.

A century later, the 1999 Orioles, like their 1899 counterparts, were long out of contention for the pennant as the season drew to a close. Unlike the 1899 Orioles, however, the 1999 Orioles finished their season at home with three games against the Yankees and three games against the Red Sox. Both the Yankees and the Red Sox were well on their way to making the playoffs, while the Orioles' players were well on their way to making tee times.

At the beginning of the season, Byron had purchased two tickets to the Orioles' final game, knowing it would be the team's last game of the century. All summer long, Byron had kept the tickets in his wallet. As the day of the game approached he called Charles to see if he was interested in going to the game.

"The last thing in the world I want to do," Charles said, "is watch the Red Sox beat the Orioles, surrounded by a bunch of drunken, obnoxious members of Red Sox nation."

"'Fenway South,' I know. It can get pretty bad."

"There's nothing pretty about it, especially with the Sox heading to the playoffs. Why are you even going?"

"It's the Orioles' last game of the century."

"I still don't see the value."

"I wanted to take Maggie, but I didn't know what to say, especially after what you told me she said. It wouldn't be fair to her."

"I agree she doesn't need to hear any more of your ghost stories, but you do need to call her and let her know you're not giving up this stupid quest of yours - what do you call it, deadball?"

"Okay, I'll call her tonight."

"Not tonight, she won't be home. She's in Ocean City this weekend."

"I'll call her Sunday, then, after the game."

⚾ ⚾ ⚾

Byron spent most of his Saturday morning dozing in his La-Z-Boy, watching television, flipping between cartoons and *Sports Center*. About noon, he was awakened by a knock at his front door.

Startled by the knock, Byron jumped off the recliner like an excited dog, kicking over an empty cereal bowl left on the floor from breakfast. Byron opened the door. It was the postman.

"I thought you guys always rang twice," said Byron.

"Boy, I've never heard *that* one before," said the postman.

"Never gets old, does it?"

"Byron Bennett?" asked the postman, turning business-like. "I have a package you need to sign for." The postman handed Byron an envelope with a delivery slip attached to the front, along with the rest of his mail.

The return address on the envelope was a law office in Baltimore – "John T. Whelan and Associates."

"Wow, special Saturday delivery. I hope I'm not in trouble," said Byron.

"Are you sure you want to sign for it?" asked the postman, raising his eyebrow.

"Sure, I've got nothing to hide." Byron scrawled his signature on the delivery slip.

"Have a nice day."

Byron's hands began to shake and his heart pounded as he closed the door. Considering the source, a letter like this almost never was good news.

Byron walked over to the kitchen and pulled a knife out of the drawer to slice open the envelope. He unfolded the letter and scanned its contents.

"You've got to be kidding me!" He headed over to his recliner and dropped down into the seat.

The letter stated:

Dear Mr. Bennett:

I am the trustee of the estate of Timothy J. Murphy. Mr. Murphy passed away on August 30, 1999.

In his Last Will and Testament, dated August 28, 1999, Mr. Murphy bequeathed to you ownership of his house and adjacent land located at 313 East 25th Street, Baltimore, Maryland.

Please contact my office as soon as possible to arrange a time and date to meet to discuss your inheritance and inform you what you must do to take title to the property. When you call, please ask for me, as Mr. Murphy's Will and Testament instructs that I present to you a package at the earliest convenience. You can reach me at the telephone number listed above.

Sincerely,

John T. Whelan
Attorney at Law

"He gave me his house. I can't believe it." *Wait a second,* Byron thought, *he gave me his house. Why on earth would he give me his house? I hardly knew him. He was such a jerk when we met and now he gives me his house? Wait, maybe Charles did this, asked a lawyer friend to write it. No, Charles isn't that clever.*

Although it was a Saturday, Byron picked up the phone and punched the numbers for the law offices of John T. Whelan, Esquire. *The few lawyers I know work weekends,* he thought. *Maybe Whelan does, too.*

A woman's voice came on the line and asked Byron to hold a moment. Piped-in, 1970's soft rock played through the ear piece, torturing Byron for the next two minutes – "Precious and Few" by Cleveland's one-hit-wonder Climax. If the call hadn't been so important, Byron would have hung up immediately.

After what seemed like an eternity, the woman came back on the line. "Hello, may I help you?"

"Yes, my name is Byron Bennett. I received a letter today from Mr. Whelan. He said I've inherited some property and I should call him."

"Oh, yes, Mr. Bennett. I typed that letter. If you'd please

hold a moment, I'll see if he's available."

Byron's whole body felt flushed.

The schmaltzy soft rock continued as the singer lamented in a billowy, pained warble how little time he had to share with his woman. The song did little to soothe Byron's anxiety.

The music ended mid-verse and a man's voice came on the line.

"Mr. Bennett, this is John Whelan. Thanks for calling."

"I received your letter and wanted to . . . ."

"Yes, how soon can you come by my office? I need to give you a package from Mr. Murphy."

"What is it?"

"I don't know. It was sealed when he gave it to me."

"I can be at your office in an hour," said Byron. "Is one o'clock okay?"

"That's fine, although it'll have to be quick because I have another appointment at one-thirty. I can give you the package, but you'll have to schedule another time to come back so we can go over the procedures for receiving your inheritance."

"See you in an hour."

Byron didn't bother to shower or shave. He threw on some jeans and a sweatshirt and jumped in his car. Within half an hour, he arrived in front of Whelan's law office on North Howard Street. The office was located on the fourth floor of an old brownstone, a few blocks south of where McGraw and Robinson once had run their sports bar, the Diamond.

Lacking the patience needed to wait for the elevator, Byron ran up the several flights of stairs, arriving out of breath on the fourth floor. Entering Whelan's office, Byron was greeted by a petite woman, perhaps ten years younger than he, sitting at a large reception desk, typing on a computer.

"Good afternoon," said the woman, looking up from her

computer. "May I help you?"

"Yes, I'm Byron Bennett."

"That was fast. We spoke less than an hour ago."

"Forty minutes to be exact, but who's counting? You guys always work Saturdays?"

"Mr. Whelan would have me here on Sundays, too, if I let him. Please have a seat. I'll let him know you're here."

Sitting in the reception area, Byron was too nervous to do anything but wait. He tried flipping through a copy of *ESPN The Magazine* with Nomar Garciaparra on the cover, but soon felt sick to his stomach. The anticipation of receiving Murph's mystery package was almost too much for him to bear.

In an attempt to calm his nerves, Byron struck up a conversation with the receptionist.

"Excuse me, do you know your phone plays 'Precious and Few' when you put people on hold?"

"Oh, you noticed. You're right, it does."

"Why don't you change it to something good? Even Muzak would be better."

"Mr. Whelan picked that song to annoy people he didn't want to talk to - like telemarketers and opposing counsel. He said only people who really needed to talk to him would be willing to sit through that song. You'd be surprised how well it works."

"Your boss is a clever man," said Byron.

"That's what he keeps telling me."

A man wearing jeans and an Orioles polo shirt, who looked to be about the same age as Byron, entered the reception area.

"Mr. Bennett?"

"Mr. Whelan?" The two shook hands.

"You're quite the mystery," said Whelan, "being added to Mr. Murphy's will days before he died. He was adamant I give you this package in person. He didn't know your address and it took some time to track you down. How well did you know him?"

"I only met him once, which is why I'm surprised he named me in his will."

"Well, you certainly fit the description he gave. He told me you used to play baseball."

"Yeah, in the minors."

"And your nickname was 'Bitty?'"

"Yes, unfortunately."

"Well, Bitty, here's the package." Whelan handed Byron a stiff, letter-sized envelope.

Byron felt around the edges of the envelope, trying to identify the object inside. "It feels like a key," he said.

The receptionist handed Byron a letter opener. Slicing open the envelope, Byron pulled out a hand-written letter in shaky cursive and a key taped to a piece of cardboard.

The letter stated:

Byron:

Here is the key to my house at 313 East 25th Street. It opens the basement door in back. It does not open the front door, which is where the tenants live.

Go to the house as soon as you receive this key, but enter only through the basement door. I am giving you my house, but you must let the tenants live there as long as they want. They are good people and always pay their rent on time.

Once you go into the basement, it will be evident what you are to do next.

Thank you for believing and for carrying on after me.

Timothy J. Murphy

"Good news?" asked Whelan, looking over Byron's shoulder at the letter.

"Yeah, I guess so."

"Good. Oh . . . there's something I need to ask you. You're not related to Mr. Murphy, right?"

"Right."

"Okay, well, since you're not family, you're probably going to have to pay some taxes if you want to keep the house."

"How much?"

"Depends on how much the house is worth. But, we can talk about that later. As I said on the phone, I have another appointment. If you'd like, we can meet next week."

"Don't let him fool you," interrupted the receptionist. "He's going to the Orioles game this afternoon."

"My snitch will make an appointment for you," said Whelan, pointing to the receptionist.

"Thank you, Mr. Whelan," said Byron.

After making an appointment for the following week, Byron sprinted down the four flights of stairs and across North Howard to his car parked on a side street. Heading north on Charles Street, in the direction of Murph's house, Byron was overwhelmed with anticipation - excitement tinged with fear. He had longed for a break like this – and now it was all happening too fast.

He needed time to think.

Byron took a detour onto East 22nd Street toward Greenmount and parked his car in front of St. Ann's. He walked up to the front of the church and pulled on the door but it was locked. After checking a side door, he ran around behind the church to the rectory on East 22nd Street – the "Anchorage," it was called, continuing the pun. Byron knocked and a woman answered the door. After a brief conversation, the woman agreed to unlock the church for him.

Byron took a seat in the same pew where he had sat for Murph's funeral mass. Byron pulled Murph's letter out of his pocket and read it again.

"Thank you for believing and for carrying on after me," Byron read from the letter.

"Thank you for believing?" What do I believe? What did Murph believe? That there were ghosts running around in his yard?

"Once you enter the basement, it will be evident what you are to do next," stated the letter.

Byron placed the letter on the pew next him. He folded his hands and glanced up at the cathedral ceiling as if looking toward the heavens to pray, but was distracted by the content of Murph's letter. *What does he want from me? Whatever it is, I'm not sure I can do it.*

Byron looked around the church at the icons covering the walls. He thought about the old ballplayers – wondering if they were ghosts or some other type of spirit. Were they restless souls, perhaps? Whatever they were, Byron needed the strength to find out. The journey that had brought him to this point hadn't scared him half as much as the possibility of reaching the end now did.

Byron rubbed his hands over the surface of the wooden pew beneath him. A sense of calm enveloped him. Nothing happened out of the ordinary, no icons twitched or winked, no divine intervention, at least not that he could tell. He knew it was time for him to go and face whatever it was Murph wanted him to do. As he walked toward the back of the church, he passed the woman from the rectory, who was waiting for him in the vestibule. He thanked her as he left.

He drove north on Greenmount and parked his car in the alley behind Murph's house. Getting out of his car, he felt a rush of adrenaline and his heart rate increased. Walking toward the back of Murph's house, he fumbled with the key as he pulled it off the index card. He opened the gate to the chainlink fence, crossed the postage-stamp-sized backyard, headed toward the basement door, and walked down the short flight of stairs, each step more purposeful than the last.

Hands trembling, Byron placed the key in the lock and tried twisting it to the right. The knob turned, but the door, ancient and warped, wouldn't budge. As he worked the key, Byron sensed he was being watched. Behind him, he noticed an old man standing in Murph's yard about ten feet away, staring at his every move like a dog watching his owner finish dinner. Byron thought he recognized the man. "Don't you work at the Stone Tavern?" Byron asked the man as he continued wrestling with the door.

"Used to. It's closed now, you know."

More old men appeared behind Byron. When he finally was able to dislodge the door, he turned around and saw perhaps 20 men standing behind him.

"Hurry up, buddy, what's taking you so long?" asked one of the men.

"Yeah, come on, kid, we've got a game to play," said another.

"Don't give him a hard time, fellows. He's new to this game." Byron recognized the voice. It was Mac.

"Mac!" said Byron. "Where did you come from? What the hell's going on here? And where the hell have you been?"

"Just open the door, Byron."

Byron shoved the door with his shoulder and pushed it open, stumbling through the threshold and into the basement. Two dozen or so men filed past him. As Byron's eyes adjusted to the darkness, he saw something he was certain had been lost to time. Shoehorned between the two outer walls of the basement were the first few rows of an old, wooden grandstand, miraculously preserved in Murph's basement. The floor was covered with dirt; there was no concrete beneath his feet. Byron was speechless. He rubbed his hand over the top of the front railing's worn, wooden surface and stared at the rows of ancient theater seats in front of him. "Amazing," he said, finally.

Old men continued filing through, one by one, walking up into the grandstand, disappearing as they reached the third or fourth row.

"Welcome to Union Park," said Mac. "Here, follow me."

Mac slipped through a narrow opening in the front of the grandstand and Byron followed him up past the first few rows of seats.

"Look over there," said Mac, pointing toward what was once the back of Murph's house.

Turning in that direction, Byron saw the most extraordinary sight. Rising before him was Union Park. Byron stood in the grandstand, looking back in time, just as an astronomer looks through a telescope, viewing light emanating from stars that burned long ago. From Byron's vantage point in the middle of Murph's tiny basement, the ancient photographs of Union Park had come back to life, rendering the park fully visible.

Byron found himself standing on the third-base side of the

grandstand, which curved around to his right toward first base. The ballpark was filling with spectators and cranks. To Byron's left was the infield and, beyond that, the outfield wall and the left-field bleachers. In front of him, where moments earlier was an unmarked alley, was home plate – in the location where Byron had imagined it would be. *My car*, thought Byron. *Where the hell's my car?*

Players roamed the field, warming up, tossing baseballs back and forth. Gradually, the sound of the ballpark filled Byron's ears as if someone was turning up the volume on an old radio broadcast – the vendors hawking their wares, people talking in the stands, yelling down at the players. It was a brilliant, crisp fall afternoon.

"I should go prepare for the match," said Mac.

"The match?" asked Byron.

"You know, the baseball game. That's how *we* say it."

"Oh," replied Byron, still somewhat confused by all that was happening around him. "Wait, you're playing?"

"I am today." Mac jumped off the grandstand and onto the field. As soon as his feet hit the ground, he no longer was the old man Byron had come to know but was, once again, a young John McGraw.

"This is unbelievable. You're John McGraw."

"In the flesh . . . well, not in the flesh, but, yes."

Byron stood speechless. McGraw waved to the crowd and cheers went up as he walked toward right field in the direction of the player's clubhouse.

"Unbelievable," said Byron, watching Mac walk away. "Simply unbelievable."

"It is that," said a familiar voice to Byron's left.

Sitting in the grandstand a few seats down was Murph,

looking no worse for the wear.

"Hello, Byron," said Murph.

"Murph! How've you been?" The question immediately seemed strange to Byron, given recent events.

"I'm better now, thanks."

"Murph, thank you for giving me this – your house – all this. But why me?"

"Mac and I talked it over. You're a true believer. You came around at the right time, as if it were destiny. I knew my time was about up and we needed someone to take my place."

"'Take your place?'" asked Byron.

"Sure, we needed someone to hold onto the house, to let the ballplayers in. I can't any more since, you know . . . ."

"So, how does it work?"

"It just does. Don't worry how for now - it'll come to you. Or, make it up as you go. Like me."

"So, will I be seeing you here from now on?"

"I don't know. Now that I'm on the other side of the fence, so to speak, I'm not sure how it works. But, now that I'm gone, I know we need a lifer so all this can continue."

"How will I know when I should let the ballplayers in?" asked Byron.

"It depends on the schedule. Sometimes the games are played here. Sometimes they're not. This year, they've been playing games from 1899, but next season, they could do something completely different. You'll get an invitation to opening day delivered to the house. That's when you'll know the year they're playing."

"How do they decide?"

"I have no idea. It used to depend on which teams could make it. But not anymore - they're all free, ever since Boileryard died."

"Boileryard Clarke? The catcher?"

"Yeah, he passed in 1959. Once that happened, he and the rest of the world champion Orioles were able to come back and play. Nineteen sixty was a great year for baseball in Baltimore."

"Is there some kind of sign you guys use? You know – to identify yourselves to each other?"

Murph thought about the question for a moment, and then he smiled.

"Ever see the movie *The Sting?*"

"*The Sting?* Yeah, when I was a kid."

"Well, you can do the same thing they did in the movie – put your index finger to your nose and kind of give a salute."

"Great, thanks."

"I'll see you later, kid." Murph stood up, gave Byron an index finger salute, and walked toward the top of the grandstand and then out of sight.

After Murph disappeared, Byron spotted a vendor walking through the stands selling scorecards. Byron raised his hand to buy one. "How much are they?" he asked as the man approached.

"Five cents."

Byron opened his wallet and handed the vendor a crisp one dollar bill.

"What the hell is this?" asked the man.

"Oh, crap, sorry, I guess you don't take those." Byron examined the new, Clinton-era, Robert-Rubin one-dollar bill, and remembered he'd made the same mistake at League Park. Disappointed at not being able to buy a scorecard, Byron shoved the money back into his wallet. Then he smiled. *The nickel, it's in my wallet.*

"Wait a second," Byron yelled to the man, searching through his billfold. "Here it is. Alright! Here you go." Byron grabbed the vendor's hand and placed into his palm the nickel he had found in Murph's front yard the previous spring.

"Thank you, sir," replied the vendor, handing Byron a scorecard. *This is fantastic, an 1899 Official Score Card of the Baltimore Base Ball Club.* Byron examined the brilliantly colored artifact published by Guggenheimer, Weil & Co., of Baltimore. *It belongs in a museum, but Charles sure as hell ain't getting it.*

In the center of the front cover were portraits of "W. Robinson" and "J. McGraw" with an advertisement for "The Diamond, No. 519 N. Howard St., Robinson & McGraw Props," boasting "Bowling Alleys, Billiards and Pool Parlors, Wine Liquors and Cigars." At the bottom of the scorecard was an ad for Von Der Horst Brewing Co., "Brewers of Extra Pale Ale & Standard Beers, 10 Belair Ave. Phone - 779, Henry Borman, Manager." *Ten Belair Avenue,* thought Byron. *I'll have to check that address out. I wonder what's there now?*

As Byron read the players' names printed on the scorecard, Mac came back toward the grandstand. He was wearing a black cap and was dressed in an off-white wool uniform with a high collar and a red "B" centered on the front.

"Did you see Murph?" asked Mac.

"I did."

"Did he explain to you how this works?"

"Sort of."

"Don't worry, you'll figure it out as you go along."

"Hey, Mac?"

"Yeah?"

"Why didn't you tell me about all this when we met last spring?"

"I did, remember? You thought I was a crazy old man."

"I didn't think you were crazy. Well, maybe a little crazy, but no more so than me. I spent most of the summer trying to find you."

"Here I am."

"If you don't mind me saying, you don't seem anything like you do in all those books I read about you. You seem - I don't know - more relaxed, maybe?"

"Death will do that to you - it gives a guy perspective."

"I can't believe I'm even having this conversation. So, why me? Out of the millions of baseball fans, why pick me?"

"Your love of the game."

"I do love baseball."

"You were able to believe in something most people would never believe in. Your faith was tested, but you never faltered."

"You were testing me?"

"A little bit, maybe. We all were."

"We all?"

"Yeah, me and the other players. But, you know, it wasn't only your ability to believe. You were lucky, too. You came around at the right time."

"Huh. Maybe I am lucky after all."

"It was nothing other than bad luck that kept you out of the big leagues."

"I always figured I was born a hundred years too late."

"Luck's a big part of the game. You of all people should know that. You spent every waking hour of every day doing everything you could to become a big-league player. But at the end of the day, you still needed some luck to make your dream reality."

"I can't argue with that," said Byron.

"So, are you ready to make your dream reality?"

"What dream?"

"Your dream – do you feel like playing some ball?"

"You mean out there?" asked Byron, pointing to the field. "With the Orioles?"

"No, Brooklyn, actually . . . . Just kidding. Yes, the Orioles.

We usually don't do this, but sometimes, exceptions are made. I've already received permission from the committee."

"What committee?"

"'The Exception To The Rules Committee.' It's ad hoc. I needed to get the approval of a few other Hall of Famers."

"You're kidding me. Who?"

"Let's see, Hughie, Wilbert, Willie, Joe, Ned, they all agreed. Although Robinson says you still owe him a baseball."

"Oh, yeah, I ran out."

"So I heard. Let's see, Cy Young, Honus Wagner, Babe Ruth, they all agreed as well. Hon and George were key because we needed approval from the first class of inductees."

"Unbelievable," said Byron. "Simply unbelievable."

"Just one thing, though. After this game, you'll be like Murph, our groundskeeper, if you will. During games, you can watch as a spectator, but you can't come on the field, unless they change the rules again."

"You'll hear no complaints from me."

"Great."

"By the way, who makes the rules?"

"Henry Chadwick, and believe me, he's a stickler."

"The 'Father of Baseball.' Makes sense to me."

"Now, when you're out there today, be sure to give it all you've got, like you did when you were a player."

"I will."

"Here, put this on." Mac tossed Byron a baseball uniform. "Be careful, it's 'on loan' from the Babe Ruth Museum, although they don't know it. I need to get it back there after the game, before they notice it's missing."

"Who's uniform is it?"

"It was mine. I had two. It may be a bit small for you,

but it's what I got."

"Thanks, Mac. Thanks for everything."

"Don't mention it, Bitty. Is it okay if I call you Bitty?"

"It is now."

"Hurry down to the clubhouse in right field and get dressed, then meet me back here. We're sitting for a team photograph in a few minutes, before the start of today's contest. You picked a good day to make your big-league debut."

Byron was about to jump down onto the field, but Mac stopped him. "Go through the stands to get to the clubhouse," said Mac. "And make sure you don't step onto the field until you're wearing that uniform."

"Why?"

"Don't ask. Just trust me."

Before making his way through the grandstand, Byron turned to Mac, put his index finger on his nose, and saluted him, like Murph had told him to do.

"You okay?" asked Mac.

"Yeah, I'm fine. Why do you ask?"

"That thing you did with your nose."

"Isn't that the sign I'm supposed to use?"

"What sign?"

"The sign for you ghosts."

"Not that I know of," said Mac.

"But, Murph told me . . . oh, never mind."

⚾ ⚾ ⚾

And so it was that Byron "Bitty" Bennett, on October 2, 1899, finally made it to the big leagues, if only for one game. But, what a game it was. In the top of the third, Mac substituted Byron at third base. He played his position with distinction, scooping up every ground ball hit to him and throwing cleanly to first base.

Knowing where to position himself, he made a spectacular catch of a line drive hit by Willie Keeler, who was playing for Brooklyn. Byron even managed to grab the belt of Hughie Jennings, also a Brooklyn player, as he rounded third trying to score. The umpire never suspected a thing. Mac, standing next to Byron along third base, gave him a wink and a smile.

At the plate, Byron drew a walk in the fifth inning. In the seventh inning, with a runner on first and two outs, he hit the ball over the shortstop - his signature hit – a single in the gap between the left and center fielders which he stretched into a double. Mac signaled for the runner coming from first base to stop at third, preventing at home plate what would have been the last out of the inning. The next batter hit a double and Byron scored his first and only major-league run – at least to date. That's because you never know what the future might bring - or the past, for that matter.

◊ ◊ ◊

Sometime long after the game ended Byron fell asleep in the grandstand. When he awoke the next morning, Union Park was gone. Byron found himself alone in Murph's basement, wearing boxers and a T-shirt, no baseball uniform. The rest of his clothes from the previous day sat folded in a pile next to him. The score-card he had purchased sat on top. The section of the wooden grandstand that remained, encased in Mac's basement, creaked as Byron stood up and jumped over the front railing and onto the basement floor below. After putting on his clothes, Byron left through the basement door, locking it behind him.

On Byron's windshield fluttered yet another souvenir, courtesy this time of the Baltimore City Police Department. *I should have known better*, he thought. *No parking on game days*. He opened the car door and placed the scorecard on the seat next to him, being careful not to mar the artifact's pristine condition. He pulled the parking ticket off the windshield and stuffed it inside his glove box.

Once in his car, Byron realized it was Sunday afternoon and the new Orioles' last game of the season - and of the century - already had begun.

He rolled down the windows and pulled his car out of the alley and onto Guilford. The wind coming into the car kicked up the scorecard sitting on the seat and Byron grabbed it as it hit the floor. He looked at the scorecard as he drove away. *What happened?* The edges of the scorecard were yellowed with age. The paper felt brittle in his hands. *Damn, it turned old, just like the nickel.*

Byron pulled his wallet out of his pocket and made sure he still had his ticket to the afternoon's game. After parking in the garage across from Lexington Market, Byron jogged south down Eutaw Street and made it through the gates as the Orioles came to bat in the bottom of the second. Byron found his seat in section 84 and tried watching the game for a while but soon found himself distracted by all that had happened the previous day.

During the bottom of the fifth, no longer able to sit still, and with the game tied at zero, Byron took a walk around the stadium, ending up at Bambino's Pub, located inside the Orioles warehouse on Eutaw Street. Exposed brick walls encircled a large polished wooden bar. On the walls of the pub hung photographs of Orioles teams through the years. In a far corner of the pub hung a picture of the 1899 Orioles. Byron examined the faces, recognizing each one, for he had seen those players just the day before.

And there, in the bottom right corner of the photograph was an image he recognized as himself. "Wait a second," he said.

"That's me. I'm an *Oriole*." Byron nervously looked around the room, hoping no one had overheard his outrageous claim. Under the caption "Baltimore Orioles Baseball Club 1899," Byron read the last names of each of the players. For him, it stated, simply, "player unknown."

Byron smiled. "Unknown, indeed," he said to himself. "If only they knew. But first, you've got to believe."

Leaving Bambino's Pub, Byron thought about Maggie.

"I'm supposed to call her tonight," he said. Then he paused for a moment and smiled. "What on earth am I gonna tell her now?"

BIBLIOGRAPHY

Books:

Charles C. Alexander, *John McGraw*, Lincoln: University of Nebraska Press, Bison Books, 1995

James H. Bready, *Baseball in Baltimore, the First 100 Years*, Baltimore: Johns Hopkins University Press, 1998

James H. Bready, *The Home Team, 100 Years of Baseball in Baltimore*, 1958

Reed Browning, *Cy Young, A Baseball Life*, Amherst: University of Massachusetts Press, 2000

William R. Cobb, Editor, *Honus Wagner on his Life & Baseball*, Michigan: Sports Media Group, 2006

Philip J. Lowry, *Green Cathedrals, the Ultimate Celebration of Major League and Negro League Ballparks*, New York: Walker Publishing Company, Inc, 2006

Blanche S. McGraw, *The Real McGraw*, New York: David McKay Co., 1953

James A. Riley, *The Biographical Encyclopedia of the Negro Baseball Leagues*, New York: Carroll & Graf Publishers, 1994

Lawrence S. Ritter, *Lost Ballparks: A Celebration of Baseball's Legendary Fields*, New York: Viking Penguin, 1992

Mark Silverman, Publisher and Editor, *The Detroit News Presents, They Earned Their Stripes: The Detroit Tigers All-Time Team*, Sports Publishing, Inc., 2001

Burt Solomon, *Where They Ain't: The Fabled Life and Untimely Death of the Original Baltimore Orioles, the Team That Gave Birth to Modern Baseball*, New York: Free Press, 1999

Hy Turkin and S.C. Thompson, *The Official Encyclopedia of Baseball, Fifth Revised Edition*, South Brunswick and New York: A.S. Barnes and Co., 1970

BIBLIOGRAPHY (CONTINUED)

Websites:

dcollections.oberlin.edu

www.around-the-horn.com

www.ballparksofbaseball.com

www.ballparkwatch.com (www.ballparkdigest.com)

www.baseball-almanac.com

www.baseball-reference.com

www.crosley-field.com

www.cume.columbia.edu

www.ebaseballparks.com

www.mlb.com

www.mudhens.com

www.projectballpark.org

www.rockymtn.sabr.org

www.sabr.org

www.thebaseballcube.com

www.washingtonheights-nyc.com

www.wikipedia.org